SON

BOOK TWO OF
THE PROCHRIST SERIES

VENSIN GRAY

This is a work of fiction. The events and characters described herein are imaginary and are not intended to refer to specific places or living persons. The opinions expressed in this manuscript are solely the opinions of the author and do not represent the opinions or thoughts of the publisher. The author has represented and warranted full ownership and/or legal right to publish all the materials in this book.

Son Of Sin
Book Two Of The ProChrist Series
All Rights Reserved.
Copyright © 2014 Vensin Gray
v2.0

Cover Photo © 2014 Vensin Gray. All rights reserved - used with permission.

This book may not be reproduced, transmitted, or stored in whole or in part by any means, including graphic, electronic, or mechanical without the express written consent of the publisher except in the case of brief quotations embodied in critical articles and reviews.

Outskirts Press, Inc.
http://www.outskirtspress.com

ISBN: 978-1-4787-2241-0

Outskirts Press and the "OP" logo are trademarks belonging to Outskirts Press, Inc.

PRINTED IN THE UNITED STATES OF AMERICA

~This book is for my mother and my sister~

Thank you!

Enjoy!

[signature]

12/31/13

A Special Thank You to…
Jennifer Hayes
And
Denise Darnall

Special Contributions from
M. Ward
R. Turner
D. McCafferty
L. Scott
S. Hill
J. Jacobs

1

I looked at the sunset over the lake, fearing it would be the last one I would ever see. Tears poured from my mother's eyes. My father was gone, nowhere to be found. My grandfather was dead. There was confusion everywhere, hate everywhere. Nowhere to go, death surrounded us, our hearts are in flame.

The White Horse. I see it. Should I go to it? *Victor!* I ignored the call of my name, and I walked toward the Horse. It's just sitting in the middle of this hell.

Victor!

I clutched my sword in my swollen hand, bleeding from all the lives I had taken.

Victor!

I ignored my name again. I declared the Horse mine. I named it *Vita*, the Latin word for Life, for I must bring life back to Earth.

Ashes everywhere screams and cries, children without parents, parents without homes, homes without a country, a country with no army, an army with no King. A king with no faith and that is why we had gotten to this point…

"Victor!"

Finally, I snapped out of my day dream.

"Man, you're sweating? What's wrong with you?" Leon sounded concerned.

Leon is my brother. Not by blood, but life has made us so.

"Sorry I was day dreaming." I replied as I snapped back to reality.

"Come on brother, we just graduated High School, and you're up here staring directly at the Sun. You'll go blind man. Let's go down stairs and have some fun!" Leon persuaded me to go back down stairs and enjoy the graduation party our family was throwing for us.

He and I graduated at the top of our class at one of the most prestigious private high schools in Ohio, University School. Leon and I played three sports a year there, football in the fall, basketball in the winter, and ran track in the spring. We won twelve state champions in all the sports combined, no thanks to me though. They were all thanks to Leon and his amazing athletic abilities.

He stands six foot three, with broad shoulders, and a V shaped body, as if he were a super hero. His eyes are light gray like his mother's eyes. His mother is not my mother. His mother is Christina, my mother is Persia. His father is not my father. His father is Ian, an ex-professional football player. Now he just owns property. My father is Victor Junior, a high school basketball coach.

So how are we brothers? I don't know, but we've called one another brother since we were five years old, and it has stuck.

"About time Victor!" my aunt Victory yelled as we returned to the party.

Victory is my dad's younger sister, but she's only a couple years older than me. She's in her fifth year in college, med-school, she wants to be a medical doctor. She has brown eyes like my grandmother Patrice.

I hugged her and walked amongst the crowd gathered at my grandparents' house, seeing friends, friends of friends, family members, distant cousins, neighbors, and most importantly, my parents.

"Hello mother… father" I said bluntly.

Everyone said that I was odd, always quiet, didn't say much. I didn't have to really. Leon was always the talkative, confident, demanding one. He wasn't arrogant; he just knew who he was already.

Myself? I stopped growing once I hit six feet. I was a bit slimmer in stature compared to Leon. I had eyes like my father's, brown. My eyes were determined eyes, because I always was determined to accomplish anything I set forth to doing. Leon's eyes were relaxed, but focused at the same time, as if he was staring right into your soul. I heard young lady's say that you couldn't stare at him too long without either falling in love, or fainting. I laughed to myself.

"Congratulations son," my father handed me a long wooden box, with a bow on top of it.

My mother was crying, as always. She rushed and hugged me. "You have no idea how proud I am of you," she said kissing me.

I loved my mother with all of my heart. She was my reason for living, her and my sister, Sa'Rah, who is leaning on our father in boredom. Sa'Rah was playing a video game on her cell phone, chewing gum in complete disregard.

"Thanks, father," I said as I took the gift from him.

It was really heavy.

"You're welcome, Third."

He called me by the nickname he and my grandfather, Victor Thomas Senior, had given me when I was a child. Third in line to the Victor Thomas name.

My sister then came and hugged me and whispered in my ear.

"Congratulations big brother! I wrote you a poem, but you can't read it now. I'll show it to you one day. You know I love you most of all right?" She said to me.

"Not more than me, dear Sa'Rah," Leon said, coming over hugging us both.

"Ew! Get off of me, Leon!" Sa'Rah yelled playfully.

We were all together, my sister Sa'Rah, and my brother Leon. I couldn't have been happier.

"Now now, no need for all of that noise," my grandfather, Victor Senior smiled.

Every time he was present, it was as if my heart skipped a beat. His voice, although soft, was demanding. You felt as if you had to respect him, even if you only knew he just a mere man. Some have written him as more than just a man, but a Legend in his own. They write that he actually spoke with an Angel, and that he's the true father of Leon. But those are all lies. And we all know the truth. Conspirators, people who are just trying to make his name bad.

My grandfather was the leader of the North East Ohio's largest church congregation. Over five thousand attended every Sunday, and hundreds of thousands watched his services live on television. He helped restore the city of Cleveland to its former glory.

Before he stepped in Cleveland, along with its suburbs, had become a black hole. Crime was on the rise, prostitution, STDS, corrupt politicians, and more. He brought back what this town was missing, a back bone. And that back bone was Christianity. No matter what denomination, he preached unity, togetherness, and Faith. His famous quote was, "*Be strong in your faith, and you will free yourself from the clinches of Satan.*" And I receive that.

My mother and father were only sixteen years old when they found out my mother was pregnant. I was born four months early, on December 20th, 2006, the same day as Leon. I always thought that was weird.

Grandfather Victor and my grandmother raised me and him, and my mother, the best they could. My grandfather, who I call Senior, became a licensed Psychiatrist. He went back to school a few years after I was born so that he could help people. He figured he did it all the time at church anyways, might as well make it official.

"Excuse me everyone. Please gather around," Senior said. He always had to give a speech. I guess he was born to speak.

Everyone quieted down, the music that was playing in the background stopped and everyone looked at Senior, waiting to hear what he had to say. He took a deep breath, as he did every time he was about to give a speech.

"Most of you know me as Pastor Thomas, or Doctor Thomas, or Victor, or silly old man."

Everyone laughed easily. He always knew that when he spoke, the audience was more nervous about what he was going to say than he was nervous speaking to them.

"Eighteen years ago, my son came to me and said 'Dad, you're about to be a grandfather.' And then he just walked out of the room. Who did he think he was?" Senior smiled looking at my father.

My father smiled back.

"Then, five months after that, I'm looking at this tiny little fellow, and I was a grandad. No longer just dad, or Pastor, or whatever you called me. I became a grandfather. I got to see one of the most beautiful things in the world. I thought I knew what love was when I saw Victoria born, until Junior gave me a grandchild. His heart barely holding on. But we prayed. We Prayed."

"Yes we did!" said my grandmother.

"And I said to God, 'Please Lord, breathe breath into this child, give him life. I beg you, oh merciful.' Let me tell you all, people were crying. Victoria was holding her brother, Victory was with Patrice, and Persy was with Persia. We were all dismayed. Then a child, no older then fifteen years old, came to me, and whispered in my ear, 'He gives power to the faint; and to them that have no might… he increases strength." Senior said slowly, quoting Isaiah chapter forty verse twenty-nine.

He looked at me with tears in his eyes, I went and stood next to him. He was a bit shorter then I. He had grayish black hair, brown eyes, and was getting a little heavier in his old age. I looked just like him. Well like my father, and my father like him. We all just stood in silence for a moment.

"Before I continue, let us pray," he said.

Everyone bowed their heads. But just as I was about to bow mine, a glimpse of a moving figure caught my eye. It must have caught Senior's too because his hand, which was holding mine, gripped tighter. I saw a Caucasian man, dressed in all black, with a black hat on. On this warm spring day, he must be out of his mind.

He looked at Senior first, and then moved his gaze to me. He held up an envelope and placed it next to a picture of me. I blinked and he was gone. It was as if no one else saw him. Senior was very quiet though he was supposed to be leading us in prayer.

"Honey?" Grandmother Patrice said gently. "Is everything ok?"

"Yes." Senior replied, snapping out of the daze

He looked at me with a troubled look. I wonder what he was thinking, but then he smiled and continued.

"As I was saying before I got caught up in my thoughts. I was going to say let's pray. But I want to continue. Leon come here," he motioned.

Leon was with his mother Christina. His father was nowhere to be seen. Actually his father stopped coming to a lot of family functions. I wasn't sure why, but I didn't ask questions.

Leon walked up and stood next to Senior.

"These two boys, or rather young men, are the best men I know. They have studied hard, both in school and church, helped in their communities, and excelled in their extracurricular sports activities. These two men you see today are going to be the leaders of the future, and one day they will be up here speaking to you all as I am speaking to you today! I know in my heart, they are the future. And I smile just knowing that I could have helped them along the way."

Senior starting clapping and everyone else joined.

"Helped?" Leon said with a big smile on his face. "Senior…"

He also calls my grandfather Senior. He probably had a closer relationship then I did with my grandfather. It used to bother me, but Leon was an only child, and Senior was his hero. So I prayed to God to get this jealousy I had in me away. And it left.

"You didn't just help us Senior. You guided us. Your way of life, your family, our family, everyone in here, you have touched in some way, shape or form. And although this may be Victor and I's graduation party, you're graduating as well! Because YOU did this. You made this happen. You, Grandma Patrice, my mother! Junior, Victoria, Victory, you have helped us all. And I speak for myself and my brother Victor." He put his arm around my shoulder. "I want to thank all of you, from the bottom of my heart, for everything you've helped us with. Give yourself a round of applause."

Christina was in tears. She came over and hugged Leon. Leon had a way with words. Master manipulator is what one opposing coach said about him.

I hugged my father and mother and the party continued. Sa'Rah was sitting down in the back frowning. I found her and sat down next to her.

"What's wrong little sister?"

She was fourteen years old, but wise way beyond her years. She looked as if she was eighteen. She was about five foot six inches with long black hair, and she was blessed with mom's green eyes. She was a beautiful little girl. I had her name tattooed on my arm. Senior didn't approve of it, but it was my decision. I guess I wanted to be a rebel. Sa'Rah loved it.

"Nothing is wrong. I just hate having to share you with all of these phony people. They aren't going to call you tomorrow you know!" She snapped at me.

"Jealous?" I asked.

I couldn't keep a girlfriend around long because Sa'Rah never liked any of them and did something to lure them away.

"Not jealous" she responded in a deep sigh. "I just don't like them gallivanting around smiling and all sorts and they have no clue who you are. They just know you're Victor Thomas' grandson and Leon's pretend brother. Yippie," she said sarcastically rolling her yes.

"Why do you talk so ill of Leon? He has never done anything but be good to you."

"I know… I apologize. But you deserve just as much spotlight. He's gotten over one thousand letters in the mail to come play sports at some stupid school and you get one letter."

"One letter? I've gotten plenty of college offers."

"Yeah? Well I'm talking about the one that man just dropped off."

"That man?"

I realized that she must have been speaking of the mysterious man in all black.

"Yes that man that stared right at you and grandfather. He spoke to me when he first came in, said something in French but it was too fast for me to decipher. But he dropped this off."

She handed me a letter she had already opened. It was a letter from the highest ranking Christian based religious studies college in the world, Jesus Christ University of Midland Michigan. Formally known as Northwood University. It was originally a business college, but in 2015 Amanda Fletcher, one of the world's top ranked Christian Activist --some call her a radical, formed JCU. People from every country begged to be a part of the school, but only one hundred students were accepted each year. They recently added sports, I heard in hopes to have Leon join their school.

I grabbed the letter from Sa'Rah and opened it.

"I've been accepted!" I said in a whisper.

I didn't want everyone to know just yet. I couldn't believe I'd been accepted. My body filled with glee. This place only accepted one hundred new students a year and I, Victor Thomas the Third, had been selected.

"Congratulations," my little sister said, tears in her eyes.

"Sa'Rah?" I said with a concerned voice. "Why are you upset?"

"Because, Victor. You're leaving me! You're going away. When I need you the most in my life."

"What are you talking about? I'm just going to college."

"It doesn't matter. Just go Victor. I will be just fine!"

"What about my poem?"

"You'll read it when you need to. Just promise me one thing. When I ask for you, you'll come?"

"By the grace of God I will."

"What's all this commotion about?"

Grandmother Patrice had wandered over.

"And sweetheart why are you crying?"

"Victor got accepted into JCU, Grandma!" Sa'Rah said quickly changing her tears of anger and despair to happiness.

My grandmother gasped and walked towards Senior as fast as she could. The music suddenly stopped.

"Everyone!" Senior said at the top of his voice. "Victor the Third has been accepted to the great Jesus Christ University!"

Everyone started to cheer. I caught a glimpse of Leon, he was looking at me smiling and gave me the thumbs up. Christina came over hugged me and kissed me on the cheeks. My mother and father came to me, and hugged me tightly. Next was Victory, she whispered congratulations in my ear. She was also accepted to JCU, but she declined to go because she wanted to be a doctor. My Aunt Victoria, my father's older sister, hugged me and told me that we'd talk later. Everyone said their congratulations.

Finally, Senior approached me.

"Hello, son."

"Hello Senior."

We stared at one another in complete awkwardness. He knew I saw that man deliver that letter. The question was, why was my grandfather so puzzled when he saw him?

"That man," He began. "You noticed him too?"

"Of course, he was staring right at us. No need to worry, he spoke French to Sa'Rah and just dropped off the letter of acceptance." I said. "I knew JCU had a history of surprise acceptance letters, but man, that was weird. No worries though, I'm very excited Senior. Maybe I can follow in your footsteps." I said in admiration of him and his success.

Why wouldn't anyone want to be like him? A humble follower of God, wonderful husband, great father, great grandfather, a good man for the community, just an all-around, genuine good man of God.

My grandfather smiled.

"Third. As much as I would love for you to follow in my footsteps, I want you to create your own. And yes, that was a surprising way to drop off your acceptance letter. You said he spoke French to Sa'Rah, huh?"

"Yes, that's what she told me," I replied, wondering why he asked.

Senior then hugged me tightly. He was happy. Everyone was happy about this announcement. I stared around the room to see people smiling, making small talk. But then I finally saw an unhappy face. In the back corner close to the kitchen, there was Sa'Rah. Staring at me, a deep piercing stare. She was looking at me as if I just tore her heart out, and ran it over with a car. Her eyes were so watery they sparkled in the light of the house. Finally, a tear ran down her face, and then at once that sad face turned into an angry face.

She turned and walked into the kitchen, disappearing into the darkness.

2

The next morning, I woke up just before the sun rose. The time when it's not totally dark outside but it isn't exactly light either. The morning sky was an orange color. That was my favorite time of the day to ride my bike. My bike was a 2017 Honda Python, a three-wheeled motorcycle.

The year is 2026. When watching movies from the 1990s and the first decade of the new millennium, this future is a lot different than what they imagined. There are no flying cars, no random trips to the moon, no one to walk on the surface of Mars. There was no 2012 end of the world, no meteor, no Ice Age, no George Jetson or robots taking over the world.

As I rode through the city, a nice cool breeze massaged my face as if the Heavens were hugging me, welcoming me into their world. The shore was a beautiful street area; freshly paved roads, no bumps or cracks in the road, refurbished houses and apartment buildings. Nice places for people stay.

Some will look at this future and say that we went back in time, using anachronistic weapons such as bow & arrows, steel swords, shields, even riding horses. Violence has gone down tremendously, thanks to the ratification of the 2nd amendment. Gun sales stopped, and thanks to controlled tracking and confiscation and harsh penalties for having firearms, there has been less deaths occurring.

The Meeting, is what it is officially called, happened in 2018. It was a meeting of the world powers to form an alliance and sign a treaty to end all wars and scrap all nuclear weapons. World leaders met in Rome, Italy and signed a treaty, international peace was at hand. It's one of the most celebrated signings in history. Since that signing, Terrorism had faded away; everyone kind of got what they wanted. Deloris Williams, the first woman president of the United States, conservative, represented us at the meeting.

Riding in a car became very different, thanks to the "Green People Act" of 2019. Emission checks were made mandatory across the states. Car pooling is different, and most people have battery operated cars, no more hybrids. People stopped using planes for long trips. It became too expensive. Instead people started using a new AmTrak train system that runs only on highly powered batteries at night, and solar power during the day. The United States worked very hard to get a centralized rail system comparable to Europe's. More teenagers started riding special motorcycles after the law passed, including myself. Some people even started riding horses to work.

That all also caused policing to become very different. Police Officers were also given battery powered cars. Their guns were replaced with specialized swords, and they were required to take training to learn to use them. Only military members were allowed to keep firearms.

It kind of became like the Roman times. Law enforcement officers gained more respect. There were still common problems like prostitution, gambling, racketeering, trafficking, and drugs, but not a lot of deaths.

Although a lot of things had been cleaned up in the world, there was one thing that forever remained the same. Religion. We managed to stop wars based on money, power, food, and control, but trying to stop a holy war was near impossible. It felt like one would be coming soon. The holy war of all holy wars, and many lives would be taken. I had dreams, lots of dreams, and the darkness was coming. I had a feeling that I would somehow be a big part of it. I hoped God would smile on me.

3

"Congratulations, brother," Leon finally said to me.

We were walking back from Euclid Creek. Euclid creek is one of the Cleveland area's parks. It has a small basketball court on the east end and it stretches about two and half miles further west.. The park is full of trees. There are high hills formed with brown solid rocks as its northern border, and picnic areas, parking, sports fields and of course the creek to the south.

It has one of the popular trails here, it's a two and a half mile walk from the entrance at the east end, and the exit to the west. Many people walk, run, hike, and bring their pets here for exercise. This is a common area for family reunions, cook outs, basketball tournaments. It's normally a very calm place, not too much negativity here, a place for people to get fresh air, the trees are beautiful, the water is clean, you could even fish. But because of the trees, at night, it gets very dark, so dark that you can't see the hand in front of your face when walking.

It was dark. Leon and I ran the trail in the park at least three times a week, normally at night. Leon preferred it. He was fearless, and with him I was fearless. He always said we knew the path so well that we didn't need light.

"Congratulations for what?" I finally responded.

We stopped running and decided to walk.

"Getting into JCU," he said with a smile. I couldn't see the smile, but I heard it in his voice.

"No congratulations are necessary, dear brother. I believe you're the reason I got accepted. They started a sports program solely for you. They wanted you to study there, and you probably gave them an ultimatum. If I didn't really want to go there I'd be a bit discouraged, but I got in, and I'm excited. So thank you." I said to him calmly.

I wasn't a simpleton. He received an acceptance letter from them, and I knew he never applied there. He sacrificed his dream of going to play for Princeton and winning them championships, a dream he had since we were children. He was drawn in by the word 'Prince.' Leon felt like he was the ultimate Prince of something, so what better for a Prince, to go to Princeton? Silly dream I know, but it was his dream, and he threw it away for me.

"Ha, so you think you got me figured out," he smirked.

"I know you better than you think I do, Leon."

"Come on V-Three," he called me by one of my many nicknames. "What did you expect me to do? Go to Princeton? Just to get some snobbish school to win some championships? When I can go to JCU, a new sports program, create history, all while guaranteeing my kid brother gets the finest education in religion the world has to offer?."

He was very good at persuading people to feel good even though they should feel guilty, like making a lie feel good even though you know you're hurting someone.

"Thank you. Seriously, Leon, I really appreciate what you did for me. I mean everything you've done for me growing up. Fighting people for me, protecting me, helping with homework, making sure I made every team that you made. You've done more for me then I feel I give you credit for."

"Ah, don't mention it V-Three," he sighed.. "As much as Grandfather has done for me and my mother, with the absence of my father. Things have been emotionally hard on her."

"Speaking of Ian, where has he been?"

"I don't know man."

Leon stopped walking. We sat at a bench area that looked over the creek. I could see hints of the moonlight on the water.

"About five years ago, I remember hearing them argue. You were over, but you were sleeping. You know I have a keen sense of hearing."

He had a keen sense of everything in my opinion.

"And my dad was yelling at my mom about, just how different I was, at the age of twelve. How fast I was, how my body was forming, my strength, eye sight, intelligence, everything. It was as if he was upset that I was healthy. I can't put my finger on why. I mean, I am a creation of him and my mother's. So why be angry? My mom said he was mad because he was upset that I am an only child. But I've told my father plenty of times that you are as much of a brother to me it was as if we both came from Christina or Persia. So I didn't mind.

"But that wasn't enough for him. So he stopped coming home early. We used to eat breakfast and dinner every day as a family. It was important to my mother to create a tradition. She would get up and cook, and we would come eat, and wash dishes. Then my father and I used to cook dinner every night, and we'd wash dishes again, and laugh as a family. We have money, we could easily afford to have our meals cooked and dishes cleaned every day, but we wanted to do this as a family. Something we could share together in a world sped up.

"Not too many families sit at a dinner table these days. They sit on the couch, watch television, and fall asleep and then the television is watching them. Parents don't talk to their children, don't know their friends, their problems, create solutions, grades, everyone is working, no one is at home anymore, and the family is dying. So my mother did what she could to make sure I was honest and open with her and my father about everything. My father used to wonder about me because I love you so. I don't know what it is, but I just feel protective and drawn to you. Sounds weird, but it is true.

"Anyway, my father stopped coming home early to cook dinner so I ended up cooking most nights. My mother and I still ate together. By the time my father came home, all he'd do is wash dishes, talk on the phone with whomever, go to sleep, and over sleep breakfast. I don't know the last time he even looked at my mother. She spends a lot of time crying. And it makes me very, very angry."

Leon and angry was like an oxymoron. He was never angry. Even in competition he held his composure. He was like a Jedi from Star Wars. They were taught to let go of all their emotions. Sort of like the Zen, letting go of attachments, and you'll never be hurt. He was never trained to do any of those things, he just did it, and he was never afraid, never cried, always happy, always encouraging, and respectful. Leon was like the perfect child, the perfect person. If Jesus was walking the Earth today, He would surely be Leon. But when Leon said he was angry at his father, I could swear I saw a hint of red in his pupils, so clear that I could make it out sitting across from him.

"I'm sorry to hear that, Leon. I had no idea."

"You wouldn't have any idea. Every time you came over to visit, my father would be there, putting on a happy face. He asked me not to say anything to anyone, not even you. He said it was just his mid-life crisis. He said he had to find himself. Said there was something he wanted to tell me, but couldn't, and wouldn't tell me. That it would kill my mother. So I let it go, never said a word, just let my mother cry herself to sleep at night. I don't know how much longer I can take it."

"What are you going to do about it?"

"What can I do? He's my father, she's my mother, I owe allegiance to them both. Till death do they part. So I can't coerce a divorce. It's out of my hands."

"Speak to Senior, he'll know what to do."

"Senior normally does, doesn't he?" Leon said with a sigh of relief.

Thinking about my problems, and knowing that I could go to him, made me feel better about the situation even before going to talk to him. It was as if Senior always knew exactly what to say at all times. The perfect phrases, the correct bible verse for the situation, Senior knew it.

"But I made a promise to my father, not to go to anyone. I'm telling you only because I trust you, more than I trust anyone else in this world. If you ever did anything to betray my trust, there would be no hope for anyone else. So I'm going to stay quiet, I know you'll stay quiet."

He then stopped talking. He looked in a direction towards the road, instead of at me. Suddenly my cell phone rang. It was my mother. I wondered why she was calling me so late.

"Hello, mother."

"Hi, sorry for calling you this late," she sounded a bit worried.

"It's fine mother, you never have to apologize for calling me. Is everything ok?"

"Sa'Rah is not in her bedroom and isn't answering her phone. She's been missing for a few hours now. Your father is out looking for her, if you get in touch with her, please bring her home. I don't want to wake up your grandfather or call the police just yet."

Sa'Rah, the ever so clever and bothered Sa'Rah. Gone from the house, missing, had people looking for her. I sighed deeply because I was very upset. She acted very strangely at my graduation party a few days ago, and now she was just gone.

"I'll find her mother. I'll bring her home."

I hung up the phone in complete disgust at my little sister's erratic behavior.

"What's wrong?" Leon asked calmly.

"That was my mother. Sa'Rah is missing. I have to go find her."

"Hmm" Leon said, as if I hadn't said anything.

He looked toward the road again.

"You can come out Sa'Rah."

Suddenly, a shadow came, and it was Sa'Rah. Too dark to tell what she was wearing, or doing out here.

"Sa'Rah? How long have you been here?"

"Long enough, Victor." She said sharply. "Leon knew I was here the entire time, didn't you Leon? You can hear everything right? You heard my heartbeat didn't you?"

"What are you talking about? Why have you been acting so weird lately? What is up? What is wrong?" I was becoming increasingly aggravated with her.

"I knew you were here. Everything that was said here, never leaves this moonlight, Sa'Rah."

He looked at her in a very peculiar way nodding his head. She looked back, smiled, and agreed.

"And yes, I did hear the heartbeats." He said to her, her smile went away.

Suddenly he was talking on his phone.

"Persia, hello. Just letting you know we have Sa'Rah, we'll be there shortly." He hung up the phone.

Old Leon, always three steps ahead of everyone. I hadn't even thought to call my mother yet to let her know we found her.

"Get on my back Sa'Rah." Leon said to her.

"I can walk myself thank you!" she snapped.

"I understand, but we have a lot of ground to cover to get you home."

He was referring to the run up to Richmond Bluffs, an upper class community in a Cleveland Suburb. That's where I lived. It's about a ten minute drive from here, it's about an hour on foot. But thirty when Leon's running, his speed. I try my hardest to keep up.

Sa'Rah got on his back. And he started running east through the darkness. I quickly followed. Running in the darkness, I couldn't talk because running with Leon, talking only winds you faster as you try to keep up with him. Just as we were approaching the road, at the corner of my eye, I saw something white moving on the basketball courts. I stopped immediately. Leon didn't notice, he was steadily running.

I walked toward the basketball courts, across the small baseball field, I climbed the small hill to the courts, and I couldn't believe my eyes. It was a stray horse. A beautiful horse. It just stood there and looked at me.

She was the horse from my daydream.

"Like her, huh?" An unfamiliar voice said from behind the horse, startling me.

I clenched my fist in preparation for a fight. Leon was long gone, I had to protect myself.

"No need to clinch your fist. I'm just asking you a question."

A short Caucasian man stepped from behind the horse, he was very thin and tiny. It was no wonder I didn't see him. He kept his distance, but I relaxed my fist.

"Victor Thomas the Third." I stuck my hand out to shake his. He didn't come forward.

"I know who you are, you can kind of say we've been waiting for you."

"We?" I asked because I didn't notice anyone else was around.

"Yes, me and her." He pointed at the horse. "She's a beauty ain't she?" He said rubbing her neck in admiration.

She was a beauty. I walked a bit closer to her, and she took a step closer to me.

"Do you know much about horses, Mr. Thomas?"

"Not much at all, sir," I responded.

"Would you like to take a seat and learn a few things?"

"Sure," I said without reluctance.

I was curious to see where all of this was going. I knew it seemed pretty insane, talking to this creepy little guy about a horse in the middle of the night. But my daydream the other day couldn't be ignored, so I listened to him. He didn't seem like a threat.

"Great, great, I would love to tell you."

We sat down on the metal seats at the basketball court. They were very cold and unwelcoming.

"You know the fastest Horse known isn't the Thoroughbred. Sure, many think that the Thoroughbred horses are the fastest, but they aren't. Thoroughbreds are the most reliable horses and can hold their top speed longer than any other horse. But the fastest known speed for a horse is fifty-five miles per hour recorded by the American Quarter

Horse, right here in the United States. This horse that you are looking at right now, she can go up to seventy miles an hour. You get a Thoroughbred to do that and its heart will literally explode and it'll drop dead.

"This horse that is before, Mr. Thomas, she's faster than an American Quarter Horse. She can hold her speed as long as a Thoroughbred and is just as reliable. But that's not all. She's as strong as the Clydesdale Horses from Scotland, a horse that Queen Elizabeth II pushed into royal servitude to carry heavy drums. You may have heard of them now called drum horses or gypsy horses.

She has just as much endurance as a purebred Arabian horse. Arabian horses have the best endurance because they had to travel long distances through the heat of the deserts. And last but not least, she's as athletic and has more stamina then a purebred Barb Horse from the Barbary Coast of North Africa. It is nearly impossible to find a purebred Barb horse today in age. But you are staring at the most magnificent work of art this world has to offer. And guess what?"

He asked a question that I hated to answer, because he knew I wasn't going to guess it correctly, but I wasn't going to say the classic cliché of *What?*

I decided to give him the what.

"What?" I asked sarcastically.

"No one has ever ridden her. She doesn't have a master, and she's still as smooth and calm as a Missouri Fox Trotter horse."

"She's never been broken huh? So how do you know how fast she is?"

"Let's just say I raced her in a vehicle once, and had to go into the fifth gear just to keep up with her."

"That is fast." I said admiring everything he'd said about her.

Although I didn't know about breeding horses, it just seemed impossible that she held the best qualities of the six horses he just named. Fast top speed, reliability, endurance, athletic, stamina, and calm, seemed pretty farfetched to me.

"I'm sure you don't believe me. So here's the deal. You give me five dollars, so I can catch the bus home, and you can take her for a spin. If you can get her up to seventy miles per hour without falling off, or your heart exploding, then you can keep her, name her, and do whatever you want. She's a smart girl, as smart as a Lipizzan Horse from Austria."

And that was seven horses she'd been compared to.

"She'll eat when she's ready, she'll sleep when she's ready. She's like an adult. Trust me, you won't have to do much with her. If you don't need her at the moment, she won't be around, and when you need her, she'll be there. Promise."

"I'm sorry, sir. As good as that offer sounds, I can't take this horse," I said to him.

As I said it, the horse neighed, and she stood her hind legs and stomped the ground very hard and huffed at me.

"Sounds like she has already chosen, Mr. Thomas."

I was in complete shock. I reached in my pocket and handed the man the first bill I could find.

"Thank you sir, but I only asked for five dollars. This is a twenty."

"Keep it," I said in complete awe.

"No, sir. No deal. I can only take five dollars, no more, no less."

He handed me back my twenty. I found five dollars in my pocket and handed it to him.

"Thank you, sir. Enjoy her," he said.

I turned toward the horse. I turned to thank him, but he was gone. He literally just disappeared into thin-air. I breathed a heavy breath; I surely hoped this wasn't a stolen horse.

We had just spent a few minutes talking, but there was no way Leon was home yet with Sa'Rah. I climbed on top of the horse. She was tall, and strong.

"Let's see what you're made of," I whispered in her ear.

Now I've only ridden a few horses in my life, and they were very slow horses, nothing fast, nothing weird. I didn't have a saddle, I didn't have any reins to steer, I didn't know how to steer with my legs. I

VENSIN GRAY

prepared myself for a very uncomfortable ride.

"Yah" I said. I refused to say Giddyup! It just sounds terrible.

As I said Yah and hit the horse with my legs, she took off so fast that I almost lost my balance. I grabbed her long thick hair on her head, and it was so thick, it felt like a rope.

She was fast. We were running up a very long sturdy hill, and she wasn't slowing down. I didn't even know if she was breathing. We were riding so fast my mouth became dry, and my jaws were flapping. We made it to Leon and Sa'Rah very quickly despite their head start.

"Steady now, girl," I said to her. We ran beside Leon. Leon stopped instantly.

"Nice horse." He said to me.

I had to catch my breath a bit. This was a very bumpy ride. I can't believe we caught up to them, and so fast.

"Leon," I said breathing hard. "I think I just lost my virginity."

All three of us laughed, even Sa'Rah.

"She's beautiful Victor," Sa'Rah said, getting off of Leon's back and approaching her.

"Strangest thing just happened. This man, this little guy, literally just gave her to me for five dollars. Crazy right?"

"Not if she was meant to be your horse," Sa'Rah said rubbing her head.

"Leon? What do you think?" I asked.

"She's a beautiful horse, brother. And she's obviously yours. You can't just go stealing horses, not like this one. What's her name?"

Ah… a name, something I hadn't thought of. The man did say I could name her.

"How about, Mere. The French word for Mother?"

After hearing that, the horse shook her head and backed away from Sa'Rah.

"You don't like that name, girl?" Sa'Rah said in a calm voice approaching her, and calming her down. "How about? Bellus? The Latin word for beautiful?"

The horse disagreed again, and backed away. I gazed at her eyes, and remembered the name I thought of in my dream.

"Come here, Vita." I said to her. She approached me with acceptance of her new name.

"Vita, huh? The Latin word for Life. That's a beautiful name," Sa'Rah said. "Can I ride her?"

I thought about it. I was Vita's first rider, I didn't want Sa'Rah getting on her and hurting herself falling off. But Sa'Rah was going to ride her, even if I said no. The horse walked toward Sa'Rah, basically welcoming her.

"I guess you have your answer," I said.

Leon and I walked along side Vita and Sa'Rah all the way until we got home.

Getting home wasn't fun, my father and mother had called me twenty times, but I didn't answer because I was too focused on the horse. The second Sa'Rah got off of Vita in front of the house, Vita ran off. The man did say once she wasn't needed, she wouldn't be there. I wondered if I would ever see Vita again.

As I walked into the house, my father hugged Sa'Rah, shook Leon's hand. He looked at me with gratitude, and for some funny reason, we all just went to bed without a word.

4

By the time I woke up the next morning Leon was already gone. He sent me a text message saying that he had to go take a jog with his mother. Christina and Leon enjoy running in the early morning. Leon loves to run period. Sometimes he takes off flying. He says that sometimes he feels like he could reach the moon. Normally after he says that I bring him down to earth. Telling him that he's only human, even though sometimes I wonder myself, his abilities are unrivaled.

He was so fast; he once ran a forty yard dash in three seconds. The men who were recording it argued over the speed. He winked at me and told me later on that he could've done it in two seconds, but he held back. He jumped abnormally high. He used to show me and me alone that he could dunk on an eleven foot rim at the age of ten years old. He was strong, agile, never tired. He was quick, durable, I mean the perfect athlete.

The National Football League tried to rewrite their rules on eligibility to get him into the league right after High School, but Leon told them that he had planned on going to college. The twelve championships we won, each of those years we were undefeated. In track, Leon ran every event, distance or speed, and we never lost. Football, he was the quarterback, broke every state record imaginable, and in basketball, let's not talk about it. He once scored fifty points by the middle of the second quarter, coach took him out of the game.

Leon made sure I made every team. I wasn't as good in basketball as my father was. Football I was just the running back. I had decent statistics but they were because Leon was every team's sole commitment. Track, I just ran speed. We had the greatest four years in sports that can only be matched, never broken. Twelve undefeated seasons, twelve state championships, and if there was a national championship, we would've won that one as well.

I got up eventually after lying in bed. I was sore after the horse ride last night. I half expected to wake up from a dream after riding Vita, but everything was real. I showered and got dressed.

I may not have been great in sports. But one thing I had a great interest in was Medieval Weaponry. Because guns were outlawed, people started taking different classes in many different skills. I learned how to use a sword, shield and more recently started learning the bow and arrow. It was very fun. I found it exhilarating.

When I picked up a sword for the first time, I was thirteen years old. After that I couldn't put it down. I took weekly training classes, because of the increase of swords and bow and arrows, you needed a license to carry them in public, and an even higher license to draw them in public even for self-defense, especially if you weren't going to use a blunt weapon.

There were a few different types of swords that were allowed by law.

You have the short sword, a long sword, and the two-hand sword. Depending on your training determines the sharpening of the blade. Since I'd been training for five years, I was licensed to carry, draw, and have a sharp blade. I never fancied a shield, but I knew how to use one. I used a long sword.

I trained at this medieval training facility west of Downtown Cleveland. It was in an abandoned warehouse. My trainer, I called him Big Red because his sword was big and red. He was this big Irish man, and he was a master at this stuff. He trained me pretty well. I think I was good. In competition, we only used wood swords, and I was undefeated in competition. I'd never actually drawn blood with my blade.

VENSIN GRAY

I didn't even know why I kept it sometimes. I couldn't imagine taking another's life.

"Where's Vita?" Sa'Rah asked as she entered my room. "I can't stop thinking about her."

"Not sure," I responded.

"When will she be back?"

"When I need her."

"What if I need her?"

"I don't understand why you'll ever need her, Sa'Rah. But I'll see if she'll let you ride her again."

"Aren't you her master?" Sa'Rah snapped at me, looking very grown up with a white blouse and long black skirt on. "You should just tell her to let me ride."

"It's not that simple Sa'Rah," I said back.

Patience is one thing I'd always had. My father really wasn't a patient person. But I was. I assume I got it from Senior. He was very calm, cool, and understanding of every one's anxiety. I tried to follow off of him.

"I just met her yesterday. Yes it was a good ride, but I don't know if she'll ever come back."

"Well I hope so," Sa'Rah said grabbing my graduation gift from my dad.

I hadn't opened it yet, and it seemed like Sa'Rah was going to open it for me.

"Don't open that!" I snapped at her.

"Too late." She said as she opened the long wooden box.

Clutching the handle of one of the most beautiful long swords I had ever seen. It was actually the new edition Silver Diamond Long Sword. It was a five thousand dollar sword! Not saying we couldn't afford it, but I wasn't sure I wanted the responsibility of owning that sword.

It was a magnificent Long Sword, three feet total in length and about two and half inches wide. The handle was six inches with a very sharp blade of about two and half feet. It was silver plated with a diamond encrusted seam through the middle, and a diamond tip, as sharp as a razor blade. I couldn't believe my eyes.

"Wow, this thing is a piece of work." Sa'Rah said rolling her eyes. "Why do even like this stuff? It's nothing but old medieval violence. These are the kind of weapons that killed people's sisters!"

She hated that I was so into the medieval ways of fighting. She stormed out of the room. I instantly called my father to thank him.

"Hello son," my father answered the phone. It sounded as if he was in his car. I heard a lot of wind.

"Father, thank you for the sword!" I said in excitement and appreciation. "It's very expensive though."

"It's not a problem Three. You will be fine with it. I hope you enjoy practicing with it. But it's really just for show. I don't expect you'll ever need to use it."

"With God's mercy I'll never have to use it," I replied.

I expect that when guns were legal, most people who purchased them just wanted protection. I can't imagine a large population of people purchasing guns just to kill someone. Sounds very barbaric.

"I have to go now, we'll catch up later."

My father hung up. We didn't have the best father son relationships. He was very distant while I grew up, more focused on his own life rather than mine. I guess it was the result of having a young parent. While I was growing up, he was growing up.

My dad was the party type I heard before I was born, even behind Senior's back he went to parties. He drank, never smoked, but was very wild. My mother on the other hand, was just a regular Jehovah's Witness girl. She obeyed her bible, wasn't very out there. Well, at least until my father got a hold of her.

Growing up wasn't too difficult. Senior and Grandmother Patrice did what they could to make sure that my father and mother at least had teenage years. My mother's mother died when I was only five years old. She died of a really bad flu one winter that went around. It killed about fifty thousand people that year.

You read about those epidemics all the time, but you don't really know how it affects you until one of your family members are lost because of it. My grandfather on my mother's side Persy, really lost his way after that. He used to attend Senior's church, but after grandma died, he just stopped. He started drinking and gambling, until he owed the wrong people money. Senior had to bail him out of the trouble he had gotten himself into. After that, he cleaned up and started going back to the Kingdom Hall.

He convinced my mother to go a few times. I remember her and my father arguing about those decisions, but it was never more than just a few angry words. They'd kiss and make up. Sa'Rah hated when they argued she did all she could to calm them down. It was like their relationship was her life I tried not to get in the middle of it.

Having teenage parents had its ups and downs. My mother was very calm and patient with me. My father was a hot head, very impatient. He physically disciplined me often, nothing too major, a spank here, slap in the hand there. My mother wasn't very fond of it, but she respected my dad's authority.

We got into a lot of arguments around the time I was thirteen. They were nearing thirty, a threshold that many feared. I was in my preteens and it was amazing how smart my mouth was, and how many times my father and I got into verbal barbs. My mother would have to hold my father back from literally killing me. Eventually I grew out of it, and I was allowed to hang around Leon more often.

Leon and I only used to hang out once and month. We talked a lot on the phone, and e-mailed, but we went to separate schools. He talked Senior into getting my dad to send me to University School, which was a life changer. We are ok now, my parents and I. Although I'm closer to Senior, I still love my father with all my heart and would do what I could to protect him.

My mother and I's relationship was a good mother and son relationship, but I was a granddads boy. I still protected my mother with

SON OF SIN

everything. I didn't like guys looking at her. When she was thirty-five she still looked like she was in her mid-twenties, and men have their prying eyes. And God knows what they are thinking. Perverts.

I found myself ending my last practice session with my usual sparring partner. His name was Brian. He was an older man, who took classes for fun. I felt like I did it for a living, with a zeal that was unmatched. The only person who matched it was an Asian by the name of Tao. No one knew where in Asia he was from. He was twenty-five, and he and I had several heated exchanges, to the point where Big Red kept us on the far ends of the practice spot.

"Good day today Victor," Brian said to me.

He was a huge man. He stood about six foot seven and easily around two-hundred fifty pounds. He played in the NFL for a few years but got injured. He was a smart man, he invested into some rental property in East Cleveland while the value was low, and it has nearly quadrupled since then, so he's sitting pretty. We had fun, but he couldn't beat me. I usually went light on him.

"I see you didn't bring your sword."

He spoke of my father's gift.

"What do you know about the sword?" I asked with a grin.

"I'm the one who told your father to get it. It was between that or the fire blade. I figured that is what you want, and the fire blade is for people who plan on using it, entering tournaments."

The fire blade was a beautiful sword that surrounded by a special lighter fluid. The top half of the blade flared up so hot it became a blue flame. It was a twenty thousand dollar sword, but you just don't buy that for show like the Diamond Blade I was given.

"Thank you, Brian. That is nice of you. Guess I won't use it on you."

Brian and I both laughed.

"Come on Victor, you don't join the tournaments. I'm not concerned."

The tournaments he spoke of were the medieval sword fighting tournaments. When you hit the age of eighteen, you can draw blood. There have been some accidental deaths, a reason why I hadn't joined it.

I was confident in my skills, but I didn't want to kill or be killed. Tao won many of the Cleveland tournaments and placed third in the state tournament. He told me that he didn't fight as hard because he knew he'd never prove himself against me. A little reverse psychology, trying to get me join, but I wouldn't.

Senior would have killed me first, and second of all, I was trying to study religion in college to hopefully become a preacher like Senior. I dreamt of being half as successful as he saving lives and teaching people about Jesus Christ.

After I cleaned up and dressed I rode to a new supermarket on the west. The area had become heavily Muslim recently. It was very peaceful and quiet, a no nonsense type of neighborhood. I always had a lot of respect for Muslims. They were very serious in their religion, not completely conformed to modernity. A lot of old school religious practices have been forgotten as time has gone on. But there, women still wore their hijab and head coverings. They always spoke to me when I came to town.

I was only known because Senior was so well known around town. My face was often on a lot of our publications inviting people to visit our church when seats were available. We had a main section for church members. It sat around 3,500 people. We also had a visitors section that was always filled to the maximum of 1,500. And even when that was full, people came and stood anywhere there was room.

I entered the new Whole foods store. It sold a lot of whole grain, healthy foods. I've always tried to eat as healthy as I can, and always loved fruit. The new store had the freshest pineapples, no matter what time of the year it was. They had the best pineapples. I love pineapples. They are a great source of vitamins, minerals, fiber and enzymes for healthy digestion. They have no cholesterol and are a great source of Vitamin C.

While in the fresh produce section, I noticed a woman wearing a purple and yellow hijab, covering all of her head. I saw Muslim women all the time wearing their practiced articles of clothing, but for some reason I couldn't stop starring at this one. I'm not really one to ever approach women, especially those who aren't Christians, but something compelled me to try to just say something to her.

"Hi," I said, as she stood across from me looking at watermelons. The summer time is their season, and they are very delicious if you pick the right one.

She looked up at me. Her face was so smooth; her nose perfectly small and fit to her face, her bone structure was like a model. She had very fair complexion, like she was Spanish, maybe mixed with black. I couldn't be sure. Her eyes were a light hazel. They were beautiful eyes. She smiled at me, one of those awkward smiles as if she didn't want me to talk, or didn't know how to respond to me talking to her. She didn't show her teeth, but she smiled and immediately looked down and returned to tending to the watermelons. She was knocking on them to determine how ripe or sweet a watermelon could be. At least that's what my grandmother Patrice had always told me to do.

"You know," I began to say. "Purple is the color of royalty."

She looked back at me, not saying a thing. She turned around away from the watermelons, towards the lemons, which I could tell she had no interest in. I knew that I should probably just leave her alone, but I was determined to get her to speak to me.

"Would you like to know why it's the color of royalty?" I asked, almost begging her talk to me.

I waited for a moment, but she was silent. I turned around to walk towards the registers.

"Why?" she said.

Her voice was soft, delicate, almost hypnotizing. I stopped instantly.

"Why is purple the color of royalty?"

Definitely Spanish, she had a Spanish accent. Not Hispanic, many people just group them all together, but there is a distinct difference in the accents between Hispanics from Latin American, and Spaniards from Spain.

"Well," I began to reply.

My heart was racing. I wanted to make sure I said everything correctly. Leon would know exactly what to say, he was very smooth with women, as if he was reading their very minds.

"Many people refer to the time called the Classical era. A point in time throughout history that interlocked the civilizations of Ancient Rome and Ancient Greece, many know it as the Greco-Roman world, where some of the literature from Aeschylus, Ovid and of course Homer wrote. During this time, Tyrian purple, better known as royal purple, or imperial purple was very hard to come by. This color, well it was a dye was created by ancient Phoenicians. Please stop me if I'm boring you."

I caught myself. I loved history, and to talk about it. I always got so over excited and often rambled.

"No, please continue," she smiled brightly, showing her beautiful teeth. They were straight and white, but the bottom row had a slight imperfection that made it even more perfect. "It's not every day someone gives me a history lesson about the color of clothing I am wearing."

She smiled as we started to walked slowly toward the back of the store.

"Well the Phoenicians created this dye, which couldn't fade. It was created from the..." I paused. I didn't know if I should tell her the nasty details, or just say it, I'll keep the details out. "Spit of sea snails. And they banded it together with the rock shell of a Stramonita hematoma, the shell of the sea snail.

"Because it was so expensive to obtain, and use, all clothing with that color at that time was deemed as a status symbol. If you could afford to purchase it, you were considered elite. Hence, why Purple is the color of royalty."

"Hmm. Did you also know that purple was controlled and outlawed in early sumptuary laws?" she replied. "And that it was considerably controlled in Byzantium, and only imperials could wear it?"

"Well, I'm impressed. So you're telling me that this entire time, everything I said, you knew."

"Yes."

"Why didn't you tell me to stop?"

"It was cute, and I wanted to see if you were going to lie. But you were right on point. So I am impressed as well. You aren't just some pastor's grandson."

"Pardon me?" I said to her, curious as to why she referred to me as a 'pastor's grandson.' "What do you know of me?"

"What don't I know of you? When my family moved here from Madrid, our welcome to the city pamphlet had a complete section on the Great Christian Pastor, Victor Thomas and his wonderful family. And of course, you and Leon were named."

She smiled at me awkwardly, as if she had heard enough about us already.

"How long have you been in the States?" I asked.

She looked at me, and then behind me. I turned around to see a large man. He was easily five inches taller than me. He wore glasses and had beard. He wasn't fat, but he wasn't all the way muscles either, like he did push-ups then ate an ice cream sandwich afterwards.

"Is there a reason why you are speaking with my daughter?"

He had a very high pitched voice for such a big man. It sounded like his lungs had been punctured. It wasn't raspy like you would expect. After he said that to me, his daughter started talking to him in their native language. I had no idea what they were saying. I could pick out bits and pieces, but they were talking so fast.

"So," he finally said in English. "You are Victor Thomas' grandson?"

He offered his hand and I shook it.

"It is quite a pleasure to meet you. I met your grandfather once, in a meeting of the leaders of the church a few weeks ago. We didn't talk long, but he is a warming presence. He commands respect without even asking for it, or wanting it."

He turned and spoke to his daughter again, and then walked away. She smiled at him, then at me.

"Mr. Thomas," she said very formally. "Would you like to have a cup of tea with me at a nearby restaurant?"

"You can call me Victor, or Three, or V-three, but never ever call me Mr. Thomas. Makes me feel old."

We both laughed a bit.

"And what may I call you?"

"I never give my name out, Victor."

She said my name in her accent and it sounded so seducing coming from her lips. I had to take a deep breath to control myself.

"Then how may I address you?"

"Maybe I'll tell you, maybe I won't," she smiled and winked at me.

I made my purchase. I only ended up buying some bubble gum. I didn't care about the pineapples anymore. I just wanted to talk to her. We walked to a small shop.

Everyone got very quiet when we entered. They knew I wasn't one of them, and I didn't pretend to be. The shop was comparable to an Arabica, a coffee house I was familiar with. There were lots of chairs in a small area, the register was up on a counter, and the counter was very long. The inside was very dim, like most coffee houses. I imagined people usually went there in to get on their portable computers, talk with friends, or see a visiting band.

"Two of your special herbal teas, large please," my unnamed acquaintance said to the cashier, who was a boy, no older than fourteen. He took her money.

"What made you think I wanted that tea?" I asked out of curiosity.

"Because I invited you to have tea with me, so you're going to drink what I tell you. Remember, I wear the color of royalty. You have to listen to me." She smiled again.

We took a small seat in the corner of the coffee house. I noticed what appeared to be the name of the place written on a napkin on the table. It was written in Arabic so I had no clue what I meant.

"What's the name of this place?"

"Just call this place Cleveland's coffee," my companion said, continuing to be very mysterious. "My name is Fawzia, but my friends call me Zia. The reason my father let me come here with you, was so that I could tell you a few things that the worlds media isn't going to allow to come out."

I sipped on the tea, confused as to what she was talking about. But the tea was very good, it was a blend of kiwi, strawberry, and I could taste the green tea in it.

"I'm sorry, what are you talking about?" I asked. "And Fawzia is a beautiful name."

"Thank you," she smiled again. "Listen, I can't talk too loud, so please listen carefully. What do you know of Madrid, Spain?"

"Madrid, Spain? Not much. I know it's the capital of Spain and influenced highly by Islam."

"Yeah, well, a few months ago you would have been correct." she said. Her voice grew more stern, and her beautiful eyes watered up. "You haven't the noticed the influx of Muslims on the west side of Cleveland as of late?"

"I'm sorry, Zia. I haven't really paid it any attention."

"Well, about a thousand of us have come in the past few months. I've been here six months, and not one word," she whispered. "Not one word."

"Word of what?"

"The Muslim persecution in Europe."

"The what!?" I said loudly.

Everyone got quiet. Zia grabbed my hand and lead me out the back door.

"The Muslim persecution in Europe, it's not being talked about. But it's like Hitler was reborn and decided instead of killing those who are Jewish, he decided to kill everyone not Christian, mostly Muslims."

"There's no way that is going on there and no one knows about it here in the States." I was skeptical.

I hated to call her a liar, but I absolutely did not believe that with today's technology, you can sneeze and it can be on YouTube, or capture tube, or I caught you movies. Let alone a twenty-first century persecution.

"Believe what you must, Victor. My father spoke with your grandfather a few weeks ago, and he asked him a few questions regarding just the total outlook of Europe. The great Victor Thomas Senior is completely oblivious to what's going on over there, so he trusted that you would be too. We don't know who we can trust in America so when we came over here, we stayed quiet. We figured if they are powerful enough to block the news from over there from coming over here, they are powerful enough to silence all Muslims in America. So we've behaved, we've been quiet, while our brothers and sisters are killed on sight. No concentration camps, no gas chambers, nothing, just brutally murdered. Women, children, it doesn't matter. Just killed."

She started crying. I was compelled to try to touch her, but she was a Muslim, and they have different respects of interactions with Muslim women and men. So I stayed back, I kept my distance.

"Why are you telling me this?" I finally asked after a few moments.

"My sister told me, the day before we left, that I would meet someone who could help us. When you continued to speak with me in the grocery store, I thought it could be you, but I doubt it. I just wanted to tell someone. Maybe you'll tell Leon, and he could help."

"Leon? Why Leon?" I said in confusion.

What did she know of Leon?

"He's the strongest of you two? The fastest? He's powerful, beyond any of our imaginations. He can, he's the only one who could stop him."

"Him? Who is him?"

She looked around, and pulled up her shirt sleeve showing her forearm, and there was a mark there. It read O, with an A under the O, but the line in the A curving with the bottom of the O.

"Him is Octavius Atavus. I'm sure you've heard of him."

"Well of course, he's a master swordsman. He mastered the art when he was twenty years old, at twenty-five, he was considered to replace the Pope of the Catholic Church and he isn't even Catholic. He's an amazing person from the stories I've heard."

"Ha." She said, starring up to the sun. "The only thing amazing about Octavius are his looks. He is indeed a beautiful, beautiful man to look at. He's a descendant of Alexander the Great. His family is very powerful in Greece. His cousins, you know them, they attend your church. They've changed their names though.

"He met me when I was fourteen. He asked my father permission to court me at such an age. My father of course said no, so Octavius had my older sister Zaviera kidnapped. My father had to let me go with Octavius, just to see Zaviera again. But once they gave her back, she had been defiled. As a Muslim woman, your hair and your virginity mean everything to you. She ran away, she told me what she told me, and then she left. Octavius was very nice, he was kind and gentle, soft spoken, relaxed, said all the right things, smiled at all the right times, until one night, he crossed the line... he tried to see my hair. No one and I mean no one see's my hair.

"My mother died before I was old enough to know anything about it, and my father explained to me, show no man your body, and show no man your hair. You are sacred. That's what he told me. Octavius said to me one night that my beauty had no match. Zaviera and I looked exactly alike, except I took my mother's eyes, and she took my fathers, dark brown. He told me that I was divine, and that only Angels should be able to touch me, and that when he's an Angel, he'll come down, and he'll create the second coming of Jesus through me. I told him he was crazy, he tried to see my hair, I fought him off, so he burned this into my skin, defiling me. My father doesn't even know this is there. I don't know Victor, I don't know what to do. I'm so sorry that I'm bringing this to you right now. Forgive me."

We stood outside the back of the coffee house for a few minutes. I had no clue what to say. I was dumbfounded, stupefied, and befuddled.

I was just told that this Octavius Atavus, a man who I admire, is basically bringing the Muslim Holocaust to the world. And she wants me to bring this to Leon. He would laugh in my face. Not that he is prejudice, but he doesn't believe in the courtship of anyone but who you are not in the same faith.

Second Corinthians chapter six verse fourteen reads 'Be ye not unequally yoked together with unbelievers, for what fellowship hath righteousness with unrighteousness? And what communion hath light with darkness?'

Leon made me memorize that the day I had kissed a Jewish girl. He was furious. I've never seen him more angry with me. He spoke of my soul. He said that he wanted me in Heaven with him. So from then on, I'd never spoken with anyone who wasn't a Christian.

"I'm sorry, Zia," I finally said. "I'm perplexed right now. I don't know what to say, or who to say it to."

"Just watch your back, and protect your church. The Muslims won't take this laying down. I'm trying to calm everything down, but they won't listen to me any longer. They aren't going to just let the United States turn a blind eye to this. I'll see you again Victor. I hope," she finally smiled after all that crying and began to walk away.

"Do not follow me," she said, and walked further down the street.

I had no idea what to make of what had just happened. There I was, just trying to tell a pretty girl, 'Hi, I'm Victor, how are you?' Instead, I got a bomb dropped on my lap. I walked around the corner to find that my bike was gone.

'What a day'. I thought to myself. I reached for my cell phone, but just as I was about to call the police, I heard some hoofs behind me. It was Vita. There when I needed her, just like that creepy little man said.

"Hey girl." I said to her.

And then it started raining out of nowhere, pouring down as if it was April. We were in the middle of June.

"What are you doing here girl?" I asked her.

She just lowered her head for me to get on her. I rode her all the way home. Although she was faster than a horse should be, the ride was very smooth, and more comfortable than my first time. When I got home, Sa'Rah ran outside to hug Vita.

And my bike was in the drive way.

Weird.

5

The next morning, while getting ready for church, all I could think about was the talk Fawzia and I had. I was so focused that my mother and I sat down and had a discussion for about an hour before we left for church. Sa'Rah and my father went to their every Sunday morning breakfast spot. They developed it about five years ago. I never would leave without mom to go to Church, and we used to take a long time, so one Sunday Sa'Rah and our father went to Denny's. They enjoyed breakfast so much that they decided to go every single Sunday. They only missed it if we were out of town.

My mother and I didn't talk about Fawzia and I. We just talked about life. She explained that leaving the Kingdom Hall was one of the hardest things she had to accept in life to be with my father. She didn't see her family as much, she missed her mother, and she missed the Hall. I didn't know what to tell her. She made this decision so long ago; life had changed so much since then.

After talking, we finally drove to church.

Church of Christ, that's all it was called. Nothing more, nothing less. There was no denomination rendered. Nothing. Just Church of Christ. You could be whatever, and go there and walk out feeling good that you went.

The church itself looked like a roman senate hall. White bricks, huge pillars, big castle like doors. Senior said he wanted an old school feeling in this church, so everything was portrayed as if it was built during the Roman times. There were tall trees and well-trimmed bushes leading down a red brick walkway towards the East and West entrances. There were ushers dressed in all white attire to greet everyone who entered.

Once you entered into the Church there was a long hallway stretching from east to west. Because this was such a big church, there were literally signs with directions. At the center of the hallway there were two entrances to the Sanctuary, one for members of the Church, and the other for visitors. The visitors, unless they were a senior citizen or physically unable to go upstairs, had to walk up a stairwell that had a semi-circle that could fit about fifteen hundred people comfortably. When you walked into the Sanctuary from the first floor, it mirrored the top rows, stretched a little further out, and back, it could fit a lot of people. It was all facing the pulpit, where of course Senior sat, along with other members of the church were going to speak.

To the left of the pulpit was where the choir sat. We had three choirs. The senior choir, which was mostly mothers of the church and older people. The adult choir, that explains itself, and then the pride and joy of our church, our youth choir, ran by a zealous jubilant Brother Phillips.

Our youth choir was composed of teens ages twelve to adults age twenty-five. Brother Phillips had them dressed well, and they could sing anything and sing it well. Our band sat to the right of the pulpit. They had a drummer, piano, organ, trumpets, violins, trombones, and a list of other instruments. We literally had an orchestra, and they worked very well with the choirs. The sound of music was an important thing at the church. A lot of people attended just to hear the music. Senior's sermons were just an added bonus.

My mother and I walked into the Sanctuary, which contained no images of what Christ might look like only pictures of various stories of the bible. The seats were pews with very soft padding covered with dark blue cotton. My mother and I sat next to my father and Sa'Rah.

Sa'Rah came and sat right next to me as always. She would always pass me notes, even though we sit right in front of Senior. Christina and Leon also joined us. Thank goodness we were family. There wasn't assigned seating, but members of the church just knew where certain people sat.

"Where's Ian?" my father whispered to Christina.

She looked at him and shook her head.

Ian had been acting very peculiar lately, as Leon said a few days ago. But he'd never missed church before. I wasn't sure what was going on with them.

I received a text message on my cell phone from Leon. It read 'I'm going to find him, and we are going to have a serious talk.'

I didn't respond. Not because I didn't want to. I didn't know what to say. Sometimes I figured instead trying to find the right words when you don't have them, just wait and if you get them, say them. If not, never say a word. Leon knew me. He would understand. I read the first note passed from Sa'Rah.

'I have a solo today.'

Sa'Rah was a part of the youth choir. She was blessed with a beautiful voice. She could hold a note. She could sing in any tune you needed her to in perfection. Awhile back a record company tried to sign her to a deal, but she said no. We didn't need the money, and she enjoyed being a fourteen year old. Besides, she only really liked to sing gospel, although I'd heard her sing some rhythm and blues songs really well.

Church eventually started at about 10:30, the normal time. They went through to provisions, welcoming people to the church, announcements, prayer, a few songs from the choir, and Sarah's solo. She sang an old song, Silver and Gold. She sang it really well, and you could hear those who had never heard her sing before marvel at her voice. After everything was said, Senior finally came from his study. He normally didn't come out before he preached. It was just one of his things I guess. Sometimes he would come out to hear Sa'Rah.

He wore his blue robe. It was a light blue color with gold markings. Everyone clapped as he was introduced, and he hugged Grandmother

Patrice, shook my father's hand, kissed Sa'Rah on the cheek, hugged Christina, and winked at Leon and me. He then walked to the pulpit, shook his assistant pastor's hand. His name was Robert Kendricks. He was fresh out of college, learning under Senior as to how to run his own church. He was from Seattle.

Senior then shook the deacons hands and acknowledged the elders and mothers of the church. Respect was a big thing for Senior, he lived by it.

"Praise the Lord everyone," Senior said in his usual calm tone.

"Praise the Lord," everyone responded.

"Today when I woke up, I had a heavy heart," Senior said. "I'll tell you all after the sermon. I must let you know, today I will not be calling alter call. If you would like to baptized today, you will come up without the persuasion of any of us. If you've been here before, you know what's about to happen! Everyone, get up, and for the next few minutes mingle with everyone. Get to know them, and as always, tell them that you are happy to be here! I love the Lord!"

Senior did this to calm everyone before his sermons, and to pray before he preached. But he didn't sound like his normal self. I believe Leon picked it up as well. He and I walked to the pulpit.

"Hello Victor, Leon."

He never called me Victor. Something was up.

"What's going on grandfather?" I asked.

He knew I knew something.

"Does this have anything to do with Octavius Atavus?"

After I said that name, Senior looked amazingly shocked and displeased at the same time.

"What do you know of Octavius Victor?" He asked in a stern voice.

"I was told a few things. I dare not speak it in church."

"We will talk later. I don't want you getting into this, Victor. Say nothing, and do nothing. I'm serious."

When Senior said he was serious, he was really serious. I didn't plan on doing anything, but I guessed the things Fawzia spoke about yesterday were true.

"What are you two talking about? And why am I in the dark?" Leon asked as we left the pulpit.

"I can't speak of it ,Leon. You heard me give my word," I responded.

He knew I was going to tell him later. But Leon might actually try to take action. He was the type that would fight for human rights.

"We'll talk later." Leon said.

After about fifteen minutes of mingling, Senior signaled for everyone to take their seats.

"It is a beautiful day outside today," Senior began. "I was talking with a young man the other day who has decided to get married. Marriage is a serious commitment, a strong commitment, so I asked him one question. I asked, what is a husband? He could not answer. Who is a husband in here? Raise your hands."

Husbands started raising their hands.

"Everyone, take out your bibles. If you do not have a bible, I want you to cover yourself. You are naked in the church. Please get an usher's attention. They will give you a bible to use or take home if you do not have one. Today, we're going to talk about the role of the husband."

Senior paused.

I knew this pause. The last time he paused like this was three years ago, when he preached about the 'Armor of God' and staying strong in your faith. He probably gained national attention from that sermon because he did it with such zeal, and I felt it was about to happen again.

"The reason I'm going to talk about this today is because we as a society have lost place in roles and values according to the Bible. What is the role of the Husband? First Corinthians chapter eleven verse three says *'that the head of every man is Christ. But the head of the woman is man, and that the head of Christ, is God.'* Now what does that tell us? It tells us that here on Earth, the head of the family, is man. So the success and failures of the family, is the responsibility of the head of the household. Families out here today, if you ever seen a family, or experienced displeasure in a family, what are a lot of common denominators? That's right, a man, in some way shape or form. The father is often gone, the husband is gone." Senior paused again, took a breath. He walked and looked at different sections of the congregation.

"I love this subject because so many men do not know what it means to be a husband. We don't want to know what it means, why not? Because now your wife is going to say 'Pastor said you supposed to treat me like this and all this stuff' and you are going to be mad at Pastor. Don't be mad at Pastor, I'm just telling you what the Bible has to say." Senior laughed a bit, makes him a bit comfortable. I asked him once if he was nervous when giving sermons, he said to me yes, because he has the responsibility to educate people on how to save their souls, he doesn't want to turn them away.

"When you go to the book of Ephesians, to the fifth chapter and read verse twenty-two it reads; *for wives, this means submit to your husband as to the Lord. For the Husband is the head of his wife as Christ is the head of the church.* Let me repeat that, *for the Husband is the head of his wife as Christ is the head of the church.* The head of his wife, powerful, powerful words there. So this means! That she must submit to her husband, as he submits to God. Patrice must submit to me, as I submit to the Lord." Senior makes a lot of references to his family, myself, my father, my mother, Sa'Rah, Leon, Aunt Victoria who isn't here today, Aunt Victory who is studying in Miami for the week, and most of all my grandmother Patrice. He loves her like no other.

"Men love to tell their wives, 'The Bible says you're supposed to do as I say.' Well we disagree. Wives you tell him, when you take off your hat and pray to God, I'll put on my prayer scarf, and pray with you. But you are a fool going down the wrong path, I will not follow. So this means, my Husbands out there, you can't go and tell your wife to do something that isn't Godly. The other evening, Patrice and I were in our living room, the grandkids were out and about; my children of course didn't visit their old parents. So Patrice and I are just having a quiet evening. I don't really remember what we were discussing, but I

VENSIN GRAY

remember the phone ringing, and on the caller I.D. I saw a number that at that moment of time I didn't want to speak. I saw Patrice going to answer the phone and I asked her 'Patrice, can you tell that person that I'm not here please.' That's a small white lie, and it's still ungodly. Patrice answered the phone, and you want to know what she said? 'Hold on a second, Victor wants to tell you that he's not here.' So for the next hour and half I was on the phone, thanks to the fact that my wife didn't submit to my ungodly request." Everyone laughed for a second.

"That was probably me calling pastor!" Said a male's voice from the visitors section. Senior looked up and laughed some more and we all laughed. There's nothing like laughter to ease the pain of anxiety. I'm always anxious when I'm in church for some strange reason. I looked over at grandmother Patrice, and she smiled at me and winked. Senior walked around some more, gathering himself. He touched the arms of one of the deacons.

"Husbands, love yourself. Same book of Ephesians, same chapter, verse twenty-eight says. *In the same way, husbands ought to love their wives as they love their own bodies. For a man who loves his wife actually shows love for himself.* That's a line right there! For a man who loves his wife! Actually shows love for himself! So Love yourself men, by showing your wife you love her. You're supposed to love your wife as you love your own body... why!? Because she came from your body, she is from your wound. God made man from dust and breathed air into his nostrils, but God made woman from man to be his 'helper'. From his rib God made her, and Adam, the first man, said 'At last!'" Senior said very loud and excitingly. "Everyone with me.

" 'At last!'" We all said in Unison.

"This one is bone from my bone, flesh from my flesh, she will be called 'Woman', because she was taken from man. At last! That is how you are supposed to feel when you've met that one. At last! Now I didn't date anyone. Patrice was my first date, and she's going to be my last date before I die. But there are men out here, who are dating two

— 46 —

or three women at one time. And even though it's not supposed to be this way, unfortunately in some cases it is. Men are sleeping in whose bed with what woman and whose daughter, never satisfied I tell you, never satisfied. Until you meet that one that is from your bone, that is from your flesh, after all these trials and errors, trials and errors, you are going to say 'At last!'" Senior gets very hyped and emotional when giving sermons that deal with the family. Not because it's more important than any other sermon, but because he believes the key to fixing societies starts from the household. Not the president's job, or anyone else, he just feels that a stable family and a good community could cure the problems with society.

"So men out here." He continued. "After you've met this woman, you've courted this woman, dated this woman, began a Godly, and I repeat, Godly relationship with this woman, you ask her to be your wife, accept her as your rib, let her become your flesh. You say 'I do' and nothing is supposed to change after that, you're supposed to keep going, keep working on your relationship with God. You might gain weight, your physical appearance might become different, but your soul and your spirit are to remain one with God and each other. So that does not mean you get to just do what you want. Colossians, chapter three verses eighteen and nineteen it says. *Wives, submit to your husband, as is fitting for those who belong to the Lord. Husbands love your wives and never treat them harshly.*

"Those verses are very important, submit, we hear the word submit again. Women submit to your husband, as he is submits to God. I've said that already, but it is so important, women out here are just following who in the world knows? Who is this man? What is this man doing? Why are you submitting to him when he has no relationship with God? What is he doing? Your family isn't where you want it to be, look at the man of the house, is he doing what he's supposed to be doing? If there is no man of the house then that's the reason why things aren't the way they are supposed to be. This new era of women, independent women, women who want to do it all alone, single mothers, raising children. I say children because, women… How are you going to raise a man? When you yourself are not a man? And women… how are you going to tell your daughter how to get and keep a good man, notice I said good man, when you don't have a good man yourself? I'm sorry; you were not made to do it by yourself. You were created from a rib, to assist the husband, the man, together, to raise a family, and people want to know what's wrong with society nowadays.

"Men want to blame women." He stopped, I'm assuming to carefully gather his thoughts about his next phrase of words. If there's one thing I've learned about Senior, just because you mean to say something a certain way, doesn't mean they are going to receive it the way you meant it. Choose your words carefully. "I'm in no place to blame man or woman; if we all do what we're supposed to do then society will be better. In Confucianism, Man is the start of everything. Everything! Kings have responsibility to their subjects, fathers have a responsibility to their son, and husbands have a responsibility to their wives. What's the common factor in there? Man, woman can't be a husband… woman can't be a father, and woman can't be a King. So why are women trying to do man jobs? Because in a lot of cases the Man is missing! Now I know some of you are in thinking 'What is going on in the Pastors mind that he's bringing up Confucianism in church. I tell you, I'm bringing it up because it's not just Christianity where they emphasize the role of man, the husband." A man after man hearts, Senior is one of the few preachers I've seen who can say such serious things, keep their composure, breathe easy and relay his message well, while still getting the crowd involved. Throughout this entire sermon, people have been up clapping, and making remarks while he was preaching. And other than the 'At Last' part, he hasn't really been super excited, just normal excited.

"Back to my original question," Senior continued after a moment of silence. "'What is the role of a husband?' Where are the potential husbands at? Also, husbands already should be listening closely too.

Find yourselves, love yourselves… take these words, and let them enter your heart, let the Lord enter your heart, and encourage your decision making, your actions, if you're depressed, pray to God and you'll be happy. If you are hurting, pray to God and you'll be healed. Husbands, if you aren't happy with your wife, first look at how you are as a husband. And if you know you are trying your best, tell her to turn to Proverbs twelve verse four.

"Now I know you women didn't think I forgot about you all. It says there that *a worthy wife is a crown for her husband, but a disgraceful woman is like cancer in his bones.* Cancer to his bones… there's no in between there, either you are a crown, or you're like a cancer. Listen to those words, it says a worthy wife IS a crown, IS a crown, but you are only like a cancer. Some may beg to differ. Either you're going to make him a King, or you're going make him feel like he's dying. There is no in between. So wives out here, who have been all for how your Husband is supposed to treat you, make sure you're that crown, don't be a cancer.

"Now what the Husband does with that crown. You're supposed to be fruitful and multiply, and if you've done what you're supposed to do. Same book, chapter seventeen, verse six says *grandchildren are the crowning glory of the aged; parents are the pride of their children.* The crowning glory, so your wife is supposed to crown you, and if you raised your children well, they will raise their children well, and you'll be glorified with the family you just built, such as my grandchildren, Leon, Victor and Sa'Rah. I couldn't be more proud. I love them all as if I had birthed them myself." He said Leon first. Although I'm his only blood grandson. It never bothers me; some ask me outside of church, does Leon and Senior's relationship bother me. And it doesn't, Leon doesn't have any family other than Ian's side. We are Christina's family, and I have no problem sharing Senior with my brother. Senior looked at us and smiled. Sa'Rah passed me a note. 'You know you're his only grandson.' I clinched her hand very hard, and looked at her, I do not like when she does things like that, it's like she challenges

Leon's importance to our family. Senior slowed up, and took one last look at everyone. This is when he comes to his final point and gives us something to think about, calls alter call, which he isn't doing today, assigns two members of the church to greet people as they leave, and release everyone.

"The subject for today is 'What is the role of a husband?' Not Man as in Jesus Christ, but Man as in the imperfect man that is living in this imperfect world trying to be perfect. We as men will never be perfect, but we as man were created to be the head of the household. To submit to God, love our wives, and support our children. The bible tells us parents not to aggravate and discourage our children. To teach them right from wrong. So men out here I beg you, to be a man. Find out what it means to be a good husband, so that when you decide to become one, or if you're already one, you know what to do. I'm going to send you out with this thought right here. Ephesians, chapter five, verses twenty-five through twenty seven; *for husbands, this means love your wives, just as Christ loved the church. He gave up his life for her to make her holy and clean, washed by the cleansing of God's word. He did this to present her to himself as a glorious church without a spot or wrinkle or any blemish. Instead, she will be holy and without fault.* Just as Christ loved the church, he gave his life for her. If we husbands are supposed to love our wives as Christ loved the church, we should treat as such as Christ treated the church, we should give our life for her."

After he finished saying that, there was complete silence in the church. Over five thousand people were speechless. Finally, Leon and I stood up and started clapping, and everyone else started clapping and praising God. The organ player started playing music, and pretty soon everyone was stomping in the aisles, raising their hands, crying. Halleluiahs were being shouted and everyone was in the spirit. After a few minutes of that going, Senior finally gained control of everyone.

"Everyone," he spoke softly. "This will be our last service for a while."

Everyone gasped and looked around.

"There have been some... problems overseas that have been brought to my attention. Amidst growing threats to Christian churches, we've been asked to cease services until further notice. Please be careful. I can't really speak on much of it, because I do not know myself. Although I would love to continue service, your safety is my main concern."

I knew he must have been talking about what Fawzia was saying. Surely the Muslims weren't threatening the churches in America. Fawzia completely spoke against it. I decided I would have to talk to Senior to see what was going on.

"God has our back, Pastor. You don't have to close church," yelled a parishioner, with a lot of people agreeing.

"I understand your concern and disappointment. Again it is only temporarily until we get a better understanding of the situation." Senior said.

After several minutes of back and forth with obvious worried and concerned members of the church, a rarely agitated Senior had Leon and I say goodbye to everyone as they bid farewell to the church.

I stood at the west entrance, saying goodbye members of the church. Some stopped and asked what I knew and I told them I knew nothing. I smiled at a few young girls who exited the church.

After most of the visitors and members had left, Elizabeth Tatopoulos stopped to talk. She was a very beautiful woman who started attending our church about two years earlier. She was European and Greek, but she had a heavy Greek accent. She stood about five foot ten, and had along neck. She looked like a model actually, long blond hair, very slim, with light blue eyes, small lips, small waist; I'd be lying if I didn't say I found her incredibly attractive.

She had spoken to me very seldom, never about anything serious. A lot of the younger members of our church and visitors tried to talk to all the time, but she didn't say a word other than thank you for coming to church. Her mother was just as beautiful, just a little older. They walked with their heads held very high, and they seemed a little snotty sometimes.

"Well hello, Victor," Elizabeth said to me, her voice deep and commanding.

"Hello, Sister Tatopoulos," I replied.

I was very formal when I'm speaking to members. You never know who you can offend by simply responding to a question.

She smiled after I greeted her.

"You know, Victor, out of all the guys that have tried to pick me up at church, you were never one of them. May I ask why not?"

That was the most surprising question I had ever heard in my life. I was speechless for a second. When I finally came to, the first thing that came to my mind was walking.

"Would you like to go for a walk?" I asked.

"Sure. Where to?"

"Just down the street."

Elizabeth and I walked down the street. I was in my church attire, a dark blue suit with a light blue shirt. Elizabeth wore a long green and yellow sun dress. Her hair was down and she had sunglasses on. It was very hot outside, but I wasn't thinking about the heat. I was too busy thinking about walking down the street with a beautiful woman.

We walked in silence for a while. It was a bit awkward. East Cleveland had become such a beautiful city. Apartments were no longer run down, and there were no abandoned houses. It was actually hard to even get a house in East Cleveland anymore.

The school system was top-notch, a complete turnaround from how things were just ten years ago. It was amazing what the work of a church and businesses can do to a city. Senior's church used to be on a different street, but people invested into a new one, and Senior said, the purpose of establishing a church is for growth, if you're going to build a new one, it should be larger than the one you had before. I miss the little church; it's now a Christian Library.

"So, Victor, do you know exactly who I am?" Elizabeth finally spoke.

"Not exactly. I know that you are from overseas. I can hear it in your voice."

"I am from London but, my mother is Greek and my father is European. He doesn't attend this church. He and my brother attend some Catholic church in Toledo."

"Oh ok. Why Catholic?"

"Because they are Catholics, silly," she said as she giggled.

Although she was very pretty, she kept a serious face. It was nice to see her smile for a change.

"Why'd you move from London?" I asked.

"That's the question I've been waiting on you to ask for two years now, Victor," she replied.

We were near a bench. She walked towards it and sat down. I followed.

"I'm sure you know about the class system. It's not as serious here, but over there, your status means everything. We were a part of the nobility in England. Very respectable people, actually in a lineage for the throne if a number of people had died." There was silence.

"You said *were?*"

"Yes were. Let me tell you Victor, in England, I attended the top schools, I was accepted into Oxford University, I was a top prep student, I was on my way. Until daddy was caught doing something he wasn't supposed to be doing. And then, just that fast, my entire life was turned over. We had to come to America when I was eighteen. I graduated from Hawken, and I attend Case Western Reserve now. Yay."

She said yay very sarcastically and almost insulting. Granted Case was no Oxford, but still it was a top school.

"What did your father do?" I asked, being nosey.

"I'd rather not say. Basically, my conversation with you today is to find out what did you think of the sermon today?"

"As normal, it was a great sermon. My grandfather always gives good sermons."

"Not his quality, about Husbands. Do you think you're ready to be a husband?"

That was a very peculiar question.

"I'm not sure. I've never been a boyfriend, let alone thought about becoming a husband."

"Ha," she laughed. "I often used to think about marriage when I was a teenager. I'm twenty now, soon to be twenty-one. I used to think about what it could be like to marry a prince or someone closer to the line to the throne. When you've had respect and power before, you want it back in a bad way. I used to get courted often, nothing serious, just occasionally group dates. I've met the young princes of England. One of them told me that I was going to be his wife. I laugh to this day because he still calls me, but we could never talk. We might as well be rich peasants. Everything was stripped from us. We couldn't even join the upper-class here in America. It's about status and power, not how much money you have. We have money, but no power, no status, nothing. The upper-class here in America is a joke compared to England. They mean nothing, they are nothing, but they are important here, to have strong families, strong ties. That is why I'm talking to you, Victor."

"I don't get it."

"I know. Look, no offense Victor, but I could marry the prince of England if I wanted to. You know who my cousin is? His name is Octavius Atavus. He's my second cousin. I'd marry him if I could just to get my status back."

"Octavius is your cousin?" I asked.

She must have been a part of the family that Fawzia spoke of. I doubted she knew what her cousin was doing over in Madrid, or she probably wouldn't just openly say it.

"Do you know what Octavius is doing now?"

"I have the slightest idea, Victor. We haven't spoken since I left

England. I haven't tried to call him or anything. He's a busy man. But enough about him, my reason for talking to you Victor is because I want an arranged marriage."

"Excuse me?" I said in complete disbelief "I'm normally not this forward, but it's been two years since we've joined your church. We've been members for almost two years now. My mother has done everything she could to try to break your mother and father up, but nothing came of that, so she settled for Ian."

"Excuse me? Did you just say your mother settled for Ian?"

No way was Ian cheating on Christina.

"Why would you just blurt that out?"

"It's not like it's a big secret. A lot of people in the church knew they were flirting."

"That's ridiculous. I don't believe you."

"Believe what you want, Victor. I want you to think about a marriage to me."

"Why would you want to marry me? And don't speak a word of this Ian and your mother thing to Leon."

"I won't. My lips are sealed. And I want to marry you because in England, two years ago, there was article about nobility and Americans, which Americans had power over here, that would have power there. Believe it or not, your grandfather would have a lot of power in England being as good as he is, and as important as he is. I was surprised. Even some of the people I thought would be on the list weren't. I believe that if your grandfather ran for President of the United States he'd win. He'd win just solely on the fact that he's one of the most highly respected religious influences of our time."

"Well I agree with one thing. My grandfather is a great man. But this talk of marriage, power and stuff. I have no power. Yes my grandfather is very influential but that's him, not me. The only person I have influence over is Leon. I could probably get him to do something incredibly stupid and dangerous to get a million hits on YouTube. What you are talking about is extremely crazy. I apologize if I come off as insulting. I understand that status and power system, both here and in England, but marrying me is not going to get you any power. If my grandfather decides to retire, I do not inherit the church. We have elders who come together and they decide on who the next pastor will be."

"Listen, Victor," she stood up.

I happened to see how smooth, shaven and strong her legs were. She put on some red lipstick that obviously was supposed to make her lips look juicier then that actually were.

"You're going to Jesus Christ University. You're going to obviously study to become a preacher. You're going to learn under your grandfather, and once he's done, I'm sure he's going to make sure the church is passed on to you. And as your wife, I'll have the money, the status, and the power. People do not tell me no, Victor Thomas the Third. And you won't be the first. I'll see you around. You have my number."

She leaned over and kissed me on the cheek. She smiled a very big smile.

"You're cute," she said as she got into her mother's vehicle. It pulled up while we were talking.

I didn't know what to think. Senior was closing the church, and I was getting hit on by one of the hottest women in Cleveland. You didn't see women like her in Cleveland often. They're all in Boston or New York, hitting on business men and professional athletes. But she wanted a power beyond my reach I believe. And the fact that she' was Atavus' cousin was scary.

It started to seem like the only good thing about the day was that it would be over soon, and I would get to spend time with Sa'rah the following day. I was hoping I could figure out why she'd been acting so strange.

6

It had been a very unusual past few days. First the day dream, then actually meeting and riding a horse that I named Vita in a dream, then meeting and actually pursuing a woman who was not of the same faith. And having her tell me about some religious Holocaust being run by a man in who I admired. On top of all that, getting a marriage proposal from one of the most beautiful women I knew.

I still had to meet with Senior about the whole closing church deal. But it was not the day for all of that. It was a day for Sa'Rah and I.

We liked to get away every few months and spend an entire Brother Sister Day together. This particular time we started off with going to breakfast at Bob Evans. Sa'rah got French toast without powder sugar, a side of eggs, and hash browns. I decided to get the Farmers omelet with some pancakes. We didn't talk about anything serious during breakfast, just joked around and had a fun filled breakfast.

After breakfast we went shopping, at a Megamall about 45 minutes south east of Cleveland. We walked around for about three hours shopping,. Sa'rah bought shoes, shirts, pants, jewelry, and office supplies. I didn't know what they were for, but she liked arts and crafts.

Finally, we had lunch and decided to see a movie. The movie went to see was called *A Kingdom in Heaven*. It was a remake of Orlando Bloom's *Kingdom of Heaven*. It was an ok movie, very long though.

After all of those adventures, we found ourselves in Warrensville, Ohio, a suburb of Cleveland, at the new Stables near Thistledown.

Thistledown is a horse track The People for the Ethical Treatment of Animals, or PETA, fought long and hard to stop having horses that were done racing killed and sold to places that slaughtered them. So they began donating the horses to the Warrensville Stables.

Sa'Rah loved horses. She used to draw pictures of them all the time. And she always wanted one, but my father never got one. He said that we would have to move out to a Ranch or get a lot of land far off somewhere to get one. My mother tried really hard for him to get her one but he didn't budge. She even went to Senior in an attempt to go over my father's head and that didn't end well for her. He spanked her, and put her on punishment for two months for that act of disrespect. Senior tried talking my father out of it, but it didn't work. My father was a stubborn person. I don't know if he was always happy, but he played the role of a family man very well.

"I think mother and father are getting a divorce," Sa'Rah said to me as we were riding.

"Why would you say that?" I asked her. It was like she was reading my mind.

"It's inevitable," she said softly, "You know them being together is my life. I love our family time. I love our family. But something is telling me that our entire family is about to experience great suffering. I don't know why. It's in my head, it's in my dreams. And with you going away to college it's going to be just me to take care of everybody."

"Sa'Rah--"

"Don't Sa'Rah me," she interrupted me. "Don't tell me I'm a kid and I have other things to worry about other than the wellbeing of this family. This family is my life. Other little girls do not have fathers, some don't have mothers, some my age are prostitutes. Some are on drugs, and others have four or five boyfriends. So don't you tell me that I'm just a kid."

She took the words right out of my mouth. I was going to tell her not to worry about those things but she beat me too it.

"Mother has been spending a lot of time with Grandfather Persy."

She continued, "She's hell bent on going back to the Hall, and dad is hell bent on her not. They are growing apart, and have been for quite some time. I believe they were holding out to at least celebrate your graduation together. But me, I believe they are going to split soon. And it breaks my heart." She started crying.

Sa'Rah was tough for a girl, she rarely cried, rarely talked on the phone, she wasn't a tomboy, but she wasn't a prissy girl, she was just Sa'Rah. Beautiful little girl, other girls tried to hang around her because she's so pretty they want to know how she does it, older girls are jealous of her, and younger girls envy her. She's really intelligent, strong minded and not afraid to speak her mind. She has conversations with full grown adults who have bills, children, mortgages, and lived a full life, and sometimes Sa'Rah is more mature than them. A lot of people call her a strange child. An article in the paper was written about "Victor's dream granddaughter doesn't accept record deal." It was her shot at fame and fortune, but Sa'Rah didn't want fame and fortune, we already had that here in Cleveland. Everyone knew us, either by Senior or Leon. We weren't incredibly rich, but we have money, respect, influence, ha, I guess this is what Elizabeth wants, that's why she wants to be a Thomas.

"Speechless?" Sa'Rah said to me after drying up tears. She wasn't one to hug while crying, she just toughed it out. "I don't know what I'm going to do, Victor. There's really no comforting in this matter. I suspected that you were going to ask me why have I been acting so strange lately, when I was missing, or during your party. I can't really answer that. I guess with you leaving going to college, who's going to be there for me? You're my brother. Sure I've aggravated and agitated you throughout the years, but that's what we do. You've always stood up for me, you've even taken the blame for things that you knew that I did, you could've easily told on me, but you took the punishments every time and never complained."

"Sa'Rah, I think that you are over thinking," I said to her. "When I'm away at college, it's just temporary. It's all in growing up. Yes it's scary. Trust me, it's really scary. But we all have to do it. I'm going to study at one of the finest institutes America has to offer. To better myself, so I can continue with what Senior is doing."

"But why does that have to be your life?" Sa'Rah interrupted again. "I understand that Grandpa is a great man. But you will always be measured up to him. No matter what you do, the accomplishments in your life, you have to live up with the great Victor Thomas Senior. And then you have to keep up with the great Leon. Doesn't any of that bother you? You are too humble, Victor!"

She and I had this argument many times before. She hated that I was always compared to either Leon or Senior. But I didn't mind being humble while others were great. I felt I was blessed to have a grandfather like Senior and a brother, blood or not, in Leon. But Sa'Rah wanted me to be great. Sa'Rah wanted me to be arrogant, and full of pride. She thought that doing that would give me the attention she thought I deserved.

Everything I did, besides medieval things, was compared to Leon. Everything I did with the Church and our community was compared to Senior. Most would crumble under that pressure, but I embraced it. I was just grateful that God had placed me in that family. I remember, Senior telling me that I wasn't supposed to be here, but prayer kept me alive.

"You have to understand, Sa'Rah, that I'm not like a lot of people. Humility takes you a lot of places in life. No one likes a loud mouth attention grabbing person. I'm quiet because I need to be. I don't get angry like others. I try to stay calm. Proverbs twenty-nine verse eleven says *a fool gives full vent to his anger, but a wise man keeps himself under control*. I'm just trying to be humble. And besides, I'm great at a lot of things."

"Like what? What are you great at that you get credit for?" Sa'Rah said challenging me.

"I'm a great brother to you aren't I?" I said with a smile.

"I guess," she said rolling her eyes.

"You guess? You know what other girls would do to have a brother like me?" I said teasing her.

"They'll have to go through me!" she said finally showing a smirk.

It was a beautiful evening. It was around eight o'clock and the sun was starting to set. The sky was a light orange color. It was the best part of a summer day in Cleveland. The time when it wasn't too hot, and wasn't too cold. It was just nice and warm.

"I'll do what I can, Sa'Rah," I said as we approached the horse check in station. "To make sure mother and father stay together."

"You promise?"

"I promise."

"Can you promise me another thing?"

"Sure"

"When you are away at college, if I need you, you'll come back immediately."

"I'll do the best that I can, Sa'Rah."

"Thank you!" She said with a huge smile on her face.

She was so beautiful. She looked just like my mother. She was going to be a great person for our community, our family and our church. We were the only grandchildren of the Great Victor Thomas. So we were kind of destined to continue the church once Senior retired. That was why it was so important for me to go learn from JCU, and she had to understand that.

Suddenly I received a text message from my father.

'Masterplan with Senior tonight.'

It's our night. Once a month, Senior, my father and I all meet at the Masterplan in Cleveland, right outside of East Cleveland. It's a bar, but we do not drink. Senior created a tradition some time ago, when Grandmother Patrice didn't cook dinner, and he wasn't cooking dinner, every Saturday night he would go and get a corned beef sandwich from there, a Pepsi and a bag of Doritos. It was his meal before preaching the next day, Grandmother Patrice called it. Sometime before I was conceived, my father started going with Senior, and when I turned 16 I was allowed to join them. It was always very fun, we used to do it every Saturday, but now, it's just every once in a while. We sit at this little booth in the back, and everyone knows us, at least the regulars. The National Inquirer tried to write up a story stating that Senior was having marriage problems so he comes here to drink. The Plain Dealer, Cleveland's newspaper did an investigation and found that he went there only for the corned beef. It was a very silly time. Senior, instead of getting angry at the articles, he just laughed at them in complete entertainment. He's the one who told me about Proverbs twenty nine verse eleven. And he said that nothing good comes out of talking in anger, speaking in anger, being overly emotional, because you aren't using the smart part of your brain, you're just speaking on pure adrenaline, and not really giving yourself time to really put an intelligent worthwhile response to something. That is why he tries not to get angry. He said growing up that my aunties made him very angry, Aunt Victoria most of all.

"Must be Masterplan night," Sa'Rah said.

"How did you know?" I exclaimed.

She was a very peculiar girl. She seemed to just know things.

"Because, Victor, I know you very well. And you have that look on your face. So it must be Masterplan night," she smiled. "Have fun!"

She hugged me tightly.

"You know I love you more than anyone else does right?"

"Right." I said. Suddenly, Vita rode up out of nowhere.

"Hey, Vita," said Sa'Rah in complete delight. "Can we ride her home, Victor? Please! Please! Pllleeaassseee!" She begged.

"Sure." I said.

I could call Leon to drive the car home. The car filled with all of things she purchased at the Megamall.

We mounted Vita. Everyone gathered around to see this beautiful horse.

"That is one gorgeous horse there, boy," said an elderly gentleman. He was Caucasian, gray hair, very plump with a big belly. He had a southern accent. I wondered if maybe his horses ran today at Thistledown. "Thank you, sir," I said in reply.

"What breed is she?" He asked, coming close to Vita.

Vita moved away a little bit. She didn't want to be touched. I whispered 'be nice' in her ear. I didn't know her exact breed, I just knew that she could do a lot of things that other horses couldn't. She was a magnificent horse. I decided to create my own breed.

"She's all-bred, sir.," I said with a huge smile on my face.

"Are you racing her?" He asked in a curious voice, as if I was going to allow him to race her.

Before I could even answer, Vita had taken off.

"No, sir," I said trying to keep balance and give him an answer before we disappeared.

Vita was on a mission. She rode as fast as she could until we got home. I walked in while Sa'Rah stayed outside to pet Vita.

Our house was large, with a porch to the right that led to the front door, and a three car garage attached to the house on the left. It was painted peach and brick red. I walked in, to the left is the dining room, to the immediate right was a little family sitting room; in between them, a stair well to the upstairs which had two bedrooms and two offices. Straight ahead was the living room, and to the left of the living room a huge kitchen with a bathroom to the left of the kitchen, and in front of the bathroom door a door to the basement which is big. It's like its own apartment in itself. It has a bathroom, kitchenette, and two rooms.

I stayed in the basement. Sa'Rah stayed upstairs with my parents.

As I walked in I heard talking in kitchen area. It was my mother, and two other men's voices. I walked further in. It was my grandfather Persy, and another man I didn't know.

My grandfather is a big man, but he lost a lot of weight after my grandmother passed. He had gray hair, balding in the middle. His facial hair was still dark brown, which was awkward. He always wore suits, shirt and a tie, always.

VENSIN GRAY

My mother, as lovely as she is, was wearing a green sundress, with her hair curled. She had make-up on, why? I Then I also noticed that she didn't have her wedding ring on. That was a problem, and would be an even bigger problem if Sa'Rah walked in and saw it.

I'd never seen the second man before. He stood when he saw me. He was about my height, maybe shorter. He was a dark skinned man, well built in stature, had dark brown eyes, and a well-groomed mustache. He was wearing a pinstripe blue suit with a white shirt and blue tie on underneath.

"Hey, Victor!" my mom said as she came over to hug me.

She was acting strange. She was never so lively and happy to see me.

"Hello, mother," I responded awkwardly.

"Hello, grandfather," I said to Grandfather Persy.

"Hello there, Victor," he said standing up.

We shook hands and hugged one another.

"Good to see you, son."

"Good to see you as well. And this gentleman?" I said looking at the man I didn't know.

"Oh this is...ah...Isaac Banks. He's a member of the Hall that daddy attends."

My mom was blushing with a huge smile on her face. I gave her a look. She wasn't behaving like a married woman. I looked directly at her ring finger. She noticed she had taken it off, and quickly moved to put it back on. It had been sitting on the table.

I shook Isaac's hand, but I really wasn't too happy to see him at the house. I knew exactly what this little meeting was about. I noticed Isaac wasn't wearing a wedding ring either. And Grandfather Persy was just going to sit back and let this all happen? Just to get my mom back to the Hall?

"So I assume you'll be going to a meeting tomorrow at the Hall?" I asked rhetorically. I knew the answer.

"I thought about checking it out," my mom replied.

"Checking it out?" said Grandfather Persy in a surprised tone, "You are coming. Victor Senior may be shutting down his church for whatever reason, but that doesn't mean you have to stop worshipping. It's time you came home, Persia."

Grandfather seemed to be pleading with her. I was getting increasingly annoyed. I didn't want to get into the affair.

"You should come too, Victor." I'm beginning to think everyone calls me Victor when I'm the only Victor around.

"No thank you, Grandfather. No disrespect, but my allegiance will always be to Jesus Christ not as just the Son of God, but as God, the father, the son, and the holy spirit. They aren't separate, they are the same."

"What if I can show you that Jesus himself said that he was not God?" Isaac challenged.

Normally I would love these encounters, not to argue, or show that I'm correct. But nothing is as exuberating as having a conversation of faith with someone else, as long as everyone can keep their composure. Having those conversations can be passionate, and some people can't control their passion and get over zealous and it becomes an argument.

"I would tell you to save it. I do not know you, and I do not want to know you sir." I said in annoyance that he feels he could witness me in my father's house, a man that my mother obviously was attracted too.

"Mother, grandfather," I said and then left the room.

I went down stairs to prepare for dinner. I showered and put on some clothes. Just some blue jeans, a nice button up gray shirt and a jacket. Riding my bike at night could be a bit cool, no matter how warm it was outside. I heard some arguing as I walked back up stairs. I should have known, Sa'Rah must've been talking to them, and she was angry.

"I don't like you, Isaac, and I want you to get out of my house!" Sa'Rah said in a commanding way, as if she paid bills. She was standing in the stair well.

"Sa'Rah!" My mother screamed at her. "You apologize this second, young lady!"

"I don't have to apologize to him! He's trying to convert me to that stupid false religion! And he's trying to take you from my daddy! Get out!" She screamed again.

This time everyone jumped at the passion in her voice. Even Grandfather Persy, who was already standing at the door as if he was preparing to leave.

"Sa'Rah," my mom said quietly.

She normal got quiet like that to calm herself down. My mom wasn't a very confrontational woman, even with Sa'Rah. She would normally just let my father handle the discipline, and she played the good parent. But she was enemy number one right now. Sa'Rah was too bright to be fooled. They probably talked, and Sa'Rah probably played coy with them at first as if she was interested in anything they had to talk about, and then once she had enough of Isaac, she snapped. I didn't really want to intervene, it wasn't my place. But since my father was gone, I was the man of the house, and it was embarrassing to have Sa'Rah act in this manner. So I walked over.

"Sa'Rah," I said getting her attention. "Apologize to Isaac. You weren't raised to be disrespectful, even if you disagree with someone."

"But Victor!" she pleaded. "They've been up here basically flirting the entire time!"

"That maybe so, Sa'Rah, but you still weren't raised that way. And you aren't mother. That is something that she is going to have to explain to us at a later time. But now is not that time. Please apologize."

Sa'Rah looked at me and smiled.

"Hello, Isaac," she said with a big smile on her face. "I apologize about my outburst. I guess I'm going to have to get used to seeing you around soon, as one day you'll be my step dad. Please forgive me, make yourself at home. Have a good night."

And she walked to her room. I shook my head smiling because I knew that was coming. My mother looked extremely embarrassed. My grandfather walked out of the door, and I turned to walk towards the basement to get my phone so I could leave. As I opened the basement door, I heard whispers.

"It's alright really, Persia," I heard Isaac say. "They were going to have to find out sooner or later."

"I know, but I didn't want them to find out this soon, even before I spoke with Junior," my mother said.

So I guess Sa'Rah was telling the truth about her feelings. She felt that they were going to split soon. Mother was going to go to a Kingdom Hall the next day. Father was definitely not going to put up with that. I'd have to talk to Sa'Rah, keep her spirits up. I grabbed my keys and when I came back upstairs, my mother was sitting on the couch. Isaac was gone.

"You heard what was said didn't you?"

My mother, like Sa'Rah knew things.

"Don't tell your father," she said to me.

I didn't talk a lot, I didn't like to gossip, and didn't want to be a part of it. I shook my head in agreement and disgust and my mother knew I was angry. I went upstairs. Sa'Rah was sleep, but she had been writing in her diary. I kissed her on her cheek. She smiled.

"I love you Victor," she said as she went back to sleep.

I heard my mother running bath water in the next room. I left the house. I jumped on my bike and made my way to The Masterplan bar where Senior and my father were waiting for me.

When I got to the Masterplan, Senior and my father were already there. I saw my grandfather's car out front, and I was sure they drove in together.

The Masterplan was a small bar, it hasn't converted to a sports bar like most bars were. Although Senior had been going there for years, it was still a pretty small establishment. It looked very basic. It's two bars, the one side, is a regular bar, and the other side is a party room. When you walk into the regular bar, you could either enter in the front on the left, or through the back. When I entered in, you could smell some tabacco smoke. Directly in front of the front door is a row or booths that sat on the right wall of the bar, it was about five booths, the biggest being the one cata-cornered that sits on the back wall and the right wall, and it's a circle booth, that's where Senior, my father and I sit. To the left of the booths is the bar, there's a long bar counter that stretches from the back wall to about four feet from the front windows. It stops at the door to the entrance of the Party Room. The booths were red with a wood square table. The bar had black bar stools, and the bar was a dark reddish color. Behind the bar was the bartender, today Stacie was working, she was a woman in her mid-thirties, she always had very imaginative hairdos. Red one day, blue the next, she enjoyed her job and she was good at it, from what I know. I've never stayed here very late, when people started drinking heavier. It was about maybe seven other people in here at the moment, a young group at the first booth, and a few people at the bar. I waved at Stacie and she smiled and waved back. In the back corner I saw Senior and my father.

I sat down next to my father. He always sat in the middle, because it was a circle. They had already ordered my food. I had a twenty ounce Pepsi waiting on me, and a two dollar bag of nacho cheese Doritos. My father always said that when he was younger, the two dollar bags were only ninety-nine cents "Hello, Father. Hello, Senior," I said.

"Hello, son," my father said with a smile on his face. "Good to see you."

He always said things like that, like he was surprised to see me or something. He knew I was coming.

"Hello, Three," Senior said to me in his normal calm voice. "How are you this evening?"

He asked the perfect question. I didn't really know how I was feeling. My personal life was going just fine. I spent the day with my sister, talked, went horseback riding, and I was eating my favorite meal with some of my favorite people. But on the other side, my mother was going back to the Kingdom Hall, which is none of my business, it is her life and her soul, she also might be falling in love with another man.

Sa'Rah hates the idea of them splitting up. I didn't like the idea, but if it made them happier apart, then it made the most sense.

"I had an interesting day," I said while finishing up one half of my sandwich.

"How so?" Senior asked. He knew something was up. I'm not sure how he did it, but he just knew the right buttons to push to get you to spill your guts.

"Spent the day with Sa'Rah, so I think we know why it was interesting."

We all laughed a little bit to ease the tension. There was a lot that needed to be discussed, The church closing, my mother's departure to the Hall, me going to school.

"Well, I have something to tell the both of you," my father said.

He hadn't even touched his food yet. Senior and I had been too busy eating our own to pay attention. He looked pretty serious.

"Persia and I are getting a divorce," he continued very carefully and very calmly.

I stopped chewing my food and just swallowed whatever was in there. It was a huge lump that went down, and it hurt. But it didn't hurt as much as hearing that my father actually saying what Sa'Rah predicted.

My fathered licked his lips, sighed, and put both of his elbows on the table. I could tell he was holding back tears. Senior just continued to eat as if my father didn't say anything. He was probably gathering the right words to say to my dad. I'm sure he wanted to talk out of passion to him, not as a psychiatrist, but as a father to a son. Or maybe, he was trying to relate? I wasn't sure. He'd been married almost forty years. My dad had been married only sixteen. I was conceived and born a bastard, Sa'Rah was the marriage child, that's probably why this will be harder on her to bear once she's told.

"Because she's decided to go back to the Kingdom Hall?" I tried to play oblivious.

I knew the real answer. They had fallen out of love long ago. My

VENSIN GRAY

father was just doing his piece. He saw Senior do everything for our family for years, and my father naturally tried to mimic that.

"That son, and other things," my father sounded sad. "We haven't really been in love in a long time. I guess we kind of grew apart, especially after your grandmother passed away. Not saying anything is wrong with her talking to her father, but he talked her into going back to the Kingdom Hall. And, as you know, I can't accept that. I won't accept it. But I wouldn't divorce her just solely because she decided to go back to her childhood faith.

"There's a man, his name is Isaac, she befriended during her quest, she's been witnessing with him, going door to door with him as if he was her husband. I know this because one day I followed them, nothing happen, but they were just so close, and the way she smiled at him, wasn't how she smiled at me anymore. They stopped to have lunch one day, and the hug they exchanged as they left is what hit me, that things were over. It was a tight hug, a compassionate one, I grew insanely angry. But I didn't do anything, I kept my cool. I went…"

He started stuttering with his words as tears went down his face. My heart went out to him, this is a woman he has loved since he knew what love was, he told me all the time he never loved or liked, or even looked at another woman as he looked at my mom. And it's hard hearing this from him because I love them both so, and as a son, I can't choose between the two, but what's wrong is wrong.

"I went to my mother and I cried. I cried for hours. I didn't know what else to do. I tried talking to her, taking her places, praying with her, just everything I could, but it just didn't work, it was too far gone, and it breaks my heart, but it's just what has to be done." My dad put his hands over his eyes and started to cry a bit more. His heart was hurting. I just looked up at Senior, he was still eating, it was as if he was deaf and didn't hear a word my father said. I didn't know what to do. I was stunned, my heart was breaking inside of me, not for me, but for Sa'Rah, if she were to see my father like this, she would be devastated.

"True love is a love of one another only when God is in it," Senior started to speak.

My father, still crying, wiped his eyes trying to calm himself.

"God is Love. And if He in all His greatness isn't brought into marriage, you will never experience true love. We all experience an emotional feeling called love, but that is only one portion of love in a marriage. For a marriage to be rewarding, it must have God's love as its driver, God's love is a love that loves even when the love isn't returned. That's Divine Love, that's the love that a marriage needs. A Christian marriage is established and held on the trust in God, and one another." Senior said that as if had practiced it for many years.

"I love you my son. You are my only boy, and my heart goes out to you. Although you are drowning in your tide, defeated by your own broken words and failures, you are in a sea of guilt as it seems like Persia is just living life very happily, her ground is breaking. God hates divorce, but he loves the divorcee and will always help those who call Him. I don't need to tell you to pray, but pray son. Love is a choice, it isn't something that we get caught up in and just walk away from it easily. God's divine love for us withstands all things and never wavers, even when we do. We do not have to measure up to anything for his Love, He loves us because He is Love. There is nothing He does that isn't because of Love. When we backslide or fail, He doesn't disdain us; instead he encourages us, reaches out and rejuvenates us. He sees everything in us, the cruelty, blindness and bigotry, but he still loves us, and he doesn't over look those things because those very things could break us. His love for us is lavish, passionate, holy, zealous and kind. I just spoke of this love Sunday. That we are to love our wives more than we love ourselves. If we could love like God, with so much forgiveness, understanding and encouragement, there wouldn't be so many divorces in the world, so many fatherless homes, and corrupted societies.

"Marriage is a divine romance between Christ and the Church. The only trust understanding of a man and a woman's attraction is the desire to build a life with one another, and that's in a true spiritual sense, not a worldly sense of attraction. God hates divorce because it's as if you are splitting Christ up from the Church. But if God isn't present son, then the church will fall. Lucifer is out here to destroy, not just marriage, but all of our relationships, he wants us to hate one another, he wants whites to hate blacks, he wants Christians to hate Muslims, he wants us to fight one another, and when we are weak, and look to blame everyone else for our short-comings, and he gets his way. Only through Christ are we to defeat him." He paused. "Only through being strong in our faith, will we free ourselves from the clinches of the Devil, don't let the Devil devise you Junior. As First Peter chapter three verses seven through eleven say…"

"In the same way, you husbands must give honor to your wives. Treat your wife with understanding as you live together. She may be weaker than you are, but she is your equal in God's gift of new life. Treat her as you should so your prayers will not be hindered. Finally, all of you should be of one mind. Sympathize with each other. Love each other as brothers and sisters. Be tenderhearted and keep a humble attitude. Don't repay evil for evil. Don't retaliate with insults when people insult you. Instead, pay them back with a blessing. That is what God has called you to do, and he will bless you for it. For the Scriptures say, 'If you want to enjoy life and see many happy days, keep your tongue from speaking evil and your lips from telling lies. Turn away from evil and do good. Search for peace, and work to maintain it.'" My dad interrupted Senior and spoke the verses himself. "Thanks Dad. I'll do what I can to see if I can find a way to save our marriage. As the man of the house, I must exhaust all avenues, before turning down the one way street of divorce." My dad spoke slowly and eloquently. He turned to me. "Son, not a word of this to Sa'Rah. I love you." He hugged me and kissed me on my cheek, and he hugged Senior tightly. "Victor, may I have the keys to your bike please?" I quickly gave them to him, and he gathered his food, and departed the Masterplan.

I was a bit confused as to what just happened. But I guess everything Senior said, basically he told my dad that he should love my mom, love her till death, and find a way to correct the wrongs.

"How do you do it Senior?" I asked him. "How do you know exactly what to say? All the time?"

"I don't know what to say half of the time, Three," he said, being humble as normal. "Most of the time I just say what's in my heart, hoping they receive what I'm saying in a positive light, and throughout all the words that I say, something hits home and changes whatever it is in their heart."

He smiled at me.

"What do you think he's going to do?" Senior asked me.

"I hope the right thing. Go home, tell my mother he loves her, and watch a Law and Order marathon."

We laughed and finished our food. We ate in silence for a while. We didn't make eye contact very much. Leon had sent me a few text messages, I told him where I was, and he stopped. He always respected our dinners here, seeing that he did everything else with us.

"So what do you know of Octavius, Victor?"

When Senior calls me Victor, it is a very serious matter.

"Better yet, how do you know of him, and what he's doing in Europe?"

I looked at him for a moment in fear. Although Senior has never struck me, he commanded a respect from me that I gave without question. I wasn't going to lie to him.

"Last week after practice I ran into this Muslim girl, named Fawzia. Her father met you a while ago, so he allowed us to converse. She told me."

"Say your words quietly, Victor," Senior cautioned.

"She told me," I said quietly, "that she had a run in with Octavius Atavus in Madrid. He asked her basically to be his woman. But she refused, and he is persecuting Muslims everywhere, and that the media is hiding it from America. I don't really see how that's possible."

"It's possible, Victor. And it's true. We've been getting threats from the Muslim community for quite some time now. I haven't reported them to authorities because I don't want it to spread here. But Octavius has started a religious war. One in which he wants all Christians to rise up against everyone else. I fear the worst. Many extremist groups will scare most calm Christian folk to fight in the name of Jesus. I did my research on him. His most trusted advisor, Lauren Craft, is about to publish a book entitled *Christian Wars*. Many believe that the book is only going to tell the history of all the wars of the past that had something with Christianity to do with it. But there is a subliminal message in it, and that message is for Christians to rise up, and fight, there's also a list, a list of everyone who is a friendly Christian, a Christian that is your brother, sister or cousin that you will fight with, and Jehovah's Witnesses is not on that list, because they will not go to war. So I fear the worst for Persy and your mother if she walks down that path." Senior stopped. This is all too much for me.

"What does this have to do with us?" I asked.

"A lot. This fall, when many of you are going to college, a lot of other young men are going to train in the arts you train in, because the war will be here in America soon. They can only hide the persecution so much longer before someone says something. They can't quiet everyone. Octavius has the blessing of the Pope and everyone Christian who signed the international peace treaty, even those who aren't Christian, and he has the blessings of our President. So I will do what I can to see if I can protect us, we must pray and pray hard Victor. But I don't want you concerning yourself with this. Have a fun summer, enjoy yourself, and go study at JCU. I'm proud of you. And not a word of this to Leon, for he may try to save the world himself."

"If this war," I said to Senior as he got up and began to gather his belongings to leave. "If this war is what you say it is, as a Christian, I will stand against it, but only an Army of God will be able to stop Octavius if what you say is true." I said in complete astonishment, and disbelief of this. I mean, yes, crazy things like this happen in movies. But to happen in actual life is unreal. I'm only eighteen years old, how do you drop this on my lap?

"Don't worry Three," Senior said to calm me down. "Everything will be fine, just pray. Do you need a ride home?"

My father had taken my bike home.

"No thank you Senior, I have a ride."

I knew Vita would be out there for me. She had to be. I haven't needed her, and she wasn't there yet.

"Ok my grandson. I love you."

"I love you too," I said.

There was a lot to take in. I didn't know what to do, I didn't know who to talk to. I am so confused. I walked outside and there she was, Vita. I hugged her, hugging her comforted me. It was as if she knew my heart was troubled. I rode her home and thought about everything Senior had just said to me. Still not believing everything could be happening over there, and not a word here in the States, just seemed impossible.

As I walked into the house, all the lights were out, but the TV was on in the living room. I thought it was Sa'Rah, but it wasn't. It was my mother and father cuddled up on the couch sleeping, while cartoons played. I forced a smile, went down stairs in my room and laid down to go to sleep. Just as I was dozing off, I received a text message from a number that wasn't stored in my phone. It read…

'I want to see you again Victor the third. Meet me tomorrow night at the coffee house for tea again'

It was Fawzia. I tried to respond, but I felt myself falling asleep.

7

The next day, I found myself riding out to the West side of Cleveland toward the coffee House at Fawzia's request. Earlier in the day I did some stretching and a light workout with Leon. We discussed things that had been going on with both of our families. He was obviously distracted by his father not being at functions he should be at. I explained that he may be going through a mid-life crisis and to just pray for him. But Leon wasn't the most patient of people. He wanted answers and he wanted them fast.

Sa'Rah and I talked for a bit, she apologized again for her actions. Our mother had a talk with her, and I wasn't so sure Dad knew what was going on. But it wasn't my business. My business was getting to the bottom of what was supposedly going on with Octavius over in Europe.

I hadn't told Leon about Fawzia yet. I mean, how could I? I didn't even know what to say to him.

"Hey, I met a Muslim woman, who told me about an Islamic persecution hidden from us? She wants to meet me for coffee."

He would assume that I would need protection. He would've come here and waited to make sure I was safe. He's a man of God, but he's always looking to protect the ones he loves. I actually hadn't told anyone, not even Sa'Rah who embraced the opportunity to meet different people of different cultures and faiths.

My dad would understand but question it; my mother would

encourage me to go after my dreams. Senior would ignore me and believe it was a phase. I wasn't sure what anyone else would say. I wondered what would Elizabeth say? She proposed marriage to me, arranged marriage, but marriage nonetheless.

Elizabeth also mentioned Ian and her mother having an affair. How could Ian do that? I'd have to talk to Senior about it when this Muslim threat calmed down. I hoped I would talk to her before Leon found something out. Unfortunately, Elizabeth was correct in a way. When you have a large church, different people visiting every day, it's hard to keep up with the many things that go on in a church. The world wasn't perfect, and neither was our church. You have your liars, your adulterers, thieves and so forth. But who were we to tell people not to come back? Especially without solid proof. But I should clear my mind of the gossip and focus on tonight.

I got to the coffee house around 8:30 in the evening, just when the Sun was starting it's decent. I walked in and immediately all eyes were on me. The young boy was behind the counter still, and the coffee house was full of men, not a woman in sight. I felt a little uncomfortable. I went and stood by the counter, the smell of fresh ground coffee was settling and it was warm and comfortable.

"You're here to meet Zia?" The young boy said to me.

He was short, about five feet four inches, with fair skin, dark brown eyes. He had no facial hair, and his hair was long.

"Yes," I said quietly. I sure hope she didn't have him cancel for her when she could have texted me again. Perhaps I should have texted her or called her to confirm arrangements.

"Here," he slid me a large cup. "Same tea you had last time. She told me to tell you she'll be a little late. Family meeting."

Same tea as last time? The Kiwi and strawberry green tea. Very delicious.

"Thank you. How much do I owe you?" I said reaching into my pocket.

"Nothing. Your money is no good here." He said to me smiling.

Maybe he knew something about me? I wasn't not totally sure.

I went to an empty seat towards the back end of the restaurant, and sat down. I drank my tea, and it was just like last time. Very good, even to be hot in the summer it was a good drink. Went down smoothly. My phone started ringing. I hoped it was Fawzia telling me she was on her way. I looked at my phone and it was Christina. I was just thinking about her.

"Hello there, Christina," I said as I answered.

"Hello, Victor the Third. How are you this evening?"

"I'm doing well. I'm at a coffee house over here on Detroit."

"On Detroit!?" she said in a shocked voice. "What are you doing there? Just finished your training?"

"No ma'am, I'm meeting up with a..." I didn't know rather to call Fawzia a friend, an acquaintance, or just some woman. I paused.

"A friend," said a familiar voice over my right shoulder. It was Fawzia.

"You're with a girl, huh Victor? And no Leon with you? She must be special."

I was blushing, I was completely speechless. I didn't know what to say.

"Well anyways, I didn't want to keep you long, I just wanted to invite you to a dinner Ian and I are having for Leon, I want to give him something that his fa..." She stopped. "His father's friend left him before he passed away. It's sort of a big thing and Leon calls you his brother. Well you are brothers, so it'll be important if you were to join us."

"Yes. Of course I'll be there. What day and what time?"

"Tomorrow at seven."

"Ok, Christina. Thank you. See you then. So long." I smiled and looked at Fawzia.

I didn't know what to say. Normally Leon does all the talking for me when we meet girls. Doing this on my own is sort of like taking the training wheels off.

"Hello Ms. Zia."

"Hello Mr. Thomas." She said with a beautiful smile. She took my tea and drank from it. Not something I would think for her to do, especially without my permission. But I allowed it, how could I say no to her.

"What have I told you about calling me Mr. Thomas?" I laughed. "And sure, help yourself."

"You want it back?" She said smiling and acting as if she would put it back in the cup.

She was wearing an off color dark pink hijab with a tight black shirt and some blue jeans and sandals.

"You two are getting mighty friendly over here," a deep voice said as five men came out of nowhere standing above the table Fawzia and I were sitting at.

The man who spoke was dark skinned with eerie dark eyes, and full facial hair well kept. He stood in the middle. His other fellows were a bit shorter than him, dressed similarly, black shirt, black pants.

"Hello, Fawzia. Who is your friend?"

Fawzia stared at him for a second, then immediately looked at me.

"You want to leave?" She asked me, getting up.

The gentlemen near her both moved out of her way as she stood up and headed towards the door. When I stood up no one moved.

"I don't want any problems," I said to them. The shop, which was once very loud and people talking went quiet.

"Well, you might have one," said the man who interrupted us the first time. "What is your name?"

"You don't have to answer him!" Fawzia exclaimed.

"Do not! Interrupt me while I'm talking!" said the man in the middle. "Excuse my temper. I'm Malcolm, this is Lamar, Yasat, Aaqib and Mahaz. And you are?"

"Victor." I said to him watching Fawzia huff and walk out of the coffee house.

All eyes were on us. I really hoped this would not escalate into

VENSIN GRAY

anything unnecessary. I didn't come here with any intentions of quarrels with anyone. Left my sword at home, and left Leon at home.

"Yeah?" said Malcolm, squinting his eyes and smiling. "I thought it was you. Look everyone!" He said loudly getting everyone's attention in the store. "It's Victor Thomas the Third! Welcome to Cleveland."

Everyone laughed. I heard some side talk and some murmuring, and I couldn't make out anything. I was focused on the five gentlemen that were in front of me.

"Excuse me," I said to him, ignoring the public embarrassment he was trying to put on me and follow Fawzia out of the store.

"Where do you think you're going? You like what you see there, huh?" Malcolm said to me.

His friends with him were either mute or very disciplined, they didn't say one word.

"You see Fawzia is my future wife. I've spoken with my father, and my father to her father and it has been arranged. It is foretold, she is my destiny. I'm not letting some spoiled brat from some coward who closes his church because of some threats try to get her before I can."

He spoke of me, and my grandfather. I don't get angry or impatient easily. I ignored his insults to me and my grandfather. He did not know me or him, and I would not fall into an argument with the fool. I merely smiled.

"May I get by, please?" I said to him in a nice calm way. Thank goodness Leon wasn't here. The shop would need a makeover.

"I guess it's true what they say about you all here. Can push you, you won't push back," Malcolm said with a smile. "Maybe you'll have to show a little heart, maybe you'll have to go through me if you want to get past."

"Malcolm!" Fawzia's father said in his low pitch voice. "I've given Fawzia permission to talk to the boy. Let him through."

Malcolm and his friends moved out of my way immediately without contest.

"I'll be seeing you," Malcolm said to me as I walked by him.

I looked back and he was finishing my tea. Man, I'm never going to get to finish that tea am I? I ignored the threat from Malcolm as I walked past everyone. The boy behind the counter waved at me as I left.

"Thank you," I said to Fawzia's father. "What do I call you?"

Fawzia's father was busy starring at Malcolm and his companions.

"You may call me nothing," He said as he closed the shop door and walked to the counter.

Fawzia was looking at me smiling.

"I'm sorry about that. They are some jerks," she said.

"It's no problem at all." I said to her, starring at her beauty, listening to her voice, it softened my soul and I was no longer thinking about what just happened. "So what are we doing?"

"Let's go to the beach."

Fawzia and I walked to the beach, which wasn't far from where we were, just a few miles north. We talked about everything but what was happening in Europe and what just happened at the shop. We talked about where we grew up, how we grew up, influences, favorite colors, favorites TV shows, books. We finally arrived at the beach. It was a warm evening, the sun was setting, and you could feel the cool breeze the night was bringing. There were mostly adults there, a few people swimming, not much else was going on.

"Where can we sit? On the sand?" I suggested, realizing I was completely unprepared for a day at the beach.

"Men," Fawzia said smiling at me again. "Fortunately for you, I brought two towels." She handed me the towels and I laid them down on the sand and we sat down.

We didn't say anything for a while, we just watched the Sun set.

"You know, I've never watched a Sunrise before. I sleep too long."

We both laughed a little bit.

"How about you?"

"I've seen plenty. A lot of early mornings with Leon."

"I can imagine how you two must work out to accomplish the things you've accomplished."

"It's mostly him."

"How do you do it?" Fawzia asked me a vague question looking at me in pure curiosity.

"How do I do what?" I responded.

"When Malcolm stood over you, you looked completely calm. You weren't intimidated, you just looked at peace. How do you do that in the face of adversary?"

"They weren't adversaries. At least not to me. I had no issues with them. Malcolm wanted me to know my place, that you're his woman."

"He wishes. He has my father's blessings, not mine."

"Well, at least he went through your father."

"He's a brute. His real name isn't Malcolm, he changed it to Malcolm, thought it make him seem cooler. He was born here in America, and given a regular American name. His birth name is Joseph. His mother wasn't Muslim. And his father slept with a lot of women. Ignore him. I'm not his woman." She said in her defense.

"Whose woman are you?" I said in a joking way.

"I'm no one's woman," she said to me smirking.

"I'm not any one's woman either, so we're in the same boat." I said lightening up the mood.

We both laughed a little bit. We sat in silence for a while. Just looking up at the stars as the night fell upon us.

"I come here almost every night in hopes that I'll see a fleet of boats, and my brothers and sisters from Europe come running out to embrace us here. But then, I get sad, because, how long before that war comes here? It's my biggest fear. It used to be that no good man would want me because I am defiled."

"Would you not say you're defiled?" I said to her with a bit of annoyed in my voice. "You're not defiled. I'm not certain how your faith is, but I'm sure anyone with half a brain would love to make you their woman."

"Ha, any man who looks at me for my outer beauty. They don't even know the first thing about me. They see something they like and they want it. I refuse to be a prize. I'm not a prize. I want a man who can stare in my soul, and tell me what I want to hear."

"Tell me what you want to hear… and I'll say it," I said in a lame flirtatious way.

"If I told you what I wanted to hear, then there would be nothing for you to work for, Mr. Thomas," she said to me looking at me.

"What did I tell you about…" Our eyes met. It was the first time we got a chance to really look at one another.

She was the perfect woman, physically at least. Her shirt was tight enough so you can see that her breasts were a nice size, her stomach was flat, her thighs weren't too skinny, and her butt sat up nicely. It was as if she was from a magazine, or a movie, not sitting right here in front of me.

The moonlight shined from her beautiful hazel eyes. I'd never had a first kiss moment. A kiss without words, without asking, no prompts or pressure, just me, the girl, our lips. I didn't know what was coming over me. My entire body felt warm, my heart beat quickened, and my breath was heavy, and she stared at me, as our faces drew closer, no one was paying any attention to us, no Christians, no Muslims, no one to judge us, it was just her and I, a woman and a man. And finally our lips met.

At first it was just a peck, then another peck, and then we opened our mouths, and she moistened my mouth with her tongue, and she grabbed my head and pulled me closer to her. We had to be kissing for about one minute but it felt like only a second, and she pulled back. Both of us breathing heavy.

"I shouldn't have done that," she said to me. "I'm so sorry Victor."

She stood up and ran off.

"Wait!" I said.

"Do not follow me!" She said back.

I sat there on the towels she had left, hypnotized by the kiss. I've kissed a girl before. It wasn't a big deal, it was just something to do. But what just happened to me was mystifying. I couldn't explain it. I continued to breathe heavy, I felt my heart beat through my chest. And all I could think about was how I wanted another. Our lips were perfect for one another. All I could do was smile. I looked around and no one was looking at me, no one paid attention to us. At that moment, I wanted the world to feel my exuberance. I leaned back and closed my eyes and just listened to nature around me. The sound of the lake water moving back and forth on shore. I started to doze off.

I was violently awoken by a shirt over my head. Still waking up and gaining consciousness, I felt a punch to my stomach. Two people lifted me up off of the ground. I heard voices but was too concerned with the pain in my stomach to pay attention to the words. I struggled but the arms that held me were too strong, even for me. I couldn't see anything. I felt myself being dragged somewhere. My legs were tied together with something, felt like rope.

"I told you Victor, she is my woman," I heard a voice that sounded similar to Malcolm's.

After I heard that voice I felt my face get struck, then my thighs, then my stomach, then my face again, and again, my arms were let go and I fell to the ground and I felt myself be kicked constantly and eventually they began to stomp on me. One hit my head and I began to fade, I saw darkness, and the pain left, and the sound left me.

I woke up some time later. My body felt like I just played ten quarters of football and I was the only one without padding. It hurt to breath, I tried to open my eyes but I couldn't. I coughed and I felt my mouth fill with what tasted like blood. I tried to spit, only to feel it drool down my chin and on to my clothes. What a night, a kiss from heaven, and a beating from hell. I felt a hand grab me and lift me up to my feet. I couldn't see. I didn't know if it was day or night.

"Young Victor," I heard a voice say to me.

I felt myself be lifted onto something. I didn't have to open my eyes to know it was Vita.

"It's not yet time for us to cross paths. But remember this through your anger. Greater love hath no man than this, that a man lay down his life for his friends. Save my so…" I faded out before I could hear the end of it.

"Vita" is all I could say before passing out.

8

"Fawzia?" I said.
I didn't know where we were at. It was very bright, all I could see was her.

She was wearing a black burga over her hair and it covered her face, it stretched all the way down to her legs. The only reason I know it's her is because of her beautiful eyes.

"What are you doing here?" I asked her.

She said nothing. Just stared at me. I took a step towards her, and she took one towards me. Finally we were face to face, and nothing else in the world mattered. My heart was pounding. She stood back, and removed her hijab, revealing to me her long silky black hair. I was amazed, she talked to me so strongly about how her hair meant everything to her, and that only her husband would be allowed to see it. But here she is, showing it to me.

My heart started racing again. She walked back up to me and put her hands on my face, and without words, our lips met again, and this time, I was more aggressive. I sucked on her bottom lip, my eyes were closed but I could see me with her. My hands went across her back and I was sure this was the woman that was meant for me. We stopped to breathe.

I felt a breath come out of me. It hurt so bad that it awakened me out of my dream. I tried to move but couldn't. I was sore everywhere. My legs, my chest, my sides, I couldn't feel my lips, I couldn't open my eyes. I just got jumped, and all I could dream about was Fawzia's lips against my own. I couldn't even smile.

Suddenly I felt a cold substance pressed against my face and a warm rag wiping against my side. The pain was sharp, but I could barely talk, let alone react to the pain vocally. I moved a little bit.

"Hold still."

I heard Sa'Rah's voice.

Hearing her voice was comforting. I didn't know where I was. I tried to open my eyes but I couldn't, my face must've been too swollen, or maybe I was too tired. I didn't try to figure it out. I just laid there while Sa'Rah tended to me. I felt her kiss me on the cheeks.

"I love you."

I drifted back to sleep.

No more dreams this time. When I awoke, I had more energy, and my body felt better. I could open my eyes. I was in my room. I looked at the clock and it showed 2 o'clock. Sa'Rah was sitting on my couch. When she noticed I was awake she jumped up.

"Hey Victor," she said in a soft concerning voice. "How are you feeling?"

"Like I was hit by a truck." I said joking around. I laughed a bit but it hurt.

"Who did this to you?" She demanded. "Better yet, hold that thought. I'll be back in a moment."

She went upstairs. I used every ounce of energy I had to get up out of my bed. I stood up too quickly because the room was dizzy, but I didn't let it stop me. I went to my bathroom and I focused to look at myself in the mirror.

The left side of my face was severely swollen. My shirt was off and Sa'Rah had put bandages on me. She did a really good job, I wasn't as sore as I was earlier. I looked to my left and saw that I had some clothes out, a towel and some body wash.

I decided to take a shower. Normally I don't like to take really hot showers, I prefer warm, but the water felt good against my skin. After

I washed up, I just stood in there thinking for a while. I thought about everything that was going on in my life.

Getting jumped by Muslims isn't the best sign for a Christian man who is trying to live the right life. Retaliation was out of the question, I guess I felt sad because I'd never see Fawzia again. I couldn't go back over there, not after this. But her kiss, it was amazing. It was beautiful, and sensual, compassionate and breath taking. The thought of never feeling her lips again saddened me.

What was Leon going to say? Who knew about this? I had to speak with Sa'Rah. I couldn't really hide my face, especially since I have to go to Christina's tonight for Leon's dinner. I hoped my father didn't know, he would overreact and try to retaliate. No matter how Christian he tried to be, he was still a man, and he was going to want retribution. Senior would be calm, and find a way to explain it. But I didn't want to talk to anyone but Sa'Rah. I love my little sister with all my heart. She took care of me, and I'll never forget it.

When I got out of the shower, I got dressed in the bathroom and came out. Sa'Rah was back and she had some food warmed up for me. By the smell of it, it was some chicken soup, and some crackers. I just got beat up, I wasn't sick.

She also had a big glass of orange juice and some pills.

"What are the pills?" I asked.

"Excedrin for your headache and Tylenol for your body, an aspirin to make sure you don't have a fever."

Was she really only 14?

"Thank you," I said to her. I kissed her on her cheek, but my lips were still swollen and I didn't feel anything.

I sat down next to her and ate as much as I could.

"Don't worry, when Vita brought you here, I brought you down here. Mommy and Daddy didn't see you."

"Does Leon know?

"No. Are you crazy? His reaction would be irrational and ungodly."

"Ha. You are correct." I said continuing to eat. I must've been hungry because I was eating this soup as if I never ate anything before.

"Thank you, Sa'Rah. Really, I appreciate it."

"You know I'd do anything for you, Victor. I told you, no one loves you as much as I do! And don't you forget it!" She said tooting her own horn, as if loving me and taking care of me bore some sort of prize.

"Well, thank you again, Sa'Rah. And I love you too."

It went silent for a while as I finished up the food she had prepared.

"Who did this to you?"

I knew that question was coming.

"I don't think it matters. Won't happen again."

"Are you going after them?"

"No."

"Then why won't it happen again?"

"Because I'm not putting myself in that position anymore."

"You can tell me what happened."

"There's this girl."

"Really!? A girl did that to you!?" Sa'Rah said in amazement.

"No. It's not that simple."

I spent the next several minutes explaining to her about Fawzia, Octavius, Elizabeth, the reason the Church was closed, Malcolm and his friends. She understood everything and listened very carefully.

"Elizabeth is a beautiful woman," Sa'Rah said to me.

She'd never liked any girl I ever liked.

"Although the arranged marriage thing sounds strange, I think she'd be good for you," Sa'Rah said smiling at me.

Sa'Rah was a beautiful little girl. Aged beyond reason, she shouldn't be as mature and wise as she was, but she was. She was like a younger female version of my grandfather.

We spent the next hour and a half just talking and laughing. Although a lot had gone on, just speaking with her made me happy.

"I trust you'll keep this talk between us," I said to her.

"Always," Sa'Rah said to me smiling.

She came to hug me, and she kissed me on my forehead.

"Thank you again, Sa'Rah."

"Anytime," She said. "Get some rest. I'm going to do some things mommy left for us to do.

"I can do my own chores."

"No. I'll do them," she said. "Just lay down. You have to be at Christina's in a few hours."

She was right. I laid down on my couch. I said a little prayer thanking God that I wasn't killed. I hoped that my face cleared up before I had to leave. It wouldn't be nice with Leon there. Finally, I dozed off.

When I awoke, I just sat up on the couch and stared into blankness. What was happening to me? I couldn't get Fawzia off of my mind. And these bruises didn't make me want to see her any less.

"Where's my phone?' I thought to myself.

I looked around and didn't see it. I looked at the clock. It was an hour before I was supposed to be at Christina's for Leon's surprise. I looked on my bed, there were some clothes already ironed and pressed for me to wear. I smiled to myself, Sa'Rah, what would I do without her?

I put the clothes on. There was a firmly pressed dark blue dress shirt, with some black dress pants, a light leather black sports coat. I looked at myself again in the mirror, my body wounds were well hidden, but my face looks like I got jumped by five guys last night. The ice Sa'Rah applied put the swelling down a bit, but my face was still very sore. I did what I could with it but there was no hiding it. Sunglasses aren't big enough. I'd have to think of a story to tell Leon or he'd flip.

I walked upstairs. My dad wasn't home yet and my mother was in the living room. Sa'Rah was in the kitchen.

"Hurry up and leave before mommy see's you," she whispered to me and smiled.

I gave her a hug, kissed her on the cheek, and went to the garage through the kitchen.

I drove my mom's car to Christina's house, or rather, mansion that's located in an upper class suburb of Cleveland. I didn't feel like using my motor cycle, my body was in no condition for that or Vita. University School was located there.

I pulled up to their house, which was a huge black brick house with a very long drive way that curved in a semi-circle. The lawn was well maintained, beautiful landscaping. I walked to the front door, which was a large glass door that didn't open like normal doors. It slid to the side like at a Walgreens except about one hundred times more expensive.

The door opened. I was a few minutes early.

"Hey Victor!" Christina said to me. "Oh my goodness! What happened to you!"

"Hello, Christina," I said forcing a smile. "No worries, I fell off of my horse and my face broke my fall." I lied, trying to laugh, but it hurt.

Christina didn't believe me. I saw it in her face. Christina was a beautiful woman. She was a few inches shorter than I, her facial structure was that of a models. She was well into her forties but didn't look a day over thirty. Her eyes were beautiful and light gray, hair long and black, her figure, to be respectful, was very well kept.

She touched my chin, I flinched because it hurt, and she took a closer look.

"We'll keep to that story. Go wash your hands and meet us in the dining room," she said.

I went and washed my hands in their restroom on the first floor. Their house was amazing on the inside, white walls with black trimming, all over were pictures of Christina, Ian and Leon, some of Leon and I, more of Senior and our family. The house was warm. The fireplace was going, even in the middle of the summer. It seemed normal in this house; air conditioning with the fireplace burning. I laughed to myself.

After wandering around looking at the pictures as if it was my first time here, I found myself in the dining room, where a long glass table was set. There were four plates set on the table; eight people could comfortably fit at this table. It was really fancy, with a chandelier above us burning with candles for light. In the middle of the table was baked chicken, glazed ham, homemade macaroni and cheese, corn on the cob, and freshly baked bread rolls. These were all of Leon's favorites.

I felt a hand touch my shoulder and I jumped.

"What's the matter, man? It's just me." Leon said.

I'm not sure why I jumped, it was just a reaction. I didn't hear him come up from behind me. It was fear, I was afraid. I knew exactly where I was at, I knew that no harm would come to me, but my heart was racing, and my fists were clinched.

"Sorry, man," I said to Leon, trying to avoid eye contact.

I turned and walked towards the chairs so that I could sit down and avoid the ensuing questions that would follow after he saw my face.

"V, what's wrong?" Leon said walking behind me.

"Nothing. Just excited to be here. Where's Ian?" I asked.

It was a stupid question, I knew that if Ian wasn't there, he was going to be angry, but it would get him off of my back.

"He's not here and probably won't be joining us," Christina said coming from the kitchen.

"And why isn't he here?" Leon said with much anger in his voice.

"That is not our concern," Christina said with a stern voice. "Please sit down, let's eat. It's a great day."

Leon and I followed the order and we both sat down. I sat to the right of Christina, who sat at the head of the table, Leon sat directly in front of me. His eyes went wide when he saw my face.

"Victor fell off of his horse, Leon. He doesn't want to talk about it." Christina said to Leon.

She's a special woman, she knew exactly what was about to happen. I did not want to explain anything to Leon.

"Must've been some fall," Leon said in complete disbelief of the story. He looked at me, and began making his plate.

We all sat there in quiet, it was an odd moment. Between Ian not being there, and my face looking like someone used it as a punching bag, I guess in some sense they did, Leon must've been full of questions.

"So boys," Christina finally broke the silence. "Any plans for this summer before going off to college?"

"Spending time with you mother," Leon said smiling.

"Spending time sword training, and spending time with Sa'Rah," I said.

"How about learning how to ride a horse better?" Leon joked.

Finally, levity in the air. We all began talking, eating, and complimenting Christina on a delicious meal. I wanted to tell them about Fawzia, but why? How did I tell them that I kissed a Muslim woman, and then five of them jumped me? I kept it to myself, especially since Fawzia and I wouldn't be seeing one another again. Which saddened me, and suddenly my demeanor went from joyful laughter, to melancholy.

"Well, I'm sure you two are wondering, what's the occasion today," Christina said standing up beginning to clear the table.

"I got those," Leon said getting up grabbing the dishes from Christina.

"Thank you, honey," Christina said to him. "I'll be right back."

Christina left the room. I stood up to help Leon clear the table.

"No, you stay there and start talking."

Leon's demeanor went from happy and supportive to angry and concerned.

"Start talking about what?"

"You take me for a fool, Victor?"

Leon never calls me Victor unless he's very serious.

"I know you didn't fall off of Vita, and if you did, your face wouldn't look like someone punched it a thousand times. What the hell happened?"

Leon never curses. His anger was building up in him.

"I think we should just clear the table." I said standing up and grabbing a few dishes.

Leon, very angrily slammed the dishes on the table and walked out

VENSIN GRAY

of the room. I understood his frustration, but it wasn't the time to make this day about me. What happened was unfortunate, but Christina invited me over for him, not for me.

I cleared the table and Leon and Christina came back into the room at the same time from different directions.

"Thank you, Leon," Christina said to him.

"It wasn't me, it was Victor. I had to use the bathroom," Leon said still calming down.

"What's in the box?"

Christina came in holding a jewelry box. The box looked more expensive than most jewelry boxes, it was glass, but too thick to see through it. The glass was blue with gold writing wrapped around it, the writing I couldn't decipher. There was a key hole in the front and in it was the key.

"What's in this box?" Christina said smiling. She was looking directly at Leon, her face was glowing. "I've been wanting to give you this for eighteen years. This is your birth right Leon."

Christina isn't a very emotional woman, as far as I know. She was tearing up. This must be a very special gift. She spoke of his birth right, his inheritance. But from who?

"Are you ok?" Leon said to Christina. "My birth right? What's my birth right?"

"Your father passed this down to you from…"

"Then shouldn't he be here to give it me?" Leon interrupted her. Suddenly Christina's face went from somber joy to remorseful pain.

"Leon," Christina spoke softly. "There's something that I have to tell you about your father."

"I want him to tell me! Where is he! Why isn't he here?" Leon spoke of pure anger. He was breathing hard, and his pupils were getting darker. I've never seen him this angry before.

"Your father…" Christina started to speak.

"Is at Elizabeth's house with Elizabeth's mom," I rudely said before she could finish.

It must have been hard for her to keep that inside, but she had to know, and Leon had to be told. They both looked at me in utter disbelief. Faces were shocked, jaws were dropped. And no one spoke for moments.

"I was told that by Elizabeth herself. I apologize, I just wanted to clear the air, no more secrecy, you both deserve better."

Leon looked at his mother, and then he looked at me. Didn't blink, didn't speak, he swallowed hard. Then he left the house.

"Leon!" Christina yelled at him putting the box on the table and walking after him.

I just stood there. I couldn't believe what I had just done. What had come over me? I needed to pray, I needed to talk to Senior because something was wrong with my spirit.

Gossip was unbecoming of me, saying something that I virtually have no proof of other than the words of a woman who is trying to marry me for increased status in this world. I sighed heavily and walked outside to see Christina standing with her arms crossed looking into the distance at nothing in particular. Leon was nowhere in sight.

Suddenly Vita appeared. Christina turned and looked at me. Her facial expression is unexplainable. It wasn't a scowl as I expected to receive; it was a mix of hurt, relief, anger and compassion.

"Go after him." She spoke sternly and walked into the house.

I followed the instructions and got on Vita. She started running the second I mounted her. She knew exactly where to go.

9

Even riding Vita I couldn't catch up to Leon. I went straight to the Elizabeth's house. It was located south east of Cleveland, middle to upper class neighborhood. The house sat on a pond. It was a medium sized house. It was a cool evening, darker than it should've been. It looked as if it was going to rain. The clouds were dark and you could feel moisture in the air. I wasn't sure if it was the moisture from the clouds or moisture from the pond.

Vita and I arrived at the house. I dismounted her and looked for signs of anything wrong. I went to the backyard where the garage was. I stopped and stared at the pond. It was a large pond; beautiful ducks were swimming across it. Other houses were circled around the pond. All of their back yards had some sort of a path to the pond, or a back porch that was built to look at it. It was a very nice neighborhood and quiet.

I looked at the driveway and I noticed that Ian's Silver Lexus was in the driveway. Not a good sign at all. The back sliding door was left open. Leon had to be in there. I slowly walked up to the door. I put my head in first. I didn't hear anything. I stepped all the way in.

All the lights were off downstairs except in the kitchen. It smelled like someone was baking some pot roast or something. I didn't hear anyone in there. I walked into their living room, where they had a very large TV, old pictures and paintings that had to be worth a lot of money, even a family portrait of Elizabeth, her mother Olivia, her father and her brother. From this picture, Elizabeth looked exactly like her mother, her brother looked like a mix of Olivia and her father. Her father was thin man, with glasses on in this photo. I'd never met him in person, and he'd never visited the church. I wasn't sure if they were still married or if he lived there. I hoped not.

This is too much drama for one day, I thought to myself.

Just as I thought that, I heard a scream from upstairs.

"What are you doing here Leon!"

I heard a man's voice.

"What am I doing here!? What are you doing here!" I heard Leon yell even louder.

I heard some tussling and a few crashes. Leon and Ian must be in a physical altercation. I decided not to go up to stop them. They were both stronger than I was, plus, I didn't have the energy. Between getting beat up last night and riding Vita over there, I was physically exhausted. I sat down on their love seat and leaned my head back. I wanted to take a nap right there despite what was going on around me.

"You are in a lot of trouble Leon!" Ian said coming downstairs with his shirt half buttoned and Leon following closely behind him.

Ian, even to be in his forties, was in excellent shape. He was about six feet two inches or so, clean shaven. He'd let his beard grow in though. He used to be clean shaven all around, and muscular.

Leon was angry, no fear was in his eyes, and the respect he had for his father was gone.

"Don't look at me like that Leon!" Ian pleaded.

But Leon wasn't listening. A woman in a white robe walked down the stairs. Very slowly as if no one was down there arguing. She sat down in a seat across from me. It was Olivia, well into her fifties but you would never guess it by looking at her. Long blond hair, light blue eyes, bronze skin, she was a beautiful woman to be any age, let alone her fifties.

She lit a cigarette and leaned back.

VENSIN GRAY

"So you two just let yourself into any home?" Olivia said with her deep Greek accent.

I looked around to Leon who was focused on his father, Ian who was looking at him, then back to Olivia who was looking at me, then I looked to the back sliding door.

"The door was open when I came in," I said trying to make a joke.

"What happened to your face?" Olivia asked.

"I fell off of my horse." I lied.

"Must've been one hell of a fall," Olivia retorted.

"I survived," I said back.

"What are you doing here?" Leon asked Ian again.

"Well I believe the answer to that was obvious," Olivia said chuckling as she smoked more of her cigarette.

"This doesn't concern you," Leon said and gave her a look.

Olivia stopped laughing instantly. She looked afraid. She'd never seen Leon like this.

"I think you should leave." Olivia said to Leon.

"You first." Leon said to Ian.

The tension was rising. Without warning, the room got really hot. I didn't know what was going on, but I knew that I was about to have to break up a fight.

"Calm down Leon," Ian said to his son. "There's a lot you do not understand."

"Do not! Talk to me like I'm a child!"

"Do not raise your voice to me son!" Ian yelled back at Leon.

"You two both can leave," Olivia said standing up.

"Be quiet Olivia," Ian said to her. "Now Leon, there is a lot that I need to tell you. But I do not know how."

"Where have you been. What is wrong with you?" Leon said to Ian.

He was staring at his father with pure disappointment. Growing up, Leon has looked up to Ian. Ian was his hero. His actions over the past few years had eaten away at Leon. Leon was finally beginning to break. That innocent, everyone loves him, non-angry boy was turning into a man, a man angry at his father. He was changing right in front of me, and at that moment, I did not know if it was a good thing or a bad thing. I'd never seen Leon angry before, not that angry, not to where the aura around him heated up so much that I was sweating.

"For too long..." Leon began speaking. "My mother and I have waited late for you to come home and you didn't show until we were sleep. For too long have we pretended to be a happy family in public. For too long I had to listen to my mother cry herself to sleep because her husband was not at home in bed with her. But instead he was here, with another man's wife!..."

Leon then said some things in a language I had never heard him speak before, and I never actually heard that language ever, dialect, nothing.

The room went silent. Ian looked at me, me at Ian, Olivia at Leon. Leon was breathing hard, he calmed himself, as he calmed down, and I felt the temperature in the room lower as well. I looked at Olivia. She was scared out of her mind, that smug, snotty demeanor turned to freight. Ian looked as confused as Leon looked.

"I'm... I'm sorry... I don't know what came over me," Leon said as he backed up.

"What is all the commotion down here?" Elizabeth said coming from the stairwell.

She looked around and gasped as she saw me.

"Victor... what happened to your face?"

I looked at Leon, and Leon looked at me, eye to eye we stared. His facial expression turned from the confusion he brought upon himself with speaking in a different tongue, to anger. His eyes squinted and unexpectedly the room temperature rose again. Something bad was about to happen. Leon started breathing heavily again.

"Now son..." Ian said.

As Ian said that Leon punched the wall he was standing next too. The room shook. Leon began screaming in the language that he spoke earlier. He grabbed his father and tossed him to the other side of the room. He landed on a sofa that was over there. Leon began flipping the furniture to go after Ian.

Olivia screamed and ran towards Elizabeth. Elizabeth came downstairs and stood behind me. I stood up immediately after Leon tossed Ian. Ian wasn't a small man, but Leon threw him as if he were a small puppy. I felt the fear in the air. Ian stood up but Leon was too fast, he grabbed him, still speaking the language loudly, and screaming at the top of his lungs.

Ian tried to tussle with him, which only made Leon angrier. Leon threw Ian in our direction and he hit the television set that was mounted on the wall. Ian bounced off of it, landing on the coffee table beneath it and the TV fell and landed on him. Olivia rushed to Ian, she pushed the television off of him. Elizabeth hugged me from behind, I felt her trembling as she grabbed a hold of me and squeezed tightly.

I didn't know what to do. I grabbed Olivia to get her out of the way because Leon was walking over toward her. He threw every piece of furniture that was in his way against the walls, breaking pictures, lamps, end tables. Leon wasn't himself. I didn't know who he was but I knew I had to do something. He picked his father up with one hand and said something to him in the language, and began punching him with his free hand in the face.

Suddenly, the room went dark. I felt myself being lifted onto a horse. I saw a male figure in front of me. It was very blurry, my face was hurting, my body was hurting, I heard a voice speaking to me.

...lay down his life for his friends. Save my son.

That is all I could make out. Reality hit me again. I was back in the room. Olivia was screaming for Leon to stop hitting Ian, Elizabeth had her face pressed against my back. Ian looked unconscious. I rushed to Leon and grabbed his arm that was holding Ian. I got Ian loose and Leon accidentally hit me in the face. Like I needed an extra lump on my face.

I fell and the room got quiet. I stood up and grabbed Leon's face.

He was in tears, he was still speaking that language and he was looking at me apologetically. I was one hundred percent sure my face was hurting and eye was bleeding, but I couldn't feel anything.

"Look at me!" I screamed to Leon who was looking at Ian. "Brother! Look at me!"

Finally Leon looked at me. He saw what he did to my face, and he looked at my entire face, which looks like a jigsaw puzzle by now I'm sure. "You want to know what happened to me? I was on the west side, on the beach, and five guys came and jumped me. There, you happy!? I didn't fall off my horse, I was jumped by five angry guys that I met at a tea shop on Detroit."

The temperature of the room had cooled dramatically. Leon backed up and looked around at what he had done. He looked at Ian, then at the walls, then at Olivia who was hugging Ian who was laying on the grown motionless. Then he looked at Elizabeth, then to me. His breathing had slowed down, and he seemed to be talking to himself between breaths.

"Tea… shop… Detroit…" is what I could make out of what he was saying.

I was too tired to tell him not to go there and exact any revenge for me.

"I'm sorry Olivia. For what I did to your house," Leon said somberly.

I felt sorry for him for the first time in my life. His heart was broken, and he just reached a level of anger that he'd never experienced, spoke a language I don't think he understood, confronted and completely demolished a man he loved with all his heart, and found out that his little brother was jumped by five angry guys. His mind must have been in a shrivel.

"I love you Victor. And I'm sorry," Leon said that in a soft voice and turned and left the house.

"Leon!" I said as I was going to go after him. But I felt an arm grab mine.

"Let him go," Elizabeth said to me. "Let him go."

Despite everything in me wanting to pursue him, I took her advice. It was quiet for a few minutes.

"Is he alive?" I said to Olivia.

"Barely," she was able to say through the tears she was crying. "I know what we were doing was wrong, I never expected Leon of all people to react like that."

"Well, mother. You had to expect a reaction of some sort," Elizabeth said. "Should I call an ambulance?"

"No," Ian said, breathing heavily.

He must've used all his strength to get that out. He sat up with the aid of Olivia.

"Water please?" He said to Olivia.

Olivia quickly went to the kitchen.

"Can you drive me home, Victor?" Ian asked.

"Not until I clean up his face," Elizabeth said to me as she pulled me up the stairs.

I found myself in her room, which, by the way, was huge. She had a king size bed on one side of her room, and a full living room set on the other, with a TV projector facing a blank wall. She had photos of her and what I assume were some of her friends from Europe, and a photo of her and Octavius when they were younger. No pictures from her in America

"Where is this at?" I asked.

In the photo Octavius was holding a sword up and Elizabeth was hugging him. They were both looking at the camera.

"This picture?" Elizabeth said grabbing it. "That was the last time I saw Octavius face to face. Don't tell anyone this, but they have gladiator games over in Europe. Not like your games here, more like back in the Roman days where slaves fought for their lives in arenas. Octavius told his parents that he wanted to do a tournament that was there. Of course his parents were against it. He was their last child."

"Last child?" I said interrupting her.

"Yes. Octavius got his name from being the eighth child. The only survivor. His parents had seven kids before him, who all didn't live past one year. Then Octavius came, and well, you know the rest of the story. The Blessed One, leader of the Christians." Elizabeth said rolling her eyes.

She stared at the photo for a little while longer, smiling and sighing at the same time.

"He had just won the tournament, he survived and killed over twenty people that day. No one knows about it, they can't know about it, he'd lose his position. But, he was my favorite cousin. He loved me like a sister then, he was my big brother, a better brother than my brother now. But after that, everything changed. It's like, he had a dream, and hasn't looked back from his conquest since."

She put the photo down.

"Enough about Octavius. What about you? What happened to you down there?"

"What do you mean?"

"Before you spoke to Leon, you just stopped. I don't know how to explain it, but your entire body just paused, I don't even think your heart was beating. And then after a few seconds you just came to."

"I don't know what you're talking about," I lied. "I was just trying to figure the best way to stop him from destroying your house and killing his father. I've never seen Leon that angry before in my life."

"You told him what I told you, huh?"

"It was on accident."

"Five guys? What did you do?" Elizabeth asked as she began cleaning out the small cut above my eye.

"What did I do?" I said smiling.

Did I tell Elizabeth that I was out there with Fawzia. Did I tell her who Fawzia was? Did I tell her that five Muslims jumped me because I was after one of their women? No. I couldn't tell her.

"Wrong place at the wrong time." I said to her.

"Well, how did you know talking about yourself when he's obviously mad at his father would stop him?"

"I don't think he was just mad at Ian," I said to her.

I wasn't a selfish person. Leon had the right to be mad at his father, but only to be mad at him.

"I believe that Ian wasn't just angry at his father. I believe he was mad that I didn't tell him the truth about what happened to me, and it all built up inside of him, and unfortunately he took it out on your house and Ian. And for that, I'm sorry. I'll help clean it up."

"Don't worry about it, I'm sure my mother will pay to have everything replaced. Just sit back. Let me clean you up. Do you have a head ache? He hit you pretty hard."

"No, I'm fine. I barely felt it through what's already there."

We both laughed a bit. She began rubbing some cream on my face. It was a peculiar smell. Never smelled any medicated ointment like it before.

"What is that?"

"Comfrey oil," Elizabeth said. "Old family remedy to heal bruises. You'll look better in no time. Can't have you looking like that dating me now can I?"

"Comfrey oil? Never heard of it."

"Well, we have a garden in the back, we grow it and make it ourselves. Ground up the root, add a little canola oil, and here you are, fast healing. Ancient Greeks and Romans used it."

"Thank you."

That was very nice of her. It felt different on my face. I stood up from the couch I was sitting on, and she and I met face to face.

"You look nice, Victor." She said to me, wiping off my clothing.

She leaned in for a kiss. I didn't return the lean. She then kissed me on my cheek. I felt it, and it was a nice kiss.

"You won't be able to resist me forever," she whispered seductively in my ear.

I smiled at her, an appreciative smile. I couldn't deny her beauty, it was invigorating.

I walked down stairs. Elizabeth stayed in her room.

"Where are you going to go, Ian?" Olivia asked.

"I need to be with my wife, Olivia. I'm sorry," Ian said to her. He looked at me, and left the house and to go to his car.

"I'm sorry again, Olivia," I said to her.

"It's not your fault. Thank you for stopping it when you did. None of this leaves this house. None of it." She said to me in a stern and demanding way.

I nodded my head in agreement, left the house and got into Ian's Lexus.

We drove all the way to his house in silence. I wasn't sure what to expect when we got there. It was an incredibly odd day to say the least.

"This, what happened, it never happened," Ian said to me. "I'll go in alone, just go home and get some rest. You look like I feel."

Ian said, laughed a little bit, and walked into his house.

I got into my mom's car and drove home.

10

When I got home it was dark out. The anxiety left my body, my heart finally slowed, and suddenly I began to feel that hit that was put on me by Leon. My face was pounding. I just smiled.

'What a day,' I thought to myself.

I got out of the car, and let the wind hit my face. I realized that Vita was nowhere to be found. I rode her to Olivia's, but then she left. Maybe she let Leon ride her over to the tea shop? No. That didn't happen.

I walked into the house. To my surprise no one was awake. Everyone's car was in the driveway. I went downstairs to my room and turned on the lights.

"Ah!" I yelled.

Sa'Rah was standing right in front of me. I didn't even hear her or feel her presence.

"What are you screaming for?" Sa'Rah said giggling.

She enjoyed scaring me, and living in this house, she often did just that. There were lots of places to hide, especially at night.

"You're trying to give me a heart attack?" I said as I laughed in relief and sat down on my bed.

I breathed heavily. Sa'Rah stopped smiling.

"What happened today?"

I swear, this girl had special powers.

"What makes you think something happened?"

"Well, you look like you just broke up a fight."

"I was riding Vita."

"Not going to work with me."

I gave up. I explained to her everything that had happened from the discussion with Christina, the special box, Leon rearranging Olivia's living room with Ian, Elizabeth and the comfrey oil. I don't know why, but I just trusted Sa'Rah with everything. I felt like I could tell her anything, she was my heart.

"Sounds like a special day for a special person," she said smiling. "Leon punched you in the face? I'm going to get him."

She touched my face.

"Elizabeth cleaned you up pretty good. You're not listening to me, Victor. She's the one for you, not the one who got you jumped by five Mexicans."

"Muslims."

"Is there a difference?" she said sarcastically.

"Sa'Rah!" I said angrily.

Sa'Rah didn't have a filter. She'd say what she wanted, and joke about who ever. Just who she was.

"I'm only kidding around."

Suddenly she got quiet.

"There is someone at the door."

Then I heard a faint knock at the door. Sa'Rah went to answer it. Normally I would that late at night but I was exhausted. When she left, I went to the bathroom. My phone was sitting on the sink. I looked and I had a ton of messages and missed calls. Seven text messages from Fawzia. Seven!? I read through them.

'I heard about what happened to you. I am sorry.'

'Are you ok Victor?'

'Victor, are you ignoring me?'

'I'm going to call around to see if you're in a hospital.'

'Not in a hospital, where are you?'

'So you sent your brother to take care of what happened? You helped destroy an innocent tea shop.'

'I'm not sure what's going on but I'll see you soon…'

Sent my brother to take care of what happened? What was she talking about? I took off my shirt and I heard some footsteps on my stairs.

"Who was at the door Sa'Rah?" I said. I was in the bathroom with the door shut.

Sa'Rah didn't answer. The door opened.

"Sa'Rah! You know to knock before…" I said turning around to see that it wasn't Sa'Rah.

It was Fawzia. She looked at me, her gorgeous eyes were watering. She was wearing an all-black covering around her body and only her face was exposed. She breathed hard and slapped me. I didn't know what just happened but I stepped back and looked at her.

"I guess my face is a magnet for violence this past twenty four hours."

"I'm sorry, but you had me worried sick," Fawzia exclaimed. "Your sister let me in. She is beautiful. Too bad she let's just anyone see her hair."

"We don't believe the same way that you believe, Fawzia," I said. "What are you doing here?"

"Malcolm and his friends. The ones who jumped you? Are all in the hospital, critical condition."

"I wish I could say I feel sorry for them but I don't."

How could I feel sorry for them? They put me in the hospital, only I didn't go to one. I was nursed to health by my fourteen year old sister.

"Word around town is that Leon is the one who did it."

"Leon!?" I said surprised. "It couldn't have been him. I was just with him."

"Had to be. This person looked like him, was fast, faster than anyone else, strong, just unstoppable. The place got hot even above the air conditioning, and the person was screaming in some language I've never heard."

SON OF SIN

Sounded like Leon to me. What had I started? Not only did he flip out at Olivia's, he was exacting revenge on my behalf. But how did he know who to attack?

"How did he pick out Malcolm and his friends?" I asked Fawzia.

"I'm not sure. He just, came in the shop, went directly to them, and the rest is just a screaming blur. Then the ambulances came, and there are a lot of upset Muslims right now."

"I have to call my grandfather," I grabbed my phone and for some reason I called Leon first.

"Hello, brother," Leon answered the phone.

"Leon, where are you at?" I asked curtly.

"I'm at Senior's."

"Stay there, I'm on my way." I hung up after that.

I looked at Fawzia. My mind was in a million places.

"I have to go, I'm sorry."

"I'm coming with you. I would love to meet the great Victor Thomas Senior."

I was in no mood to argue. When I walked outside, I half expected Vita to be out there waiting for me. She wasn't. I jumped into my mother's car and we drove to Senior's.

The drive to Senior's was quiet. Fawzia didn't speak, I didn't try to spark up a conversation. A lot had happened over the past few days and I was trying to bring it to a close before a lot of bad things happened. Me getting jumped, Leon finding out about Ian and Olivia, and an attack on the Muslims. I didn't want a war starting, especially not one that I had something to do with.

When we got to Senior's, Leon was already outside. I got out of the car immediately.

"Leon!" I yelled. "Why did you go to that restaurant and fight them? Haven't you done enough today?"

"What are you talking about?" Leon responded with a puzzled look on his face.

"That place I told you about, where I was jumped, why did you go there?"

— 109 —

VENSIN GRAY

"I didn't go anywhere, brother..."

"Don't brother me!" I snapped at him.

I'm not sure what was coming over me, but I was angry. For the first time since I was jumped, I was actually angry. And I wasn't holding back on my words.

"I think you need to calm down, brother."

"Or what? You're going to beat me up to? You put five guys in critical condition."

"I do not have a clue of what you are talking about, Victor!" Leon screamed back at me. "I've been here talking to Senior since the episode at Olivia's house. Why don't you believe me?"

"He's telling the truth, Three." Senior came out. "He told me about what happened, everything. Thank you for stopping it when you did. And who is this?" Senior motioned to Fawzia who was standing behind me, and looking directly at Leon with astonishment, fear or lust. I couldn't tell by looking at her.

"It wasn't him," Fawzia spoke of Leon. "The man who did this, his eyes were as black as a starless night sky. Not light, not gray, not bea..."

She stopped speaking, then closed her eyes tightly.

"I'm sorry, Leon," I said to him. He didn't respond, his eyes were on Fawzia. "Senior, Leon, this is Fawzia, a friend I met over in a grocery store on Detroit after training. She's opened my eyes to a few things that are happening in the world."

"It is a pleasure to meet you, Mr. Thomas," Fawzia said lowering her eyes and sort of taking a bow to Senior.

"Please, Fawzia, I am but a man, no need to bow your eyes to me," Senior said to her. "I met your father once, good man."

"Thank you," Fawzia said smiling. As her met eyes with Leon her smile went away.

"Is she the reason that you were beat up?" Leon said looking furious.

"Leon," Senior said.

"Yes Senior?" Leon answered with complete respect.

"Go help your grandmother in the house. She's arranging a few things for a get together, she could use an extra hand since I left." Senior said and smiled at him.

The grandmother he was referring to was Grandma Patrice. Without question, Leon went into the house. When he was gone, Senior spoke to us.

"Tell me, Fawzia, what happened to Victor the third's face?"

Fawzia was quiet for a moment. She wasn't there, at least I hope she wasn't there to witness what happened. Or maybe she was, maybe she set the entire thing up, to get back at some Christians for what Octavius was doing over in Europe.

"I'm not entirely sure." Fawzia finally spoke. "I remember that Victor and I were at the beach together, and I left. I got home, and I get a phone call telling me that Victor may need to go to a hospital, and that he was somewhere down on the beach. I ran there immediately with my father but Victor was nowhere to be found. There was blood on the sand where the scuffle happened but no Victor. Just some horse tracks and a strange man on the beach dressed in all black."

"Dressed in all black you say?" Senior's eyes lit up. "Did you speak to him? Did he say anything to you all?"

"He didn't look our way, it was as if we weren't even there. He just stood there staring off into the distance. I called Victor several times and texted him, and finally when I was tired of him not responding, I took a taxi over here."

Senior was silent for a long time. His face, his eyes, everything went blank. I didn't know what was going on.

"Senior?" I said after a few minutes of the awkward silence.

"Yes, Three, yes, I'm sorry." Senior said coming to. "Tell me what you remember from your encounter."

"I don't remember much, Senior. I remember being woke up violently, drug, beat up, I lost consciousness, then some hands lifted me up onto Vita, and he said a scripture to me. I didn't catch it all until I was at Olivia's."

"A scripture you said? What scripture?"

VENSIN GRAY

"It went 'Greater love has no man than this, that a man lay down his life for his friends.' That's what it was."

"Greater love has no man…" Senior mumbled to himself. "John fifteen thirteen. That's all he said to you?"

"No. I didn't make it out when he first said it, but at Olivia's, I had an out of body experience. I guess that's the only way to describe what happened, but it replayed the ending that I thought I passed out before hearing. He told me to save his son."

Senior took a big breath, and his face looked puzzled. A look of excitement, I haven't seen this look from Senior in, ever.

"Are you ok?"

"I'm fine, Three. I'm fine."

"Mind telling us what is going on, Mr. Thomas?" Fawzia said sensing his reservation just as I.

One thing I know about Senior is that he's not a reserved person, if he knows something, he'll tell you if it wouldn't harm others.

"Nothing that I can prove right now, Fawzia. Three."

"Yes, Senior." I responded.

"You said that there was someone who fought the men responsible for what happened to you?"

"Fawzia told me, I wanted to see if Leon had done it."

"Yes, someone who looked very similar to Leon." Fawzia spoke. "Came into the tea shop on Detroit, and went directly for the people responsible for Victor. He was fast, strong, and unstoppable. I'm not sure they even got a hit off, it was a very quick fight, and all of them are in the hospital now, critical condition."

"How are things over that way?" Senior asked.

"Well, everyone believes it to be Leon. No one knows what they did to Victor. So there are very angry people over there right now. Not sure what's going to happen but…"

"I will go speak with them," Senior said interrupting her.

"I'm coming with you," I said.

"No," Senior shot back forcefully but calmly. "Stay here, or go home and get some rest. I will handle this. Tell your grandmother I'll be back soon. Fawzia, take me to where your leaders would normally meet."

Fawzia agreed and walked toward Senior's car. As she walked past me, her hand touched my face, it was so soft and inviting and any sense of anxiousness I had in me faded away with one simple touch, my world felt better. Senior and Fawzia drove off into the night. I felt a hand on my shoulder and I jumped.

"It's just me, brother," Leon said calmly. "You're so jumpy. Normally you're very reserved, those five did a number on you."

"I'm sorry, Leon," I said again, still feeling bad for accusing him of something he already told me he had no idea about.

"You apologized once, that is all that was needed. How is your face? I got you with a good one."

"Yeah, you did," I said laughing uncomfortably, trying to feel better. "What happened to you?"

"I don't know. I'm trying to figure that out myself. Whatever it was, it felt natural."

"Like turning into the Hulk?" I said.

"No," Leon said laughing a bit. "More like, coming up for air when you've been under the water for a long time."

"Well, my long time is twenty seconds, yours is a lot longer."

"You know what I mean. That sensation you get when you hit the surface and get that breath into your lungs. That how I felt, I felt like I was breathing. Like there is something inside of me that's trying to come out. I don't know rather to fear it or embrace it. So afterwards, I just rode Vita here, and prayed with Senior and Grandmother. I felt solace during the prayer. Then we all ate, relaxed and Senior and I played a few games of Chess. Then you called. I need you to trust me brother. I've known you all my life, I've never told you a lie, I've never done anything to make you think that I wouldn't be honest with you. So don't think I'm going to start now. Ok?"

"Ok. And again Leon. I'm…"

"Don't say sorry again or I'm going to hit you again."

We both laughed and embraced in a brotherly hug.

"I need to get home to my mother. I'm sure she's worried."

"I took your father there. He said that everything that happened, didn't happen. Olivia concurs. I don't know how he's going to explain his limp or his bruises to your mother though. The only thing that I can think of that could relate to the beating you gave him is that he fell off of a very tall tree and hit every branch on the way down and lived to tell the tale."

We both laughed again.

"I hope he's not angry with me."

"Might be too scared to be angry."

"Well, let me get home. Mind if I take Vita? She think she's faster than me."

Suddenly I saw Vita running down the street and Leon took off after her, he caught up to her and mounted her at full speed and waved goodbye. What a day.

I walked into Senior's house. Grandma Patrice was sleep on the sofa in the living room with the fire place going. It was a cool night in Cleveland. I felt so weak, and so tired, I used all of my energy to stay awake and focus on all the events that happened. I laid down in front of the fire, I stared at it long and hard until the flames looked like they were moving. They made human figures and then they collided.

I kept my eyes open as long as I could but sleep was defeating me.

11

The next two and half months of the summer all kind of blended in to one another. Senior spoke with the Muslim leaders on the West side of Cleveland, explained what happened and that the person responsible for what happened to Malcolm and his friends was not Leon. He gave his word and they believed him without question.

Leon and I trained more together for a month until he had to go up to Jesus Christ University for football training. It was their first year of having any collegiate sport, just to see Leon go there and show off his skills. He and I talked a lot more; he didn't have any more instances where he turned into the Hulk. I told him until we found out what was going on with him that's what I'm calling him. We jogged Euclid Creek every night, and continued playing basketball when we had the time.

Ian and Christina, in public had been seen together, looking just fine, but in the background they were not. Leon and I were both confused as to why Christina wouldn't get a divorce. Furthermore, the box that held Leon's gift went missing the day Leon had that Hulkish episode. I didn't take it, Christina didn't take it from herself, and Leon left before any of us. Christina was pretty depressed about it but Senior assured her that it would show up.

It seemed that only he and Christina know what was in there. After hearing Senior, Christina calmed down about it being missing.

Speaking of marriages, my mother and father seemed to have

found a middle ground. They didn't argue anymore, they didn't fuss or fight, they smiled in public and at home. Mom even joined us on Sundays. Although no church had been going on, we all gathered at Senior's house and just had discussions and bible study. You can shut down the Church, but you can't stop Christians from coming together anywhere to worship Jesus and be amongst one another.

There wasn't any news from the actions that were happening overseas, but from what I could get from Senior, it was getting pretty bad and would ultimately hit the United States soon. Many men and women who were supposed to go to college were being recruited into a group called 'True Followers of Jesus Christ'. According to Senior it was a training group for Christian Soldiers loyal to Octavius. I asked Senior if we should be worried but he assured me that Jesus has the greatest Army of them all.

Sa'Rah seemed to be worried, many of her classmates as young as fifteen were seen joining Octavius. Sa'Rah and I spent a lot of time together this summer, every day we had breakfast with one another. She would cook one day, I would cook another. She even invited me to her and our father's Denny's breakfast on Sundays.

Sa'Rah told me that I was going to be special, and that no one would match my skill. She talked as if she was a dying eighty year old war hero. But that was my sister and I loved her to death.

She invited Elizabeth over to the house quite often. Her and Elizabeth had conversations about life. Sa'Rah asked her to tell her about Greece and Europe and Elizabeth would come over, and answer every question without a problem. I wasn't sure if they were really friends, or if Elizabeth was using Sa'Rah to get to me, or more likely, Sa'Rah was using herself to bring Elizabeth and I closer.

Fawzia and I spent a lot of time together when we could. Because of the day that I was jumped, I would go to the west solely to train and then leave. But we often met on the south side of Cleveland. There was a town called Parma, which held no real religious allegiances, just a town which you can be as you want to be.

We often just walked around there, and didn't worry about anything. She told me that Malcolm and his friends made a full recovery and were now training extremely hard and recruiting men to their cause to eventually get Leon back. Not sure how that was going to work out for them knowing the Hulk. But it would be fun to watch.

Fawzia and I talked about anything and everything. We even touched on the subject of us leaving and having children and leaving the world behind. Religious persecution, judgments and everything. But it was only talk, I wouldn't walk away from Jesus, and she wasn't leaving her Mohammed teachings. But her company was soothing, and kissing her was like that breath of fresh air Leon spoke of. It just felt like I was supposed to do it. We spent majority of our time talking or kissing, nothing else in between.

She told me about her hopes and dreams before the war started over in Europe. She spoke of how Octavius' presence was illuminating but darkening at the same time. She missed her sister, who she believed was over in the states, but didn't know where, or even how to find her.

She said her father was trying to get her to marry a Muslim over in Spain once he made it over here but she confessed to me that her heart only held me in it. Hearing words like that made me feel good for some reason. I mean, my family loved me, but her desire and love for me was different. It was like I woke up in the morning just for that love. I had to earn that love from her. She never said it, but I saw it in her eyes. I never said it either, never told a woman that I loved her before and I didn't know how I would tell her.

"You brought me here, and now you're just going to sit there and stare at the water and not talk to me?" Fawzia broke my thoughts up.

I brought her to a different part of Lake Erie, a beach behind a senior community center. It was a very beautiful part of the lake. It was quiet. It was the eve of the day that I was leaving to go to Jesus Christ University. It was a warm evening, and we got there just in time to see the sun set over the lake.

"We made it in time." I said to Fawzia.

I was wearing a University School t-shirt and some basketball shorts and flip flops, Fawzia had on some all black leggings and a plain purple shirt and of course her hair covering. She stood next to me, my arm was around her waist and we stood on these rocks and watched the sun set.

"My grandfather brought Leon and I here many times when we were children," I began speaking. "He told us that we are brothers, didn't matter what society tells us, close friends didn't quite describe us. He told us, that we were brothers, and that was that. He told me that Leon's blood runs through my veins, I never quite understood what he meant by that. But I learned that when I was a baby, I was near death, and Senior pulled one of the doctors to the side and the doctor reluctantly put a pint of Leon's blood into me, and here I am today. No one knows about that. No one, not even my grandmother, not even Leon, just my grandfather, Leon's mom and me. This is where Leon and I really began to embrace brotherhood. This beach."

I looked around and she looked with me.

"It's beautiful." She said smiling.

"You're beautiful." I said to her.

She smiled at me and gave me a soft kiss on my lips. As we kissed the wind blew and I felt a mist from the water that slammed against the rocks. The sky grew darker as the sun descended. It wasn't our first sun set together, but it could be our last.

"I don't know what's going to happen when I go to college tomorrow night. I'm not sure we'll have time to talk, but I promise that I'll do all I can to talk to you. And I'll text you every morning, and every night"

"And I'll answer every message." Fawzia said to me, looking at me in my eyes, reassuring me that she was mine.

We never fully said that we were a couple. But in essence we were.

"I love you, Victor Thomas the Third," she said that to me, and instantly my heart stopped.

I looked back at her. I was full of glee. I was speechless, hearing her say it was amazing, my hands started to tremble and my legs went numb. I was in love. She must've felt my hands shaking because she hugged me tightly.

"You don't have to say it back," she whispered in my ear.

"I love you too," I said back to her.

It was the first time in life I ever told a woman that I loved her. It felt weird, I saw it happen all the time growing up. Kids telling kids I love you, just for sex, or a sense of comfort, but me, I said it because I felt it, and I meant it.

"Promise me that you'll be here when I return."

"I promise you, Victor, I'll be here," she said back to me in a soft voice.

She pulled back, and she kissed me again, and this time, I felt a light on me. The Sun was finally about to fully be down and its final light was on us as if it was a spot light. I didn't know what her hair looked like, but I didn't care. Her face pressed against mine was all I cared about. Her lips touching mine, our souls intertwining, and our body's aura colliding was all that I was concerned with. Our kiss became more passionate, she grabbed my head, and my hands were on her back, one of my hands moved up and touched her head covering and she stopped kissing me. Her eyes watered up.

"I love you, Victor. You're leaving and I'm going to miss you. I have to go."

She walked away off of the rocks and up the hill. I didn't follow her, her father was supposed to pick her up, and I guess he was up there.

I just sat on the rocks. The last time she left me after an embrace I was woken up violently. This time I wouldn't be. This was my neighborhood. I laid there on the rocks, my heart was pounding, I couldn't be any happier. I felt blessed. I had a great mother and father, the greatest grandfather to ever touch this planet, the best little sister, an amazing brother, a taboo relationship with probably one of the most beautiful women in the world, and I would be attending Jesus Christ University to learn how to take over for when Senior stepped to the side.

"Dear God." I started praying. "I know that I don't often pray to you on my own. I don't get much alone time these days. They say when you pray, you're supposed to just talk to you like you're right in front of me. This is me praying to you Jesus. I don't often get to thank you for all the blessings that you have given me. I truly appreciate them. I know that things are rough for Fawzia and her people, though we may not believe the same. I'm sure there is a reason why you brought her into my life and I thank you for that. Perhaps one day she'll believe as I believe, but if she doesn't, then so be it. I want to ask you for the courage and direction when I'm at JCU. I'm terrified of college, I hope I selected the right one. I hope that I do what I'm supposed to do, and ultimately I hope that I start the correct way into becoming a good man like my father and his father. My heart beats for you, Jesus, and your Will will be done through me. I am but your vessel, Jesus. Anything you need done, you give the word and it will be so. I love you, and this is my covenant to you, that I will give my life for you, no matter what. Protect my family, keep them in your thoughts. I love you, Jesus. Amen."

When I finished that prayer, I saw a shooting star directly over my head, and suddenly I felt my heart beating faster and faster. I started breathing heavy and sweating on a cool night. The wind blew harder and harder and finally a big wave hit the rocks and I fell into the water. While under the water I tried to swim back up to get air but something was holding me down. They felt like hands grabbing on to my arms and legs. Once I couldn't hold my breath anymore I sucked in a bunch of water, the pain in my lungs was excruciating, and I started to panic.

I began to see a light.

"Calm yourself, young Victor," a voice said to me. "Breathe."

I started to breathe just fine underneath the water. I was bewildered. I didn't know what was going on.

"The hands you feel are that of Satan's. He fears you, he wants your life, but he cannot have your life. I accept your covenant."

"Jesus?" I asked out. I didn't see anything but a bright light, nothing more.

"I am the way, the truth and the life. I command you, Satan. Let him go!"

I woke up on the sand coughing up water. The sun was out. I must've lost consciousness under the water that long and the waves brought me to land.

Was I dreaming?

12

I went home to sleep a few more hours. I couldn't decide if what happened was a dream, or if it was real. When you're under water for a long time and your brain is without oxygen, you can hallucinate. Maybe I hallucinated. That would be the last time I went to sleep on a beach.

I walked around my room, most of my clothes were packed up into a truck. My mother, father and Sa'Rah were all driving me to college. I looked at the posters on my wall, championship trophies, gold medals. Photos of my family and I, this room, wasn't going to be mine anymore. It seemed like just yesterday Leon and I were on the basketball court for the first time as University School students. And suddenly we were grown. Prom was over, graduation was over, college was about to start and life would begin.

The decisions you make from here on out are you own. Your parents can no long come to the rescue. It can be scary if you look at it from a standpoint of your parents are your pillars. But if you are your own man or woman, you choose your own destiny. My destiny was to follow in the footsteps of my grandfather. Big shoes to fit but I believed in my heart that I could do it.

I ended my moment of crossing over to adult hood and nostalgic thoughts. I finished packing up the things I would need and I made my way over to Senior's. They were having a little barbeque going away party for me. I texted Fawzia that morning but she hadn't returned it yet.

I made my way to the back yard where everyone was.

"Hey Three!" yelled my Aunt Victory.

She came over gave me a hug and had my father take our picture.

"Good luck in college! Remember how you were raised, and don't get down on yourself if you do get caught up in the college life, ok?"

"Ok, auntie," I said to her.

She gave me a hug and a kiss and made her way over to Grandma Patrice.

"Hello, Three," said Christina. "Leon says that he's sorry he can't make it but he said that you're going to love it up there in Midland."

"Thank you Christina." I said to her, she appeared to be in dampened spirits. "What's wrong?"

"Growing up is what's wrong. My babies are off to college and it makes me happy and sad at the same time to give you all out to the world."

"Don't cry, Christina."

My mom said coming over to hug her.

"You can have Sa'Rah."

They both laughed.

"Speaking of Sa'Rah, where is she?" I asked my mom.

"She's down by the Lake. But quick take a picture with me and your father."

I got by my mom and my father and Christina took the photo. Suddenly I was swarmed by members from the church, and other friends and distant family members wishing me well. We all ate some delicious barbeque that Senior and my father prepared.

"I remember when your Aunt Victory went off to college," Grandma Patrice said as she and I sat down on some lawn chairs away from everyone. "I didn't really know what to tell her quite honestly. I didn't go away from college. Married your grandfather right after high school and here I am, mother of three, grandmother of three. I don't regret anything, but sometimes I wish I would've gone."

"Well, you still look like you're in your twenties grandma. You can still go," I said joking around with her.

"You are silly," my grandmother said laughing. "I was a popular cheerleader in high school and no one in the world would've thought that I would've ended up with Pastor Thomas. But he is a fine man isn't he? You should know. You look just like him. I just want you to be careful up there ok, Victor? I don't know what's troubling you, but a few months ago I watched you fall asleep on the floor staring into a fire place and you looked as if you were watching a movie. You don't have to tell me what is going on, and I don't know what is going on with you and that young lady you've been gallivanting around town with. I just want you to protect this ok?"

She made a gesture to her heart.

"When that is involved, you sometimes tend to lose sight of reality. Decisions you make are blinded with passion, no matter what is going on around you, Victor. I want you to really try to remain calm during situations that would make even the strongest men panic. Remember Jesus is always with you, even if it feels like he's not. Keep your composure, remember how you were raised, and most importantly, pray and give thanks to God always."

I figured I shouldn't tell her what happened the last time I prayed.

"And if you get home sick, come home for a day or two, we all love you here."

I got up and gave her a hug. My grandmother Patrice was a very interesting woman. From what I gathered growing up, women like her didn't marry men like my grandfather, they married men like Ian. She was unique to say the least. A strong woman. I loved her with all my heart.

"Hey there, Victor," Grandfather Persy came by to chat.

"Why is everyone calling me Victor all of a sudden?" I asked him as I gave him a hug.

"That's your name isn't it? I wish your grandmother was here, she would have loved to have seen this day. But I'm happy and I know that you are going to do well in college. I'm sure everyone is giving you speeches, I just wanted to stop by and say that I love you and be smart and Jehovah be with you."

He gave me a hug and walked off. He looked like was about to cry.

"Hey honey!" Aunt Victoria came and gave me a big hug. "I'm so glad I could make it!"

"Hey, Aunt Vicky," I said to her.

"Man, college. I'm proud of you. About to be a man out here."

I just smiled, didn't know how to really take that.

"Jesus Christ University, awesome college, I visited up there to give a speech, and they are really nice up there in Midland. You're going to love it. Here get a picture with me! Hey, big head, come take this picture."

She was gesturing for my father.

"You're not calling anyone big head are you?" My father joked back.

He took the picture, and then Aunt Victoria walked off with Aunt Victory.

"Just do your best out there son," my father said. "I did the best I could to raise you the best way I knew how. Obviously, you coming into the world was unexpected. And I'm sure there have been times where I was less than a father that you deserved to have, but just know that kids don't come with instruction manuals, and just like you're learning to do things and what you like, I had to learn it as well. I love you son, don't ever forget it."

My dad hugged me, my mom snapped our picture and he walked away.

"I guess it's my turn." My mom said to me smiling.

I loved my mom, although it didn't always show based on the lack of time I spent with her, but you have to leave the nest someday right?

"I saw you talking to your grandmother Patrice. I wish my mother was here but Patrice has been a great influence in my life. And I love and appreciate her. You know, her and I are a lot alike. We were young beautiful girls and we married a Thomas. Only God knows why."

We both laughed.

"I know I haven't been a great mother. And I know the stuff with me and your father, church and the Kingdom Hall is looming over you and Sa'Rah, but I don't want you to bother yourself with that while you are away. I want you to make smart decisions, and do what's in your heart. Don't second guess yourself, have fun, learn as much as you can, and be who you want to be. I love you baby."

My mom hugged me and Senior took the picture. Where he came from, I had no idea.

"Don't worry, Three," Senior said. "I don't have much to say. Other than put Jesus first and pray. I know you're going to be just fine. I love you."

"I do have a question, Senior," I said to him. "If you have a moment."

"I'll always have a moment for you, Three," Senior smiled.

"Well, you know I'm going to Jesus Christ University to become a Minister like you. I mean, I know I'll never be able to do what you do, but I want to try really hard."

"Three, you're going to touch more lives than I ever have. And even if you just touch one, that's good enough for anyone," Senior said interrupting me.

"Thanks. Senior. But I just want to know, what do you do that makes you different from other Pastors and preachers out here? I mean there are mega churches everywhere, but people wouldn't call our church a mega church, they wouldn't call you a Pastor preaching to the masses. What do you do?"

Senior looked at me, and gathered his thoughts for a second, a practice that I wanted to master. Instead of just blurting out the first thing that came to mind, he took his time to think of a reasonable responsible response.

"What do I do, huh?" he said to himself. "Other pastors, they go to class, they do their ministry, and then they get behind the podium and are looking at all these people looking at them, they have their own ideas and own agenda, not to say it's against the Will of God, but who's to be certain it is? And they preach, and they preach grace, or they preach the gospel, or they preach hellfire and brimstone, they try to market their church, get more Members, more money, and a bigger church, some churches do hellfire and brimstone, preaching conviction, and often time troubled minds are scared to go there, or their hearts aren't strong enough, then you have those are so smart, they feel like the pastor is judging them, and condemning them, a man, condemning another man, who are all short of the glory. I'm different because I just try to teach. That's it; it is not in my hands to judge anyone, not in my hands to do God's work. God will judge everyone. Even me, I'll be judged differently because I am in the position that I am in. But was Jesus not a teacher himself? How many people did Jesus condemn or convict? How many people did he save or heal?

"You see" He continued, "people may try to get you with the 'oh, God is going to toss you in the Lake of Fire, or continue living your lifestyle and God will always forgive you.' Jesus spoke of iniquity, not Sin, but a multitude of Sin. When someone has complete knowledge of what they are doing, and continue doing it without remorse and without conviction, which is what gets you to the fire and brimstone. Not to say that it's wrong to preach a certain way, just do it from the heart, Three, be a teacher, and remember you always can learn more. I've read the bible several times in life and still learn different things every day."

Senior gave me a hug and suddenly everyone in the family was around and we all took a few group photos. Except, it wasn't a complete group. When we all scattered and I looked for and found Sa'Rah at the bottom of the lake sitting down with her feet in the water.

"Didn't want to join the party?" I said to her as I removed my shoes and sat next to her with my feet in the water.

"I had a dream that you drowned last night," Sa'Rah said to me.

"You have a very vivid imagination. It's just fear," I said to her lying. I believed I had drowned the previous night.

"What have I told you before? You can't lie to me," she said looking at me with our mother's eyes. "What happened?"

"I said a prayer to God, and then I fell in the water, couldn't get out then woke up on the beach."

"Bad things happen to you when you go to sleep on the beach."

"Trust me, I know."

"Something else happened. While you were under water."

"How do you know?"

"I don't know."

"I felt hands, holding me down, pulling me towards the bottom. And then, it was like Jesus spoke to me, and told me that the Devil wanted me, and then He told the Devil to release me, and then I woke up on the sand."

Sa'Rah just smiled.

"I'm glad the Devil didn't get you. That would suck," she said very sarcastically. "Look at them, they don't even know you're gone."

"Why are you acting like this, Sa'Rah?"

"Why not? They throw you this party, and I'm sure they all gave you all this great advice, but do they know what it is like to be you, Victor? Do they know what you've been through? Do they care? They don't care. This is tradition, graduation, send offs, all this stuff is just tradition, they aren't doing this because you are special. They are doing this because it's just what is supposed to be done I guess."

"What is wrong with me having a sendoff, Sa'Rah?"

"Nothing. It's just that they are going to go off and live their life just as normal, and I'm going to be affected the most. My brother is leaving me."

"I'm not leaving. I'm going to learn so I can be a better, smarter, more responsible man when I get back."

"You're leaving me. The second you leave mom and dad are going to get a divorce, and things in Cleveland will begin to fall apart while you and Leon are off in Midland and somehow I'm going to have to hold this family together until you're ready to do your duty to God."

"My duty to God?"

"Yes, your duty to God. We all have a duty to God, and yours is going to be leader of this family. Grandpa Victor and I won't be around forever to lead us."

"You are something else you know that?"

"Don't do that Victor!" Sa'Rah shouted at me while standing up in the water. "Don't talk to me like I'm some average child. I am not!"

"Look, Sa'Rah, growing up is scary. I'm scared, sooner or later I'm going to get married, have children. Leon and I won't be able to hang out like normal, you and I won't get to be you and I anymore because I'm going to have my own family, and other responsibilities, and that is what life is."

"Well, I'm ok with you getting married, as long as it's with Elizabeth. I've been prepping her to be your wife. Don't let my hard work this summer go to waste."

Sa'Rah had set the record for most mature girl on the planet. She was beyond my years in maturation. She reminded me of a reborn Senior. I just shook my head.

"Well, thank you for your permission, young lady. Now can we go up there and spend some time with the people that are only here because they're supposed to be?"

"Sure," she said softly.

It was a very warm day. It felt great outside. The sun was right above our heads, nature was singing to us. It was a wonderful day to be with family and friends.

"Make me a promise, Victor," Sa'Rah said.

"Anything."

"When I need you, you'll come home."

"I'll be on the first plane home, love," I said to her kissing her on her forehead.

She started crying and grabbed me and cried on my shoulders.

"Come on now, Sa'Rah."

She bawled into my shoulders. If anyone was going to miss me, Sa'Rah was going to miss me. We were unique people on the planet. We shared the same mother and father, we had a connection. I wasn't the crying type so I let her cry.

"I'm sorry, brother," she said wiping her eyes. "Just remember who loves you the most."

She walked back to the Party. I followed her. My dad noticed that Sa'Rah was crying and she ran to him and cried some more and he took her in to the house. Everyone was saying their little 'no don't cry sweethearts' and other comments. I kept walking around. I checked my phone, still no text from Fawzia. I resent the same text thinking maybe she didn't get it.

"Hey there, Victor," I heard a familiar voice say to me.

I turned around and it was Elizabeth, looking as plain as I'd ever seen her look in my life. Normally she was very dressed up and ready to impress anyone. But her hair was in a ponytail, she had on a white t-shirt, with some tight blue jean pants on and some flat shoes. She looked probably the most attractive I'd ever seen her, because she didn't look like she belonged in a magazine.

"Hey, Elizabeth," I said to her giving her a hug.

"I didn't come to stay long. I just wanted to give you this."

"What is this?"

She handed me a book.

"It's my journal. Read it when you get lonely. And there will be nights that you get lonely. Trust me."

She gave me another hug and kissed me on the cheek.

"I'll always be here for you," she whispered in my ear.

She smiled showing her perfect teeth, and gorgeous smile. I laughed to myself. I had two very beautiful women that I could be with.

Elizabeth went and hugged Senior and walked off. I looked at the journal. I opened the first page and it read.

'This if for when you get lonely, Victor. Read me. You'll be surprised at what you'll learn. ~Elizabeth.'

"Someone has a secret admirer," my mother said to me. "She's beautiful. But it's time to go.

Everyone said their goodbyes. Sa'Rah eventually stopped crying,

SON OF SIN

and my mother, father, Sa'Rah and I drove to Midland.

When we arrived on campus we entered in from the north entrance. It was a heavily wooded area. There was a high school north of the school, but you would never know the school was back there if you weren't looking for it. It was hidden well. Probably why JCU decided to take over the old Northwood University School.

Driving in from the north we passed a few baseball fields and soccer fields looking for the office building. We finally circled around and passed a parking lot by what looked like one floor dorm rooms connected to another set of dorm rooms and the cafeteria. Finally, we arrived at the office building.

I went inside. The lady inside was nice, she told me that the freshman dorms were filled up and I had a room in the apartment complex near the river at the south entrance to the school. My family and I drove some more, passing more classroom buildings and one that looked to be an auditorium. The campus was very clean area and reminded me a lot of University School only a lot larger. We passed the gymnasium, swimming pool, track field and football field and finally we arrived at my apartment.

There were seven complexes with what seems to be four apartments in each one. Mine was the very last one facing the river. My father helped me set up my room. Since I was the first one there, I took the room all the way in the back with its own bathroom. I hoped I didn't have to share it, but if I did, that would be ok.

After setting up my room, my parents hugged me goodbye. Sa'Rah didn't cry this time, she just hugged me, gave me a kiss on the cheek and left. After they left I just laid in the bed, checked my class schedule. For some odd reason I only had one course, it was called 'ProChrist' studies. I had no idea what that was, but what was even more peculiar was that my first class was the next day.

Leon was away, the football team had an away game to start their season. No one seemed to want to talk with me, so I went back to apartment and checked my phone to see no text message from Fawzia. I sent her a goodnight text and read Elizabeth's journal until I fell asleep.

13

The first thing I did when I woke up the next morning was check my phone. There were still no text messages from Fawzia. I had messages from Sa'Rah, my mother and my father, Senior and a missed phone call from Leon, but nothing else. While I appreciated the love and attention I received from my family, there was void in my heart. I wanted to hear from Fawzia. I needed to hear from Fawzia. Maybe she was busy. I sent her another message, and hoped she would get it.

I noticed that the only class on my schedule was at eight o'clock. I looked at the clock and it was nine. Late on my first day. This wouldn't be good. I took a quick shower and grabbed a cereal bar and ran out of the door. I noticed more people were moving in.

I barely made my way around campus. I went up to the main classroom area but couldn't find the class. I turned my schedule around and there was a map of the campus, the class room was my campus dorm room. I was confused. I ran back to my dorm. When I walked in I noticed a man standing up. He was around my height, Caucasian, clean cut, he had on khaki pants with white dress shirt on and some black shoes.

"You're late," he said to me.

His voice was accented, but I couldn't put my finger on what language.

"I'm French if you must know my accent."

Did he just read my mind?

"No, I heard your thoughts."

He did read my mind. He wasn't even looking at me. Who was this guy?

He turned around. He was the man that delivered me the acceptance letter.

"My name is Marcel Le Blanc. It is my pleasure to meet you, Victor."

"How did you…" I started to say.

"I'm sorry. I wish I had more time to explain how I heard your magnificently loud thoughts. I do not have the time or the patience right now. We must get to it. Take off your clothes."

"Excuse me?"

Who did this guy think he was?

"I think that I am Marcel, and I know that I am your ProChrist instructor. And I think that you should just do what I say. Jew."

"Excuse me?"

"With the excuses. One day when you get the chance, ask your grandfather why I called you a Jew. When we met almost twenty years ago in that bar, that's what I called him. He still frequents that bar."

He was speaking of the Masterplan.

"How do you know my grandfather?"

"I know a lot about you, Victor the Third. You can say that I sort of paved the way for you to be here. Do you think that your grandfather thought to put Leon's blood in you all on his own? Not a snowball's chance in hell would he have thought of that. And do you think that the Doctor would drain a pint of blood from a newborn baby to put into a dying newborn baby? Again, snowball's chances. So it was me. Now where you are is your training room. You didn't think all these rooms were yours did you? And what is ProChrist training? Well, it's hard to put a thought to it, but basically what ProChrist training, at least this ProChrist training, is to try to make you the most skilled fighter on Earth. We only have three months, or ninety days to do it, so the less you ask, the better. Today we'll get the talking out of the way, and tomorrow at two in the morning we'll begin your training."

"Did you say two in the morning?"

"Did he stammer, Victor Thomas the Third?"

I turned around to see a tall woman, a few inches taller than myself, with red hair and dark green eyes, and a few freckles on her face. She had a slight Irish accent, she was wearing a robe as if she just gotten out of the shower.

"Did he not tell you that time is vital?"

"I don't know who you people are," I said in complete disbelief.

"I still think that we should have recruited Leon instead," the woman said to Marcel.

"Leon doesn't have Jesus' blessing, he does. Now not another word of it," Marcel said back to her.

"Jesus' blessing?"

"Enough! Take off your damn clothes! Leave your underwear on," the woman shouted at me.

Intimidated, I quickly obeyed. I removed the clothes that I had on all the way until I was in my underwear. While I stood there, the woman circled me several times looking at me. She finally stopped in front of me.

"He has eight percent body fat. He's in excellent shape already," she said to Marcel. "When we are done with you, you'll be in perfect shape."

"My name is Helen. Not Helen of Troy. I, like Marcel and like your grandfather am a ProChrist. Do not interrupt me with questions, Victor Thomas the Third I will break your face."

She must've known I was going to jump in and ask about my grandfather being this ProChrist warrior.

"Not a warrior. ProChrist is just a term, each person had their own agenda from God to complete. Yours just happened to be a warrior."

She walked around and removed her robe, revealing a sculpted body from a magazine. She looked a Viking warrior, her arms were chiseled, as well as her legs and her stomach had more abs then I could count. She was wearing a black sports bras and some biking shorts with black socks. If Wonder Woman had red hair, she would be her.

"Now that I have your attention. The next ninety days will be the toughest ninety days of any human's life. The first and last person to endure this died in a week. I'm not quite sure you will survive this, Victor Thomas the Third, but I have been given strict orders to just go with it. I hope you quit, I hope that you give up, go home and never return," she said smiling at Marcel. "I hope that I never see you again after tomorrow. I hope that you call your grandfather, and he tells you to come home because he doesn't believe you can be a ProChrist. Maybe in four years we'll recruit your sister, she'll definitely last. But you. I don't think so, nothing but a benefactor of Leon's greatness."

She was trying to get under my skin. I would be lying if I said she wasn't.

"What does this have to do with anything?"

"A war is coming Victor," Marcel answered me. "And like any war, you need leaders, you need strategy, and you need purpose."

"And what war will I be fighting in?"

"Not just fighting, Victor. Leading," Marcel said walking towards me. "You're going to be leading this war. You can say that the fate of the world rests on your shoulders. Big burden to carry but it was the same with your grandfather. He didn't complain, he did his duty to God just as you will do your duty to Him."

"Did you not make a Covenant with Jesus recently?" Helen said to me.

"How do you know that?"

"Who do you think rescued you from the water, Victor?" Marcel said to me looking in Helen's direction.

I was silent at first and stunned. I didn't know what was going on, who was going on, what I was doing here. I was scared, but only for a second. If Senior could be this ProChrist, then why couldn't I? If she believes that Sa'Rah can endure this, then why can't I endure it? I'm not just a benefactor of Leon.

"Thank you," I said to Helen. "And I can endure anything you throw at me."

Helen looked at Marcel again and smiled.

"Are you sure about that, Victor? You are about to learn how to eat like an ancient Greek Olympian, nothing but meat for protein, and carbs for energy. You will consume more water that would kill most of the world's top athletes and you will throw up every single day. You will drink red wine at night, enough to put you to sleep, and water from Heaven in the morning to replenish your nutrients. You will learn how to operate on just four hours of sleep a night. When you wake up, you will use half an hour to bathe and eat, then you will meditate for two and half hours. After that, the fun begins."

She laughed.

What she was saying didn't sound so bad. Well, the four hours of sleep sounded pretty gruesome but I believed that I could handle that.

"Ever heard of Sparta? And I'm not talking about the movies. I'm talking about the actual Military Sparta. Fitness began at birth. If you were born a Spartan you would have died and Leon would be King right now. But you are here, and you will endure what they endured. You will be disciplined like them, you will learn to ignore pain, and you will be physically fit and tougher than any opponent, even the Great Octavius. You will be fed just like a Spartan, you will be given just enough so that you won't get sluggish from a full belly, but to give you a taste and make you desire more. And last from Sparta you will learn their military Phalanx formation training to lead your men and women in battle. Again, do not interrupt me. I'm just getting started.

"You will learn Kung-Fu. You will learn the principles of fighting from Sheng Hun. One, your form or posture, your body structure or shape. Two, force, your force or theirs? Whose energy in what direction? Three, application, how do you deal with that force? Time of the posture. And four, philosophy, making the best use of the fighting principles you know. You will learn the seven animal styles of fighting.

SON OF SIN

Xiong or bear, which is clarity, definition and fluidity, you learn how to harness the power of mass, body physics, strength and stamina. Tong Long or praying mantis, establishing footwork to achieve a point of vulnerability against your opponent. Bai he or crane, balance, quick footwork, this will teach you take downs and most importantly blade work. She or cobra, learning to deliver hard, fast concessionary strikes with timing unlike anyone you'll face. Man or mongoose, learn how to be evasive, avoid danger, regain balance and control when fallen. Lung or Dragon, mythological creature or not, you will learn to use stealth and the spirits. And last but not least, Fu, or tiger, you will learn ferocity, courage and strength. Sound like fun?"

"Sounds like a lot. But I will learn it," I responded.

"Well I'm not done yet, Victor Thomas the Third," she said still smiling that sinister smile; she's going to enjoy torturing me. "Ever heard of Ninjutsu? Or perhaps a ninja? Well you're going to learn the eighteen disciplines of the ninja. With a particular focus on Kenjutsu which is sword techniques with an emphasis on Kendo, kendo is the way of the sword. Also focuses on shinobi-iri and bajutsu which are stealth, horsemanship. When I said that I'm trying to turn you into the ultimate fighting machine, I wasn't lying."

"What is this, the Matrix?"

"This is not the Matrix, this is the real world, there are no computers, no alternate dimension, and it is what you see. You will spend the next ninety days, eighteen hundred hours of awake time going through the most vigorous training regimens allowed by only the laws of humanity, and while you sleep you will learn as well, three hundred and sixty hours of learning in your ear. So no this is not the Matrix, you will hurt, and you will bleed and you will hate me when it is over. We are going to break you down to the very soul of your existence and build you back up, and you will fight me, and you will fight Marcel and ultimately have to kill one of us before we give you a passing grade. Any more smart remarks?"

"No," I said looking down.

"Good. You will also learn different variations of swordsmanship, fencing, Japanese style, Chinese, Philippines and Korean, you will also learn how the gladiators fought, Romans, Germans and Italians, new age, old age, the only thing your medieval arts training has done is taught you how to properly hold a sword. That's it. You will learn how to use a compound bow, you will learn how to create your own arrows, which arrows are best for the type of environment you are in, you will learn how to fletch, make a bow string, you will wear a bracer, finger tab and thumb ring. You will learn how to patch up a wound, stitch up a cut, handle fractures and breaks. You will learn physics, air movement, reading the movement of animals. There is a lot more but quite honestly, I'm tired of talking and I'm sure you are tired of listening, be up at two tomorrow if not, you will not like me. Ever. Good bye."

Helen walked out of the apartment, she seemed angry. I think she just realized that ninety days would be impossible for me to learn even one of the things that she spoke about let alone all of them.

"Warriors across time have gone generations and not mastered one of the things she just mentioned. Not even archery." Marcel said standing up. He had an iPod in his hand. "This right here is what you are going to listen to while you sleep. Every night, you will be given a meat to eat and some red wine for your heart. This has tons of lessons on it that you will listen to while you sleep. This iPod may seem normal but it will only activate when you are sleeping. Four hour segments for each lesson. It will violently wake you up after it is finished so be prepared.

"Every morning and every night you will be given a half an hour to bathe and eat and do any personal things you need to do, so you should make those minutes matter. Helen left because although it will be a difficult task, you have been given a blessing from Jesus and you will learn everything you need to learn within the time limits that we have. I wish there was more time, I really do, but there isn't.

"There are going to be moments in which you want to give up, and when Helen senses that she's going to work you harder. Stay focused

Victor, stay focused. At the end of the training with Helen you will train with me, you will learn the Angelic language, the language you heard Leon speaking a few months ago in pure anger, you will learn how to read it, hear it, understand it, write it and speak it. Do not ask how he spoke it involuntarily, you'll find out soon enough. Also you will learn the Angelic martial art, no stance; you could close your eyes and defeat any opponent, without looking at them. Just sensing them is enough. You'll learn it. I know this is a lot to digest in one day, but time is of the essence.

"I'm not sure what you know about Octavius, but his war could either be the end of freedom as you know it, or the beginning of something much more evil. I'm hoping it's the former, and not the latter. Good day Victor. Oh, and I have your phone, you'll get it at night. Read up." He tossed me Elizabeth's journal.

I looked around the apartment and it was empty, no television, no clothes, nothing but a bed, iPod and Elizabeth's journal. This was going to be a trying semester of school if I have to learn everything she just said I had to learn in such a short period of time. I didn't know what was happening; Octavius' war must be more serious than I thought. I hope everyone at home is ok. After just sitting around doing nothing for a few hours I finally opened up and started reading Elizabeth's journal. It was a story, a story about Octavius written by Elizabeth. Her journal is about her cousin? After reading about who he was and how he was I started dozing off. I didn't know what time it was, I put the iPod headphones in my ear and dozed off thinking about Fawzia and what she was doing, I miss her.

14

"How did you get here Fawzia?"

Fawzia was in my dorm room. Except it wasn't my dorm room. I didn't know where we were. But Fawzia was there and that is all I cared about.

"I've loved you since I first laid eyes on you," Fawzia said to me.

She was wearing a blue hijab head covering but she was wearing silk robe. She came closer to me, she smelled of warm apple cinnamon. She kissed me and her lips tasted of ice mint. She aggressively kissed me. More aggressive than she ever had, she rubbed my face, and placed my hands on her buttocks, and I grew excited, and I squeezed her bottom firmly, she stopped and stepped back and looked deep into my eyes.

"Tell me your dreams… and I shall see them come to pass…" I said to her, but it wasn't my voice…

A blistering shock hit my ears and I woke up in a panic. I took the headphones out and threw them. I sat there breathing heavily.

"What was that?" I said aloud.

Marcel did warn me that the iPod would wake me up violently. I barely slept. What a weird dream. Whose voice was that talking to Fawzia? Not enough time to think. I had thirty minutes to myself. I noticed my phone was sitting on the table. I picked it up, still no messages from Fawzia. I had a message from Sa'Rah.

'It's going to be hard, big brother, but don't give up.'

It's official, she has special powers. There was some food on the table, some cut up fruit and a piece of toasted wheat bread. I ate it, showered and when I got out of the shower I put on some clothes that were sitting on a mannequin that I assumed was mine. There were some black jogging pants, some all black running shoes, and a scrub like black shirt.

"Took you long enough," Helen said to me.

She startled me, I didn't hear her come in.

"That took you forty five minutes, I said thirty minutes. Now you can't meditate for as long as you need to. Come outside."

I walked outside. It was raining, and raining hard. It was very dark out. I had to remember it was two or three in the morning. It was cold for the end of summer. It felt like freezing rain.

"You read about Octavius last night, right?" Helen asked me.

She was wearing the same thing she had on yesterday, as if it wasn't freezing.

"Yes, I read a little about Octavius," I answered. "What does that have to do with anything?"

"Know your enemy Victor. Know your enemy." She walked over near two trees and pulled off a branch and started peeling it. "Come sit down right here Victor. I'm going to teach you to meditate."

I walked over to the trees. I was very tired but my ears were still ringing. The shower woke me up a bit. I was hungry but my skin felt like it wanted to crawl inside of me to warm up. I sat down in between the trees. All I could feel was the wind blowing, the rain hitting my skin, I was drenched.

"I want you to concentrate hard. Control your breathing and focus, ignore the elements, they are not there. Close your eyes and listen to me. Your breath is the essential force. It is the center of activity in our bodies. Breath and mind are one being, when your mind is disturbed, your breath is disturbed. When you're anxious, you breathe with haste and hollowly. But when your mind is at ease, your breath is deep and smooth".

I sat with my legs crossed on the grass. I was wet. I couldn't clear my mind. All I could think about was this bad weather. The rain, the thunder and the lightening. How could I focus? How was this going to help me learn everything she told me I was going to learn? This was stupid. I was cold, hungry, tired. My ears hurt, and my girlfriend hadn't written me back in a few days. What was she doing? That dream was incredible. I'd never felt so alive, in such lust, it was the first time that I thought about her in a way that exceeded that of just kissing and embracing. In my dream I wanted to make love to her, in every sense of the word. Her smell, her touch, the taste of her lips. I felt my back being struck.

"Clear! Your! Mind!" Helen said as she hit me three times with the branch that she had taken from the tree.

"What did you do that for!?" I yelled as I quickly stood up.

She kicked the back end of my knee and I went down.

"Clear your mind. If your mind was clear, you wouldn't have felt those."

"Anyone would've felt that."

"You have to ease your mind and breathing, Victor Thomas the third. The more completely your mind is at ease, the more in depth your body is at rest. Your respiration, your heart rate, circulation and metabolism slow down in a deep relaxing state of mind. It is a very important part of being alive and staying alive."

She motioned for me to sit down.

For the next two hours I tried really hard to clear my mind, focus on the present, focus on myself and what was happening. I went maybe five minutes without getting hit. She continued to hit me, each and every time it was harder. She kept telling me to go home, give up, but I didn't let it get to me. Eventually my back went numb. I felt the blood pour down my back. My shirt was useless. I was breathing heavy, but eventually, I was able to remove all thoughts from my head. All I thought about was air, and how the wind against my back soothed the pain, and how the cold rain washed away some of the blood. My heart was beating so fast, because I couldn't focus on thinking about nothing, I was focused on bracing for the next time she hit me. But she didn't.

"Get up."

I stood up.

"Take your shirt off." I did as I was told.

I felt her rubbing some cream on my back. It smelled familiar. It smelled of Elizabeth, the comfrey oil she had applied on my face. It was a relaxing smell. After Helen was finished applying the Comfrey oil on my back, she had me follow her to the river.

The heavy rain had flooded the river a bit, some of the water was on the road in which cars traveled to get into the school.

"Take these in each hand," she handed me two poles about four feet in length. They had to weigh around one hundred pounds apiece. "Run across the river with these. Fifty times. You have one hour. Any time left after you finish you can rest."

"Did you say fifty times?"

"One hundred times. And you can't swim, better hold your breath if your head can't stay above water."

I ran to the river. The Tittabawassee River. It was about one hundred and fifty feet from shore to shore at width. I didn't know how deep it went, obviously deeper with the rain. The river had trees running parallel to it. The water was dark, and from shore to shore there was no smooth entrance into the river, you just had to step in.

I breathed hard and began running across the river, my feet were stepping on rocks at the bottom, and the deepest point came to my shoulders. I slipped a few times due to fatigue, or wind, or the waters. I had to keep the poles in my hand. The wind was picking the water up, and the rain was hitting me in the face. I couldn't breathe, each and every time I crossed the river the poles got heavier and my arms got weaker.

It took me two hours to complete it one hundred times. My body felt like it was about to fall apart. It was day time by the time I finished. It was still raining so hard you would think it was the fall or hurricane season in Michigan. I stumbled to a bench where I sat.

"Get up," Helen said to me.

She handed me a wooden sword. I could barely lift it, my arms felt like noodles.

"Show me your stance. You think you're so good at sword fighting, I want to see how good you are."

"I can't lift my arms," I cried out to her.

"You think your enemy cares if you're tired? They do not care. Show me what you got."

I got into a typical defensive sword stance. I was tired. If she was going to attack, I would just block and counter until I felt enough energy had returned to me.

She attacked first. I blocked it, then she attacked again, and again, and again. Each time my arms grew weaker and weaker and I could no longer block her attacks.

"You're dead! Again!"

We repositioned ourselves and she defeated me again.

"Again!"

We did that for an hour to the point where I couldn't breathe. My body felt terrible, my arms were sore, my legs were tired. Helen kicked my calf hard and I felt my entire body be lifted from the ground and my back broke my fall. Then she thrust down with her sword. I was able to roll out of the way.

"Your enemy will have no sympathy, Victor Thomas the Third. You must understand that, you must apply it, and you must find that extra ounce of strength you have to keep yourself intact.

"Your enemy will be vicious, ferocious and without sympathy. Your followers will only go as far as you go. You have a heavy burden to lift, Victor Thomas the Third, you sure you can handle it? At home there's a big comfortable bed waiting for you, warm blankets, and some hot cocoa. What are you doing here?"

She was trying my patience. I was getting tired of her calling me Victor Thomas the Third. I was getting tired of her telling me I could go home. My body ached, my arms felt like wet spaghetti noodles. The sword felt like it weighed half a ton. I was hungry, I was thirsty, I was aggravated, and my girlfriend was ignoring me.

"Stop calling me Victor Thomas the Third," I said to her calmly.

She smiled and looked at me.

"Make me," she said.

I gathered all the strength I had in me. I was going to show her that all my training wasn't for nothing. I gripped my sword and ran at her with pure anger and absent mind of defense. She parried my high attack and kneed me in the stomach. It was the worst pain I'd ever felt in my life. I would have preferred to get jumped by Malcolm and ten of his friends than to feel that.

I dropped to my knees instantly and coughed hard. I was gasping for air that wouldn't come. She kneeled down beside me and touched my right rib cage.

"Ahhhh!!!!" I screamed in agony. It felt like shards of glass were ripping through my insides.

"Yep, cracked a rib," she said feeling around my abdominal area. "Let this be a lesson to you, Victor Thomas the Third. Never, ever fight in anger, gets you nowhere but a cracked ribbed." She squeezed my rib that was cracked and I gritted my teeth and hid the pain. I didn't want her to know she hurt me too badly. "Here, drink this and eat this, you have ten minutes and we're to our next lesson." She dropped a few pieces of jerky meat on the ground next to where I was kneeling and placed a gallon of water next to it. Without hesitation I ate the jerky and drank the water within seconds of one another. After drinking the water I didn't feel the pain in my stomach anymore. I stood up; the rain had subsided a little. You could see in front of you more clearly now. We were fighting by the river in a huge field.

"Ready for you next lesson?" she asked. It wasn't even nine in the morning and I felt like I'd trained for five days for a marathon.

"I'm ready," I said to her with false confidence. I wasn't sure if I was really ready. If I died doing this, I was going to be pretty upset.

"Get in pushup position."

I got down in pushup position.

"Down."

I went down when she commanded me to.

"Down, down, down, down, down."

She said down at least four hundred times. My arms were getting more tired by the second. Then she started walking on me as if I were a stair case. When I went down, she stepped on me to come back up, and then stepped off when I went back down.

For the rest of the day she tested me, pushed me, different exercises, styles of fighting, showing me different moves, explained aptitudes, reasoning for this style, or that style. She fought me, she beat me up, and she kicked me and punched me. I never rested for more than ten minutes. She told me that the enemy would not be merciful. She succeeded in making me want to quit. She made me want to go home, to that warm comfortable bed. But every time I thought of quitting, I tried even harder.

By the time the first day was over I could barely walk. She refused to help me walk to my apartment. It was around ten o'clock, or maybe later, there weren't any times given during training. I had thrown up three times. I felt like my arms were going to fall out of their sockets. It was the hardest day of my life.

When I got in, I noticed my phone was ringing. It was Sa'Rah.

"Hello," I barely said.

"Don't give up big brother!" Sa'Rah said to me. "I know it's hard. But nothing worth having is achieved without effort! I love you!"

And she hung up the phone before I could say anything. I looked at my phone. No messages. I sent a text to Fawzia. She was all that was on my mind. I showered for ten minutes. When I got out of the shower, some food was sitting at the table with some red wine. I ate the food, didn't care where it came from. And I drank the wine. I had never drunk anything alcoholic before, but it tasted bitter. It felt good going down.

My mind eased and numbed a bit as I drank more of the wine. Then there was no more wine to drink. I looked in the cabinet and to my surprise there was nothing but red win in there. I didn't even read to see what type of wine. I popped the cork, and drank two bottles all by myself.

Thoughts in my mind drifted to making love to Fawzia. Another dream would be nice. I wished I was at home with her. I wished she was in bed with me. I wished I could hold her, smell her, taste her lips and look into her eyes. I reluctantly put the iPod headphones back in my ears and drifted off to sleep.

15

"What are your dreams?" I said to Fawzia in a voice that isn't my own.

"My dreams?" Fawzia repeated as she stared deep into my eyes. "My dreams are that one day, you are staring into my soul while making love to me."

"That's a bold statement from a virgin."

"Well, I'll have to lose it sometime. I don't know if I'll ever find a man worthy enough to be my husband. So why not to you?"

"What is it about me?"

"You're eyes are gorgeous…"

The iPod shocked my ears again. I threw the headphones across the room again as I had last time. My stomach felt sick. I felt like I had to throw up. My body was as sore as it has ever been. My back was hurting, my arms and legs were bruised. My head was pounding, my mouth was dry. It felt as if I was about throw up everything in my body. I mustered enough strength to get up, I had to try to focus but the room was spinning. I only had thirty minutes to get ready and I could barely walk straight.

Once I finally stood up, I started to dry heave. I was dehydrated, it must've been all that wine. The table, it had a small glass of water on it and some meat and fruits again. I took the water and drank it as fast as I could. I don't know why, but that was most refreshing glass of water I'd ever tasted in my life. All of a sudden I didn't feel any more pain.

My sore muscles loosened up and my stomach settled, my headache went away and the room went from a spinning blur to a standstill.

"Surprising how one glass of water can change your life, right?" said Marcel's voice behind me in his obvious French accent.

"What did I just put inside me?" I asked him. "Was it laced with pain killers?"

"That is the water from Heaven Helen mentioned. Just eight ounces replenishes your body to full strength. "

"It's amazing!" I said out loud in pure excitement. I felt a rush in my body. I felt like I could do anything. This training won't be so bad after all if I can feel like this every day.

"One day at a time, young Victor. That is all I ask of you is to last every day. And every morning, this is what awaits you. Now quickly shower and put on today's gear. You still have a long way to go."

I showered as he said, I was so happy, so energized, I felt like a new man. After the shower, I looked at my phone, no text messages from Fawzia. I decided to send an 'I love you' text to everybody in my phone. That is the euphoria I was feeling.

"Don't get too excited, Victor. You didn't lose yesterday, your body just absorbed everything that was taught to you yesterday and now you are feeling the after effects of one day's training. Imagine how you'll feel after ninety. I say survive every day because yesterday was probably the easiest day of them all. They are only going to get harder…" Marcel said as he left the apartment.

For the next few weeks, Marcel didn't tell a lie. Every single day I felt like I was on the brink of death. Broken bones, shattered egos and my brain being pumped full of information that I don't remember. Martial arts, archery training, eating right, pushups, pull ups, and river running were things that I missed. These other things Helen had me doing were probably against the law in most modern countries. She begged and pleaded for me to give up every day. I bled from my ears, my nose, my pores, I often crawled into bed forgetting to eat, drinking myself to slumber only to awaken to a fresh glass of Heaven juice.

That thirty minutes in the morning was what I looked forward to the most. I drink that and I have thirty minutes of peace and quiet, no one yelling at me or beating me.

Communication with my family was sparse. Other than the I love you text messages I sent every morning, I didn't talk to anyone much. Sa'Rah understood and she was ok with it. I did get disturbing news, she was right; my parents were seeing divorce lawyers. I hadn't had a chance to talk to them. Normally at nights I would play voicemails throughout the day. Leon was extremely concerned he never saw me. But I sent him a text assuring him I was ok and everything was ok and just told him I was on a special assignment. He's been in my apartment before looking for me but obviously he never found me, I was away in training for twenty hours a day.

Fawzia didn't write at all. She may have sent a text every now again, very short one word text messages. And just those brightened my days up. I was very lonely. I hadn't had fun in weeks. I hadn't talked to anyone. She was in my heart so any message from her was worth it.

I asked her what took her so long to text and she acted as if she didn't know what I was talking about. I often ignored her dodging my question because it was Fawzia. But as time grew, and her texts were less meaningful, I found comfort and companionship reading Elizabeth's writing. It wasn't all about Octavius, she wrote about her own life, poetry, past boyfriends, hopes and dreams. She was right. Reading this for a few minutes at night helped my mind.

Senior had texted and called with concerns of my absence and how late I text everyone or how early. I wished I could tell him what was going on, that he would understand, but that was a lot to put on Senior's heart. If I was going to be a leader I must walk this path alone, through blood, sweat and tears.

As Sa'Rah texted me, nothing worth having is achieved without effort. Her spirits were dampened and there was nothing I could do about it. She hadn't asked me to come home. She wanted me focused on the goal at hand, which I was sure she was well aware of even without me telling her what was going on.

Elizabeth happened to be one of the recipients of the 'I love you' text messages and her reply was always 'I love you too, my brother in Christ.' She wasn't allowing herself to be sucked into my happiness every morning.

Often after I had wine, I would pass out praying to God that I lived through the night. I didn't think I would make it after a few nights of this training. The only thing that disturbed me were the voices in my dreams, why Fawzia was looking into my eyes and what did that mean.

16

"*If you understand this, Victor,*" Marcel's voice said in a dialect similar to Leon's raging dialect. "*You now speak and understand fluent Angelic. And the iPod is actually working. You must understand me Victor. This war is bigger than you; it's bigger than anything you can imagine. This war is the beginning. What type of beginning is up to you.*"

The next few weeks passed by easier than the first. My body and mental capacity was coping with the adjustment in my lifestyle. I went from being free, having fun and doing what I wanted to do, to living a much more disciplined detailed oriented life. It was taking less wine to get to sleep in the evenings. I wasn't throwing up as much. I was rationing my food supply better. I was more focused during training. I was becoming more competitive in our sparring. Swords weighed next to nothing, and I was a great aim with a bow.

Meditation was when I got to really rest and reenergize. I sat there, and I blocked out everything around me. It was like I was sitting in space looking at myself, being at peace with who I was, and what I was trying to accomplish. I often reflected on my life, I'm only eighteen years old. Why was I here? Why was I destined to be a leader of some army fighting in a war I didn't even know about against someone who seemed to believe he was God's chosen one to purge the world of non-Christ believers.

I missed my family. I missed running in the mornings with Leon at Euclid creek. I missed us playing basketball and winning every game all the time until the point where people would fight just to play on our team. I missed Sa'Rah, and having our day together. I missed seeing her smile as she rode Vita across the city. I missed my father's presence, my mom's warmth, and Senior's spiritual security. I missed church and praising Jesus with my church family. I missed going to eat real food, fattening food with soda, and grease.

I missed getting ice cream with Fawzia. We would go to small ice cream shop on the south side of Cleveland. A mom and pop ice cream store, she would get an Oreo Cookie ice cream cake, and I would get a banana split and we would eat, laugh and enjoy one another's company. We went twice a week. We used to stay up on the phone all night if weren't together. We used to dance when no music was playing. We used to kiss under the moon light. We watched sunrises and sunsets.

Now, for some reason that I did not know, she wouldn't even talk to me. But didn't tell me that she didn't want to talk to me. She wouldn't let me go, but also wouldn't give me any closure. I was trapped between yearning to hear from her, yearning to hear her say that she loved me, to wanting her to tell me she didn't want to talk, so I could begin to mend my heart. Being stuck in the middle is no fun.

To find more comfort, I read Elizabeth's journal more. I was past Octavius, and on to Elizabeth's life. I felt like I was getting to know her, to know her personality, prides and insecurities. I didn't know why someone as beautiful as she would have insecurities.

She enjoyed jogging, she had braces as a kid, and she once kissed the prince as a young girl. Her mother taught her to marry for position as a young girl and it has stuck with her since. She fell in love only once in life and that passage went:

He wasn't a man of any particular position. He wasn't even all that handsome. There was a certain spirit about him that I couldn't ignore. Or maybe it was his work ethic. He tried extremely hard to impress me. Being someone of no importance, wanting to talk to someone like me is insulting. But I gave him the chance. We didn't work out, we were too different, our directions in life were light years apart. He was ok with mediocrity, and I wanted to be Queen. He broke my heart and I broke his. Just because you have a feeling for someone doesn't mean that you are meant to be with that person. Maybe it's just supposed to be a moment, even a brief one means something. We were an example of two wrong people meeting at the right time and it ended ugly. We argued, we fussed and we fought, and one day he grabbed me, and Daddy wasn't having that. Gave up everything, and we had to move to America. All because of a relationship that should've never happened.

Reading her writing was a soothing melody to my troubled heart. I didn't know Elizabeth well before I read her book. I always thought of her as just this extremely beautiful untouchable woman from Europe. But reading this, I felt like she was more human than I thought. You know how we look at celebrities, as these untouched forces of nature. But the bottom line is that they are humans just like us, they breathe, they bleed, they eat and they sleep. They are no better than the next person.

According to Sa'Rah, our parents weren't going to finalize the divorce until they had spoken to me. But because I was incapacitated, there was no way to talk to me in depth about their decision. I wondered how Senior was handling this. I wondered if Sa'Rah was holding up well in school. She was a special soul. She sent me text messages of encouragement all the time. She was who I was protecting. Thinking about her got me through the training.

When I got home from training, my phone was ringing. It was Fawzia. My heart jumped. We had a conversation for twenty minutes. I was excited to hear from her. Although the news wasn't good news.

Octavius was in America. His war hit New York City and Los Angeles. It hit those cities without warning. Thousands of Octavius' men wearing the cross symbol with O in it for Octavius, rounding up non-Christians, meeting with Church leaders. Churches stopped services as the Muslim population, and actually the entire population that wasn't Christian had some things to say about Octavius. I only heard this from her. I haven't been on the internet, watched TV or checked news on my phone. I am completely disconnected and off of the grid.

After the phone call, after the shower, I drank one bottle of wine and went to sleep. I was ready for training to be over so that I can see my family.

17

"Good morning, Victor." Sa'Rah's voice through the phone said with a great joy to finally talk to me after months with of just text messaging.

"Hello, Sa'Rah!" I said with a cheerful voice.

I drank the water so I could be re-energized. I decided I was going to use my entire thirty minutes talking to Sa'Rah, I missed her dearly.

"I've been dreaming of your training. Sometimes I cried myself to sleep because I know that you are in great pain every day. How do you adapt and continue every day?"

"What do you know of my training?"

"I feel like my dreams are real."

"Well this time I guess they are. And it's been a rough two or three months. I'm not sure what day it is but I know it's coming to a close soon."

"Mom and Daddy are sleeping in separate rooms. Mom has their room, and Daddy is in your room."

"How's that going for you?"

"I don't know, Victor. It's like no one is understanding the importance of family. And now that you and Leon are gone, it's just me here from our generation and no one listens to me. Senior is just letting them do this."

"Well I'm not sure how much control Senior has over the outcome of Mom and Dad's marriage Sa'Rah." I said. "Look, when I get home,

I'll get to the bottom and things, and I'll see what I can do to help. I don't want you focused on that. What you must understand is that they love you more than anything else in the world. They just might not love each other anymore."

Sa'Rah was silent for a few moments.

"Sa'Rah?" I said.

I heard some crying in the background. It broke my heart to know that she was sad and there was nothing I could do about it. This family is her life, she loves all of us. She sacrificed being a famous singer just to keep us as normal as possible. I loved that girl, with every ounce of blood I had in me. When I got home, I'd see that things change for the better for her.

"I'm here, brother," she said, sounding a lot like Leon when he calls me brother. "I'm sorry to call you this early. I know that you have a lot on your plate up there."

"No," I said looking at my plate of food. It was a piece of meat, and some fruit, nothing at all like I used to eat. "I don't have much on my plate at all."

I laughed to myself.

"I just wanted to hear your voice. I wanted to tell you that I loved you. I don't want to be a distraction to your training, and I don't want to be a distraction to your ultimate purpose in this life. I love you, Victor," she said sobbing.

"I love you too, Sa'Rah, and you're not a distraction, you never have been, and you never will be."

"Tell me you love me again please."

"I love you."

"I love you too. Goodbye." She said as she hung up the phone.

I didn't feel right. Nothing felt right about that conversation. I quickly bathed, ate and put on the day's attire.

Before walking out of the door I sent a quick text message to Leon and Fawzia.

'Bro, meet me at my dorm at exactly nine thirty, do not be a minute late!'

'I love you, Fawzia'

The past few weeks of training had been more of a perfecting training. I wouldn't call myself a master of anything, but I was darn good at everything that was taught to me. Sparring became tiresome for Helen. I was stronger, faster, quicker, and light on my feet. We fought in the forest with blind folds on, listening to the elements around us. Feeling for trees, noticing the wind, picking up the faint difference in smell, how you could smell sweat or blood from many feet away to determine where your enemy was.

Even though I learned mixed martial arts, the focus was always on sword fighting. I asked her why the sword and she said because I'm fighting in a war with swords, bows and arrows, not hand to hand combat. The hand to hand combat was to be just coordination for the sword, different styles and techniques I could learn from the many different marital arts that I learned. And in case of a hand to hand combat, I could stand my own ground. She said that I was learning ancient techniques and having ancient training is because I was going to be fighting, or rather leading an ancient war.

Fawzia and I had talked more and more the past few weeks. Not much on the phone, but she did leave a voicemail saying that she loved me. I listened to that voice mail every day since she left it, once in the morning, and once in the evening. It warmed my heart to hear her voice. I didn't feel so lonely anymore. She still only texted me when she wanted to text me. She'd go a few days without replying, which sucked, but when she did reply it was a good feeling.

I hadn't talked to anyone else other than Sa'Rah and Fawzia. Since Fawzia was talking to me and texting me, I hadn't been texting Elizabeth or reading her journal. I planned to make it a point to read an entry. I couldn't lose focus.

It was close to the end of training for the day. I couldn't remember feeling so beat down. Not since the first day of training when my body was ill prepared for the suffering it would go through. It was as if Helen put forth an extra effort.

"Why so hard?" I said breathing heavy.

"Because I think you've gotten arrogant, you think that you're ready," she said back to me.

"I apologize. I did survive for months."

"That you did," Helen responded.

"You think that I could take a day off?" I asked her. I knew how important it was for me to continue with my training. But I had a bad feeling about Sa'Rah and I wanted to go see her. Give her a hug, and assure her that I loved her.

"Absolutely not!" Helen said as she blindly struck me in the face with her boot.

I hit the ground. I didn't have any energy to dodge it. My focus was on Sa'Rah. I lay on the ground, my face was hurting almost as bad as when Leon punched it and I felt it hours later for the first time. Grass was in my eyes and dirt was in my mouth. Maybe a few months ago this would've bothered me. But this time it was merely a minor annoyance rather than something disgusting.

"Training is over."

She walked away angry.

When I was finally able to pick myself up, I walked home. Leon was waiting at the front of my door. I'm not sure what time it is, but great timing.

"I got your text brother," Leon said to me.

He looked his normal self, didn't get any larger playing college ball. He was wearing his Jesus Christ University football outfit, a gray hoodie and gray jogging pants. Jesus Christ University has eleven wins and zero losses. Leon was the quarterback and his numbers were outrageous. Surprisingly, Octavius' war wasn't hitting the United States like I thought it would. Nothing was really shut down, still no mass news coverage of it. Nothing.

Authorities were saying it was just a disturbance on the east and west coast that they were handling. Isolated incidents are what they were being called. I was not even sure if Leon knew anything about it.

VENSIN GRAY

"You look like you just got ran over by a truck! Are you alright?" Leon made a remark as to my wellbeing. If only he knew this is how I looked after training every day he wouldn't be so surprised.

"It's good to see you, Leon," I said to him as I gave him a hug. I gathered what little strength I had left in me to give him a firm hug.

"You look the same." I said smiling.

"I wish I could say the same about you. Look at you!" Leon said analyzing me.

I didn't think that I'd changed physically much, but mentally I was a completely different person. Maybe my look is different.

"Is everything alright? Your text message seemed pretty important."

I forgot all about the text message. This is a guy I used to see every day, I haven't seen him in months. I was wrapped up in the moment.

"I need you to do me a huge favor."

"Anything, name it."

"I need you to take Vita, and go to Cleveland as soon as possible and check on Sa'Rah for me."

"What's wrong with Sa'Rah?"

"A lot is going on, don't really have the time to explain, just do that for me. Go straight there, and bring her back here. Can you do that for me?"

Leon looked at me for a moment. He knew I wouldn't ask him to do something so sudden unless it was serious. Suddenly Vita came walking towards Leon. Must've known I would need her.

"She'll be here by tomorrow, you have my word. I love you, brother." Leon said as he mounted Vita and road off.

"I love you too." I said quietly to myself.

The strength I had gathered up for Leon left as he left. I limped into the apartment. I showered and ate what food was on the table waiting for me. I never asked where it came from; I just appreciated it being there. I put on my night clothes, drank a bottle of wine and found myself on my hands and knees.

"Dear God," I began praying, "I'm asking you for strength for

Sa'Rah. She's young, and smarter than she should be. Instead of worrying about what boy likes her, or what shoes she's going to wear with whatever outfit, she's worried about me and my purpose in life. She's caught up in the drama with our parents' divorce. I'm asking you to give her strength, give her comfort, and show her that you are the way Lord. That you are the way… Amen." I said, not entirely finished praying but I felt my eyes closing and the iPod headphones were in my ear.

Sleep was calling me, and I couldn't help but answer.

18

The next day of training felt worse than the day before. I wasn't focused at all. I was desperately waiting to see Sa'Rah. Helen knew my mind wasn't focused and took it upon her to hurt me more than she's had to in a long time. She didn't speak to me afterwards; she only looked at me with great disgust and walked off in to the moonlight.

It was cold out, November came swiftly. It was like only yesterday I was first coming up here an anxious young man wanting to see his future. But I had become a well-trained warrior destined to lead an army against unknown forces.

When I walked to my dorm, I didn't see anyone standing outside of it. There wasn't any hint of Vita, Leon or Sa'Rah. I walked into my dorm, nothing out of the ordinary, just my food. I ate my food, and checked my phone, no messages from Sa'Rah or Leon. Fawzia hasn't responded to any of my messages sent to her either. I sighed deeply and took a shower. I opened up Elizabeth's journal and began reading the next entry.

After the failed relationship with Matthew, I decided that I would like to know what makes a good relationship. What are the key essential elements that are needed? I think the first and most important thing is direction. Where is each person headed? Can a young woman primed for success get with someone on the downslope of life and expect it to work? After that, of course you have communication, honesty, respect, loyalty and responsibility. Those go without saying. But should they be the same? Should they laugh at the same jokes? Like the same movies, read the same books? Wouldn't they get bored out of their minds? I think that a good relationship is the proper balance of togetherness and individualism. Such as, just because you're in a relationship doesn't mean you should be with someone all the time and know what they are doing at all times during a day. You should still have your own individual life, just now intertwined with another. Sure, you should talk, and let others know important stuff. But if you stopped at a grocery store to pick up some lettuce should you have to tell them and make sure where you're at? Not at all. If you wouldn't do that if you were single, why do it when you're in a relationship? I think people get caught up into changing one's self to make their partner like them more or feel better and that's why no one last. Because one day, you're going to look in the mirror and not like who's staring back, not like what you see. You should still be able to be yourself. Always.

I smiled after reading that passage. Elizabeth was a bright woman, and her journal entries kept me sane the past few months. I was going to have to thank her when I got home. I probably should've called her to go see Sa'Rah. But I didn't want to put that responsibility on her. I looked at the calendar and tomorrow would be the ninetieth day. My last day of training, then I could go home, see Sa'Rah if she wasn't up here yet. See my family. I missed them.

I drank a bottle of wine and went to sleep.

"It's good to see you. I thought that I wouldn't see you again," said Fawzia.

"I'm here."

Words came out of my mouth, but again, was not my voice. Fawzia walked up to me, and removed all of her clothes. From head to toe and kissed me softly at first. Then her kisses grew more aggressive as we fell back.

I looked around and we were on the beach that I took her to the last time I saw her. We were on a blanket. It was cool outside, the wind was calm, the water gently hit the shore. The stars were lit up in the sky. She smiled at me. I caressed every inch of her body, and she closed her eyes and bit her bottom lip in ecstasy.

"I want you," she said to me, her voice trembling with desire and passion. She licked her lips and kissed me.

"Say my name..." I said to her.

"..."

My dream was interrupted again with the shock of the iPod. It doesn't bother me anymore; I just know to get up immediately. What a dream. I need to see Fawzia first thing when I go home tomorrow. I checked my phone. Twenty nine missed calls. Another call came in, it was my father.

"Hello?" I said.

"(silence)" No one said anything. Did he accidentally dial me?

"Dad?" I said again.

"Victor...Are you sitting down son?"

Something was wrong, he sounded as if he was fighting something, fighting an emotion but I couldn't quite put my finger on what.

"I'm still in bed, Dad. What's going on? It's great to hear from you."

"I wish that I was calling for something better than what I'm calling about."

"What are you calling about?"

"Your sister."

"What has Sa'Rah done now?"

Leon must've came, and she must've ran away or something. Her and I needed to have a long talk.

"You sister passed away sometime yesterday. She was found in her bed. Not breathing..." My dad stammered on those words.

My heart dropped. My face went numb, and the world stopped spinning. Time stood still and I could feel every pump in my heart.

"Son." I heard my father say but I didn't respond.

What happened?

"Son!" I heard my father scream into the phone.

I still didn't reply. My hands were trembling. I felt sick instantly. I ran to the bathroom and threw up. I didn't know what I had in me to throw up but whatever was in there is gone now.

"Victor, talk to me." My father said.

"I'm here, Dad." I said wiping my mouth. "How did she die?"

"I'm…" My father said, and then paused. "I'm not sure yet son."

I wasn't a crier. I couldn't think of the last time that I did cry. Not against anyone crying, I just didn't do it. My eyes didn't get watery, I didn't throw a tantrum. I was just stuck.

"I'll see you soon, Dad," I said as I hung up the phone.

I checked my missed messages, some were from Senior, Grandmother Patrice, my mother, my father, Christina and even Elizabeth, but none were from Leon. I didn't know what I had to do to get home, but I would do whatever was necessary.

I ate my food that was prepared for me and I drank my water. The water did nothing for my troubled mind. I was still very confused about life. My sister, dead. The sweetest little girl on the planet, the very reason I went through this training, was to protect her, protect her future, and to be that protector of our family. She's gone. I took a shower. I didn't pray. I was angry at God. How could God do this to me? How could He take her?

But everything happens for a reason right? I thought to myself. I put on my attire for the day, which ironically was all black. I went outside. It was raining, very hard. The last time it rained so hard was my first day of training. I sat down in my usual meditation spot and I crossed my legs, and closed my eyes.

The only thing I could see was Sa'Rah and I playing. Helen was near me. I felt her presence, she was saying something, but I didn't pay any attention. She hit me with her stick, but I ignored the pain. I only wanted to think about Sa'Rah. My sweetie, my baby sister, my other, my life. I saw her smiling.

I saw us running around the house, playing little games. I saw the many pictures of her and me after my sports competition, when everyone went to Leon, she came to me. I felt her hugging me. I felt her love and her warmth. I felt her spirit, she may have been unique, and awkward, but she was my sister. I heard her singing, laughing, and crying. But now she was without life.

"I love you, big brother!" I heard her say that in my head.

My mind went blank after I heard that and I felt the next hit Helen put on my back. That angered me. I focused, whenever Helen was going to hit me, she took a quick small breath. An untrained ear wouldn't notice it for it was small and subtle, but I heard it. She swung her tree branch and with one motion from my arm, I broke it in half.

Her breathing quickened. She was angry. I stood up and without looking at her I dodged a few attacks she threw my way. Helen was more experienced than I. No way could I beat her in a fight without being as focused as I could be. I had to get home, and fast. I had to be there for my family. My dodging of her punches and kicks aggravated her, especially since I haven't thrown a single shot back. She was breathing hard, and attacking without breathing. She was going to tire herself out.

She brought out her sword, too soon in my opinion. She swung it with pure anger and emotions. I had her. My timing had to be perfect, she swung up high, I dodged to the left and I brought out my sword, our swords hit, she did a spin attack with her sword, I parried it and her arms flailed apart, I stepped to the right and with my left knee, I struck her stomach with my knee as hard as I could, just as she did me when I attacked her so blind and recklessly. I didn't feel bad for hitting a woman. Helen beat that out of me. I didn't care who was in front of me, if you were attacking, you can be put down.

Helen gasped for air. I stood over her. I sheathed my sword. This was the first time I ever put a hit on Helen and it was a good one. I smiled at my accomplishment. Then I walked away. Helen didn't try to stop me. I saw Vita in the distance. She came to me. I mounted her and turned to look at Helen who was gone.

"Thank you," I said.

I had to thank her. If it wasn't for her, the news of Sa'Rah would've paralyzed me. Instead, I used tactics, and without too much effort, put down an enemy. The training wasn't for nothing.

"Home girl, let's go home."

19

"Don't be nervous." My dad spoke in a soft voice looking at Sa'Rah and I. We were sitting on an airplane readying to fly to visit Aunt Victoria in South Carolina.

"Why do we have to fly to see her!" I screeched.

"Because she's giving her first company speech today and I promised her I would bring her niece and nephew."

Aunt Victoria was a public relations director for a charitable foundation that helped homeless children and hungry families. She was giving a speech as to why if every working person donated one dollar to the fund per month, they would raise over a billion dollars in one year to help their cause.

"But, Daddy I'm scared," I said to him in my miniature ten year old voice.

"Don't be scared, big brother," a six year old mature Sa'Rah said to me. She leaned over and kissed me on my cheek.

"I love you Victor," she said to me. "But when it's our time to go, it's our time to go…"

When I came to I was groggy. I was on Vita in front of my house in Richmond, Heights. I didn't even remember the ride there. I didn't feel it on my body, normally after a few minutes on her I got sore, but not today. It was an extremely beautiful day to be such a horrendous day. There were plenty of cars there. I was sure if Sa'Rah was still here she would ask all of them where were they at when she was alive.

That's just how she thought.

I looked around, there weren't any police cars. I assumed they came, discovered no foul play and left. I didn't want anyone in my family to see me so I snuck around to the back of the house and made my way to the second floor and let myself into the bathroom that was connected to my parents' bedroom. I guess my ninjitsu training did work. I did it without effort or thinking.

The doorbell rang, and whoever was in Sa'Rah's room walked out crying and went downstairs. I walked into her room and shut the door behind me and locked it. I didn't want to be disturbed. I took a deep breath and walked around her room. I never took the time to look at all the pictures she had in here, pictures of her and me, her and dad, her and mom, her and everyone in the family. She really took family to heart, it was her pride and joy. It appears that no public authority has been here yet; the room still had everything intact.

I took it upon myself to look around, I looked everywhere, in every direction to avoid looking directly at Sa'Rah's dead body on the bed. I reached under the bed and found an empty bottle of sleeping pills. No. She wouldn't! I thought to myself. I didn't want anyone else to think anything so I put the pills in my pocket. Diary. Where is Sa'Rah's diary. I have to read her last entry. I searched everywhere in her room, sock drawer, closet, everywhere. I couldn't find it.

Finally, I looked at Sa'Rah. Her body was motionless, lifeless, she looked cold. Her skin color wasn't the same skin color. She was lying down in her dark blue pajamas Grandmother Patrice bought her for Christmas. She had a locket around her neck with a picture of her and me when we were younger. Her eyes were closed and her mouth appeared normal. She looked at peace. My muscles tightened up. Where was Leon at? Why didn't he get here? I clinched my fist together. Then I began to calm down. I can't get too angry. There are a lot of questions that needed answering.

"Who closed this door?" I heard my father say outside of the door. The doorknob shook. He must've been trying to come in. "Who locked the door!?" My father said in a panic. "Maybe she's in there!? Maybe she's alive!?" My father shook the doorknob more vigorously. "Sa'Rah!? Sweetie, you in there!?"

I didn't move, I didn't respond. I just stood over here, looking directly at her. Hoping that by some miracle she'd come back to life, open her eyes, smile and claim this as one big joke for attention. I leaned over and kissed her forehead. I felt for a pulse, but nothing was there and her body was cold. My little sister was dead.

"Calm down, Junior!" I heard Senior exclaiming to him.

I heard more footsteps come up the stairs.

"Give me the keys! Where is the key to her room!?" my father cried out.

"Here," I heard my mother hand him some keys.

After fiddling around with the wrong key he finally unlocked the door and opened it with much aggression only to see me standing here. I didn't look his way.

"Three?" my father said in an excitingly disappointed way.

Excited to see me, disappointed to see that his daughter is in fact deceased. I felt my mother rush and hug me. I didn't hug her back. Her and my father were a part of the reason my sister may have taken her own life. Their divorce, something Sa'Rah didn't understand, was killing her, something they didn't understand. I understood, I just didn't let it bother me. It was their life, but Sa'Rah and I thought differently.

"I've been here only a few minutes," I responded as dryly as I could.

I felt my mother's tears on my arms. My father came to hug me as well. I was their only child now, their love and protection of me just multiplied by two. I would rather it had been my life lost instead of hers.

"Would you all mind giving me a few moments alone with Sa'Rah please?"

"Sure. But how did you get in here?" my father questioned me.

"I learned a few things in college, Dad." I said to him trying not to sound disrespectful. "Who found her?"

"Your mother did. Son, are you ok?"

"Besides the obvious, I'm fine," I said letting my anger get the best of me.

"Be mindful of your father, Three," Senior said to me in a stern voice.

"Apologies, Dad."

"No, it's ok, Son. It's…" He said, eyes watering up. "It's really good to see you."

He gave me a hug. Everyone was crying. I looked around the room, Senior, Grandma Patrice, Christina and Leon were in the room with us. Seeing Leon made me grit my teeth.

"When did she pass?" I asked.

"Had to be sometime last night, she was with Senior most of the day yesterday."

"Yesterday?" I asked Leon to come here two nights ago, he should've had her and brought her to see me yesterday. "Would you mind giving Leon and I a moment with Sa'Rah please?" I said to everyone.

My dad shook his head reluctantly and everyone left the room.

"Where were you?" I asked Leon the second the door shut. I stopped him from coming close to me to give me a hug of comfort.

He stopped and looked at me. His eyes showed a sign of guilt.

"I asked you specifically to come here to see her. Now look at her," I said to him demanding and calmly.

"I…" Leon began speaking. He licked his lips and his bottom lip kind of hinged up.

He was about to lie to me. I don't know how I know this, but I just knew it.

"I just didn't make it bro," he said to me. Looking me directly in the eyes, he lied. I didn't let it bother me at this moment.

"Ok," I said to him. I didn't show any outward signs towards him as to why he lied. I'm sure he had a good reason. Just nothing I wanted to hear at the moment.

I walked out of the room and I heard him speaking to her.

"I'm sorry, Sa'Rah. I love you," Leon said and he began crying.

"You and I have to talk," Senior said to me standing at the staircase.

There was a lot that we did need to talk about. But now wasn't the time. I wasn't in the mood for talking about anything.

"When are the authorities going to come to examine her?" I asked ignoring Senior's directive for us to talk.

"Your mother and father just called them. They are on their way. But we need…"

"I don't want to talk right now, Senior," I said interrupting him.

I began to feel tired. I hadn't felt so tired in a long time. It wasn't a fatigued tired, it was more of a headache tired, like I was fighting something, I just didn't know what it was.

"I don't mean to be disrespectful, Senior, but I just want to go get some sleep. The funeral, it has to be at the church. I don't care what anyone says, or any threats, it has to be at the church." I said as I walked away. I would defend anyone who tries to interrupt her service.

I went and hugged my mother and gave her a kiss on the cheek. I hugged my father and Grandmother Patrice and Christina. Leon came out of Sa'Rah's room wiping his eyes and I just looked at him, no expression, just a look.

I descended to my room in the basement. My father had been staying down there, his clothes were everywhere. He had been sleeping on the couch because my bed looked exactly like I left it before I went to college. I went and took a shower. I stood in there for about an hour. For the past three months all my showers had been five to ten minutes. I never had a chance to really get into the shower, to stand still and let the hot water pour down my head, and down to my back and shoulders. I didn't know what soap I was using at the college but I got a chance to use my own soap, smell like I wanted to smell, wash my own hair. I was able to keep myself well groomed while I was down there, but it wasn't how I would have liked it to be.

After I left the shower I went into my kitchenette. I went into the refrigerator and there was a plate of fried chicken wings with a note on top of them.

'I know it's been a long time since you had some of these!' ~Sa'Rah

It was hand written by her with her name on it and her signature with a smiley face next to it. Even after death she amazed me. My heart started pumping fast. I knew what I was fighting. I was fighting the urge to cry, to let the built up emotion go. But I dared not even let one of my eyes get teary.

I wished that there was some wine there. It would have been nice to have some with the last meal my sister ever made for me.

I walked back to my room. I sat down on my bed and suddenly I felt lonelier than ever. No Sa'Rah, Sa'Rah was gone, no one to come and keep me company on days like this. Fawzia didn't even know I was town, I didn't think she would even care if she did. Leon, I didn't even want to look at him. I was just alone. Even though it was midafternoon and sunny, it felt dark and rainy.

I heard footsteps coming down the stairs. Whoever it was about to get sent right back upstairs, I didn't want to be bothered. I stood up and to my surprise Elizabeth walked into my room. She looked at me, her eyes watered immediately and ran to me and clinched me and began crying harder than anyone upstairs.

"I…" she said, trying to talk through her tears. "I spent almost every day with her." She began crying more.

We sat down on my bed and after a few minutes of crying on my shoulder she finally pulled herself together. I didn't say anything because I didn't know what to say. I was hurt like she was hurt, I wasn't going to tell her it was going to be ok because it wasn't going to be ok, Sa'Rah was gone, and there will forever be that void in my heart, and no one will be able to fill it.

"I'm so sorry Victor." Elizabeth said wiping her eyes and clearing her throat. She didn't have any make up on, and she looked beautiful. It was dim in my room, I had heavy curtains around the few windows that was down here. And it was as if her eyes glowed.

"I'm a mess, and I can't imagine how you must feel," she said as she looked me right in the eyes.

I didn't say anything. A few minutes went past and Elizabeth got up to leave.

"When Sa'Rah was six years old," I started saying. Elizabeth stopped at the door. "My dad was having us fly to South Carolina to hear my Aunt Victoria give a speech for her charity. We were sitting on the plane."

I paused, and Elizabeth came and sat next to me and put her arm around me for comfort. It was nice to feel her touch.

"We were sitting on the plane and I'm whining and complaining and my dad is just sitting there, and finally he told me not to be nervous. Sa'Rah, she was reading a book, I don't remember what book, but normal six year olds shouldn't be reading books on an airplane as if they were in their thirties. So she says to me, don't be scared big brother. I love you, and when it's our time to go, it's our time to go. And she kissed me. Six years old." I said smiling to myself at the memory of my younger sister.

"You're different," Elizabeth said to me. "Everyone upstairs is a mess, even Leon is crying but you're down here and you look completely calm. You've changed." Elizabeth said looking at me right in the eyes.

At that very moment, I felt vulnerable, if she tried to kiss me, I wouldn't resist. As our eyes drew closer together, she turned, and grabbed something from her bag.

"Share this bottle with me?"

She brought out a bottle of wine; it was as if she read my mind. It wasn't the wine that I drank in college, it was a white wine.

"Only if you share these wings with me," I showed her the plate of wings that Sa'Rah had made for me. "Sa'Rah made them. Left me this note."

I gave her the note. Elizabeth's eyes watered back up as she walked into the other room. I didn't follow her, I would let her get herself together.

After a few minutes she walked back in with some wine glasses and we shared the wings and drank the entire bottle of wine. It was a good time despite the sad nature that brought us together. Was this Sa'Rah's master plan? Did she do this to get me and Elizabeth to spend some time together? No. Can't be, she wasn't that bold… was she?

"What's wrong, Victor?" Elizabeth said to me after she noticed I paused.

"Nothing. I just wanted to thank you for your diary. You were right, it did get lonely in college, and it kept me company."

She gave me a hug after that. She got up and went towards my bathroom.

"You mind if I use the girl's room?" she said as she smiled.

"Be my guest just leave the toilet seat up," I said joking back with her.

While she was in there, I cleaned up the food we ate, the chicken was delicious and the wine calmed the sad mood. It didn't mask it, it didn't make me pretend like Sa'Rah wasn't there, it just helped sooth the wound a bit. Like putting a band aid on a cut after you cleaned it up. I was tired, I wanted to lie down but it would be rude to do so while Elizabeth was here.

"You need to clean that up," she said coming out of the bathroom. She was a beautiful woman. She was wearing a blue shirt with some black jogging pants. She looked like a track runner.

"Thank you for coming by, Elizabeth," I said to her.

"Thank you for letting me cry on your shoulder."

"It's been a long day already, and I'm pretty tired."

"Ok. Well I'll let you sleep."

"No."

"Pardon me?"

"I was hoping that you stayed," I said.

I didn't know what came over me, but at that moment I didn't want to be alone. I had been alone for past three months, and she was really the only constant thing that kept me company through her words.

Fawzia and I barely talked, and when we did talk, and then we just stopped I felt even lonelier after that. So I wanted company tonight. I wanted Elizabeth.

"If you don't mind."

"Of course I don't mind." She said as she walked towards me.

I kissed her on her forehead. And I lay in the bed. She didn't immediately lie down, she went and turned off all of the lights. I heard her wrestling with something and finally she lie down with me.

"Are you sure you want me to stay?" she asked again looking directly at me.

"Yes." I replied.

She got underneath the covers with me and put her leg over mine. She had taken off her jogging pants. Her skin felt so soft and smooth. She kissed me on my cheek. I tried to turn my head to kiss her back, but I felt myself drifting off.

20

Sweat was pouring down my face. I was groggy at first and I saw a few figures in front of me. I stood up and squinted my eyes. I closed them tightly and re-opened them. My blurry vision became clear. There were four people about fifty feet from me. This place was a rocky area with fire on both sides as far as you can see. It looked like we were in the Grand Canyon, or some canyon of some sorts with stone walls on both side and fire surrounding the platform we all were on. I walked closer until the people became clearer. There were two huge men holding one man down on his knees. The two huge men were both tall and very burly. Standing in front of the man on his knees was another man, not too much taller than I, he was wearing a robe of some sort, the only thing I could see was his hair. I heard him talking.

"You were a fool to come here alone," he said to the man on his knees.

"But I'm not alone," said the man's voice…

"Son…" I heard my dad's voice say to me. "Victor!"

I awoke from my dream. I rubbed my eyes. My neck was extremely stiff, I rubbed it. When I finally came too and opened my eyes I saw that my father was here with me. No one else was around, it was a little bright in my room, I must've slept till morning.

"I need you to get up and get some food in you," my father said to me looking at me with great concern on his face. I could imagine how he felt. I was the last of his children. He was going to be more protective of me.

I looked around, there was no trace of Elizabeth.

"When did Elizabeth leave?" I asked my father. Suddenly I felt extremely hungry. Like I hadn't eaten in my entire life.

"She left about four nights ago," my father said to me. I looked at him in confusion. "You've been sleep for five days, son."

"Five days?" I said in complete disbelief.

"Today is your sister's funeral. Your mother made you some breakfast, eat up, take a shower, get dressed and let's get out of here, it starts in two hours," my father said as he got up and walked out of my room.

I looked at my table in the center of my room and there was a plate with eggs, sausage, bacon, and two slices of toast, some milk and a glass of orange juice. I ate that very fast, I was starving. After eating the food I cleaned up in the bathroom, I had to stand in the shower for half an hour. I got dressed, for the occasion I put on an all-black suit, with a black collarless dress shirt, black pants and black dress shoes and a black suit jacket. I looked at myself in the mirror and sighed deeply.

Sa'Rah was gone, and I was about to truly say good bye to her. I never would've imagined that I would say good bye to her, except for when I was closing my eyes for the final time, and she would get dressed to say good bye to me. No parent should ever have to bury their child. I could imagine the heartache my parents were going through. I dared not ask. Hopefully they were praying.

I walked up the stairs to see my mother and father waiting on me in the kitchen.

"It's good to see you up and about honey," my mother said to me. She was wearing an all-black dress with a hat that had a cover for her face.

My father was wearing a black suit with a white dress shirt and a black tie. He looked like he hadn't slept in five days. He looked extremely tired.

"Dad," I said with a concerned voice. "When's the last time you slept?"

"He hasn't slept," my mom said quickly. "He's been watching you downstairs like a hawk. Making sure you were ok while you rested. You look refreshed. Did you enjoy the breakfast?"

"Yes. The breakfast was great, Mom. Thank you for making it."

My dad didn't say a word. My mom looked at him and he seemed completely out of it.

"I want to drive. You two sit in the back," I said. I figure that we could all drive to the funeral together.

I grabbed the keys to their car and got into the driver's seat. I checked my phone. I had a ton of messages, but none from Fawzia. Not a one. I sighed to myself. What was she doing that she couldn't even send me a message? She hasn't heard from me in five days and she was ok with that? We were going to have to have a long talk, her and me. We had to talk about where the relationship was going because if she didn't want it to go anywhere, she could let me go. My heart yearned for her, I missed her smell, I missed the feel of her lips on my face, and not talking to her, it felt like another part of my heart was gone. No Sa'Rah, no Fawzia, what was I going to do? As I thought that to myself, a message came in from Elizabeth.

'See you soon.'

I just smiled to myself. I looked at the rest of the messages she sent me. She texted every day to see if I had awoken. I had some strange e-mails from Leon apologizing. I'm not sure what is going on with him, couldn't think about that though. I just had to get to the church. I'd missed the church, it had been a long time since I'd been there.

While driving my parents to the church, it was really quiet in the car. No music, nothing. They sat in the back, my father fell asleep and my mom just leaned on him. Did Sa'Rah really do it? Did she do the drastic to get the family to come closer together? Or was this just a Band-Aid on an open wound?

When we arrived at the church, the parking lots were full. People were filing in. I dropped my parents off at the door. As her family, we were going to go into the church last. I found a place to park in the family parking section. When I walked towards the door I saw everyone.

My Aunt Victoria was talking to my father; my grandmother Patrice was hugging my Aunt Victory. Christina and Leon were together talking with Senior, and Grandpa Persy was hugging my mother. We were all there. I took a deep breath and walked towards everybody.

"Victor!" I heard my Aunt Victory yell. She ran and hugged me. "It's so good to see you walking after being sleep for so long." She hugged me tightly. Then everyone in the family came around me.

"How are you Victor?" I heard Grandpa Persy say.

"Are you ok?" Christina said.

"I missed you," Aunt Victoria said.

"Everyone," I said after they all bombarded me with questions. "I'm alright. I appreciate your concern but I'm fine. Today isn't about me, it's about celebrating the life of Sa'Rah. I am fine." I said annoyingly. I understand that I slept for five days. But today isn't about me.

The Ushers came out and escorted us in. As we walked through the door through the center aisle to view Sa'Rah's body. I heard everyone start crying. I felt a hand touch my own. It was Elizabeth. I stopped and gave her a hug as her tears ran down her face and onto my own. I kept a cool face. I'm not sure why I was the only one not crying. Did that training harden my heart? I was sad, probably more sad than anyone here. When I finally walked up to her body it was me and me alone. My family had stopped, cried and walked off.

I stood above her and I looked at her face. Cleaned up by the mortician, her eyes were shut, her hair was long and straight, her hands were held together on her stomach, she was wearing a white dress. Her locket of her and I was around her neck. I took out Elizabeth's journal. I had brought it with me. It kept me comfortable in college. If by some miracle, after she's buried she can read this while waiting to be judged by God, it will give her good company. I put the journal underneath her hands and I whispered in her ear.

"Enjoy this in the afterlife sister." I kissed her on her forehead. "I love you. Goodbye my angel." I said. After I did that it was as if the entire church started crying at the same time. I turned and I walked back to sit with my parents.

"I wish…" Senior began to talk at the podium. "I wish we were opening church today for the first time in months, for something less tragic than someone being taken from us at such a young age."

Senior spoke with elegance and authority, he was calm. You wouldn't have known his only granddaughter was the one not ten feet from him.

"A merry heart maketh a cheerful countenance: but by sorrow of the heart the spirit is broken. The heart of him that hath understanding seeketh knowledge, but the mouth of fools feedeth on foolishness." Senior spoke a verse of the Bible. "That was Proverbs fifteen verses thirteen and fourteen. Listen to these words, the heart of him that hath understanding seeketh knowledge. Seeks knowledge. Untimely deaths of the young always hits our hearts hard. I look at every one of you, and everyone wants to know why this happened? Let's not sit here and think about Sa'Rah's death. Instead let's celebrate her life. Let's get to know the loving, caring, kind young lady she was."

My phone vibrated in my pocket.

'Young Victor, it is Marcel. You're training is not over.' Marcel texted to me.

'Not now, at my sister's funeral.' I responded.

'More will die if you do not finish.'

'It will have to wait.'

My phone then made a loud noise and interrupted Senior. Everyone in the congregation turned to look at me. My phone was on vibrate. I didn't even look at the text message I just turned my phone off. Senior continued. He spoke about Sa'Rah as a unique person with a beautiful voice. My phone went off again, this time louder and ruder than before.

"Victor!" Senior snapped at me. "Please turn off your phone."

"I'm sorry." I responded. Looking at my phone that was just turned off. It was off, but I could still see the message.

'Your sister's death means nothing if you do not finish your training.'

VENSIN GRAY

That angered me. My phone rang loud again.

'Niagara falls, three hours.'

I stood up, and I walked out of the church with everyone looking at me. I was embarrassed and angry. I didn't know what was so important about Niagara Falls, but my sister's death meant something. When I walked outside Vita was waiting on me. Without hesitation I got on top of her and road off. I heard Leon and Elizabeth calling for me as I rode off. It was a cool day, it was sunny. Niagara Falls was about three and a half hours away.

As we got closer to Niagara Falls the sky was getting darker and the wind was more chilled. I could see my breath in the air. It started snowing out of nowhere. It snowed hard too. Vita didn't seem to mind at all she kept at her alarming speed that no horse should be able to keep up with for this long.

When we arrived at Niagara Falls, New York, you couldn't see anything, it was literally a white out. By the time Vita had stopped, we were at the actual water falls. The water falls were a semi-circle with water flowing from the west toward the south. I looked, and listened, I didn't hear any water, and it was freezing cold.

"Grab your sword, Victor," I heard Marcel say to me in a language that wasn't English.

I looked at Vita. Vita had my diamond sword tucked in her saddle. I grabbed the sword. I didn't know where Marcel was but I heard him. In a blink of an eye, the white out went away revealing a completely frozen Niagara Falls. It was beautiful. My breath was taken away.

"Don't be afraid to speak back to me. You know the language, Victor," Marcel said to me appearing to me out of thin air. He was wearing a black shirt with black pants and black boots. He looked as if he was ready for combat. His sword was unsheathed and he was walking towards me.

"Speak to me in the language Victor."

"How do you know I can speak this language?" I said to him in perfect tongue of the language he spoke to me.

"This is the language of the Angels. It's very important that you are confident in your ability to speak it and understand it."

"How can I know this?"

"You didn't think the iPod was there for your entertainment did you?"

"Why am I here?" I asked of him.

"I told you, your training isn't done. You need to know what it's like to have your sword go into another person's flesh," Marcel said that to me and I got irate.

"You made me leave my sister's funeral for this!" I screamed at him.

"It is the most important part of the training. All those hard days, days in which you stopped breathing but survived. Days in which you crawled home, would all be for nothing if you pause in the middle of battle and get killed because you don't know how to kill. Watching it on television means nothing."

"I'm not about to kill anyone, Marcel," I said to him in a very egotistical tone.

"That's fine," Marcel said walking over to the frozen water. He stepped on top of it and looked back at me. *"I'm sure your sister won't be too lonely in hell when her brother joins her soon."* I unsheathed my sword as quickly as I ever did and I was running towards the frozen water as fast as I could.

I attacked high with anger and he dodge it easily. I slipped on the ice and almost lost my balance. I had to calm down. I wasn't going to beat Marcel in an angry motion. We began to spar on the ice. I tried every attack I knew, high to low, low to high, left to right, everything I learned. I was the obvious aggressor in the fight. As we were sparring, we were stepping back and forth and the ice began to crack. How this ice was formed? I did not know.

"How did you do this with the ice!?" I screamed to Marcel.

"I did nothing, God did everything." He said while pointing up to the sky.

Suddenly, lightning struck the ice we were on and ice began to break in to chunks and you heard the waters beginning to roar. As I stood in amazement at the fact we were fighting on ice, Marcel went on the offensive, he was faster than Helen, but not as strong with his hits. He was less predictable with his movements. I went on the defensive and blocked his attacks.

"*That's good, young Victor!*" Marcel said to me as he stood straight up and didn't look at me as he dodged my attacks and countered.

"*How are you doing that?*" I asked. He wasn't looking, he wasn't paying any attention but was fighting me as if he was looking directly at me.

"*Use your senses Victor. Know your enemy,*" he said to me.

We sparred more and he cut me on my left shoulder. I grabbed my shoulder and I noticed blood was coming out of the wound but it wasn't that bad of a cut. We were on a block of ice that was going towards the falls. I was facing the falls and his back was to it.

"*You're being too naïve right now. You will either kill me, or join Sa'Rah,*" he said.

I raised my sword for a high attack, he positioned his sword to block it, I spun around with a seemingly apparent leg sweep. He jumped to avoid the sweep. I stopped mid-way between the sweep and position my sword in a backwards lunge. I felt it resist as I lunged backwards. When I turned around, Marcel was looked at me, blood poured out of his mouth. He dropped his sword and smiled.

"*Now, Victor. Now you know,*" he said as he fell backwards into the falls.

I was stuck. Never before had I stabbed someone, the feeling of my sword going into another humans flesh felt terrifying. The blood that poured out of his mouth didn't feel good at all. There was no satisfaction in it. He said kill or be killed. I didn't want to die.

"I'm sorry, Marcel," I said out loud. I fell to my knees ignoring that I was about to fall over the falls as well. Just as the block of ice was getting ready to go over. I felt an arm go around my torso.

"I got you brother!" Leon said to me. "I'm not letting you go down!"

I looked over at him, he was tied to a rope and we both fell into the water. But we didn't go down. Leon was holding on to me. He was strong enough to withstand this water. I was in a daze. I didn't know what was going on. We were being pulled towards land. When we got to land, Vita pulled us from the falls. Standing next to Vita was Elizabeth. She ran towards me and hugged me.

"Oh my god!" she screamed. "Are you ok!? What were you doing out there Victor!?" She said holding me tightly.

"Are you alright?" Leon said to me. His suit was wet.

"How did you know to find me here?" I asked them.

"We followed you after you left. We lost you in that white out but I caught up to Vita and I knew you wouldn't be far off. This rope just happened to be lying around." Leon said walking close to me. "We lost Sa'Rah. I wasn't going to lose you. Especially not to some water fall," he said to me hugging me tightly.

We spent the next several moments drying off and getting some food at a local restaurant. My sword that my father gave me was gone. It just assisted me in killing Marcel. I ate sparsely. I was hungry but I wasn't hungry. I wanted to look at the falls, I wanted to find Marcel. I wanted to see for myself.

"We should get you home." Elizabeth said to me. "You don't look too well."

I didn't feel too well either. I was a murderer. Who was I becoming? I left my sister's funeral to murder another man. I blanked out. I felt Leon help me to Elizabeth's car. He laid me down in the backseat and Elizabeth began to drive. Next to us was Leon on Vita. I closed my eyes. All I could see was Marcel's face and blood pouring out of it, and him falling down into the falls. I tried to open my eyes again but I couldn't. I eventually fell asleep.

21

"Victor Thomas the Third…" Helen said to me looking down on me.

Blood was pouring from my nose. I was losing consciousness. My breath lessened and the air around me became harder to breath. My heart rate slowed down and I felt the will to live slipping from my grasp.

"One day, you'll know how to do things. You won't know how you know how to do things. You'll just know them."

I looked at myself in the mirror in my room. My shoulder was cut pretty badly. I took a bottle of peroxide and gently poured it over it. Next I put on a latex glove and checked the cut to make sure the bleeding had stopped and nothing foreign was in there. You don't want to close up a cut with anything that's not supposed to be in there in there. I poured some alcohol in a small bowl and dropped a sewing needle and tweezers in there to disinfect it. I then took the sewing needle and the surgical suture I had and I began stitching my cut up.

I have no idea when I purchased all of these medical things. One thing I vaguely remember Helen telling me before beating me unconscious was that I should always have medical supplies on me at all times. I made sure everything was closed up good and I put on a shirt, finished cleaning up and walked upstairs where I found Senior, Grandma Patrice, my mother and my father, Aunt Victoria and Victory, Christina, Leon, Ian and even Elizabeth were sitting down or standing up in the kitchen looking at me.

"Hello everyone," I said slowly.

"You have some explaining to do, son," my father said with an obvious attitude.

"What do I need to explain?" I respond back to him with attitude. I was annoyed. I didn't want to have to answer any questions right now. I just wanted to be left alone. "I apologize for interrupting Sa'Rah's funeral…"

"You should be!" My father barked at me interrupting me.

"Junior!" Grandma Patrice said to him with a look on her face for him to relax.

"And…" I said with a deliberate slight to my father. "For missing the rest of her funeral. I had some unfinished business to attend to."

"What business? With that Muslim!?" My father yelled.

"What Muslim?" Leon questioned abruptly and unprovoked.

"Junior!" Grandma Patrice said even louder standing up. "You were not raised like that!"

"You missed your sister's funeral to be with some woman you can't be with?" my father said completely ignoring Grandma Patrice, his mother.

I would have loved to tell them about the training, I would have loved to tell them that I was a warrior, battle tested, and a killer now. I'm not proud of either, I just wanted to be a normal teenager, who plays video games, questions what he's going to do after high school, date several girls, get my heart broken, break some hearts, get married and have children. Or just eat cereal and watch TV all day and get fat. I would love to do that. But I can't. And now isn't the time for alternative plans. Instead of telling them, I'll show them.

My father, his actions, his voice elevation, his seemingly failing way to try to calm down, wanted to strike me, wanted to prove his fatherly bravado over me, all he needed was the right push.

"You weren't even there to say goodbye when we put her in the ground," my father said quietly not looking me.

"What's it to her?" I said with a childlike attitude. I pray that my father forgives me after this. "It's not like she was going to say goodbye back."

There was a gasp, then complete silence.

"AHHHHH!!!!!" My father yelled at the top of his lungs and came charging at me with full force. The way he was running towards me, arms spread, he was going to try to grab me. That's exactly what I wanted. I quickly stepped to the left, and with a football player like swim move, in which I pushed his left arm away from me with my right hand, and with my left, I dodged him and gently pushed him letting his momentum carry him into the living room in which he flipped over the sofa and crashed into the coffee table. My Aunt Victory was about to rush in to see if he was ok, but I grabbed her and gave her a look of don't. I walked in there.

"Grab me and take me downstairs, tell them to wait." I whispered in his ear. "Do it with force, like a man, like my father."

My father, with tears in his eyes, stood up and grabbed me.

"We're going to have a talk Victor," my father said to me with force. "Wait here." He told everyone as he took me down stairs and slammed my door after him.

When we got downstairs he let go of me quickly and sat down on my bed breathing hard. He looked at me with admiration.

"You've changed son." He said to me. He had blood on shirt. I walked into the bathroom to get some cleaning material.

"Take off your shirt father," I said to him.

He took it off very gingerly. He had a small piece of glass in his side.

"I have changed, the change was necessary." I said to him as I cleaned his cut. I looked at it, it didn't need stitches, I cleaned it really well. My dad winced a bit from the stinging of the peroxide, I bandaged it up really good and made sure enough oxygen could get through the bandage to begin healing it.

"Am I going to have to call you nurse?" he said laughing a bit.

"Hopefully that's all you'll have to call me," I said smiling back. It had been a while since he and I had some alone time.

"You haven't slept in a while father. You need some rest. I'll make up for missing Sa'Rah's funeral."

"How will you do that?" he asked as he laid back in my bed.

"You'll see," I said to him. I don't think he heard me, because I noticed a change in his breathing, he was fast asleep. He needed it. I put the covers over him and turned out all of the lights. I walked up stairs to see the family.

"I hope you didn't hurt him too bad, brother," I heard Aunt Victoria say.

I got sad at the sound of that. She referred to my dad as brother. I don't have any more sisters to refer to me as brother.

"Don't worry," I said when I appeared in front of them. "I was gentle."

It went silent in the room again. Elizabeth came and stood next to me.

"Don't worry, my father fell asleep. He needs some rest."

My mother walked up to me. The way she was standing, her facial expression, her hands were in a slapping position. She reached back and slapped my face. I could've dodged it, but embarrassing one parent today was enough.

"Don't you ever! Disrespect your father like that again," she screamed to me and stormed downstairs in the basement. I'm glad that I was expecting that or I'm sure that would have stung.

"Anyone else want to take a shot at me?" I felt Elizabeth's hand on my face where my mother had just slapped me.

"Stop being so smug, grandson," Senior said to me in a calming voice.

"I want to make up for missing Sa'Rah's funeral," I said as the rest of the family stood up and walked towards me in the kitchen. "I have an idea. The weather forecast says that there will be a blizzard this weekend. Let's light up some candles in the church, pull out some hot chocolate, no electricity except for the microphones and instruments…"

"Let's have the winter concert praising Jesus," Senior said finishing my thought.

"Sa'Rah wouldn't have wanted it any other way," Grandma Patrice said with great joy giving me a hug and kissing me on my cheek.

Everyone got on their phones. Friday was just a few nights away and we had to get a lot of preparations done. Everyone had small talk and left the house. They were so excited about the concert.

"What about security Three?" Senior said to me.

"I'll handle security," I responded to his concern.

"With the war finally hitting America, the Muslims aren't as understanding anymore to us being allowed to continue our faith, praise and worship. This concert will be a slap in the face to them."

"They'll just have to understand. And they will understand," I said to him, assuring him that they will understand. Even if I had to go and see Fawzia's father, someone would listen to me.

"I'm sure you'll pull it off," Senior said to me. He looked at me. He knew who I was. He knew it. I knew it, the eye contact we just had was what he needed to connect the dots. If only I could tell him that Marcel was no longer with us. He sacrificed himself so that I wouldn't freeze in battle.

For the next several hours, Elizabeth helped me clean up the living room and set up preparations for the winter concert. She was excited about it. She was a good friend to me, a better friend then I deserved. I knew what was on her heart. And for some reason, my heart was still on Fawzia. This concert gave me a reason to go see her.

"Make sure you order a lot of cleaning supplies," I said to Elizabeth.

"Why?"

"Because there's going to be a lot of spilled hot chocolate and marshmellows," I said.

"Why will there be spilled hot chocolate and marshmellows?" She said laughing a bit.

"Because Jesus is about to be praised again in Cleveland!" I said with a big smile on my face.

"Hallelujah!" Elizabeth shouted.

We stood up together and met eye to eye. We stared at one another for a moment. I looked deep into her eyes. What a beautiful woman.

"One day." She whispered to me. "One day." She said. She grabbed her bag and walked out of the front door. She turned and smiled at me. "One day." She said one last time holding up the number one with her index finger.

I just smiled.

The next few days I was at the church setting up for the concert. I was fielding phone calls, getting equipment. Once word around town spread that we were having a concert, people were RSVP'ing as if we sent out invites. Once it was determined that there were going to be a lot of people coming, we rented outdoor projectors and speakers and set up areas around the church where people can watch and listen to the concert as if they were inside of the church. We got tons of flameless candles to set up both inside and outside. I wanted an old school feeling, I wanted people feel like they were sitting in front of their fire place listening to good Christian music on the radio drinking hot chocolate and eating graham crackers. The hot chocolate and graham crackers were Sa'Rah's favorites to eat during the winter, sitting in front of the fireplace. She would often fall asleep there. This concert was of course for worshipping Jesus, but I was putting it down as Sa'Rah's idea. I purchased security radio ear pieces and designated a few trusted church members to help me with security. My main concern was Muslims being insulted by this.

The eve of the concert, I found myself on the west side, in the grocery store's fresh produce section looking for a good pineapple. I didn't know what came over me, but I missed the taste of fresh pineapple in the morning. While I was searching for the best one I noticed a familiar person. Dressed in purple again, it was Fawzia. My heart started to race, suddenly, all the training I had had left me. I was anxious, and nervous. What would she say to me? How will she react when she sees me? Did I ask her why she hasn't responded to my messages? Or just be happy that we've seen one another.

"Fawzia." I said calmly as I stood behind her.

She turned around, saw it was me and looked down immediately. I barely saw her face, she appeared to be ashamed or embarrassed. Perhaps she and Malcolm had gotten married.

"Is everything ok?" I asked her.

She didn't respond, she just walked down another aisle. I followed her. She was exactly as I remembered, she smelled of morning roses, and glowed like the moon on calm waters at night. She hastened in her walk until I grabbed her arm. She breathed heavy. But not a breath of frustration, a breath like she missed my touch.

"Victor," she said, her voice sounding more American and less of the Spanish accent she had. "What are you doing here?" She said trying to avoid eye contact with me. "This concert that's being paraded all over town, you know that Malcolm and his friends aren't going to allow it to go on."

"They can't stop it," I said arrogantly. "Are you with Malcolm? Is that why you haven't been talking to me."

"No, Victor," she said shrugging her shoulders removing my hand for her. "Facts are facts, you are Christian, and I am Muslim. We can never be." She said, her eyes watering up as she finally made contact with me. It was as if everyone in the grocery store avoided this aisle that smelled of herbs and spices. Everything went silent, as she looked into my eyes, she saw the love. She saw how I missed her.

"I don't care about that," I said. "What has been my grandfather's saying?"

"Be strong in your faith…" she slowly responded.

"And you will be freed. He didn't say be strong in Christianity, he said be strong in your faith," I said as I embraced her and kissed her lips. She kissed back, but for only a second.

"Stop it, Victor!" She said a little louder then I think she would have liked. She dropped her basket and walked towards the front of the store.

I wanted to follow but I dared not to. I looked inside of her basket. She had avocados, DHA eggs, broccoli, yogurt and spinach. Always eating healthy.

I purchased my pineapple and left the store.

When I went home, I decided to stop at Euclid creek. I sat and watched some old friends play basketball. I resisted the urge to play. I ran the trail and did some pushups and sit ups, I barely broke a sweat. But it felt good to work out again. I drove home. I ate my pineapple and I showered. I laid down with a huge smile on my face. Tomorrow I would be back in church again. Amongst loved ones, with the Spirit.

22

I woke up the next morning feeling refreshed. It was the first time in a long time where I went to sleep when I wanted to go to sleep and woke up when I needed to wake up. I looked around my room and smiled. Today was going to be a great day. I felt it in my soul. I decided that I am going to call Fawzia. I always get anxious before calling her, I don't know if she's going to answer, and if she does answer, what am I going to say? I know I should be confident when calling my girlfriend. Not even sure why I still call her that. But I decided I wanted to call her.

"Hello?" Fawzia answered the phone sounding like she just woke up.

I froze up. I didn't think she was going to answer.

"Hello?" She said again, this time more alert then before.

"Victor, what do you want?" She said sounding as if she was exhausted by me contacting her continuously. Just when I was going to say something, her sounding that way took all of my excitement away.

"I just…" I said with a sudden reluctance to speak. "I just wanted to tell you that I missed you."

"That's nice," she replied sarcastically.

I was growing impatient with her.

"What did I do to you?"

"What are you talking about?"

"What did I do to deserve the way you've been treating me?

Ignoring me, talking to me periodically when you felt like it. What is going on?"

"Nothing is going on."

"You're lying!" I screamed over the phone to her. I was enraged. Something had to be going on. "There's another man. Isn't there?"

"Victor…" she said as if she wanted me to stop.

"Be honest with me. Are we still together?"

"What do you think?" she said with an attitude. I didn't know what to think, that's why I asked. What is it with her?

"What do you mean what do I think? Do you still love me? Because it feels like you hate me."

"No, Victor. I'm really just indifferent about you," she said and ended the call.

I stood there in silence. Indifferent? I thought to myself. That's worse than hate, she doesn't care or doesn't not care, it's as if I didn't exist to her. I had to calm myself. I meditated for a few hours to gather my thoughts and my feelings. I came to the realization that she and I were no more. The incredible summer we had, all the time we spent together. The kissing, the hugging, and the affections we shared. All felt like it didn't happen. My heart just broke in two more pieces. The two women in whom I relied on were gone. Sa'Rah was gone from this world, and Fawzia was just disconnected.

After meditating, I decided to make my way to church. It was a very windy outside and the snow was coming down very hard. I was hoping that it would ease up by the evening so that the concert won't be ruined. What am I saying? It could be raining shards of glass and people would still come tonight. We had choirs from all over the city coming to sing, solo artists, anybody who enjoys praising Jesus and singing are trying to come. We got a huge donation of homemade hot chocolate, Styrofoam cups, napkins and graham crackers for the event.

When I arrived at church, we had a few snow plows clearing out the parking lots, the projectors were being set up and the speakers were already out and being tested. When I walked inside of the church, there were hundreds of people working vigorously to make tonight a success. The flameless candles were being brought out. Seat assignments were being handed out, all money that would be received was going to go to the Muslim war recovery fund for Muslim's effected by Octavius' war. They do not know it yet, but they'll be happy when they see the check in the mail.

I was a bit troubled. I wasn't as focused as I should've been. All I could think about was Fawzia's indifferent comment. Was there anything worse she could've said? I didn't do anything wrong. I spoke to her when I could, I was honest and open. Maybe she was just mad today. She did kiss me back, and even though it was brief, it was there, and I felt it, and I felt the love in her heart.

"Don't forget your training brother," I heard Sa'Rah say in my head.

It couldn't have been Sa'Rah, she's not a Jedi, she doesn't have after life mind tricks, but perhaps it was my conscience using Sa'Rah's voice to tell me not to stray away from my training. I had to focus.

"Hello, Three," Senior said to me. "You look disturbed."

He could always tell what's going on with someone.

"Walk with me."

We took a walk around the church, talking about me and Sa'Rah, me and Fawzia, and just me in general. We didn't discuss my new knowledge of him being a ProChrist as I am. It wasn't the time. I had to be focused on the evening, making sure it went perfect.

"That's just how it's been, Senior. I'm not sure why I love her, not sure what's going on. But I'm holding on to what little bit of hope there may be left. I know we're not supposed to feel this way about one another, me believing in Jesus, and her believing in her ways. But I figure, just as my Dad got my mother, I could get Fawzia." I said explaining to Senior my thought process.

My mother was a Jehovah's Witness before she got pregnant with me, she wasn't as into it as she is now so she came over rather easily, but now, it seems like she's devout on going back, even at the cost of my father's heart, and even, Sa'Rah's life.

"Well," Senior said as we took a seat on the top row of the sanctuary. "I'm not quite sure that you'll get Fawzia as your father got your mother. Your mother and her parents were in a conflict of such with the brothers of their Kingdom hall, so when your mother got pregnant, the opportunity came for them to leave, and they did. They never truly stopped believing in what they believed in, which is ok. I can explain to someone one thousands ways my reasoning and justification for what I believe in, and they won't see it as I do, just as they can do the same for me, doesn't mean they are going to make me not believe in what I believe. Your mother never fully committed herself to what we believe, she just dealt with it for the sake of the family, but her heart was always at the Kingdom Hall. And you want to know why you're so drawn to Fawzia?"

"Why is that?" I said while digesting everything he just told me.

"Fawzia, the name itself means victorious," he said. I looked at him and we both started laughing.

"That would make sense," I said while laughing.

"Let me go get dressed. Love you, grandson," Senior said while hugging me. He walked off.

For the next several hours I sat up there and watched everyone prepare the church around me. A few hours before we were expecting everyone to be here, I drove home, the roads were worse than before, but not much traffic. I got dressed. While looking at myself in the mirror. For some strange reason I got down on my hands and knees.

"Dear Jesus," I began praying. "Thank you for the opportunity to have this concert tonight. I pray that you bring everyone in safely and lead them home just as well. I hope today, the singing in your name, and the praise touches lost souls and bring them to you. Thank you for the wonderful family that I have, thank you for Senior, Grandmother Patrice. Thank you for Aunt Victoria and Aunt Victoria. A special thank you to my mother and father, who have lost a child but still find enough strength to love and guide me. Sa'Rah may be lost in the flesh, but her spirit and her soul still lingers in my heart, and I ask that you bring her to you Lord. In your name I pray, Amen."

"That's a good prayer, son," my father said standing behind me. "You sounded like your grandfather there." He looked at me. "Sa'Rah bought you that shirt." He commented on the shirt I was wearing, it was a black dress shirt with horse designs in it. "Ride with me to Church? Your mother isn't coming."

"Why isn't she coming?" I felt insulted, this was my idea, why wouldn't she come and show her support?

"She doesn't feel she belongs."

"No use making her," I responded.

I didn't feel like losing the focus of tonight on my mother's absence.

My father and I rode to the church. We had a good conversation in the car. He was just explaining to me how much he loves my mom, but how he has to get stronger in his faith of Jesus Christ, and the constant back and forth with her, and her decision to go back to the Hall is what was bringing him from his duties as a Christian. I just listened to him talk. I said my piece when I felt it was needed, but for the most part, my father just wanted to vent to his son, and I was happy I could listen.

When we arrived at the church, the parking lot was almost full. We had complimentary valet parking because of the snow. I had arranged that with the security I put into play. My father went into the church, I put my radio in my ear and made sure everything looked good on the outside. The snow had slowed down over here to a light fall, and the wind stopped. There were thousands of people outside standing and looking at the projectors on the east and west side of the church. The streets were full. You would've thought we were doing a countdown for New Years at Times Square. The police came. They wanted to make their presence known. It's always necessary when there are a lot of people grouped together. But for this occasion, all we were doing was praising Jesus; no police officer would be needed.

I walked inside of the church. It was warm in there. I walked into the Sanctuary and it looked like there were no seats available. There were people everywhere I looked, dressed comfortably. Some people were big on tradition, so there were ladies with skirts and dresses on. Senior wasn't big on dress code though. I stood in an aisle area. I drank a little hot chocolate as I listened to one of our Elder's welcome everyone to the church. We had a little bit of everyone in here today, Catholics, Pentecostals, Baptist, and others. I just smiled to myself.

"We have a special song today we are going to play. This is for the Thomas family," The elder said as the lights dimmed and a projector came on.

On the screen there was Sa'Rah. This was last year; she got national attention for how she sung this song. It's an original from Chris Tomlin, 'I Will Rise'.

"There's a peace I've come to know. Though my heart and flesh may fail. There's an anchor for my soul. I can say 'It is well'" She sung as people started clapping and shouting as if Sa'Rah was really there. "Jesus has overcome. And the grave is overwhelmed. The victory is won. He is risen from the dead… And I will rise when He calls my name. No more sorrow, no more pain. I will rise on eagles' wings. Before my God fall on my Knees, and rise… I will rise."

She sung the entire song and held the last note to the point where even the person holding the camera started clapping and you were looking at her feet for a second. After the song was over, people started clapping really hard.

I wasn't in charge of the music. That was Brother Phillips. But what I did suggest was to find a Christian band who could emulate the 'Triumphant Entry' played at the Commissioned live concert reunion back in the early two thousands. While people were still cheering for Sa'Rah's song, you heard the bass come in lightly, and the guitar, joined by a light drum, and a melody from an instrument that I couldn't tell what it was, maybe the keyboard, or a trumpet, or another instrument with a gentle sound, but for the first minute a fifteen or so seconds it played the light sound building up to the rest of the band coming in, and it got louder, and it streamed, and then there was a portion of the song that repeated the notes in a fashion that it went high, low back to high and back to low.

Everyone was standing up and cheering, you heard the Hallelujahs, people were waving their arms. I looked over to the left and I saw Elizabeth up and clapping. Her hair was down. She had on a light blue blouse, some blue earrings, and a black skirt on and some blue stockings. She turned around and saw me, she smiled her bright smile and waved at me. She must've felt me looking at her. I don't know what just happened but when she turned around and waved, my heart jumped. For the first time, I wanted to be with Elizabeth. I felt an urge to go give her a hug.

"Victor, come in," I heard the radio go off in my ear. Just as the band was finishing up, the applause was loud; I could barely hear my radio. I walked out of the Sanctuary to the hallway because I sure outside was just as loud.

"This is Victor," I responded.

"There's a big group marching down Superior. I left my post. Last I saw there were near seventy ninth moving towards Superior and Euclid."

"Weapons?"

"Their swords are out."

I sighed deeply. I was hoping to avoid this.

"Do you want us to call the police?" Said another security official that agreed to help.

"No. I'll handle it. Has anyone seen Leon?" I said. I hadn't seen him all night. I saw Christina, but no Leon.

"Negative, no signs of Leon."

Where in the world is Leon?

"Ok. Stay on your post and let me know if there is any more movement."

"You're going by yourself!?" yelled another security official.

"I'll be fine. I repeat, stay at your post."

This was what I sort of expected. I didn't want to shed any blood so I didn't bring my sword on purpose. Instead I brought an iron rod that I had lying around for years. It was about five feet in length, it was pretty heavy, it was study enough to put someone's lights out with one hit but not do any real damage. I grabbed the pole that I had put away in one of the churches closets and walked outside. As I knew, Vita was waiting on me.

I got on Vita and we rode off. We intercepted them at the bridge over Martin Luther King Boulevard. There were about fifty men with their swords out. They must've marched from the west side. They were tired and irritated. I had the advantage already. I dismounted Vita. The wind picked up and the snow began to fall harder. The men stopped. One of them walked towards me at the center of the bridge. It was Malcolm.

"So we meet again, Victor," Malcolm said in a very calm but arrogant way.

"What are you doing here Malcolm?" I said to him.

"I'm paying tribute to Jesus. Move out of our way, or we won't be as kind to you this time."

"Well this time I'm awake. And we don't have to do this, Malcolm."

"Oh we do."

"No one is stopping you from worshiping Allah. So why come between us?"

"No, no one here is stopping us from worshipping Allah. But you are hiding the fact that my brothers and sisters are being cut down in the millions by one of your own."

"He's not one of us."

"You're all the same to me," Malcolm said growing angry. He was ready to attack me.

They all were wearing the same thing, dark brown wool like jacket with black pants and black boots, no head gear. This was Malcolm's little army. It was only fifty of them. I don't think they have the skills that I have. I believe that I can take them.

"I don't think you brought enough men Malcolm." I said turning my back to him.

"Victor! Watch out!" I heard the radio in my ear.

I knew he was going to attack, I forgot the radio was in my ear. It made me just a slight bit hesitant, but I caught myself. I blocked his sideways sword attack with my iron rod and parried his high attack and countered with a kick to his ribs. He went down on his knees.

"Oh my goodness…" said the security official on my radio.

"I need you to go back to the church," I said to him.

"But, Victor."

"No buts. Just go back to the church and enjoy yourself. I'll be fine. Do not, and I'm serious, do not tell anyone that this is going on, I want them to enjoy themselves. They deserve this." I took the radio out of my ear, and I saw my security official ride off in his car towards the church. I put my radio on Vita.

"So we're really going to do this, Malcolm?" I said. When I turned around he was walking back towards his men.

"Go get him!" I heard him scream to a few of his men.

Only three came out. They outnumbered me so they were going to come with a lot of confidence and attack without much thought of defense. The first attacker I side stepped him. Blocked the attacker from my right and parried the hitter on my left, I turned and hit the attacker I side stepped on the right clavicle with the point of my rod, then I swung the rod tripping my right attacker, by this time, the left attacker regained his posture after I parried his attack and he came at me aggressively with his sword up for a high attack as if he was carrying an ax, I positioned my rod to hit him in his stomach. He groaned and hit the ground. All three lied on the ground, two of them in agony, one just didn't have the heart to get back up. There was silence for a moment, then Malcolm and everyone was running at me all at once. This was going to be interesting.

Malcolm was the first to arrive; I dodged his attack and elbowed him in the face. There were too many swords around for me to dance all night, especially without backup, I would have to use the bridge to my advantage. I fought, dodge, blocked, kicked, put men down, tripped and stunned some. There were so many. Perhaps I over estimated my abilities. I was growing tired. I should've brought my sword, but had I brought my sword there would be a lot of bloodshed, a lot of death and an outcry in the morning. I may have broken a few bones, knocked out some teeth, but everyone would wake up in the morning.

Just as it seemed as though I was getting too tired to be on the offensive, someone in all black clothing, moving too fast for me to see, hit one of Malcolm's men and he fell hard. It was still about twenty to thirty of them still up. They attacked both of us, I was on the southeast side of the bridge, he was on the northwest end and together we put down all of the men. He didn't have a weapon, from what I saw of him, he was moving just like Marcel when he was dodging all of my attacks. He had on a black derby hat, with a black trench coat, black pants, and a black shirt, black everything.

He was fast, faster than Marcel, and he countered with such precise accuracy, I was caught watching and almost got my head cut off. That woke me up from star gazing. I quickly ducked the sword aimed at my head, countered with a knee to his chin, and the only person left standing was me, the other man and Malcolm. Malcolm and I stared at one another long and hard. He then turned and helped one of his men up.

"We're leaving," Malcolm said.

When I looked for the man who helped me, he was gone, vanished. I had no idea who he was, or where he came from.

"Thank you," I said out loud. If I ever saw him again, he couldn't say I didn't thank him.

I looked at the Muslims helping one another up from the ground. I felt bad for them. Octavius is a man of power and numbers, and with the help of governments, it was hard for any Muslim group to counter his war. I don't care what religion you are, or what religion you aren't, it doesn't give any one man the right to persecute anyone. I grew angry.

"Malcolm!" I screamed as I jogged to him. His men got into defensive stances.

"He just wants to talk," Malcolm said as he stepped forward as the rest of them made their way down the street. "What more do you want from me? You took my woman, your people are killing my people, and now two of you just put down my best men." He said sounding defeated.

"Let the Christians here worship Jesus. No more threatening Churches, and I give you my word, I'll do my best to stop Octavius." I said to him holding out my hand to shake.

Handshakes may not mean much to people who want proof, contracts and signatures. But to me, a handshake means my bond that I will hold on to until death. Malcolm looked at me weird for a second. But he saw it in my eyes, the purity and the determination in them. He put his hand out, and we shook.

"No more threats to churches. I hope you hold up to your word," Malcolm said as he turned and walked away.

I don't know what it is about gaining a level of respect for someone you fought in battle. I gained a new level of respect for him. He did jump me, but that was just child's play. I had his girl, he wanted her back, he wanted to make a point. This, this right here was something deeper. I saw it, he was hurting. I would be hurting if people who believe in Jesus were being cut down just because they believed in the almighty. I grabbed my radio from Vita.

"Everyone, come in," I said on my radio.

"Is everything alright, Victor?" said one of the respondents.

"Everything is fine. I need you all to get in your cars or trucks. You are going to see several men walking northwest on Superior. Get the wounded, and take them to the hospital on the west on Twenty- Fifth Street. Come back and take the rest home."

"Are you serious?"

"As serious as I've ever been," I responded... I put the radio down, mounted Vita and rode back to church.

I was going to try to enjoy the rest of my evening.

23

I rode Vita back to the concert. It was very crowded out despite the cold weather. I found a spot further back on the west end of the church where I could at least hear the music faintly. Everyone was out here worshipping Jesus, they were screaming, small talk, love, chants, it had it all. I got off of Vita and sat back on the ground and lay back near a large stone to prop my head up. I have a feeling that Malcolm and I are going to work well together. I must admit, if there was a persecution against Christians by any group, I would stand up against them.

As a Christian myself, I couldn't see myself accepting what Octavius was doing as right. He was striking down millions of Muslims, other Christian factions, Jewish people, atheist, Buddhist, didn't matter what religion you were, what you believed in, all that mattered was what he believed, and if you didn't believe like he believed, you're dead. From my talks with Fawzia, he was killing men, taking young male kids and turning them into his slaves, he and his men raped women and then killed them. He was ruthless. He claims that they were ruthless with Christ, so he'll be ruthless with the non-believers. Of course any true Christian would not agree with him that killing someone else proves a point.

He killed in the name of Jesus but truthfully he killed for his own lust for power, didn't matter, he had to be stopped. I'd have to find a way to do it. Right then I just wanted to enjoy the rest of the concert, what I could hear of it, but I dozed off.

When I awoke the parking lot was emptying out. I must've been tired after my exchange with Malcolm and his men. I got up and walked back to the church. When I walked inside I saw several members of the church cleaning up.

"There you are!" I heard Elizabeth say from the other side of the sanctuary. The accent of her voice couldn't be missed. "Where did you go?"

"Hello, Elizabeth," I said to her. "I had to go take care of something. Safety precautions."

"Safety precautions, huh?" she said smiling at me. "Well, a few members volunteered to clean up a section of the sanctuary, I'm still surprised Pastor allowed us to drink and eat in here."

"Well the food and drinks are minor compared to the purpose of this evening," I said to her as I began to help her clean up her section. As I expected, there was hot chocolate and graham cracker crumbs everywhere.

"You know when I first moved here, you would never find me doing this," Elizabeth began talking. "In London, I was waited on hand and foot, anything I wanted, at the snap of my finger and just poof, it was there. People knew their places and I knew mine. But… America has really humbled me. We're not the power we once were over there, no lineage to the throne; we just have wealth but no power, no real connections, just a lot of money." She said as she began to clean more. I didn't say anything back to her. "And when I waited to approach you, and you basically ignored me, it was a shock. Most men would divorce their wives of ten years to spend one night with me, and I throw myself at you and you looked right through me." She said as she paused and our eyes met.

"How do you do it?" she asked.

"How do I do what?"

"How do you just not show any emotions for Sa'Rah's death. You haven't appeared angry, disconnected, sad, nothing. I've only known her for a few years, and I really got to know her this summer, and what's sad is." She said while gathering herself trying not to cry. "What's sad is, I never had a friend, and most of my friends from Europe distanced their selves from me when we were basically removed from any part of relevance. Here, either I'm too pretty, or too rich, or too smart, or perhaps I looked down on the possible friends here. And my best friend became a fourteen year old girl. She didn't act fourteen, sometimes I wondered who was more mature between the two of us. And she loved you so much, and you haven't shed a tear for her." She said a bit choked up.

Instead of responding I continued to clean up. I didn't have to defend myself to her, or anyone else. I loved my sister. I sent my best friend, my brother to come here to check on her and he failed. What more could I have done? Could I have come? I believe not, I believe that I would've gotten my legs broken had I tried to leave. That training was my destiny, and death was Sa'Rah's destiny, I just have to accept it.

"I'm sorry, Victor." Elizabeth said to me after a few moments of awkward silence.

"It's quite alright," I said to comfort her. "People show emotions in different ways, sorrow isn't always everyone's reaction to death. She lived her life, and she did what was needed to be done, and God took her when He felt it was time for her. I can't argue with God. I don't care who my grandfather is."

We both laughed a bit.

"Your grandfather is everything he was advertised to be. When we first moved here, we knew that your family was the family to get close with to get anywhere here. Pastor introduced my father and mother to some important people and we were able to extend our wealth here and give back to the communities and be charitable. Something I never knew about back home."

"You know when I first met you, I thought you were a supermodel for some magazine. I looked on the internet for days to see if you were." I said embarrassingly.

"I couldn't tell. You never spoke to me."

"Didn't think you would be interested."

"And why not? You're Victor Thomas Senior's grandson. Probably the most influential family in Ohio, wealth, no secret crazy stuff, no illegal drugs, just good Jesus worshipping people. You're important…"

"Everyone's important, whether they are Victor Thomas Senior's grandson, or just some poor kid trying to find something to eat. We're all important. And I don't know why I didn't say anything to you. Never thought about it honestly. All my life Leon took the lead and I followed humbly."

"You see, that's what makes you special. I grew up a brat, when I came here I had to clean my own room, learn how to garden, and wash clothes. That is peasant's work."

"We are all servants of the Lord." I said. Elizabeth just smiled at me. "We should do dinner one day."

"I would like that," Elizabeth responded with excitement.

"And what I would like is a ride home," my father said walking into the conversation. "Hello Elizabeth. Son…You ready?"

"Yes," I responded.

I looked at Elizabeth.

"I'll call you."

"I'll be waiting," she responded. She gave me a hug and my father and I left out of the church.

"Tonight was a great night son," my father said to me. "It was good to see your sister sing at the beginning. I miss my little girl."

"I miss her too, Dad," I said while turning into our housing complex.

"She was an amazing young girl. Smart, funny, talented. She reminded me of a young female Senior. I love you son, but I think that your sister was going to be the one to take over for Senior whenever he decided to hang it up."

"Don't worry, Dad. I've often thought the same thing."

"Your mother, she's taking it hard. I think I'm going to take a week off of work and take her on a vacation. She's always wanted to visit

Europe. We just never got the chance to go. But now that our only child is grown, we can pretty much go anywhere." He said reluctantly.

"I'm not sure that Europe is the best place to go right now, I said. Knowing about Octavius and his war. I don't want my dad leaving the city.

"You don't think so? Well, you might have a point, it takes a lot of planning to just get up and leave the country. Not even sure if your mother's passport is renewed. Perhaps I'll go and rent all of our favorite movies, take her to a hotel with a fireplace and a hot tub, and just sit, eat, relax and enjoy each other's company. Turn our phones off and just be husband and wife."

"I think that idea would be much better than Europe. I think Mom would really enjoy that."

"Think she'll enjoy this?" He brought out a small box as I pulled into our garage.

The box had two rings in there, a male ring and a lady's ring. They looked similar. They had diamonds on the top of a woven yellow gold band. The inside of the band was normally sleek with the inscription, 'semper tuus ero' inscribed into the lady's ring, and 'semper tua ero' inscribed into the male's ring. "It means 'I am forever yours' in Latin. The last time your sister and I went out she had me buy these. Said it was necessary." He looked at them and smiled. They were beautiful rings.

"She'll love them."

"I hope so, son. I hope so. Do you think she still loves me?"

"Well, the day I accidentally made you break the coffee table," I said smiling.

"Accidentally. Ha… sure," he said sarcastically. "Don't think I forgot about that. I'll get you back." He said grabbing my shoulder and smiling.

"She slapped me pretty hard and told me not to disrespect you. If that's not love, she just doesn't like me," I said laughing.

He joined me.

"I love your mother, with my entire heart, son," he said to me. "I knew it the first day that I laid eyes on her in high school. We rushed, and had you, and then we married, had Sa'Rah. And life changed. I don't know where it all went downhill; it was slow rather than sudden. I saw it happening, she saw it happening, and you know Sa'Rah saw it happening. You, didn't really pay too much attention to us. You were so busy with Leon. Just know that I'm going to try my hardest son, my hardest to fight for this marriage, to be like my mom and dad, to last forever, through any and everything. Sickness and health, until death son. Until death," he said looking at me.

"Sa'Rah would've wanted it like that." He said as we walked into the back door through the kitchen.

My mom must've been up because the alarm wasn't set, and some lights were on. We turned the corner and to my surprise there was a man without a shirt on in the house holding two glasses and a bottle of wine. My dad was standing behind me and I felt him place his hands on my shoulders. He was trembling. The man dropped the glasses as they shattered on the floor I heard footsteps coming from upstairs. In my mind, I was praying and hoping it was one of my aunts, they had keys to the house and aren't strangers to coming over and sleeping over when they wanted to. They never had male company but there is a first time for everything.

"Is everything ok honey?"

My mother's voice rang through my ear as I felt my father's clinch on my shoulder tighten. My mother came into the view of the kitchen and saw my father and I. She gasped and put her hands over her mouth. She was wearing this man's shirt I presumed and it fit her like a short skirt.

I closed my eyes immediately. The man that was in there was familiar to me. His name was Isaac, and I met him some time ago when I had to stop Sa'Rah from yelling and screaming at everyone.

Mom, is this how we were to find out? After my dad just poured his heart out to me about his unwavering not giving up love for you. This is how you repay him. By having another man in his house?

I kept my cool. I concentrated really hard. Using my training, I blocked out all sound and listened for heart beats and breathing, there were three heart beats, the fastest one was behind me, my father's, it was pure anxiety filled with anger, sadness and pain, he was choked up in the breaths he was taking. My mother's was just as fast, it beat of fear and was breathing very fast. The third one was an anticipation breath, as his heart beat was slightly elevated.

My father was about to attack. He let go of my shoulder and tried to get around me but I stopped him grabbing his arm, using his momentum I spun him back around me.

"Let me go, Victor!" my dad screamed in pure anger and embarrassment. "Let me go!"

"Victor…" my mother began to say.

"Get out!" my father yelled.

"Just listen to me!" my mother screamed back, but her screamed didn't compare to the hurt I felt in my father's voice.

He was shaking, I wasn't going to let him fight this man, or fight my mother if that was in his intentions. I don't know what he's thinking, when someone is this hurt and angry, you have to assume that the worse was going to happen.

"Just let me…"

"Get OUT!" My father screamed even louder and held the out word longer until he was out of breath.

My mom jumped.

"Let's just go, Persia," Isaac said grabbing her arm and leading her out of the door.

Feeling my dad's body and temperance turn from anger to sadness, I released him. He just fell to his knees, he was weakened. He didn't have any fight in him at the moment. I looked at him, and I began to grow angry. I walked outside. His car was parked at our neighbors. He helped my mother into the front seat of his truck; he had a gray Nissan hybrid truck. He didn't hear me walk behind him. When he turned around he jumped backwards startled.

"Are you here to fight me?" he said catching his breath.

"I've fought enough for one day," I said dryly to him.

I didn't want to fight him. I didn't need to fight him to make a point. I looked at my mother; she looked back at me and burst into tears. I didn't feel sorry for her, she brought this on herself. "If I ever see you over here again…" I said looking at him. I didn't finish my sentence, the threat was made. It's one thing for someone to have an affair, it's another to have an affair in the house my father lays his head. That disrespect will not be tolerated. He understood as he got into the car and drove off.

I walked back into the house. My father wasn't in the kitchen any longer. I walked past the stairs and I heard a faint sound of him crying. He was in Sa'Rah's room from the sound of it. I walked up stairs. I walked into he and my mother's room, and the lights were off but the bed wasn't made up, it looked as if someone was in it. Although the bathroom door was closed, there was a glow in there.

I opened the door to their personal bathroom, when I opened the door I noticed candles lit with rose petals, and the Jacuzzi was filled with an aloe smelling bubble bath. I blew out all of the candles, cleaned up the rose petals, and drained the Jacuzzi. My father probably saw it, that's why the door was closed, no need for a reminder in the morning.

I took the sheets off of the bed, and their comforter and put them downstairs in the wash room, I was probably going to throw them away or donate them to a family in need. I cleaned up the broken glass in the kitchen and I made the bed up with their spare linen they kept. Afterwards I looked in Sa'Rah's room and my father was asleep on the bed, holding a family portrait of Sa'Rah, my mother, he and I. I turned the light out.

"You still love me," my dad said, sounding of a man trying not to fight tears. "Right, son?"

"With every beat of my heart, Dad," I responded as I closed the door.

I couldn't see my father like that. And I was sure he didn't want to be seen like that either. I walked down the stairs and noticed in the trash can was the box that held the rings Sa'Rah had told him to buy. I grabbed them; perhaps he'll use them another time. I took them downstairs with me. What a long day.

    I showered and went to sleep.

24

The next morning when I woke up, I took a shower. While I was in there, I was thinking about how I could fix what happened last night. Was there a way to fix it? Was there even a reason to fix it? My mother and Isaac have been flirting for quite some time now and last night was the straw that broke the camel's back.

I got dressed and went upstairs only to see my mother in the kitchen. She was washing some dishes that were in the sink. She had on clothes now. Looked like running clothes, an all-white jogging suit with black running shoes and her hair in a ponytail. She must be getting ready to take a jog.

"Good morning, Victor," my mother said to me in a very dry voice. "You must have a lot of questions."

"Good morning, Mother," I said to her as I kissed her on her cheek.

She was already sweating; she must've already had her jog.

"I do not have any questions. It's none of my business," I said to her as I began preparing breakfast before my morning meditation.

"You have to have some questions," she said. "Sa'Rah always had questions."

"But I'm not Sa'Rah," I said calmly back to her. "Sa'Rah is dead. And we should accept it, and move on with our lives."

"I miss her, Three. I really do. And Isaac was helping…"

"Don't do that," I said interrupting her.

"Don't do what?"

"Don't make what you and Isaac is doing anything about Sa'Rah. Don't put that on her. What you're doing with Isaac started before she died, and is continuing." I was aggravated by her trying to justify what she's doing with Isaac by putting it on Sa'Rah's death. I wasn't going to allow it. I couldn't allow it. "And if I were you, I wouldn't try to use that excuse on dad." He would not tolerate it, or be as calm about the rebuttal as I was.

I grabbed some fruit out of the refrigerator, an apple for their antioxidant compounds that prevents damage to cells and tissue, an orange for vitamin C, pineapple for its source of manganese, a grapefruit for its lycopene and ability to speed up metabolism, a banana for its soluble fiber and potassium, strawberries as a source for flavonoids, a pear for its source of dietary fibers, and some prunes for a small amount of proteins. Again, I have no clue how I know all of this, I'm assuming that I was learning all of this while sleep in my training, and that sometimes I'm just going to react without consciously remembering how I know why I am knowledgeable of this.

"Who bought all of this fruit?" I asked my mother.

"I did," my mother said softly, "Sa'Rah gave me a shopping list of fruits to buy for you. There are more in your refrigerator down stairs."

I smiled to myself.

"Where is your father?"

"He's not upstairs?"

"I checked. He wasn't in there."

"Did you try Sa'Rah's room?"

"I can't bring myself to go in there."

I went and checked the garage; my father's car was gone. I looked around the kitchen, there was no traces that my father had been in here to eat anything. My mother had been cleaning but she hasn't gotten to the counter top yet, when she cleans, she does the dishes first, then the cabinets, then the counters, to the floor.

"He's at Denny's," I proclaimed.

"How do you know that?"

"A hunch."

He needed the peace. It was his and Sa'Rah's favorite breakfast place, why wouldn't he go there to relive it, even if he was alone. His heart had taken a beating lately. The loss of Sa'Rah and now his wife with another man, and he walked into it. It's one thing to have suspicion or to hear rumors, but to see those rumors proven truthful is torturous. I rinsed off the fruit, cut them up into a bowl and began eating them.

"Slow down. The food isn't going anywhere," my mother said to me.

I was eating extremely fast. I was so used to showering, dressing and eating in thirty minutes. Time to me was incredibly precious and I didn't want to waste another minute. I didn't slow down. I just looked at my mother. Our eyes met for the first time, I'm not sure if she was avoiding me. But when our eyes met, and I looked into my mother's eyes, I saw Sa'Rah's eyes. They had the same eyes, green; it was as if I was staring at the older Sa'Rah. I lost focus for a second and I had to release the gaze.

"You have your father's eyes," my mother said sadly. "Beautiful, dark brown determined eyes."

She took a deep breath.

"I'm going to take a shower," she said and then walked out of the kitchen.

I finished eating.

After I finished eating I went outside, it was drizzling, but the sun was bright. I always found that odd, the sun would be out, but you could still feel rain drops. I walked to our back yard, which was fenced in to stop people from falling down the hill that lead to the creek. It was about a one hundred foot drop. It was Euclid creek, but not the park, just the creek that stretched all the way north from Lake Erie south to Pepper Pike.

I found a nice place behind the fence that wasn't too steep, but private enough where I wouldn't be bothered. I sat down, crossed my legs and began to control my breathing. I heard the birds around me, squirrels playing, bugs crawling and flying insects buzzing. Then, concentrating harder, I heard the faint sound of water traveling, and then no sound. I was in complete concentration. The world around me no longer existed.

My thoughts were only on Octavius, Malcolm, and the war. I didn't think about Fawzia, I didn't think about my parents, I didn't think about Sa'Rah, or Marcel, or my training, nothing. I wanted to find a tactical plan to confront Octavius and find a way to stop this war before more unnecessary bloodshed happens.

When I finally came out of my meditation the sun had been covered up by the clouds and the air had cooled off. No rain, but you felt the moisture in the air. I walked back into the house. I smelled my mother's perfume in the air faintly. I looked into the garage, her car was gone but my father was home.

I looked in the kitchen; on the counter was a bottle of alcohol. I grabbed it, I looked at it, it was a pint of Jack Daniels. There was nothing else in it. I smelled the bottle. The very smell of the liquor burned my nose hairs. I looked at the labeling, forty percent alcohol by volume. Well, if my father drank the entire thing by himself, he was passed out somewhere.

I looked around in the kitchen more. In the sink area there was a strong smell of the liquor. He must've poured some of it, if not all of it down the drain. I walked up stairs to see my father lying in his and my mother's bed.

"I didn't drink any of it," my father said.

"I know."

"I bought it, but when I smelled it, I just poured it all out in the sink, came up here and prayed. Where were you?"

"Out back."

"I looked, I didn't see you."

"Down by the hill that leads to the creek."

"What were you doing down there?"

"Meditating."

"About your mother and I?"

"No."

"Oh."

"Sorry. You and my mother, is between you and my mother."

"You've always been that way, son," my father said smiling getting up looking at me. "Senior wants us all to meet at his house tonight. Sort of like a family meeting."

"Ok. I'll be there."

"I hope so," he said. "Was your mother here?"

"You didn't see her?" I asked. Looking at the clock on the wall, it was nearly three o'clock, I had meditated for hours.

"No. I went to Denny's and when I returned, I just noticed she had been here, I didn't get a chance to talk to her."

"Do you want to talk to her?"

"Of course I do. She's still my wife. At least for now."

"Well, maybe you'll talk after tonight."

"She's not coming to the meeting."

"Why not?"

"She doesn't know about it."

"Why doesn't she?"

"Senior sounded like he wanted it to be just us for now."

My cell phone rang. It was a number I didn't know.

"Hello?" I answered.

"It's Malcolm. Turn on the television, any channel will do."

I quickly turned on the television in my parent's room. The president of the United States was making an address to the country.

"My fellow Americans," Deloris Williams started off saying. Deloris was a stout Caucasian woman. She had brunette hair, light brown eyes, and determined face. She was in her forties, and was voted in by a record setting number of women voters. Her voice was confident, intimidating but welcoming at the same time.

"It has been brought to my attention that war will soon be stepping foot on American soil. This war is a persecution of religious practices. It is a battle for the rights of Christians throughout the world, so that we can practice our beliefs freely and without judgment. It has been fought and resisted across the Atlantic Ocean for over a year now, and soon it will be here.

The leader of the resistance is Octavius Atavus, a personal friend of mine.

He and I have talked about this war extensively over the past few weeks. About what it means for America, for Christians, and for other religious sects. It will be dangerous. It will be difficult. But it is necessary. For too long we have suffocated our true thoughts, watered down our practice and compromised our beliefs. We have let others dictate the path of our lives.

This injustice goes on no longer.

Octavius has made us aware of a secret military strategy that has been planned for many years to attack us at the heart of our very freedoms. Today I stand before you to say, you should know your neighbors. They may not be who you think they are. Many enemies have tried to take away the freedoms of American, and the many great men and women of our military lost their lives to defend those freedoms. Over these long and troubled years, we have learned that freedom isn't free.

Octavius has been capturing and questioning not just Muslims, or Jews, but Christians as well. He will find anyone who stands in the way of the freedoms of our world, and who dares try to destroy the very roots of American society. Octavius has this government's full support and cooperation. My full support and cooperation.

From this date forward, America is in a federal state of emergency. As Commander-in-chief, I give Octavius the authority to capture and question, and prosecute anyone who challenges our freedoms. Octavius has permission to use his own men that he has brought over, who have all sworn an oath to America, and to protect America.

And now, I will let Octavius speak to you."

The people in the audience cheered ignorantly. President Williams spoke of Octavius capturing and questioning people regarding the very freedoms of our world. What she skipped out was how he was brutally killing millions of people overseas, and now that war is here, and she just gave him permission to be the judge, jury and executioner.

"Friends in high places huh?" Malcolm said to me on the phone. I forgot he was even there. I didn't respond. My father's face looked pale.

"Hello, Americans," Octavius said. His accent sounding much like Elizabeth's. "I am Octavius Atavus. I am a living descendent of Alexander of Macedonia, or what most people may call him, Alexander the Great. I've visited America many times in my life. I've visited the beautiful architecture of Columbus, Indiana. I'm seen the Monterey Peninsula of California and its deep Spanish and Mexican roots. I've been to New Orleans, Louisiana whose unbeatable spirit is moving and the food and music is soothing. I've rafted the Colorado River while enjoying the natural beauty of the Grand Canyon. I've celebrated New Year's many times at Times Square in New York, though cold, the bright lights warmed my heart. I've seen the Sante Fe Opera in Sante Fe New Mexico, I've hiked in the Mountains of Sangre de Cristo. I did not see Yoge Bear at Yellowstone National Park, although the bear I did see looked very hungry, but the scenery was beautiful and the air was fresh. I've swam on the beach of Cape Cod in Massachusetts and of course I've walked The Strip in Las Vegas, Nevada. I want you to ask yourself this. Have you done all of that? Have you went out and lived your life? How many of you go to work every day and disdain your existence? Just because I wasn't born in America doesn't mean that I'm not as American as the next person." He paused and looked at the audience in which was flashing pictures left and right throughout his speech.

"I stand before you today," he continued, "with great humility and reluctance of this authority that has been given to me. I often wish it had fallen upon someone else's lap. But it has fallen on my lap and with this authority I will conquer all that stand in the way of the very freedoms that make this country and other free countries in the world great. You have those that you may call your neighbor, those who may call you friend, those who seek to destroy you from within. I will quote to you a passage from the New International Translation bible. Second Corinthians chapter ten 'By the humility and gentleness of Christ, I appeal to you, I, Paul, who am timid when face to face with you, but bold toward you when away! I beg you that when I come I may not have to be as bold as I expect to be toward some people who think that we live by the standards of this world. For though we live in the world, we do not wage war as the world does. The weapons we fight with are not weapons of the world. On the contrary, they have divine power to demolish strongholds. We demolish arguments and every pretension that sets itself up against the knowledge of God, and we take captive every thought to make it obedient to Christ. And we will be ready to punish every act of disobedience, once your obedience is complete.' I will repeat 'We demolish arguments and every pretension that sets itself up against the knowledge of God, and we take captive every thought to make it obedient to Christ. And we will be ready to PUNISH! EVERY! ACT! Of disobedience, once your obedience is complete." He said the second verse with much more emphasis than the first half of the message.

"The devil is in full force to attack your freedoms. His biggest armies? The Muslims, the Jews, the atheist, anyone who does not believe in Christ. I implore any American who dare calls themselves Christian, to stand up, take arms, and demolish any argument and every pretension that sets itself up against the knowledge of Christ. Take no prisoners, punish every act of disobedience. Ephesians six eleven, 'put on the full armor of God so that you can take a stand against the devil's schemes.' Romans thirteen twelve, 'The night is nearly over; the day is almost here. So let us put aside the deeds of darkness and put on the armor of light.' Ephesians four fourteen 'Then we will no longer be infants, tossed back and forth by the waves, and blown here and there by every wind of teaching and by the cunning and craftiness of men in their deceitful scheming' Ephesians six thirteen 'Therefore put on the full armor of God, so that when the day of evil comes, you may be able to stand your ground, and after you have done everything, to stand.' Second Corinthians six seven, 'in truthful speech and in the power of God' with weapons of righteousness in the right hand and in the left.' James four seven 'Submit yourselves, then to God. Resist the devil, and he will flee from you.' And if there is someone who calls themselves Christian, and they refuse to take up arms, if they refuse to put on the armor of God, they are in league of the devil, and the devil must be slain." He said and walked away from the podium wearing an all-white suit with a blue cape with gold trimming tailing behind him. He left with thunderous applause by the audience.

"You still there, Victor?" Malcolm said on the other end. "The president just gave the most dangerous man in the world permission to kill whoever he sees fit. Still want to keep that promise to me?"

"My word is still my bond, Malcolm," I said to him.

"There will be an outbreak after that message. Which will play right into Octavius' hands. There will be attacks after attacks and soon the so called true Christians will take up arms, and kill without penalty, convict without trial, and be celebrated. Is this the end of the world as we know it?" I remained silent. I was in shock as to what I just heard and saw on American television. The president just used her power to do what she wants to protect American people and gave power to someone who is going to kill American people. Is this the war I was trained for? "Victor?"

"I'm here, Malcolm," I said breaking my silence. "My father and I are on our way to my grandfather's house in Bratenahl. Do you know where his house is?"

"It's my job to know where my enemy's base is."

"We are not your enemy. Meet me there."

"Should I bring my weapon?"

"Do you think it'll help you against me?" I said sarcastically.

"I'll bring it. I'll see you there," Malcolm said as he hung up.

I looked at my father and he was sitting on his bed in shock. I didn't have time to comfort his disbelief of what just happened.

"Father," I said to him. "It's time to go."

My father didn't say anything. He looked at me in complete confusion.

"Did that just happen?" he asked me.

"It did. But don't worry, everything will be fine. We have to get to Senior's. Meet me in the garage in ten minutes." I said reassuring to him and stern with my command.

I left the room and dialed my mother. I had several text messages coming through from several people asking me about what just happened. Nothing from Fawzia but I didn't concern myself with it.

"Victor, did you just watch the…" my mother answered.

"Yes. Where are you?" I said interrupting her.

"I'm at your grandfather's house."

"Senior's?"

"No, my father."

"Stay there, do not go near the windows, lock the doors, and if anything happens, call me. I will be there soon."

"No son, we're going to the Kingdom Hall for a meeting. I'll see you at home afterwards."

"I don't think that's a good idea right now."

"It's ok, honey. Everything will be fine," she said sounding as calm as she'd been in the past. "I'll talk to you later, be safe out there."

She hung up the phone.

I didn't think she was at Grandfather Persy's house. I dialed his number next.

"This is a surprise," Grandpa Persy said as he answered his phone. "How are you doing, Victor?"

"I'm doing good Grandpa. Did you just watch the news?"

"Yes I saw it. Nothing new to me, people have been trying to kill us since we started. Now they just giving them power."

"Is my mother over there?" I hated to be so direct with him. I don't call him as often as I should. But we never really had that type of relationship, I would normally check on him through my mother.

"No, your mother hasn't been over here since she came over half naked and crying last night because your father kicked her out of the house. I'm glad that she has Isaac in her life. What kind of man kicks his wife out the house like that?"

"Ok Grandpa. Thank you. I love you, I'll talk to you soon." I said as I hung up the phone.

I didn't have time to tell him what really happened, he may actually know what really happened and may just be angry because my father kicked her out. My mother lied to me. She's with Isaac right now. Well I hope he keeps her safe, if anything happens to her, I'm holding him solely responsible. I went to my room and grabbed my old steel sword. It wasn't as sharp as I would like it to be, but it'll do. I put it in its sheath and carried it upstairs with me to the car. My father was already in the passenger's seat.

"Why do I have to drive everywhere?" I asked him smiling trying to ease the tension.

"Because you're younger and more alert," he said back to me smiling.

"I am more alert. I'm not sure about younger, you look younger than me," I joked. "We have to get to Senior's fast. So I'll be driving fast."

"Let's go," my father said putting on his seatbelt.

We pulled out of the garage and we were on our way.

25

The ride over to Senior's was normal. There were a few more police vehicles and horses in the street. But there was no fighting, no people gathering in the street as I expected. Pulling into Senior's house, it was very normal out. I saw Malcolm hiding behind a tree near the front yard. My father didn't notice him. All my father and I discussed was Octavius' speech.

"I'll be in, in a moment father," I told my dad when we parked.

The drive way was full. Christina was there, Aunt Victory and Victoria were there, and even Elizabeth's car was there.

"Ok, son," my father said as he walked into the house.

I walked towards Malcolm and noticed he brought two of his men with him. My sword was in its sheath around my waist. Malcolm and his two men were armed, but didn't seem to be in an aggressive stance. I never saw these two men of his before. Although I do not remember many of them from the night on the bridge, these aren't apart of the five that had jumped me.

"Hello, Malcolm," I said to him as we shook hands.

"Victor," Malcolm said back. "These two men are my most trusted. This is Azeem."

He pointed to his left, Azeem was a smaller man, looked to be in his mid to late twenties, he was clean shaven, and wore the garment that Malcolm wore, black shirt, with black pants and black shoes. He was very thin, lighter than I am.

"This is Wajeeh."

Wajeeh was about half a foot taller than I am. He looked as if he should be playing professional football, around my age, curly hair, and darker skin with a full goatee. I shook both of their hands.

"We don't really have ranks here but if I am the leader, Azeem is second in command and Wajeeh is third. Azeem is good at tactics and planning, Wajeeh is good at implementing the strategy. What is your strong suit other than fighting Victor?"

"Everything," I said to him, I was trained in everything. I noticed that some of the neighbors were looking at us.

Even through Senior's bushes and fence they were looking and pointing and talking amongst themselves. "Let's go out back."

They followed me to Senior's private path on the beach. The last place Sa'Rah and I had a conversation.

"Are we to really stand up to Octavius and his massive army?" Azeem spoke. "Octavius has millions at his command, and not to mention those who he told to take up arms today. They may not be trained, but they can make a mess."

"We won't sit here and let him massacre innocent people are we?" I said to them. "I'm a Christian, I believe in Jesus Christ as my Lord and Savior, but I won't condemn you and execute you for not believing in the same. This war, his war, is not a war of the Lord, and I wouldn't be a true Christian if I let him slaughter innocent people. American or not, Christian or not, doesn't matter to me. So yes, we're going to fight him, and anyone else who thinks this is the answer."

"You don't look like much of a fighter," Wajeeh said. "Are you sure he's the one that took out every one on the bridge."

"Careful what you say Wajeeh." Malcolm said to him. "This is him, and he's better than you think. Give him the respect you would give me." Wajeeh said nothing; he shook his head in agreement. "Where are your men Victor?" He asked the very question I was thinking of myself. I don't have anyone other than Malcolm's people to help with this cause. I needed to get to work, find people to support my cause, get them trained, and get my own people who could help with what's to come.

"I don't have anyone as of now Malcolm. But I'll get help," I spoke honestly to him.

"Well, from now on, my men are your men," Malcolm said.

Wajeeh and Azeem both knelt down before me. It was embarrassing.

"Don't kneel to me. Only kneel to your God," I said to them.

"Don't take that from them," Malcolm said. "It's a sign of respect and honor."

"We don't have too much time for this," Azeem said. "I'll tell you what I know General." He referred to me as General. "There is a massive naval fleet preparing to set sail for Cleveland from Rondeau Provincial Park in Canada. Somewhere around one hundred thousand warriors. They aren't our friends. They are coming to take over a single city in the United States, all they need is one City, and then they can expand from there. When Octavius started this war, this plan was set to motion. Hundreds of thousands of Muslims have made their way to Canada, and have been training for this moment. I don't know when they are to set sail, but it will be in a few months, maybe less. They aren't coming to befriend Malcolm or his men, they are coming to cleanse everyone out, and start anew."

"They'll need more than one hundred thousand," I said. That's a lot of men, but they are vastly outnumbered.

"They have more than that. But if one hundred thousand attack, and then another one hundred thousand come, and more keeps coming. Cleveland's defenses will be over-whelmed. Not to mention if Octavius men know about this, which I'm sure they do, it's going to be a battle on both sides. We do not have the numbers. All the people you love here in Cleveland, they will be killed, the women, the children, everyone. And if Octavius wins, you'll be killed." Marcel never told me that I would be planning a defense for Cleveland. I've learned tactics, I've learned how to defend, how to fight and how to lead. But training is different from real life.

VENSIN GRAY

"How many men do you have Malcolm?" I asked.

"A few hundred," Malcolm said humbly.

"But that number is to grow vastly after Octavius' speech," Wajeeh said. "Malcolm's father was a well-connected man. Knew a lot of people who will fight for his son."

"Malcolm," I said. "It is important to tell your men, and your people, whatever they do, only defend themselves, do not attack first. That is what Octavius wants. The president figures that speech will outrage the nation, someone will throw the first blow publically and then it will justify her putting us in a state of emergency. Do not throw the first punch."

I just thought of Octavius' plan in a matter of seconds. Azeem and Wajeeh took to discussing this with Malcolm and they agreed with me. After several minutes of talking and planning. Azeem gave me a look.

"You're Fawzia's friend right?" he asked.

"I guess you can put it that way. Why?" I asked him. It was an out of the blue question.

"Whatever you did to her, her father is infuriated," Azeem said.

"I agree. I've never seen Baasim that angry before," Malcolm said. "What did you do?"

"I haven't done anything to Fawzia," I said to them.

"I believe him," Malcolm said. "I will call you when we have an update of things to come. You should work on getting yourself an army, and fast, and in secret. If Octavius makes a visit here first, we're doomed." Malcolm said as he, Azeem and Wajeeh all left quickly.

I'd have to meditate on this later. I didn't even know who to contact about help. I looked at how calm the water looked, and how the Sun was directly above me. I wished I was a fish, they didn't have to worry, just swim all day and try not to get eaten.

I walked into Senior's house with all eyes on me.

"Who were your friends?" Leon said to me with a scold on his face.

"Hello everyone," I said as I made my rounds to hug everyone in the living room. We all sat down. "That was a friend of mine, Malcolm…"

"Malcolm?" Leon rudely interrupted. "The Muslim who jumped you?"

"You were jumped!?" my father yelled out.

Everyone started questioning me about what happened. I looked at Leon, why would he do that? Why is he making this about me?

"Everyone, everyone. Please calm down," Senior said taking control of the room. "Three, please tell us about Malcolm."

"Thank you, Senior." I said looking at Leon. "Malcolm and I had a little scuffle…"

"He jumped you and left you for dead," Leon said interrupting me again.

"Leon, please." Christina said. I understood Leon was angry, perhaps a bit jealous that I was talking to Malcolm.

He and I hadn't really had a chance to hang out. He still hadn't told me where he was during the concert. We'd talk about that, and why he kept interrupting me later.

"We had a scuffle, it's been resolved. I told him to meet me here to discuss what the president and Octavius just declared. I asked him to do his best to make sure life is ran as normal. No one fighting anybody."

"That was smart of you," Senior said standing up. "I've known about this for quite some time now. The reason why I shut down the church and Sunday operations was for the protection of the congregation. I gave my word to a few influential leaders that until this war is stopped, then I won't feel right holding church while there are people being slaughtered. May not make sense, there's no defense of it in the Bible, but I didn't want to hold church and on the way out, someone or a lot of people got killed. The Muslims are just like us, just trying to hold on to the customs in which they believe. Unfortunately there is a Christian, or a claiming Christian in power to threaten their very freedoms. Well our freedoms. We aren't taking up arms and fighting anyone."

"Isn't Octavius your cousin?" Leon said directing his question to

Elizabeth who was sitting next to me.

"Yes," she replied.

"What's his problem?" Leon continued to question her.

"I don't know Leon. I'm not Octavius," she said sounding a bit nervous.

"And she shouldn't be questioned as if his actions are a reflection of her intentions," I said to Leon.

"Why is she even here?" Leon said. "Who are you with Victor? Her or that Muslim girl?"

"I invited her here, Leon," Senior said.

"I'm sorry, Senior," Leon said calming down. "But it's funny, you can speak up for her, but not for yourself. Why do you have your sword Victor?"

Everyone looked at me. I'd always carried it around, it was nothing new.

"It's never been a problem before," I said to Leon.

Had Sa'Rah been there, they would be arguing at how and why he continued to call me out.

"Three's sword isn't the problem right now, it's Octavius' sword. And we have to find a way to get it dulled down, hopefully the people here in America won't buy into this."

"Please, Daddy," Aunt Victoria said. "There are people who aren't Christians who are going to claim to be if they can take arms and fight somebody. This is a disaster waiting to happen."

"I agree with Victoria, Dad," my father said. "Just like aggression in young men who play sports or violent video games, they are just looking to satisfy that hunger. Octavius just gave a free pass to kill whoever you see fit."

"Including us," Aunt Victory said. "We aren't taking arms, then we are the so-called Christians. We either have to hide, or take up arms with Octavius. If he finds out Victor Thomas isn't agreeing with his war, he may make a point of you."

"Over my dead body," Leon said standing up. "Someone has to protect Senior."

Leon looked at me with anger in his eyes. I ignored him. I didn't know what his deal was, but I wasn't letting it get to me.

"I won't need any protection, grandson," Senior said touching Leon on the shoulders.

Leon went and sat next to Christina. I got a text on my phone from Aunt Victory.

'What is with him?'

I ignored it. I would talk with her later.

"Who are you texting Victor?" Leon said to me. "Your Muslim friend?"

"Yeah, who are you texting son, this is important," my father said to me.

I put my phone in my pocket and smiled at Aunt Victory. She laughed a bit.

"I'm going to be meeting with other leaders of the church tomorrow; we're all going to discuss what Octavius has said. Presently, from what I know, the Pope has giving him authority over the Catholics, and he is the most powerful Christian right now, and that speech, right now, won't do anything until someone does something stupid in retaliation. I'm sure the newspapers and the media is going to do its best to embezzle whatever is going to sell papers. Which is war, regardless of the casualties. I just want you all to be careful. Don't talk about your faith in public, do not tell anyone what church you attend, and don't talk to anyone about what they do. Our purpose right now is to keep quiet, stay out of the way. But continue to live your lives as normal as possible," Senior said. He seemed more worried than he was letting on.

"I'll have to do some praying, but God will give us the answer, God will show us the way. And whatever you do, do not be the one who starts this war."

"Yeah, Victor. Keep your sword in your sheath," Leon said smiling trying to make it appear to be a joke.

Everyone but me laughed. He wasn't joking. For the next several minutes, everyone engaged in small talk. I did my best to avoid Leon. I spoke mainly with Aunt Victory and Elizabeth about how weird he was acting. She has never seen him act like this. I told her that I wasn't sure. After the talking was dying down a bit, Leon approached me.

"Why don't you tell us all about your time at college?" Leon said to me.

"Yes Three, tell us about college, you barely talked to any of us while you were away," Aunt Victoria said. Everyone gathered around Leon and me.

"Yeah, Victor. Tell us about college. Tell us about the time I saw you barely able to walk, going back to your dorm? Tell us why you weren't in any classes, and people didn't even know you attended the school. Tell us why you never came home to visit. Didn't call anyone, you and I never hung out one time while you were there. Every time I came to your dorm you were gone."

It was a logical question. He made good points. It would be tough to tell them that I received this so called ProChrist training from a guy that I killed. Senior would understand, but I don't want to talk about it in front of them before he and I had a chance to talk about it. I stood there looking at everyone looking at me. I didn't know what to say.

"Better yet, tell us why Elizabeth and I had to rescue you at Niagara Falls the day of Sa'Rah's funeral?"

"You were at Niagara Falls?" my father said to me looking at me confused. "You left your sister's funeral to go to Niagara Falls?"

"Maybe that's why Sa'Rah is gone," Leon said. "No love from her brother."

As angry as I was before he said that. I reached a level in which Leon and I were going to have to talk privately. Whatever I did to him to make him act like this has to be discussed. He's my brother, my heart, I love him, he's stood up for me, he's had my back, he's supported me, but that doesn't justify him acting this way and saying the things he's saying.

There was a hard knock at the door just before I was going to open my mouth to say something. My father answered it. It was Fawzia and her father. Fawzia walked in, eyes looking directly towards the floor. Followed by her father.

"Baasim," Senior said walking towards him, shaking his hand. "What are you doing here?"

"I apologize for interrupting your family's meeting," Fawzia's father spoke. "Hello Mr. Thomas."

"Are you here to discuss what Octavius just said?" Senior asked him.

"I've had my run ins with Atavus before," Baasim said. "I'm here to discuss Fawzia."

Senior looked at me confused. I looked at Fawzia, but she didn't look back at me. I didn't know what was going on.

"Please have a seat then," Grandma Patrice said standing up offering a seat.

"There is no reason to sit. But thank you Mrs. Thomas," Fawzia's father said looking at me very angrily.

"Victor Thomas the Third," my father said to me. "What did you do?"

"I haven't done anything," I said to my dad.

"How do we know that?" my father yelled. "Like Leon said, we didn't hear from you for three months, you come back here, your sister's dead, you leave her funeral, what is going on with you!"

Everyone was staring at me. I didn't know what was going on. I understand that I was gone for a long time, but it wasn't to be with Fawzia. I didn't know how to answer any of their questions. I looked at Senior for help. But he looked at me, he shook his head. He didn't have any answers.

"What is there to discuss about Fawzia sir?" I said to Baasim.

"I'm disowning her." Baasim said, his voice was a bit choked up.

He was fighting the emotional of pain. Fawzia started crying instantly.

"What did you do to her, Victor!" my dad screamed at me.

Everyone in the room jumped a bit but me.

"Junior, calm yourself," Senior said to him. "Give him a chance to explain what is going on. What is going on Baasim, that is a very serious gesture."

"She..." Baasim said. "Is with child."

Everyone gasped in the room.

"And I'm here to give her to the father of her child."

Everyone's eyes were on me. I looked directly at Fawzia. She looked up and our eyes met. She glanced at Leon who had suddenly become really quiet. My heart started to race.

"Dad," I said to my father.

"Yes, son. You have some explaining to do," he said to me trying to calm down.

"The day that Sa'Rah was with Senior, the day before you found out she passed away overnight. Did Leon come?"

"No, son. Why would Leon had come?" my father answered sounding confused.

"Leon," I said looking at Leon who was standing a few feet from me.

He didn't look up at me.

"I sent you here, the day before Sa'Rah died. Where did you go?"

"Don't make this about, Leon!" my dad yelled at me.

"Is it true, Victor?" Elizabeth said to me. Her eyes were tearing up.

We stared directly at one another. It was quiet for a few seconds, I heard Fawzia crying some more as everyone awaited my answer.

"I'm still a virgin," I said quietly looking down.

Fawzia began to cry even harder. My emotions ran rapid. I felt Elizabeth's hands on mine, but it didn't nothing to comfort the betrayal I was feeling. Fawzia, the first girl I ever fell in love with. Risked everything for, was almost killed for, is pregnant by Leon. My brother, the one who told me that if I did anything to betray his trust, he wouldn't trust anyone else in the world.

"Leon!" Christina said standing up. "Wha?"

Christina couldn't get the words out of her mouth. Her eyes watered and she began crying. Grandma Patrice and Aunt Victoria ran to her. Senior and my father were looking at him. Baasim looked at him in disgust. Elizabeth was talking to me, but I didn't hear any words that she was saying. My anger meter just broke.

"I sent you here to save my sister!" I said to Leon in the Angelic tongue.

Everyone stopped and looked at me. Senior's face was shocked. I knew Senior and Leon were the only ones who could understand what I was saying.

"I sent you here to save my sister!" I said to Leon again in Angelic tongue.

My heart was racing, my blood was boiling, I was more angry than I had ever been in my life. I walked towards Leon. My father began speaking and walking towards us, I didn't hear anything he said. I had tunnel vision, I could only see Leon.

"Tell me you didn't sleep with Fawzia!" Continuing in the Angelic language.

A shocked Leon looked up at me, and then to Fawzia. I looked their eyes. Guilt was over their faces. I breathed deeply.

"I trusted you!" I screamed to Leon as I struck him with my fist. I snatched my arm from Elizabeth. Nothing was going to calm me down. I heard voices, but I didn't hear anything. Leon stumbled over and looked at me. *"I trusted you with my sister's life!"* I yelled to him and struck him again.

"I don't want to hurt you," Leon said to me in perfect Angelic tongue. *"How do you even know this language?"* Leon asked, getting up from where I had knocked him down.

I'm sure he thought he could beat me, but he couldn't. He was just guilty. I wanted him angry. I cleared my mind and was finally able to hear what was around me.

"Victor stop!" I heard Fawzia yell.

Everyone looked scared. I turned and Baasim was gone. Senior went to help Leon up, my father was looking at me, and everyone looked shocked as to what just happened. I wasn't finished. Not even close.

"Why should I stop Fawzia?" I said reverting back to English. "Why shouldn't I hurt him? You don't know what I went through in Michigan. You don't know how every day I would crawl back to my dorm, bleeding, in pain, barely breathing, and the only thing that got me back to my dorm was the hopes that you had texted me? Called me? Something. But I got nothing! I was gone for three months and we talked maybe twice. The only thing that kept me company was Sa'Rah and Elizabeth's journal. Sa'Rah is gone now! And I sent Leon home to check on her the day before she died, and what does he do? He goes to visit you?"

I stood quiet for a second.

"Tell me your dreams, and I shall see them come to pass." I said, "Now I understand those dreams I had, they were reality. I dreamed of you, and in the dreams I was Leon. And this entire time I thought I did something wrong to you. And you say that you feel indifferent about me. Indifferent?"

Everyone looked at Leon. Leon looked at me, he was getting angry. I saw it in his movements. He wasn't angry enough for me. Not yet. I looked at his mother, who was crying.

"Like father like son huh, Leon?" I said looking at Christina, who looked up at me. I just hit a chord with her, and Leon knew it.

"How dare you!" Leon screamed to me in the Angelic language. Leon was stronger and faster than me. I was going to have to use those to my advantage. He charged me, just like my father, I used his momentum against him, I stepped to the side and threw him near Fawzia. She stepped in between us.

"I'll go through her to get to you," I said to Leon. He gently touched her arms to move but she didn't. Elizabeth got up and grabbed her hands and led her out of the way.

"Leon! Victor!" my dad yelled. "Stop this non sense! You're scaring everyone!"

"Three. Please. Listen to your father," Senior said to me.

"Not this time. Not today. My sister could be alive if he had done what I asked him to do."

Leon was still angry, I don't know why, but when he's mad, you feel it in the air. It got really hot. Leon came to attack me. He swung angrily, all towards my face. I dodged every hit while leading him away from everyone. When we were finally in the front room, I decided to go on the offensive. Leon wasn't going to tire out, I would get tired of dodging hits before he tires out. His stamina isn't of this world. He threw a left hook, with my forearms I blocked it and hit him in the chest with my left elbow. He tried to counter with a right punch to my stomach, I hit his arm down with my left hand and with my forearm, I hit him in the nose. Blood started pouring from his nose. He looked at me; he was surprised at how fast our last exchange just went. I heard my father and Senior behind me. Leon's back was to the largest window of the house. I saw my father and Senior's reflection in it.

"Maybe," Leon said wiping his nose. *"Maybe Sa'Rah would be alive if I was her brother instead of you."*

After Leon said that I attacked him with full force. I kicked his shin, he stepped to the left and threw a wild right hand punch towards my head, I aggressively parried it, he lost his balance, I rose my right foot up and kicked him; he flew backwards out of the window. I stepped out of the window. I don't know what came over me. But my anger was pouring out of my sweat glands. I wanted to take Leon's life. I grabbed the handle of my sword.

"Victor!" I heard my father scream.

"Victor no!" Elizabeth yelled.

"Leon watch out!" Christina screamed.

"Three! Sheath your sword!" Senior called out.

I didn't pay attention to any of them. My sister was dead because he decided to go sleep with the woman I loved. The only vengeance I needed was to make him suffer. I drew my sword and rose it up above my head with both hands. Leon's eyes caught mine, he just looked up at me, his nose was bleeding, and tears ran down his eyes. It didn't stop my anger. Good bye brother. I said to myself. I swung my sword down.

"Noooo!!!"

I could collectively hear everyone behind me scream. I heard a clash of metals together right when my sword was about to strike Leon. My sword was cut in half. The sword that was used to cut it looked exactly like my diamond blade my father had bought me for graduation. I looked at the person wielding it. He looked very similar to Leon. He was a few inches taller than I. His eyes were black. He wore a black shirt, a black trench coat, black pants and black shoes with a black derby hat.

"Oh my God." I heard Christina say. "It's Leon…"

26

Breathing heavily, I stepped back and looked at my sword. It was completely cut in half, a difficult task for anyone to cut steel. I smelled the burning of the metal. I looked at the person wielding the sword that cut mine in half. He was looking at Leon on the ground.

"*Stand up Leon,*" the man said in angelic tongue.

Leon looked at him and stood up.

"*Who are you?*" Leon responded getting to his feet.

I was backing up, looking at my family who was looking at me in disappointment; Senior was looking at the man who saved Leon. I felt ashamed.

"*Calm yourself, Young Victor. Today, I am not your enemy.*" He said looking directly at me. Should I attack him? What if he's a threat? "*I would control my thoughts if I were you. Marcel trained you well, but not well enough to take on me. Not yet at least.*" He said reading my thoughts just as Marcel once did. "*You haven't told them about your time in Hell I see Victor the Victorious.*"

"*Who are you?*" Leon screamed at him.

"*Control your tongue!*" The man screamed at Leon.

His voice, the power of it raised struck fear into me, Leon took a step backwards.

"Hello Christina. I see you haven't told Leon about his, true father. And Victor, I see you haven't told anyone of Leon's bloodline." We all looked at Senior and Christina.

"Leon, it's…" Christina started talking. "It's been…"

"I am not Sin!" the man screamed at Christina. "Do not call me that name again."

"Hello, Xin." Senior said to the man. "What are you doing here? Where is Sin?"

"Who is Sin?" Christina asked.

"Does this ring a bell?" Xin went into his pocket and brought out a necklace. It was gold, with woven like silk in strands with angel wings as a pendant; it was the most beautiful necklace I had ever seen. "I took the liberty of adding the pendant on myself. It's only fit for my brother's s…"

"I would rather tell them myself, Xin," Senior said interrupting Xin.

"Very well. Have at it," Xin said to him walking towards me. "I believe this belongs to you. Took a tumble down the falls." He said smiling.

His teeth were as white and straight as I've ever seen teeth look in my life.

"Why don't you go have a drink?" He said to me.

Suddenly, Vita rode up next to me.

"Son, where are you going?" My father shouted out.

"Let him go," Senior said to my father.

I got on Vita, I looked at everyone. I caught eyes with Christina who was fixated on Xin. Aunt Victoria and Aunt Victory were both waving at me and standing by Grandma Patrice who was holding on to Senior's hand. Senior looked at me with one of those 'We have to talk later' looks. My father looked confused. I looked to Elizabeth who had tears going down her face. Then I saw Fawzia who was looking right at me. She looked incredibly sad. Then I looked to Leon, my brother, who I just tried to kill. Our eyes locked for a long time, and Vita took off running.

"I love you!" I heard Leon yell in the angelic tongue.

"I love you too." I said in my head.

SON OF SIN

Go take a drink? I thought to myself. I rode Vita to the Masterplan. It had to be the place this Xin was talking about. I walked into the front door. It was unusually crowded for it to be early evening. The sun hasn't even begun to descend yet. I sat up on the bar stool at the bar. The bartender was unfamiliar to me. He was a middle aged Caucasian man, thin with medium cut brown hair. He wore a white button up shirt, some black dress pants and some really nice black dress shoes.

"What's your poison?" he asked me.

"I'm not old enough to drink," I responded to him.

"Non-sense man. If you weren't old enough to drink you wouldn't have sat up here," he went and got a shot glass and poured me a shot of brown liquor. He sat it in front of me and tended to the other people sitting at the bar. Eventually he made his way back to me.

"What's your name?" He asked me.

"Victor," I responded.

"I'm Mark," he said sticking out his hand.

We shook hands.

"Mark Warman is the name. And if you aren't going to drink this, would you mind if I did?"

I shook my head no. I was in no mood to drink anything. I was full of mixed emotions, I was just angry enough that I almost killed the closest person living in my life. He also slept with my girlfriend, who ignored me to the point of insanity. He also didn't get here in time to save Sa'Rah, he made a detour that could haunt him for the rest of his life. Maybe that's why he was coming at me like that today, maybe he wanted me to attack him, and maybe he wanted to be punished. Elizabeth, what am I going to do about her? She just saw a side of me that I didn't know I had in me. Not to mention what my aunts and grandmother think about me. What about my mom, where is she? I hope she is ok. This war, recruiting, I need help. Where Is Helen?

"You know, the last time I saw someone looking like you looked, they just lost someone important to them," Mark said to me. "My father had passed away, and I wasn't ready to let him go. I was in the early

VENSIN GRAY

thirties, working a decent job, no children, and my dad just, passed on. I didn't understand it at the time. I was angry, I was lost, and this was the man who had guided me through everything in life. And in one second I was alone. Want to know who guided me Victor? God. God showed me the light my young brother."

"Your father died not too long ago huh?" I said to him, he looked as if he was in his mid-thirties, could pass for last twenties. He was dressed way too neatly to be a bartender at the Masterplan.

"My dad died over fifteen years ago," he said. I felt confused.

"How old are you?" I asked him.

"Never ask a gentleman his age," Mark said smiling at me. "We'll talk soon. I have to tend to the other patrons. Your drink is still there if you want it."

I looked at the liquor that was in front of me. I smelled it, it smelled like the same exact liquor my father had. I reached my hand out to grab the glass to taste the liquor. Perhaps it would calm my nerves, perhaps it would help me feel better about everything that had just happened.

"I don't think you want to drink that, Victor Thomas the Third," said a familiar voice behind me, it was Helen.

She grabbed the drink and drank it very fast and motioned for Mark for more.

"Helen!" I said excitingly. I never thought I'd be glad to see the woman who almost killed me every day for two months.

"Hello, Victor," she said to me. She wasn't dressed like a warrior today, she had red shirt, some blue jeans, and her hair was sleeked down. "I owe you for kneeing me in the stomach." She said as she smiled. "The war is starting sooner than I expected."

She took more drinks from Warman. She drank them very fast and looked at me.

"I'm not totally confident that you are ready, but Marcel thought you were ready before your training, so I'll carry out his wishes."

"Marcel's…" I said, hesitating, how am I going to explain to her that I killed him.

"Marcel is where Marcel needs to be. Think nothing else of it," Helen said as I heard a glass hit the table where Senior, my father and I would normally sit.

I looked back and there was a man back there, dressed very similar to Xin. His face was hidden in the shadow.

"Don't concern yourself with him," Helen said to me.

"I need to start get an Army," I said to Helen. "I have information about an attack from the north."

"You're going to need more than an Army to take out Octavius and the ones who are sailing from Canada," Helen said smirking.

"How do you know about the ones sailing from Canada?"

"It's my job to know," she said as she drank more shots. "And don't worry about gathering an Army, worry about keeping people alive. The rest will sort its self out on its own. Tomorrow at first sunlight, your horse will be there to get you, she's going to take you to a place that you will get further instructions. Be up, be ready. Take your friend Malcolm too, it'll be a nice ride for you two." She said as she stood up.

"I must bid you fair well now, Victor Thomas the Third," she walked over to the man in the shadow and sat down at the table with him. Warman joined them as another bartender, one that was familiar to me showed up. She was a fair skinned older African American woman.

"Hello, Grandson," I turned to see Senior sitting down next to me. "We have to talk."

"How is everyone?" I asked.

"They are in shock," Senior said as he told the bartender he didn't want anything to drink. "Your aunts are tending to your grandmother. Elizabeth followed your father home to make sure he made it there safely. Christina took Fawzia home with her for Fawzia is in the care of our family for now."

Senior said as he paused and just stared in the distance with a blank face.

"What about Leon and that Xin guy?" I asked trying to break him

VENSIN GRAY

out of his moment of silence.

"You won't be seeing Leon for a while," Senior said. "He wept at learning some things about himself. He wept harder knowing that he had hurt you. I told him this before he left, I told him, from Proverbs eighteen verse nineteen, *A brother offended is hard to be won than a strong city. And their contentions are like bars to a castle.* What that means Three is that the closer two people are, the more difficult it becomes to reconcile differences once one has deeply hurt the other. I know you are angry with Leon grandson, but you will have to find it in your heart to forgive him."

"I've forgiven him already," I said calmly. "Doesn't excuse what he did, I asked him to come home to basically save Sa'Rah, instead, he goes and sleeps with a woman that I was in love with. I'm not even sure how long it's been going on. But that wound is deep. He is still my brother, and we will talk. What did he learn about himself?"

"As you know, Leon wasn't normal. He is a lot like his father," Senior said slowly.

"He was a lot more than Ian," I said.

"Ian wasn't his father," Senior said looking at me.

"Ian wasn't his father? Then who was his father?"

"His father, is a man, or rather something else, and everyone knew him as Leon. But his real name was Sin. Sin was from Heaven. This is going to sound crazy but Sin is an Angel."

That explained a lot. After my training with Marcel and Helen I was going to believe anything Senior had to say. But Senior would never lie to me.

"I believe you," I said reassuring my grandfather that I believed him. Leon was exceptionally gifted in everything.

Not being totally human makes more sense than luck.

"I have a lot of explaining to do to Christina and your grandmother. This is something I kept from them since Leon's conception. Sin was my best friend. He saved my life on several occasions. Helped form the man you have in front of you today. He predicted that you would be important to Christianity. I often hoped that it would be in a different way. But I can see that you have improved in your combat the way you easily handled Leon. You looked a lot like Sin in your movements. I miss him. I could really use him now, with Octavius, and what he's bringing to America. Life as we know it is about to change…"

"You would think for the better," said someone in a thick French accent.

I turned around and it was Marcel!

"Marcel!" Senior and I said at the same time.

"Hello, Victors." Marcel said as he sat down in between Senior and I, he motioned for a drink.

"It's been a long time Victor the Victorious. How have you been my friend?" he said to Senior.

"I killed you," I said in complete shock.

"Obviously not," Marcel said sarcastically.

"My friend," Senior got up smiling and hugged Marcel. "It has been too long. I was just telling Three about Sin."

"I know. I heard everything," Marcel said as he drank a shot of whatever the bartender poured him. "And you can't kill me young Victor."

Marcel smirked.

"Why did you call him Victor the Victorious? I didn't know you were a warrior Senior," I said to him.

"I'm not, grandson," Senior said to me.

"Oh, don't be modest," Marcel said to Senior. "Your grandfather saved Sin's life. You see, your grandfather was in a place between Earth and Hell, and his survival was based off of Sin's success against Xin. Well, Xin had overwhelmed Sin, and in an instant, your grandfather showed courage beyond the capacity of the word and pushed Xin out of the way and almost died. But of course Sin didn't let that happen. If it wasn't for your grandfather's judgment, Sin would be dead, he would be dead, and a battle would've gone for naught."

"Don't be modest, grandfather," I said to him smiling. "You did all that!? That's amazing."

"What's amazing is this drink," Marcel said. "Are you sure you two don't want to try this?"

"No thank you, he's fine and I'm fine," Senior said.

"You won't get to see Leon for a while," Marcel said. "He's going to learn about his Angelic origins. Xin is going to teach him to use his power, by the time he's finished Leon will be stronger, faster, quicker, than before, hell, he'll even be able to fly. Xin needs him to be at his peak. He has a mission for him, that he will fail without you, young Victor."

"What do you mean?" I said to Marcel.

"You've had the dream." Marcel said. "You saw the four bodies, you felt the heat, when the time comes, you'll have a decision to make. And like your grandfather made the decision that his life was meaningless without Sin's, you'll make the right choice. I'm sure of it."

"You've trained him well," Senior said.

"I didn't have much to do with it. Helen did," Marcel said to Senior.

"You met Helen!" Senior said to me. "How was she?"

"Mean," I said.

Senior and Marcel laughed.

"Don't worry Victor the Victorious, you'll meet her one day," Marcel said to Senior.

"She's right over there." I said pointing to the table she, Warman and the other gentleman were sitting at. But no one was there. I didn't even notice them leave.

"Who's over where?" Senior said to me.

"They were just right there," I said.

"Who is they?" Senior said.

"Nobody," Marcel interrupted. "Young Victor, it's best you go home right now, get some rest. You have quite a day tomorrow. I have to speak with your grandfather about a few things. We will talk soon." Marcel said.

"Ok," I said to Marcel.

I stood up.

"I love you, grandson," Senior said to me hugging me tightly. "Be careful out there."

As I walked out, I heard Marcel ordering two corned beef sandwiches. I wish I could've stayed. Vita was nowhere to be found. It was late and it was dark.

"Need a ride?" I heard as a car pulled up.

It was Elizabeth. I got into the car.

"How did you know I needed a ride?" I asked her.

"Your father told me where you probably were going to head," she said. "So I just waited out here until I saw you come out."

It was warm in her car, and it was nice to see her.

"So that was Fawzia. She's very pretty."

"Let's not talk about her," I said. I didn't hate her, just not a subject I wanted to touch on at the moment.

Elizabeth drove me home. For the most part we were quiet on the ride home, had small talk here and there. I tried to avoid talking about anything that just happened. I wanted to go home and sleep. I texted Malcolm to meet me at my house at dawn. Hopefully he isn't a late riser or I would have to leave him.

"Here we are" Elizabeth said as we pulled into my driveway.

"Thank you for the ride home, Elizabeth," I said to her. "You've been a better friend than I deserved to have. Truly." I said as I closed her car door and went into my house.

I didn't look back. My heart was confused at the moment. I still had love, anger and sorrow for Fawzia and Leon's betrayal. And on the other end of the spectrum, I felt Sa'Rah's love in every one of Elizabeth's actions. I didn't want to hurt her or lead her on, or go to her just because I might be vulnerable. When I walked into the front door, I noticed a bunch of suitcases and a few boxes and my father sitting in the dark on the recliner chair.

"Your mother is leaving," my father said.

"Are you ok?" I said to my dad.

"I just need prayer son. But your father will be fine. Jesus will get me through this." He said in confidence.

I went to my room, I'd let my father be alone right now. I was still surprised about finding out Leon was half angel, slept with and impregnated my girlfriend, or rather ex-girlfriend, my grandfather fought in a war, and Marcel, despite me shoving a sword in his stomach and falling over a waterfall, looked alive and well.

It was too much for me for one night. I laid down, and instantly fell asleep.

27

The next morning when I awoke, the very first thing I did was call Leon. It went straight to voicemail. I wanted to make sure that yesterday wasn't a long dream, or rather nightmare. Fawzia sent me several text messages apologizing and expressing her disbelief that she was carrying an angel's child. She also admitted she was scared when I was fighting with Leon. She thought that I was going to kill him.

Normally text messages from her would ease any tensions I had, but she only exasperated me. I just wanted her to leave me alone, never talk to me again. I'm not solely blaming her, Leon had his part in it too, they didn't have to lead me on, and she could've told me that she was talking to someone else, not having me believe that we were something we weren't.

I looked through the rest of my messages; I had a message from almost everyone I knew. I only responded to Elizabeth's. She told me that she was worried about me; I let her know that I would be fine. It was still dark out. I took a quick shower and got ready to leave. I walked upstairs.

My mom's suitcases and boxes were gone. My father was on the couch sleep. Must be tough to sleep upstairs, in one room, is the last room your daughter was alive in, and the other, a bed you shared with your wife who has left you.

I took the moment to call my mother. She didn't answer, but I left a voicemail letting her know that I loved her.

I walked outside on the porch. In my peripheral vision, I saw a fist coming at my face to the right. I blocked it with my right hand and quickly hit the person throwing the first in the ribs with my left. When I looked it was Malcolm. He was doubled over laughing and coughing at the same time.

"You're good, Victor," he said rubbing his rib cage.

Had I known it was Malcolm I would've eased up on the hit.

"I could've seriously hurt you, Malcolm," I said with a bit of anger.

He didn't scare me. I assumed there are people out there who might want me dead.

"Don't worry, I can take a hit," Malcolm said dusting himself off.

He was wearing black leather jacket, black jeans and brown boots. It wasn't snowing but it was a bit cold out, I had on gray JCU hoodie, some black jogging pants and black boots.

"Where are we going?" Malcolm asked.

"I'm not sure. I was just told that Vita would take me there," I said.

"Vita?"

"The name of my horse, means life."

"She's a loyal horse."

"There's no better horse on earth."

"My men are excited to work with you, especially the ones that you kicked their butts on the bridge."

"I kicked yours too," I said jokingly, calming down from earlier.

"I let you win. Had to build your confidence up. Did you bring your weapon?"

"Always," I said as I motioned towards my sword in the sheath. I brought my diamond sword; it was the only sword I had that I trusted. "Be confident Malcolm."

"I am confident that Allah sent you here for a purpose. Our paths didn't cross for nothing."

"Well, have you said one of your fifteen prayers today so we can leave?" I said laughing at him.

"It's only five and yes I have," Malcolm said as he mounted his horse. "Did you sprinkle water on your face and prayed to your three different God's yet?"

"I believe in the Trinity."

"So your God has three heads?" Malcolm said as I mounted Vita.

We looked one another and laughed. It was all in jest. I respected him, and he respected me. Vita took off running. She was running so fast that Malcolm's horse couldn't keep up.

"Slow down girl," I said to her.

She slowed down to a trot.

For the next few hours we headed southwest. I didn't know where we were at one point. Malcolm and I spent the time talking about our lives. I explained to him what happened to Fawzia. He told me that his father didn't disown her. He merely gave her to the man that got her pregnant. He told me that he never actually had a chance to talk to Fawzia, he just wanted to marry her because he felt it would've been strong in bonds to combine families. He told me why he changed his name. Malcolm X was someone he greatly admired. He asked me how did I become so good at fighting, I didn't want to tell him I had special ProChrist training, but I also didn't want to lie, so I told him for ninety days I slept four hours, and trained the rest.

While we were talking we heard sword fighting. We looked, and in between two houses there were several men fighting what looked like a Muslim, or rather they had on Keffiyeh, a head covering for Muslims, the Keffiyeh was white with a black ring around the top to hold it down. They were wearing white pants, and a black shirt with black sandals. It wasn't that cold down here, and it looks as if snow hasn't fell here yet. I had no idea what city we were in.

"We should help," Malcolm said. To him, it was a bunch of people against one Muslim.

"I don't think we have the time Malcolm," I said to him.

"Nonsense," Malcolm said. He dismounted his horse and walked towards the fighting. The Muslim was handling himself well. I couldn't let Malcolm go there by himself. I dismounted Vita who huffed, she was angry.

"I'm sorry, girl," I said as I rubbed her neck. "I'll be back."

"Looks like you got some friends," I heard one of the men say.

There were seven of them, and one Muslim.

"We don't want your kind here. So we're going to hold you until one of Octavius' Captains get here." One of the men said.

Or should I say boys? They all appeared to be in their mid to late teens, around the same age as me. I could easily take every one of them down without a problem. But now would be a good time to examine what I'm going to have to help Malcolm with about his fighting.

"I don't need your help!" the Muslim screamed out to Malcolm.

It wasn't a man, it was a woman. Malcolm stopped in his tracks. The seven men turned to look at us.

"Come here to die too?" said the tallest of them, brunette hair, brown eyes. Of the seven, he seemed in command. To his left there were five others, two African Americans, and three Caucasians, and to his right, one Latino.

"No one is going to die today," Malcolm said with force in his voice. "Let her come with us and we won't hurt you."

They all laughed, I'm assuming they believe their numbers are superior to ours. Malcolm looked at me and smiled. Suddenly the tallest guy turned and attacked the Muslim girl. She dodged him, he was swinging his sword as if it was a baseball bat after a fly. The other six ran at us, we were in between two houses that were closed off on the end where the Muslim girl was fighting with a garage and two tall gates. I just leaned back against the house and watched as Malcolm was fighting. His stance left himself open for attacks, and he gripped his sword too tightly. He swung with anger, not controlled, and didn't pay attention to his defense.

Three came at me, very similar to when Malcolm's men ran at me, no order, pure adrenaline, probably not a thought in their mind about what they are going to do when they got here. I didn't want to make a point today to them, I took out my sword and with three blocks with my sword, and three counter strikes, I cut all three of them on their hamstring. I hit their hamstrings because it would be incredibly painful for them to stand up and proceed to be any use in a fight. Malcolm had managed to stay alive, though his arm was bleeding, he had gotten cut, I interrupted his fight with another three blocks and three counters, the other three were on the ground. The tallest guy threw a punch at the Muslim girl, she dodged it and did a round house kick to his face. He hit the ground hard.

"You heathen Muslims!" he said as he got up, spit at us, and ran off. His friends crawled behind him.

"I told you I didn't need your help!" the Muslim girl screamed as she swung at me, I stepped back and dodged her attack but she caught Malcolm in the face.

"Hey!" Malcolm said. "Ouch!"

She kept trying to hit me but I dodge and blocked each hit. I wasn't trained in her art of fighting, but I believe it to be krav maga, Israeli self-defense martial arts. She wasn't using it correctly now for I wasn't attacking her.

"Calm yourself, woman," Malcolm said to her.

She stopped attacking me and did a fake low kick towards Malcolm, he went low with his arm to block it, and then she round house kicked him just like she did the other guy. I shook my head and walked towards Vita. As I was walking, I looked at her face, she looked exactly like Fawzia. Except her eyes weren't the same color. Fawzia's eyes were light hazel, hers was dark brown.

"Zaviera?" I said to her as she turned quickly and looked at me.

"How do you know me?" she said.

"I know your sister," I said to her.

"You know Fawzia!?" she exclaimed in excitement. "That's the only reason I've come this far in America."

She and Fawzia had the same accent.

"How is she?"

"Pregnant," Malcolm said.

Zaviera's face went from pure joy and happiness to angry.

"Pregnant!?" Zaviera said with malice.

"By his brother," Malcolm said pointing at me.

"We don't have time for this," I said. "You're staying here or riding with Malcolm, we have a place to be at. Malcolm can explain everything on the way."

I mounted Vita. Malcolm and Zaviera mounted his, and we took off. I rode ahead of them. I heard them talking with one another but I didn't listen for the words. I tried to meditate while riding Vita, not easy, but I got my breathing in control. I closed my eyes and tried to become one with the air around me.

When I opened my eyes, we were in a heavily wooded area in front of a small brick house with a beautiful garden to the east. It had a stone walk way to the front door.

"This place is beautiful," Zaviera said getting off of the horse.

"I'm sorry." Zaviera said to me. "For everything that Fawzia put you through."

"There's no need for you to apologize for anything she did," I said to her. "Let's see what this place is."

"Wow," Malcolm said when he finally came to.

"How's your arm?" I said referring to his cut.

"It's just a scratch," he said.

The front door opened and a woman walked out. She was about my height, very slender, fair skin complexion with blond hair. She was wearing a blue robe. She walked towards me.

"You're almost as handsome as your father," she said to me. "Come in, all of you, I've been expecting you."

"Who is this woman?" Malcolm said to me as we all followed her into the house.

"I have no clue," I whispered to him.

"There's no use whispering." The lady said, "I hear everything. Now come with me."

She motioned to Zaviera.

"We must get you cleaned up and get you out of those. Disgusting masculine clothing."

The décor was beautiful; she had exotic looking furniture, tables, pictures, and lights. Malcolm and I sat down on some chairs that were facing a fish tank. The fish tank was pretty big, had a lot of fish inside of it, I didn't know the names of them, I just saw the fish. After about an hour of sitting, Malcolm walked off to explore the rest of the house. I used that time to meditate. I found that meditating calmed me down, and during my meditation, I could find ways to get closer to Jesus, maybe hear His words through my conscience. Sometimes I could meditate for hours and not even realize it.

"Victor," I heard the lady say to me.

When I came to I was looking at Malcolm, Zaviera and the lady all standing in front of me. Zaviera and Malcolm were wearing different clothing. Zaviera had on a black with gold trimming hijab on her head; she wore a white dress that stopped at her knees, with black pants on underneath, and a black shirt under the white dress. On her feet she had on what looked like boots but fit like shoes. She also wore a thick black robe that hung like a cape but you could fit it all around you. Malcolm's attire was very similar minus the dress, he had on a white shirt and loosely fitting black pants.

"Enough with your deep breathing exercises follow me."

I stood up, I looked at them, on each one of their left chest there was a circular patch that looked like a bulls-eye. The differences were, Malcolm had a dot in the middle, and three circles around it. Zaviera had two.

"Those dots are their ranks," the woman said to me as we walked down a very dark corridor, it was as if she was reading my mind. "Malcolm's rank is second to yours, Zaviera's is second to his. Putting it in English, you are, in sorts, the general, Malcolm is second in command, and Zaviera is third."

"I don't even know, Zaviera," I said. How can I trust her to be third in command of anything, I don't know who she is.

"You don't know Malcolm either, except for the fact that he's tried to kill you twice," she said as she opened a door to a small room with a manikin on it.

"These are your clothes, similar to there's except I made some, modifications for you."

I began to put on the clothes. I started with my pants and shirt, which, the best comparison I could come up with was fit me like Under Amour clothing, it was as tight as my skin, it was black, it was a top that was long sleeved, and the pants went down to my ankle. Over my pants I put on a very lightly feeling black pants, they were loose, I'm not sure what material they were, it felt silk like. I put on a white shirt with a similar dot diagram to Malcolm's and Zaviera's except I had four circles. On my left arm, I had a golden bracer for shooting arrows. The cape like robe, was closely related to a medieval robe, without arms, something that could cover your entire body with a hood. It was black with white and gold trimmings.

"You are going to be a good commander, Victor," the lady said to me. "I designed your aunt's and your father's prom outfit. I was told to create this for you and your friends out there. But I couldn't stop there, I had to make one thousand more."

"One thousand more?" I asked.

"Follow me," she said as she walked out the back door of this small room.

We went outside for me to see several men and women dressed very similar to me. This area was a big area all surrounded by thick trees, you couldn't see in the distance. They were all standing around and talking until they looked over at me, and instantly got into formation and stood straight up in attention.

"Looks like we have our Army," Malcolm said as he touched my right shoulder and walked towards them.

It was extremely sunny outside today, a nice day if any to be outside during the winter.

"They are fighting with us?" I asked to the lady.

"They are fighting for you. You are their general," she said to me. "Now I'm sorry if I'm curt with you, but I have several other things to do. I'll be quick, I'm not sure if you know how rankings go, but your rank is general, we don't deal with stars, so you'll have to tell who is who by your ranks. You're the general, Malcolm is the colonel, Zaviera is your major, the one circle is your captains, you have ten of them, and the one dot with the big circle are all just soldiers. Your insignia is the green dot you have in the middle, every army, every place, needs a logo to distinguish them from anyone else. So when you see the one dot and one big circle around it that is your insignia. My suggestion for you is that you put them to work, get a base to work out of, and prepare yourself. You have another hour here and then you must leave."

She turned and walked away.

I had no idea who these men and women were. I didn't know Zaviera but I had to trust her to be my third in command. I don't even know why I'm the general. I don't want to be the general. No time to reflect. I walked up and down the rows of men and women. None of them made eye contact with me.

"Where are we going to put all of them for now?" Malcolm said to me.

"You need to come up with a plan," Zaviera said to me.

"We have to think of how to feed them," Malcolm continued.

"And how to hide them from Octavius."

For the next several minutes Zaviera and Malcolm were going down a long list of things that we need to do, think of, address, from feed, training, planning.

"Ok, I get your point," I said to them.

They instantly became quiet. I looked at them as if I said something wrong.

"Sorry, Victor," Malcolm said. "As second in command, she basically told me that I have to respect your words without question. And when you speak, I'm quiet. The nature of ranks I guess. I'm not used to it, but if it's going to save lives, make things easier. I'm all for it."

"Same here," Zaviera said. "But I'm not calling you sir."

I laughed a bit.

"Well, we can't stay here to devise a plan," I said to them.

I thought of the only place I could send them that would make the most sense.

"Zaviera, your sister is at my brother's house in Pepper Pike. I want you to take these men and women to University School, have them wait there for further orders while I think. Here is the address for where your sister is staying."

I gave Zaviera the address.

"Take everyone but the captains."

Zaviera took the soldiers through the house, I'm not sure how she was going to get them all there, but I had to get them somewhere.

"When we were coming back here, about twenty buses pulled up out front. How did you know that?" Malcolm said to me.

"I didn't know that."

"Then how were they all going to get to University School?"

"I didn't know. I put that up to Zaviera."

"Well that's smart."

"Hey, shut up," I said to Malcolm laughing.

During our entire exchange, there were five men and five women staring at us. I guess it's time to grow up.

"Captains."

"Sir!" they all said in unison.

I was going to have to get used to this. It made me feel very uncomfortable. But I did understand why it's necessary to have ranks, and following orders and a general level of respect that is due from each soldier.

"Colonel," I said to Malcolm, smiling still getting used to being a general. "Take this."

I handed him my family's emergency credit card that's linked to Senior's account which had a lot of money available to everyone.

"I want you, and the captain's to get tents, firewood, water, fruits and some lean meats for the soldiers to have. I don't care how many stores you have to go to, get it done. I'll be there in a few days."

"But, Victor. You don't think the president of University School is going to notice that there's an army just relaxing on their sports fields?" Malcolm said.

"I'll make a phone call. Now get out of here," I said to Malcolm.

"Sir yes sir!" the captains said as they left out.

I took a deep breath. I walked to the front yard and mounted Vita. I had no idea what I was going to do, but I had to come up with something, and I had to come up with it fast.

28

Over the next few days I stayed in the house. My cell phone was turned off the entire time and all I did was train and meditate. The only person I talked to was my father. I wanted to disconnect myself from the outside world. I had to come to terms that although I'm only soon to be nineteen, I have a lot of people relying on me to be successful.

When I finally decided to reconnect with what was going on with the outside world, the second I turned on the television, I saw protest, and people arguing, senators and representatives questioning President Williams' use of power and how Octavius could get the power he held. There had been a huge increase in missing persons reports. Nothing violent had occurred, just peaceful protest and questions. It seemed that President Williams had enough backing from both the Senate and House of Representatives that nothing was going to remove Octavius' power.

It was close to sunset. I walked into the kitchen to see my father cooking. Smelled like he was baking some chicken, had some broccoli and cheese going, and a salad.

"Hello, Father," I said to him.

I was fully clothed, I figure it was time for me to go see the army and talk out a plan with Zaviera and Malcolm. I received a box in the mail, it was from Marcel, it had a bow in there, some arrows, a smaller back up sword I could use just in case I get disarmed. Some patches for promotion for my soldiers, according to Marcel I could have two colonels, four majors, and sixteen captains. He wrote a letter to me in detail by saying these soldiers aren't getting paid, the only promise to them is that their families will survive the upcoming turmoil that will bestow the world. So they aren't here for pay raises, promotions and power, they are here for their families.

"Hello, son," my father said to me. "Have dinner with me before you leave out?"

"I would love to," I said as I put down my bag by the front door and sat down at the dining room table with my father.

He had baked some chicken, had some broccoli and cheese, a garden salad with some homemade dinner rolls. It was delicious. We ate in silence for a moment, but we began talking. He was telling me how he got a lot of phone calls regarding where I was at. Elizabeth had stopped by, Senior even stopped by but I was nowhere to be found. He touched on my mother; he said that they have been having small talk here and there, nothing serious. He did mention that he asked her not to go out witnessing right now until the Octavius thing blew over. That's something I had never thought about. I would have to keep an eye out for her.

"Son, I want you to be careful out there," my father said to me. "I don't know much about going into battle with weapons, and spears, and lives that are at stake. As a basketball coach, the best thing I could tell my young men to do was do their best. Biggest difference is, if they did their best and lost, they get to go home, and cry it off, if your people don't do their best, they'll die, or worst, you'll die. I'm extremely worried son. But Senior and I have talked, and it's in God's will for you to be who you are. I always knew that Leon was really Leon's son. I just hoped he was Ian's son. Leon, or rather, Sin, was a good man. In the short time that I knew him, he opened my eyes to things, I was only a few years younger than you when we spoke. His voice had power. He commanded your respect without asking for it. He was knowledgeable and impartial. If you grow up to be a man like him, I know he's an Angel and what not, but if you can grow up to be like he was when he was here, I'd be a proud father. Because I see a lot of his qualities in you."

My dad said smiling.

"I understand that, Father," I said. "Although I've never met Leon's father. I know you, and I feel like you're a great man, and my mother, despite what you two are going through, is a good mother, and Senior, and Grandma Patrice, Aunt Victoria and Aunt Victory, Christina, I mean all of you, helped in raising me. So anything good you see in me, or me in the future, you should attribute that to yourself."

I said as I stood up and drank some water. I went and gave my father a hug.

"What does Deuteronomy thirty one six say?" I asked my father.

"Be strong and courageous. Do not fear or be in dread of them, for it is the Lord your God who goes with you. He will not leave you or forsake you." My father said while looking in his bible.

"If I have God on my side, you shouldn't worry at all, Dad," I said to him.

He smiled as I picked up my bags and left out of the front door. As I suspected Vita was outside waiting on me. I mounted her and we rode as fast as we could to University School's athletic fields. When I arrived the wind had settled down, and it was a warm night for it to be winter. Thanksgiving had come and gone and no one noticed it amongst the ruckus of Octavius.

"It's the general!" I heard someone yell.

"Form your line!" The same person screamed as I rode through the fields.

They were all around the football field training, the tents were set up at the softball fields, and it looked like food was being served at the soccer fields. I dismounted Vita.

"It's about time you showed up," Zaviera said to me. "Thank you for telling me where Fawzia was. It's been a long time since I saw her; we had a really good talk. But now's not the time for that."

SON OF SIN

"You're welcome about your sister. I'm glad I can help," I said to her letting her know that her personal information was still important. The soldiers began lining up in single filed lines.

"Who thought of all of this?" I said to her referring to the eating, sleeping and training.

"I did," Zaviera said. "Had to keep them loose and limber. One thing Fawzia told me was that you are reliable. She did love you…"

"Let's not discuss her," I said interrupting her. "At least not now. Where do I set up my tent at?"

"Yours is already set up," Zaviera said to me. "That's your strategy tent."

She pointed at an open tent near the fifty yard line of the visitor's sideline.

"In there you have a projector, a computer with full internet access, and a white board. Your sleeping tent is the one all the way to the back."

"Thank you," I said to her. "Where is Malcolm?"

"He's taking a shower in the locker rooms. The headmaster of the school has allowed us unlimited access to their locker rooms to bathe. I guess your phone call worked." She said as she smiled at me. She had a gorgeous smile just like Fawzia.

I walked into the strategy tent and sat down at the desk. There was a projector pointing at a huge whiteboard, underneath the white board were markers and erasers. I had two computers on my desk, a desktop computer and a laptop computer.

"Excuse me, sir," one of the captains said as they stepped into the tent. He was a few inches taller than I, he looked Asian and Caucasian, a mix of the two, he had a short haircut, broad shoulders. He was lean but appeared strong like a football player would.

"Sir, permission to speak freely."

"What's your name captain?" I said to him.

"Bob Dembo, sir."

"Captain Dembo, I have a question, what is it about ranks?"

"Ranks sir, are extremely important. It is very serious sign of respect. Majority of the men and women who get promoted to their various ranks worked extremely hard to get there, I'm not sure what you endured to get the rank of general, but whatever it was, you should feel you deserve the rank. Most people respect the rank and not the person. I used to tell my troops that you do not have to respect me, but you will respect my rank."

"What I endured huh?" I said to him.

I was not sure what he had endured to receive Captain. I'm sure it was gruesome. But what I endured, I almost died every day for ninety days, I'd lost my sister, my brother, and the love of my life.

"Speak freely Captain," I said to him after a moment of silence.

"In normal circumstances, a captain would never say this to a general. But these aren't normal circumstances. I took an oath to serve under you. I couldn't help but notice that you are only a few years removed from puberty. I have served in the Marines and the Army, and I took an oath to serve under you for the protection and future of my family. I do not have any religious ties; I'm not one of importance. I'm speaking to you, giving you advice so to speak, to let you know this isn't a game. I saw how you and Colonel Malcolm were joking around. This isn't a joke sir. You have the responsibility of a thousand men and women lives under your command. My suggestion is that if you need to grow up, that you do it and the sooner the better."

After he said that, it dawned on me. It was time for me to grow up. That is what I was doing these past few days that I was away, growing up. I was thinking of what needed to be done.

"Remove your insignia," I said to Dembo in regards to his one circle insignia Captain's badge he had on his uniform.

"Sir?" Dembo said looking at me in disappointment.

He removed it and handed it to me. I handed him a two circle Major's badge. He looked at it.

"You're promoting me?"

"Why not?" I said to him. "You spoke up for your fellow soldiers, and I don't think we have a lot of time to test you in other things. So I'm just going to go with my gut. Get everyone in formation. I will speak with them."

"Yes sir!" Dembo said as he accepted the promotion and walked outside of the tent. I heard him getting everyone in line.

"Good to see you back," Malcolm said as he walked into the tent.

"You didn't ask for permission to speak," I said jokingly to him. "Come out here, I'm going to speak to everyone."

Malcolm and I walked outside to see all the soldiers lined up and in attention.

"Here's a microphone sir, so everyone here can hear you," Dembo said to me handing me a microphone.

I had never got up and spoke in front of a large crowd before. I'd seen Senior do it hundreds of time with no problem. I had never been so nervous in my life, but I had to put the nerves aside.

"I am your general," I started off saying. "I haven't had the chance to introduce myself to you all because this is very new to me. I have responsibilities on my lap. Often times, we as people complain when we have a lot of responsibilities that is bestowed upon us before we're actually ready. Life has thrown us all a pop quiz, I don't have the luxury of time to complain, to whine, to pout, the only thing I can do is grow up. Max Lucado said that you are valuable because you exist. Not because of what you do or what you have done, but simply because you are." I said as I paused and looked a lot of soldiers in the face. "With that being said, I'm telling you all now, that you will not be fighting in this war that is coming here. Instead you will be assigned to work in what I have designated, Safe Zones. What Safe Zones are, is basically what it says, it's going to be a place, not too much bigger than this school, where you will guard and protect the people living inside of it. The parameters are this, there are no parameters, anyone who can make it to a Safe Zone, has passage to be in the Safe Zone. The people who will come to the Safe Zone are people that do not believe in what Octavius is saying, because if they did, they would feel safe anywhere.

Wars aren't won by brutes, wars aren't won by smart people, wars are won by purpose. And our purpose in this war is to save as many innocent lives as we can. You will get your orders soon."

I handed the microphone to a Captain.

"Tell them to eat and rest tonight," I said to the Captain.

"Sir yes sir!" The captain said enthusiastically.

"Are you insane?" Malcolm came to me. "We need them, they are about as good as we're going to get when it comes to fighting."

I ignored Malcolm. As a General, I hate to think this way, but it was my order, and he'll have to respect it. I motioned for Zaviera and Dembo to join me in the strategy tent. Malcolm spent a few minutes complaining about my decision, and how he thought we could use them.

"Are you finished?" I said to Malcolm.

"Yes, sir," Malcolm said with defeat in his voice.

"I've promoted Dembo from Captain to Major. He will be in charge of the Safe Zones." I said as I pulled up a map of Jesus Christ University. "Major Dembo, you've traveled, you know more about the geography of the U.S. than I. I want to establish ten Safe Zones, I want seventy-five to eighty soldiers in each one. You see how JCU is heavily wooded? With two main entrances? I want you to put a roadblock at those entrances, keep the fresh water of the river safe. All Safe Zones should be near a fresh body of water, an area that you can use the natural terrain to your advantage. Post look outs, keep the surveillance going, swap out the guards, and make sure they get enough rest. Everyone who comes to the Safe Zone must have something to do to. JCU has dorms, places to eat, places to train. Try to find farmers, gardeners, and other people to tend to the natural upkeep of the Safe Zone, I'm not sure how long they'll need to be established, could be weeks, could be years, make sure it can be done. I'll go over more of my instructions for the Safe Zone later."

"Victor," Malcolm said. "You just can't go into places and tell them what to do and how to do it and when."

"I can and I will and I have," I said to Malcolm with a frustrated voice. "I know we're friends, but continue interrupting me, and we won't be. Just trust that I know what I'm doing. A thousand highly trained dead soldiers does nothing for us in this war. But if they are protecting those who will ultimately be the future of this country once the smoke clears, that is what is important here. Understood?"

"Yes, sir," Malcolm said.

"Zaviera," I continued. "Over on the west side of Cleveland there is a sword training facility. I want you to go there, and start recruiting for our army here. Give anyone who joins this insignia and make them take a quick oath of loyalty to our cause. We'll go over the oath later. Send them here where Malcolm will get them trained. Malcolm, we don't have a lot of time to train everybody on everything, but we have time to train everyone on one thing. Zaviera, once you've done that, I want you to give these to Azeem and Wajeeh."

I handed her a Majors badge and a Colonel Badge.

"I can't give someone a higher rank than I," Zaviera said in confusion.

"The Colonel one is for you, and your badge will go to the other one," I explained to her. "Malcolm, get your men here, and get them training. I'll gather as many men and women as I can from my end and send them here. Let me know as soon as you can in regards to when the Muslims will attack from the north, or when Octavius will attack from the south. I'm assigning five soldiers to go with each of you. There will be no discussions about it, Azeem and Wajeeh will get five as well."

"How many will you keep for yourself?" Malcolm asked me.

"I have two Colonels, and three Majors, that's who I have," I responded quickly.

Truthfully, I trained alone, I know how to fight alone, I didn't need anyone to guard me.

We spent the next several hours going over specifics for the Safe Zones, rules and regulations for them. I left the locations up to Major

Dembo. He would notify me when they were ready for people to start coming. He took eight hundred soldiers with him to begin preparations. The five that will go with each of them, that left one hundred and fifty soldiers here under my direct command. Malcolm went to get his men ready and fitted for their uniforms, he found some seamstresses to start making clothing for us.

With the remaining soldiers, I put them all at different points in the Cleveland area to be look outs for what was going to come. I put several of them to scout the Mentor Headlands beach area for escape routes, and for them to give me reports and suggestions. They were all trained very well, in a lot of the things I knew about. I respected them, got to know a few of them. It was my job, as Dembo put it, to save as many lives as possible.

29

Over the next month, life seemed different in America. The weather was the same, the snow fell in the north, and it got a bit cold in the south. But the atmosphere was strictly fearful, as people disappeared left and right. How others were silenced. The police acted as if they were powerless, perhaps they were powerless. The military was in control of a man not even from the United States. There were no Christmas cheers, no Christmas spirit or shopping, no Hanukkah. Sports stopped, as people began staying home and not veering too far away from their neighborhoods. Those who claimed to be a part of the new Christian wave of Octavius; they walked with their chest out, feeling untouchable. I didn't pay them much attention.

Tensions had grown as both sides are waiting for the other to throw the first serious punch. There have been fist fights, some drunken madness, but nothing too serious, no bloodshed. The nation was paralyzed with fear. No one wants to be that person that officially gives Octavius the reason to begin his onslaught.

The Safe Zones had been set up, the first one in Michigan, at JCU had been established and it is being spread across our families and close friends of a safe place people can go. Most people feel safe right now, they don't believe that Octavius is going to do them much harm. Right now, as I see it, it's Octavius' Christians versus what I call true Christians. True Christians don't try to do God's work for Him. For second Corinthians five ten says *'For we must all appear before the judgment seat of Christ, so that each one may receive what is due for what he has done in the body, whether good or evil.'* God hasn't asked any of us to do His job, which is to judge right and wrong and be impartial.

Seemed like Octavius was doing that on his own. Someone had to stand up against him. And that task had been given to me.

My father and I had spoken to many Kingdom Halls in regards to their witnessing. It's not that we didn't believe in what they were doing, but because we feared for their safety. I had my soldiers spread across the city, in regular clothing, watching and reporting what has been going on. Zaviera has gathered quite the following, based on rumors that I had my own Army to stand against Octavius and anyone against the freedom of religion. We had an array of different people join our cause, some confused people who didn't know what to believe, Muslims, Christians, and others, men and women alike who were for fighting for what they believed in.

Over the past month, Zaviera had massed almost five thousand people, who have given an oath, not to me, not to Jesus, but just for humanity, that God gave us all free will, and with that free will, we will do what we please, as long as we respect life, liberty and the pursuit of happiness. The American way ironically.

Malcolm had gathered over five hundred of his best men. Malcolm, with all respect for his beliefs, didn't want women in his unit. He felt that men should be fighting and protecting the women. He was very adamant about that, he respects my authority, and I wouldn't make him have women in his unit. I assigned different units to different areas. Malcolm wanted his men to be the ground unit, first in battle. He quoted me a verse from the Qur'an that says *'Those who believe fight in the cause of Allah...'*

He and I spent many hours speaking about our respective religions. Though neither one of us would conform to the other, gaining knowledge and respect was worth it. Major Dembo had found the nine other Safe Zones locations and sent men there to garrison them and prepare them. I knew that ten was not enough, but it was a start.

SON OF SIN

When the Safe Zone at JCU was one hundred percent operational, I was sending my family there. According to Azeem, the Muslims were going to launch their attack from Canada soon, and Octavius was actually in Ohio, down near the Southern border.

It was a calm day, snow was on the ground, the sun wasn't out, but you could see clearly. For the past month I had been following my mother on her Saturday witnessing trips. The Jehovah's Witnesses believe that nothing worse can be done to them, they spoke to me and said that there women have been raped, dogs have been let loose on them, they've been attacked with guns, swords and other weapons, they didn't believe that Octavius, or anyone else could do much worse than what they had already endured to spread the words of what they believed. I could only respect them. But I could protect my mother.

It was a Saturday, and I was sitting on top of a bar. My mother was walking with another woman, down the street, a suburban neighborhood, a Rite-Aid at the corner, with houses lined up all the way down the neighboring street with two side streets connected from the south to the north.

"So this is where you hang out at on Saturdays, Victor," Malcolm said as he knelt down next to me as I watched my mother start from the west side of the street going towards the east on the north side houses. "Looking at pretty ladies, huh?"

"Be careful what you say, that's my mother you're talking about," I said to Malcolm jokingly.

I was used to people giving my mother compliments, I'm sure in their mind their thoughts weren't always pure, but who was I to control what they think?

"Why are they knocking on doors?" Malcolm asked.

"They are Jehovah's Witnesses."

"But I thought you asked them to stop that for now."

"I did. They are stubborn with their worship and beliefs. I can't make them stop."

"I can believe that. Why do you fight Victor? I'm sorry for asking, but you and your family, you're good Christians, and you have this man who gets the power over the greatest power in the world, and instead of joining him, like I'm sure majority of your people will, you stand against him, a small man against a giant. I can't say that if I was in your shoes, I may not fight Octavius, but I wouldn't stand against him."

"It was never an option. In fact I wasn't given an option. This is what I was born to do. It was foretold to my grandfather. Maybe not in this exact words, but it was told that I would have an effect on this world greater than that of most men. I can't see myself killing in the name of Jesus. Even now, if I have to take a life, it won't be in the name of Jesus, it'll be in the name of protecting what I believe in, which is that everyone has the right to life, and believe in what they believe in. My father told me a long time ago that a great man, told him not to fear people who have different views of Gods and practices, but fear those who do not believe in anything, who are lost and do not respect life. I fear that Octavius doesn't respect life, and someone has to stand up to him." I said.

It was quiet for a moment, I looked and a door was slammed on my mother's face as they began walking to the corner house of the first connecting street that ran north.

"Why do you fight?" I asked Malcolm.

"The Quran says *'And slay them wherever ye find them, and drive them out of the places whence drove you out, for persecution is worse than slaughter... but if they desist, then lo! Allah is forgiving and merciful. And fight them until persecution is no more, and religion is for Allah,'*" he said. "Allah tells us to stand against those who choose to kills us for what we are. Not to sit back and accept being persecuted, we are to attack until the persecution is no more, and that Allah shall be religion."

"That's a good way to look at things..." I began to say before I was interrupted by a loud scream of a woman.

I instantly looked towards my mother and the woman companion she was with had been stabbed in the abdomen.

"No!" I said as I jumped off of the roof of the building.

She was about four houses down from me.

"Victor you won't make it!" Malcolm screamed as he jumped with me.

The roof I was on was about fifteen feet from the ground, I landed on some snow that eased the fall and I was running as fast as I could towards my mother. The man who had just stabbed her was walking towards my mother who stood there shocked. Malcolm was right; I wasn't going to make it. The man raised his sword, my mother dropped to her knees, I ran even faster, I heard a projectile flying in the wind. As the man's sword arm began to go down towards my mother, an arrow pierced him in the back near his heart. He fell forward, I got to my mom in time to move her from him falling on her.

"Victor!" my mom said crying as she hugged me and wept into my shoulders as she watched her friend cling on to life.

She was gasping for air as blood poured from her stomach. She was a young woman, looked as if she was a few years older than me.

"Hold on lady, don't die!" Malcolm screamed to her.

I looked up at where the arrow came from and saw the same man that had helped me on the bridge. I heard doors opening and people walking out of their houses.

"Oh my God!" I heard one man scream. "You killed Adam!"

"Get your swords son!" I heard another man yell.

I looked up to where the man who shot the arrow was and he was gone. I heard Vita gallop behind me. This situation was not going to be good at all. About fifteen men came out of their houses, some kids around my age as well, ranging from all races and sizes.

"Brittany!" I heard Isaacs voice yell.

"What did you do to her!" he said as he ran to her body.

"Malcolm," I said to Malcolm as he stepped away from the woman, noticing everyone circling us.

"Sir?" Malcolm said hearing the authority in my voice.

"Take my mother, and take her to my father's house, tell them to meet me at Senior's, send every available soldier there. And do it with haste," I said to him.

"I'm not leaving you!" Malcolm said.

"That's an order!" I screamed at him.

Isaac began crying over Brittany.

"That's his brother's wife," my mom said slowly, still in shock.

Malcolm grabbed my mother and mounted Vita and rode off faster than anyone could see.

"You bastards!" said a very angry man behind me.

He was about six foot four, and a bit over weight, looked mixed, black and white.

"You killed an innocent man!"

"I didn't kill him, but that man killed this woman," I responded.

"That woman shouldn't have been knocking on his door to spread this Devil worship!" said another man, shorter than I, Caucasian and lean.

"You don't know that its Devil worship, have you ever read their studies? It's not one hundred percent different than yours!" I screamed at them.

"Isn't that Victor Thomas' boy?" said another man, my height, and completely overweight, with a beard, no shirt and his stomach hanging over his pants.

"That's his grandson. Siding with them Muslims and these Jehovah's Witnesses." said the six foot four man. "Octavius gave us the right to detain you!"

"I don't want to hurt any of you," I said to them as I stood straight up.

Isaac was still crying over Brittany who had fallen to sleep, never to awaken again, near my feet, an elderly Caucasian man who took an arrow to the heart from an impossible distance.

I looked at Brittany, she was a beautiful young woman, she was a larger woman, but full of life and full of spirit, I followed her over the past few weeks and her and my mother seemed to get along great.

Stabbed only because she believed in what she believed in and wanted to share it with others. I felt myself getting angry.

"It's too bad Adam didn't get to kill that other little Jehovah's Witch," said a man behind. I lost focus.

"God, forgive me," I said out loud as I drew my sword and struck that man down quicker than anyone could react to me saying 'God, forgive me.'

There was silence and blood on the snow. I looked at the man that I had put down, he was looking at me, his eyes were faint and his breath was fading, and stared right at me, I was breathing heavy, it was the first time I struck someone with a fatal blow since Marcel. Now is not the time to feel merciful.

"Get him!" yelled a man.

They all converged on me at once, very sloppily, I was going to make this quick, and try not to kill anyone else. I dodged two sloppily thrown lunges with an ax, I cut someone's knee, another's shoulder, some else's back, I put down about seven of them before the others looked at me in fear. I didn't kill anyone else but there were three body's, one woman who bled out into the snow, an old man with an arrow in his back, and another man's whose body was cut from the abdomen to his thigh, my slice of his was fatal and he bled. The other men were crawling away.

"Did you think Octavius was joking!?" I yelled at Isaac. "Did you think that his message to people was going to go ignored!? You almost got my mother killed! You did get someone killed!"

"Shut up!" Isaac said to me as he charged me in anger.

I slapped him as hard as I could in his face as he fell to the ground in total shock as to how fast I hit him. He cried some more. I heard police sirens coming near.

"Sir!" I heard one of my soldiers say. "We need to go right now."

I grabbed Isaac and got into the SUV the soldier was driving. There were three more soldiers in the SUV.

"Are you ok General?" a soldier asked me.

"I'm fine. Drop me off at my grandfather's and take him wherever he needs to be. Any news on my mother?"

"They were intercepted and taken directly to your grandfather's house. Your father is in route there now sir," said the soldier sitting in the passenger's seat.

"Thank you," I said.

I was exhausted. I used all of my mental energy trying to save my mother from getting killed. I felt myself dozing off in the back seat as I lay my head back. I just started this war.

30

"Why did you kill me?" a man's voice said to me.

I opened my eyes and all I saw was darkness. Then, he flashed in front of me. It was the man that I had killed when he raised his sword over on Meredith.

"You raised your sword," I said in return.

"But I have a family, two sons and a daughter nearly eighteen. What will you say to them?"

"I… I don't know."

"How will my wife provide for them? Who is going to teach my son's how to be men?"

"It was either you or me."

"I wasn't going to attack. I don't even believe in what Octavius is doing, I was only out there because the rest of them."

"Why were you armed?"

"Because you were armed."

"I'm sorry."

"It's ok. Just take care of my family."

"You have my word."

Then it was darkness again, everything faded.

When I opened my eyes this time I was inside of the SUV in front of my grandparents' house.

"We are here, sir," I heard a soldier say to me. I got out of the car and walked towards the door of Senior's house. A soldier came to see me.

"Sir, I intercepted Colonel Malcolm and your mother, sir," she said to me.

She was a few inches shorter than I, Caucasian with light blue eyes, very fit.

"Have you ever killed a man soldier?" I asked her.

"Sir, yes, sir," she said.

"Do the visions ever go away?" I asked her.

She got quiet, and her eyes looked down and glossed over for a moment but she came to.

"No, they do not," she said sadly. "Sir."

"You did a good job. Now I must place another task on you. I want five SUVs gassed up and ready to head to the Safe Zone in Michigan within the next two hours."

"Yes, sir," she said as she walked away into her SUV and drove off.

"Glad you made it out of there safely," Malcolm came and said to me. "But it's all over the news."

"What's all over the news?" I asked him.

"Come with me," Malcolm said as Elizabeth's car pulled into the driveway.

"Victor we need to talk," she said as she got out of the car dressed in all black tights as if she was about to go jogging, with her hair flipped back and a hat on her head. "It's important."

"In a second," I said to Elizabeth as I followed Malcolm into the house.

We went into the living room where we found my father, Grandmother Patrice, and Senior all standing up looking at the television. The news was on. It showed me standing up, and striking down the man in cold blood.

"This is obviously edited," I said to them. It only showed me and the one man, and two people on the ground, Brittany and Adam.

It showed me being circled, but it just shows me striking him down, it didn't show him raising his sword or anything.

"This isn't good," Senior said. "They are saying that you killed that

SON OF SIN

woman and the other man before killing the third person."

"I didn't..." I started to say.

"You don't need to explain Three. Your friend Malcolm has told us everything. We just got your mother to relax. She's pretty shaken up," Senior said to me.

"Thank you for saving her, son," my father said to me in gratitude.

"You don't have to thank me for saving my own mother," I said to him.

I didn't save her though, someone else did. No time to explain that now.

"You all are going to want to hear this," Grandmother Patrice said as she turned up the television.

Octavius was set to speak.

"Three people were slain today," he started off saying, wearing his white outfit with blue trimmings. "Three people were slain because of what they believe in. All three of them were good Christians, spreading the word and faithfulness of the Gospel, and they were slain in cold blood by a so called Christian and his Muslim cohort. I am not privy to all the happenings in Cleveland, but I will be on my way there soon. It brings great sorrow on my heart to say this, but the executioner of these three innocent people, is no other than your own Victor Thomas. Second Corinthians fourteen and fifteen says *'And no wonder! For Satan himself transforms himself into an angel of light. Therefore it is no great thing if his ministers also transform themselves into ministers of righteousness, whose end will be according to their works.'* I will be traveling to Cleveland, to meet with this Victor Thomas, and I will bring him to justice. Until then, every Christian has my complete authority to strike down anyone who doesn't stand for Jesus Christ!"

"Which Victor Thomas is he talking about?" my father said. "Obviously not me, but let me talk to him."

"Not a chance," Senior said. "Not a chance son, you're not going to talk to him. I will talk to him. Explain the situation."

"Words aren't going to get through to this man, Dad," my father said. "He's coming here to bring you to justice. What do you think that means? You think he's going to put you in some jail, no he's going to kill you."

Grandmother Patrice sat down with tears in her eyes. Elizabeth rushed over there to her. No matter what was going to happen, her husband, son or grandson, all named Victor Thomas, was going to have to face Octavius. Senior wanted to go because he was a minister; he was the most well-known of all of us. My father wanted to go to protect his father and his son.

"And what do you think they are going to do to you!" Senior yelled out. "You think I'm going to let you go talk to him knowing that he's going to strike you down. Who do you think I am!?"

My father and grandfather began shouting at one another.

"Malcolm," I said.

"Sir?" Malcolm came to me.

"Call Azeem, find out if there is any movement, get Zaviera here as soon as you can…"

"Sir," a soldier said interrupting me.

"Yes?" Malcolm said to the soldier.

"There are several media cars trying to gain access to the driveway."

"This is just great," my father said sarcastically. "I'm going to talk to them."

"No, son, I am," Senior said to him.

"Dad!" my father yelled. "I've lost Sa'Rah and Persia, I wouldn't be able to live with myself if you or Three went."

"I'm sorry, son. But I'm not asking you," Senior said to him.

My grandmother grabbed my father who started crying.

"Send cars to Christina's, and my aunts, call them, let them know to get essential things, and prepare to leave," I said to Malcolm.

"Christina and Fawzia are already at the Safe Zone sir. Zaviera sent them yesterday." Malcolm said.

"Good," I said.

Eric Anderson, a well-known car dealer in north east Ohio, he owned four dealership lots, over a hundred cars and SUVs on each lot, each lot equipped with its own gas pump. He gave us and our cause access to his entire inventory and gas. He had two conditions; the first was that we put his wife, his mother, and his four daughters into a Safe Zone. I told him that he could go as well. But his second condition was that he fought alongside me in the war. That is how we are able to transport people back and forth to the Safe Zones. We took all of the dark cars, and had the darkest tint put on the windows. We didn't decorate them in any way, if you are to look at them, you would think it's just a normal car.

Senior began to walk out of the front door.
"Guard him," Malcolm said to the soldier.
"Yes, sir," the Soldier responded.
"Any other orders sir?" Malcolm asked me.
"Get your men to that beach."
"Yes, sir," Malcolm said.
"Oh, Malcolm."
"Sir?"
"Send an SUV to the man's house that I put down today, he has a wife, a daughter, and two sons, have them taken to a Safe Zone."
"How do you even know this about him?"
"Colonel," I said looking at him.
I didn't feel like being questioned.
"Yes, sir," Malcolm said in complete confusion.
"Can we talk now?" Elizabeth said to me.
"Yes," I said to her.
I lead her to the back yard. The sun had started to shine over the Lake. The air was still brisk; it hit every one of my nerves in my body with chills.
"What do we need to talk about?" I asked to her.
"I never told you what my father did for a living," she said to me.
"I don't know how that is relevant," I said to her.
"What he did, he built the ships that the Muslims are going to sail

across Lake Erie in to attack us from the North."

I was shocked. Not at her father building the boats, but the fact that she knew what was happening.

"How do you know they are sailing from the North?"

"My father told me and my mother everything. My brother is over there right now, he wants to fight with them. My father tried to get him to change his mind, but as they were building the ships, my brother talked with them, and believes in their ways, and wants to fight their fight, and they are going to let him."

"Your brother has a right to fight for what he believes in."

"Don't give me that, Victor!" Elizabeth screamed at me.

She was scared, I could see it in her.

"Is that all you had to tell me?"

"It may not be a big deal to you. But it is to me. My cousin is about to start massacring everyone, my brother is fighting for a Muslim Army. The man I love is leading an Army against them both." She said as she stopped and looked at me.

She was the second woman to ever say that she loved me. The first one didn't go over so well, I was not quite sure how to accept this. I didn't want to make the situation weird. I just looked at her and smiled a comforting smile as she blushed a little bit calming down.

"My father felt guilty so he built another boat, a boat for you."

"What do you mean for me?"

"Well not specifically for you, but for whoever was going to meet the Muslims at that beach. That's just the first beach they are going to, they are going to try to take Cleveland and the surrounding cities, one city garrisoned means they can build and grow right here on your soil. My father built a ship, but not a fighter ship, an escape one, it's loaded and equipped with jet skis and speed boats. It's designed like a cruise ship, it can hold anywhere from two to three thousand people, it's faster than a cruise ship though. It's going to be sitting out on the west. Just something I wanted you to know, in case you needed to get out of there."

The wind blew and our faces grew nearer to one another.

"Victor," my grandmother Patrice interrupted. "One of your men is asking for you."

"Thanks," I grinned and said to her.

Elizabeth and I looked one another and laughed a bit. It was nice to laugh in these troubled times.

"Thank you for this information, Elizabeth. I want you to go with one of my men, they are going to take you to a safe place, and I promise I'll see you there."

"Not yet, I want to talk with my cousin."

"You think he'll listen to you?"

"Doesn't matter, he will hear me."

"Afterwards, please, you, your mother and your father, need to get with my men so they can take you."

"I will," she said.

I walked back into the house. My father wasn't in the living room. And Grandmother Patrice was looking out of the window.

"Sir," said a soldier, "It appears that your grandfather is being overwhelmed with questions. Sir."

I walked out of the front door, there were news vans from at least eight different stations out front, cameras and lights, more than twenty people trying to ask Senior a question at one time. I walked up to the middle of them where Senior was standing, Elizabeth by my side.

"Who is this?" said one of the reporters holding a microphone to Senior's face.

"I am the Victor Thomas that Octavius will see when he comes here," I said as they all turned their attention to me.

Senior looked at me in total fear.

"I am Victor Thomas the Third, my father is Victor Thomas Junior, and my grandfather is Victor Thomas Senior. I am the Victor Thomas in the video. What the Video doesn't show is how that woman lying on the ground was stabbed by the very man who lay near her with an arrow in his back. I am not denying that blood is on my sword, because it is, but only by the man you saw, who raised his sword and I attacked before he could. I'm not sure why our President has given such a power to Octavius Atavus, but I can assure you it is not the Christian way according to the Bible."

"The Bible speaks of love and forgiveness, and that the judgment of all men is through God. Octavius is not God. Octavius is man, and as all men, he has fallen short of the glory. And if he wants to come here and speak to me, he is more than welcome to. My ears are ready to hear what he has to say, and my sword is ready to defend anything I need to. His war is instilling fear in all of America and the world. Well I'm here to tell everyone, since Octavius loves to go to the Bible to get his point across, Second Timothy, chapter one verse seven says *'For God hath not given us the spirit of fear; but of power, and of love, and of a sound mind.'* Do not fear Octavius, all Christians know that what he is doing is wrong, and eventually, the true Christians will prevail."

I turned to walk back towards the house, they continued to ask questions.

"Get them out of here," I said to my soldier.

Over thirty of my soldiers had converged to Senior's house. Malcolm must've given them the order. My soldiers began to get the news crew out of the drive way. I walked into the house with Senior and Elizabeth.

"Are you sure you're ready for this, grandson?" Senior said to me.

"As ready as I'll ever be, Senior."

"No! No way," Grandmother Patrice said. "You're not going to talk to him. None of you are."

"I have to, grandmother," I said to her calmly. "If I don't go talk to him, he'll find all of us, and then there won't be any talking. You have to understand. I will be better off than my father or Senior."

"Sir," I heard Zaviera say walking into the front door. "You asked for me?"

"Yes," I said to Zaviera. "What is the status of everything I asked Malcolm?"

"Your Aunts are on their way here, they want to see you before they leave. Malcolm sent someone to pick up your grandfather Persy. The man you struck down, his family is in route."

"Good," I said. "Senior, grandmother, get prepared to leave, take only the essentials."

"What do you mean leave?" Senior said as Elizabeth answered her phone and walked out of the back door to talk.

"This place isn't safe anymore. I've had a Safe Zone established, you two, my father, my mother, Aunt Victoria and Aunt Victory will be taken there along with other people who wish to go. Some may already be there. I'm not asking you all, I'm telling you all that you're going."

"Ok," Senior said as he led my grandmother upstairs to begin packing.

"It's time Zaviera, we have to get to Mentor Headlands Beach, that's the first one reported that they are going to go to. There will be a cruise ship to the west, with jet skis, and speed boats near to us, I want you to question everyone, whoever knows how to operate those, they are on retreat duty, once I give the word, with haste, get people to that ship and come back. I want your finest archers covering them."

"Yes sir, I will begin preparations immediately," Zaviera said as she began to leave.

"That was Octavius," Elizabeth said as she walked back in.

Zaviera stopped and looked at Elizabeth.

"How does she know Octavius?" Zaviera asked.

"He's my cousin," Elizabeth answered.

"How can we trust you?" Zaviera exclaimed.

"I trust her. And you will," I said to Zaviera.

"He will see me tomorrow morning, at the Federal Building downtown. Then he wants to see you. I'm going to try to talk him out of it."

"Ok," I said.

"Might I make a suggestion?" Elizabeth asked.

"Go ahead," I said.

"There's an airport over there, Burke, I'll have access to my father's money, I could get you a few planes and pilots, if you have to retreat, they can fly you anywhere you'll need to go. "

"That's actually not a bad idea, sir," Zaviera said to me.

"It's not," I said. "But just in case, have a few charter busses down there as well as a backup, as well as any SUVs we have left in the city. Call Eric; tell him to suit up, he's coming with me to see Octavius. Thank you Elizabeth."

"You're welcome. I have to go, get my mother and father ready. If I don't see you tomorrow, please don't kill my brother."

"If I see him, you'll see him," I said to her.

"You have your orders." I said to Zaviera.

She and Elizabeth both left.

I was alone in the living room for the first time in a long time. I walked around looking at the pictures on the wall, family photos, and child hood art. I looked at a picture of my father when he was just sixteen, in his basketball uniform, my Aunt Victory holding me as a baby when she was still a kid herself. Aunt Victoria's graduation, Grandma Patrice and Senior's wedding photo. A baby picture of Sa'Rah. Leon and I holding up the state's championship trophy for football our freshman year, our first championship together. It hit me right there, I haven't seen my brother in almost two months, and haven't seen much of him in the past six months, I went from spending nearly every day with him in some capacity, to never seeing him. I don't even know where he is at. I sighed deeply.

I sat down on the floor and crossed my legs, I closed my eyes and blocked everything out, it could be the last time I ever meditated.

Let me find some peace in this moment.

31

I meditated for a few hours and then my aunts came over. My father and mother came from downstairs and shortly after Grandma Patrice and Senior came down. We were all in the living room when it hit them, they may never see me again. My aunts both hugged me and kissed me on the cheek, and told me that they loved me. Grandmother Patrice hugged me, but couldn't look me in the eyes. She hurried off to the car.

My mother hugged me tightly, and she wept into my arms, I couldn't lie to her, I was going to see Octavius in a few hours, and after that, if I survive, I have to lead my army into battle against two forces that greatly outnumber us. The chances of me surviving are low. I hugged her, and I kissed her, and assured her that God was watching over me. My father said some words of encouragement; surprisingly he seemed really proud of me. That gave me strength.

Senior and I didn't talk; we didn't hug or shake hands. We looked at one another, and then his eyes dropped, as he got in the SUVs in the middle of the night, and they drove off into the night. I had three soldiers in each vehicle.

I was going to miss my family. It takes a village to raise a child, and my family was my village. Through faith, through love and joy, they all chipped in and raised me the best way they knew how. A piece of my personality came from every one of them. I thanked God for my family. I wished I could've said goodbye to Leon and Sa'Rah though, that would make things seem more complete. I didn't fear my task that was appointed to me by God. Jesus had to walk His path, be crucified for us to be saved, if God asked me to do this, I would gladly do it. My life belongs to him; I'm just borrowing the body.

I slept at Senior's house. I had soldiers outside all night. I told them that I didn't need them but they preferred to stay. I slept only a few hours. When I awoke, I took a shower, got dressed in my gear, I ate breakfast.

"Dear God," I knelt down on my knees in the living room, on the couch with all of my family's pictures around, Christina and Leon, Senior and Grandmother Patrice, Grandpa Persy and my mother, my father and Sa'Rah. "I pray to you this day, asking you for courage and strength. Honor and understanding, selflessness and righteousness. I ask that you put your hand on this world, and have it be as you see fit. Your will, will be done. I love you God. As I close my eyes, guide me with your hands to salvation. In Jesus name I pray. Amen."

I walked out of the front door.

"Sir!" five of my soldiers said in unison.

I breathed hard.

"No one is coming back here," I said to them. "At least, no one should be. One of you stay here, help yourself to anything in the house. If anyone does come, send them to the Safe Zone if they are a friendly. A foe? Put them down. The rest of you, come with me."

Vita walked up. I mounted her, the rest got in their vehicles, two got on motorcycles and we rode to the Downtown Cleveland Federal Building. Today was Sunday, a few days before Christmas. Downtown was completely empty of regular people. All I saw was Octavius' military colors and men in the streets as I went south. It was a gray day outside, no sun, no wind, no snow, just a day.

His military was everywhere, his colors were white and blue, they all stood in formation on every street in a straight line, if I tried to take any other route I would have to go through them. They stopped me from going any further on the street. My caravan of men included me on Vita, two motorcycles, and two cars and one SUV. As I stopped in front of the stairs of this tall building, it was maybe thirty or more floors. I got off of Vita to see Eric escorting Elizabeth out of the building.

"Victor!" she said as she ran to me and hugged me. "I saw my cousin. He means to kill you!"

I hugged her back.

"I know," I said to her. "I am ok."

"But I'm not," she said to me looking at me, not crying, but almost. "I'm not ready to lose you."

I smiled at her.

"Are you done with your talk with your cousin?" I asked her.

"Yes," she said.

"Good, I need you to get to the Safe Zone." I said to her as I motioned for one of my Soldiers to come to her. "Get her to Michigan. Put her with my family."

"Yes, sir." he said to me. He walked her to the SUV.

"Is your family there?" I asked her.

She shook her head yes.

"Make sure she isn't followed." I said to one of my soldiers on the motorcycle.

I walked down to Elizabeth who was getting in the car. She appeared greatly saddened and I want her to feel better. I took out Sa'Rah's rings. "Do you see these?" I said as I showed them to her.

"They are beautiful," she said.

"Hold on to them for me," I said

"Ok."

"I'll be back for them."

"Promise?"

"Promise," I said to her as I hugged her.

She started letting tears flow from her eyes. I wiped one of them away as I leaned in and kissed her lips. Her lips were soft, and sweet, and passion went through me. It was a quick kiss, but a necessary one.

She licked her lips, stopped crying, breathed hard and smiled at me. I closed the door to the SUV and it left with my caravan following it.

"Must be hard to let her go like that, sir," Eric said to me.

"Not really," I said to him. "She's going to a good place."

"Ready to go in and handle this guy?"

"You're not coming in with me?" I said to Eric.

"Why not, sir?"

"I have another task for you. I want you to take food to the army on the beach, make sure they eat, make sure they laugh, take a little wine too, make sure they have a good time, sing and dance. I need you to elevate their moods, calm their tensions and ease their fear."

"Right, sir," he said to me reluctantly as he began walking down the stairs.

"Oh yeah," I said to Eric. "Take this. Give it to Malcolm." I took off my General's Badge and gave it to Eric.

"Sir?" he said to me looking sad and confused.

"Someone has to lead everyone if I'm gone. Fight with honor." I said to him.

He shook his head in agreement. And turned and got into his vehicle and drove off.

I walked through the doors of the Federal Building. In the front lobby there were over one hundred of Octavius' soldiers. They all stood in attention and stood in a line that leads directly to the left bank of elevators. Two men walked in front of me, and two behind me. They didn't take my weapons from me. I was armed with my diamond edged sword, a bow, a quiver with a few arrows, a backup sword that was sheathed to a thin shield that hung on my back like backpack, and a small knife on my thigh.

"The Lord is my shepherd," I began to recite Psalm twenty-three as we walked between all the soldiers, eyes straight ahead.

We entered into an elevator as the soldier pressed floor thirty one. They stood on the four corners of the Elevator, I was in the middle.

"I shall not want. He maketh me lie down in green pastures: He leadeth me beside the still waters. He restoreth my soul: He leadeth me in the paths of righteousness for His name's sake. Yeah, though I walk through the valley of the shadow of death, I will fear no evil: for Thou art with me; Thy rod and Thy staff they comfort me. Thou preparest a table before me in the presence of mine enemies: Thou anointest my head with oil; my cup runneth over." I said as the elevator stopped and the doors opened.

I saw Octavius for the first time in my life face to face. He was an inch shorter than I, with long dirty blonde hair, his eyes were the same color eyes as Elizabeth's, and he was in excellent shape. He had on his usual attire of white garments with his white cape with blue trimmings.

"Surely," he and I said in unison. "Goodness and mercy shall follow me all the days of my life: and I will dwell in the house of the Lord forever."

"Follow me," he said to me as he turned and walked into an office with glass as the walls.

I walked into the room and there were two chairs that sat facing one another eight feet apart. All of his men stood in front of each elevator. No one coming in, no one going down. I felt my phone vibrate; I got a message from a number that was unfamiliar to me. It said to use the window. I looked out the window and it was a beautiful view of Lake Erie. The waters looked calm, birds flew, and it looked peaceful.

"And when I looked up," Octavius said as he closed the door and closed the blinds to the room. "I saw a man standing in front of me, with a drawn sword in his hand. And I went up to him."

He walked towards me. "And I asked, 'Are you for us or for our enemies?'"

"Neither," I said to him. "Bust as a commander of the army of the Lord, I have come." I responded to his Joshua chapter five verses thirteen and fourteen reference.

"You know your bible," he said to me.

He was armed with a sword as well.

"Have a seat." He said as we sat down in front of one another.

He looked at me and smiled graciously.

"My cousin loves you," he said to me. "She offered herself to service to me, if I would spare your life. But of course I didn't accept it. That is my cousin, and I love her. And after you die, there will be others. But before I bring you to justice, I'm going to do something very cliché."

He said as he stood up and walked around the room.

"An Angel came to me Mr. Thomas. As clear as I am talking to you right now. He was a bit taller than I, fair in the skin, good looking man, determined face with black eyes, wore a black coat, a black shirt and black pants, and spoke to me in a language I never heard, but I could understand every word. And he told me to go start God's war. These people society has accepted, these Muslims, these Jews, these pretend Christians, they are the first to go. Then the remaining sycophants, miscreants and degenerates will follow. He said he would control the media, control the attention, get me the Pope and get me the President of the United States, after those dominos were in place, I could do whatever I wanted to purge the world of the insufferable madness we call acceptance."

"Why the Muslims, Jews and Christians first?" I asked him.

"The Hindus, the Buddhist, atheist and others, they don't believe in an Almighty. They believe in a way of life, I will crush them with relative ease. The Muslims, the Jews and the pretend Christians, they believe whole-heartedly in an Almighty, and that belief gives them strength, it's what gives you strength to rise up against me."

The angel he described sounded a lot like Leon's Uncle. Leon's Uncle is also who I believe is to be the one who helped me onto Vita after I was jumped by Malcolm, fought with me on the bridge, and shot the arrow that saved my mother. How could it be the same person? It couldn't be. Perhaps it was Leon's father, this Sin guy, perhaps he's the one that visited Octavius. But Senior and my father spoke so highly of Sin.

"I rise against you because you are wrong," I said to Octavius. "My mother's side of the family is Jehovah's Witnesses, we don't believe everything the same, and does that give me the right to go kill all of them? God gave us all free will to do as we please and to be judged by God and God alone."

"Why not?" Octavius said smugly. "You think I've spared my family who do not believe as I believe? If anyone in my family was a Jehovah's Witness, I would kill them if they chose not to change their ways. In the book of Ezekiel, chapter eight, God gives Ezekiel a vision of men worshipping an alter that is not of The Lord. They turned their back to God. Starting from the middle of verse seventeen, God said 'For they have filled the land with violence, and have returned to provoke me to anger: and, lo, they put the branch to their nose. Therefore will I also deal in fury: mine eye shall not spare neither will I have pity: and though they cry in mine ears with a loud voice, yet will I not hear them.'"

"God said that He will deal with them. What you're doing is wrong." I said to him growing angry. "What about Fawzia?"

"Fawzia!?" He said surprisingly as he turned around and looked at me. "How do you know Fawzia?"

"I fell in love with her," I said smiling. "Then she broke my heart."

"Fawzia," he said as he took a deep breath. "Her sister was delicious."

He turned to me smiling.

"Fawzia was going to be my queen; she was going to be the queen of the world once it's in my hands."

"She's a Muslim. She believes in Allah," I said to him.

"She would've believed in anything I told her!" Octavius said. "But her sister, I defiled her, that's what she told me, she saved her. And Fawzia left my grasp. Her father took her from me. He won't be taking her again once I find her."

"Why won't he be?"

"He's dead."

"You killed their father?"

"Yes."

"Do they know?"

"I don't care. How is Fawzia?"

"Pregnant."

"You got her pregnant!" Octavius screamed. "Good for you. At least now when you die, you'll have someone to carry out your name."

"By my brother," I said regretfully.

"Now that is interesting," Octavius said. "Where is your brother? The great Leon. Truthfully, he was the only man I feared could stop me in this world, he's disappeared. Now here you are. Your swordsmanship is great. I watched the entire video, the man didn't even get his sword out of his sheath before you killed him, he barely raised it. Then, everyone else, you didn't kill another person, merely injuring them to not return. You're good, almost as good as me. Leon must've taught you to move that quickly. I was hoping to meet him before I sacked this town. The fleets of Muslims have no idea I know they're coming, you should join me."

"Was that your cliché moment?" I said as I stood up and looked out the window he was looking out of.

"It was." Octavius said. "I need you to promise me two things, Mr. Thomas."

"And what are those two things?"

"If some how you survive, take good care of Elizabeth, she is, in many ways my sister. I promised her that I would give her brother a quick death, I don't want her to hurt."

"And the second?"

"I have a son, nearly fourteen years old, living in Egypt. No one knows of him, I want you to find him, and keep him at your side."

"Why can't you do that?"

"Because if you survive this. That means I'm dead."

"And what of my family, if I don't survive."

"I'll see to it they'll see you soon in the afterlife."

"I see," I said with a deep breath as I stepped backwards.

I felt it in his voice; he was waiting to attack me. He was finding the moment. I will give it to him.

"Sounds like you think you've drunk the wine of the wrath of God," I said making a reference to the fourteenth chapter of Revelations.

"What you don't get," Octavius said looking at me from the corner of his eyes.

"I am the Wrath of God!" he screamed as he unsheathed his sword and attacked me.

I was prepared; I dodged his initial attack and unsheathed my sword. He was too fast and too smart of a fighter to play with and try to let get tired by swinging.

We fought across the room, there was nothing but space, and two chairs and no way out. He was on the offensive mostly. I wanted to wait to see if his men would come in to help him when they heard the noise. I suspect they will. When I went to the offensive, he struggled to defend, he was an offensively powerful fighter but when it came to protection, he lacked the skills. I was balanced, I could defend and attack. I cut him several times on his arms and legs, just scratches, nothing serious. But it annoyed him. His back was against the wall, I went up for a high attack and he threw sand in my face. I dropped my sword and stumbled backwards. He pulled back on the string of a bow, I heard him release it, I back flipped over the chair and the chair blocked the arrow for me. I back flipped again over the other chair as I heard him release another arrow. I quickly pulled my short dagger from my thigh holster and cut it in the middle, it was aimed at my face.

I opened my eyes, they were burning. He had picked up my sword and ran at me with both his and my sword. I brought out my shield and blocked his attacks, I brought out my back up sword and went to offensive, I blocked his attack with my shield, parried his other attack and kicked him hard towards the glass wall that his men stood behind. He dropped both of the swords. His men ran into the room. It was two of them, one ran towards Octavius, the other towards me with his arms raised, I hit him in the face with the shield and pierced his stomach with my sword.

I remember the text that told me to use the window. I'm assuming it meant to jump out of it. Because there were too many men to try to use it as a way to exterminate his men. I put my back up sword in the shield's sheath and put that on my back. I grabbed Octavius' sword and threw it at the window, it pierced the window, but didn't break it, just cracked it in all directions. More of Octavius' men were running in, I put them all down permanently with relative ease. The elevators, all of them lit up and I heard more running out. You could fit about fourteen armed men in there comfortably, and there were eight elevators to this floor, there could be over one hundred men running in here. Impossible odds, especially if Octavius gets up.

"Here's your sword," Octavius tossed it to me.

"You fought well." He said as his men stopped at the door.

"Kill him," he said calmly as they all charged at me.

I grabbed the chair and threw it as hard as I could at the window with Octavius' sword in it. It broke the window as I ran behind it as I heard several arrows being shot at me. I was outside of the window. I'm not so sure this was the best of ideas, there was nowhere for me to go.

I began to fall. My only thoughts were of Elizabeth and Sa'Rah. I would see Sa'Rah soon. I felt two arms grabbing me. I looked up. It was Leon!

32

"Leon!" I screamed at the top of my lungs as we flew through the air.

"Calm yourself, brother," Leon said to me.

He sent me that text. I looked up to see him, shirtless with huge white angel wings. We flew over Lake Erie, as the wind hit my face. I had to concentrate to breathe. We flew several miles east towards Mentor Headlands State Park beach area. Leon landed us on the most west edge of the beach. When we landed I just looked at him. He wore brown sweat pants and black shoes, no shirt, with huge angel wings at his back. And the necklace his uncle gave him around his neck. We stood there starring at one another in silence.

"Thank you for saving me," I said to him finally.

He didn't say anything back. The sun had come out and I felt it warm my face, it was still pretty cold out.

"This is where you'll have your war," Leon said to me as we looked in the distance east.

I couldn't see them but I'm sure that my army was over there.

"Octavius couldn't fight you honestly could he?"

"I'm not so sure anyone could match me one on one," I said to him trying to get him to laugh.

It was an awkward feeling. I hadn't seen him since I tried to kill him for sleeping with Fawzia. Leon was different; he was calm, as if he found peace or a purpose.

"You always said you felt like you could fly," I said to him. "How did they get those wings on there? Staples?"

Leon finally cracked a smile.

"Being an angel, I can walk in the spirit world, or the world of man, as either an angel or a man. And no, they did not staple these on," he said laughing. "I'm sorry again, about what happened with Fawzia."

"It was in God's will," I said to him.

"God? Ha," he said smugly. "Look at the Lake brother, is it not calm? But we know what approaches, we know what see's to set itself on our shores. I am not a man, but I am not an angel, I am part of both."

"So you're a Mangel?" I said trying to cool the seriousness down.

"No," he said back to me. "Earth is a planet in need of a leader. Octavius began the process, but he was never to lead."

"Who is to lead then brother?"

"Jesus is the son of Man. I am the son of Sin, Earth will become New Heaven, and Cleveland will be my Jerusalem, and I its Jesus. And I will reshape the world into a glorious paradise until Jesus decides to return."

"That's blasphemous," I said to him at his ridiculous statement.

"For a man yes. Not for an Angel," he said as he spread his wings, they had to stretch seven feet wide. They were thick and feathery like an eagle's wing. "How is my mother?"

"She's in a safe place," I said to him.

"I looked for her and Fawzia, they are gone. So is my fathe…" he paused. "So is Ian. Where are they?"

"They are in a safe place."

"I looked for Senior, I didn't see him. I wanted to tell him goodbye before I left."

"Where are you going?"

"I have to finish some business my uncle couldn't finish. This may be the last time we ever speak, and I wanted to tell you that I love you, and no matter what happened, you are my little brother, and I love you," he said as he placed his hand on my shoulder.

"You were only born a few minutes before me," I reminded him as I place my hand on his opposite shoulder.

"Yes but I was fully developed, nine months, you were early, writhing in agony, facing death, and then, you had angel blood put in you and look at you now."

I never thought of it like that. Leon's blood was added to mine, and that blood corrected any illnesses I had at the time and I survived and grew to be, who I am today.

"I guess that's right," I said to him.

"Goodbye, brother," Leon said to me as he walked into the water.

"Oh," he said as he took out a sword from basically thin air.

It was a large golden sword with angel wings at the grip.

"I believe that I could best you one on one," he said as he smiled and walked into the water.

He walked straight out until he was fully submerged. I didn't know where he was going to finish his uncle's unfinished business. I thanked him for saving me. But I had to get to my army.

I walked about a mile east to see my army camped in the parking lot at Mentor Headlands State Park Beach. They were all eating at picnic tables that were lined up in rows stretched across the parking lot. Music was playing, people were laughing and joking around, just as I instructed Eric to do.

"It's the General!" screamed one of the soldiers.

The music stopped, everyone looked at me and began to stand up.

"As you were," I said to them all.

Everyone looked a bit uneasy.

"It's good to see you're alive," Zaviera said to me. "You're bleeding!"

"I jumped out of a thirty first floor window," I said to her as I walked by everyone looking at me.

"How are you alive?"

"You wouldn't believe me I told you," I said to her.

"Sir," Azeem said to me. "According to scouts, they'll be here in the morning, and Octavius' army will be here sometime tomorrow afternoon."

"That gives us some time," I said to Azeem.

"Time for what sir?"

"To break bread," I said to him. "Eat everyone! Enjoy each other's company, laugh, be joyous and grateful."

I walked into Malcolm.

"This is yours, sir," Malcolm said to me handing me my General's badge back. "Octavius is dead?"

"No," I said to him.

"Well I'm glad you're not," Malcolm said. "You have warm water and soap in your tent, and fresh clothes. Suit up. We eat tonight, war tomorrow."

He was smiling. It was a smile of courage, Malcolm was ready for this, he was born for this, to fight for what he believed in. I looked at him and shook my head in agreement.

I went into my tent. I washed up, patched up a few wounds, and put on my gear. I left my weapons in my tent. I walked out and joined everyone smiling, eating and drinking. It was an odd day to say the least. I fought someone that I looked up to and admired, I jumped out of a building window, and was caught by an angel, my brother, who then just walks straight into the water. I tried to take my mind off of tomorrow, I'm not sure if any of us will survive. I didn't see the ship Elizabeth promised, but I did see some jet skis and some boats while we were in the air.

Amongst the talk at the tables, were religion, missing sports, why are we fighting, many different topics and subjects. I got to know quite of few of the soldiers I was responsible for. Some looked eager, some looked nervous. I think it's a time for me to talk to them.

"Everyone," I said.

They all stood up and walked near me. It was nearly few thousand of us, not as many people I had thought would show.

"The General speaks!" Malcolm said to silence those who didn't hear me.

"Talking with everyone, I can see that there are some doubts about us against these two forces we will face tomorrow. I know that many of you aren't Christian or Muslim, or a religion at all. But I do know one thing, we are all people, we are all humans. We breathe air, and we bleed red blood. And just because we have differences in beliefs doesn't mean that the person next to you isn't your brother, or your sister. It doesn't mean that their family they are protecting isn't your family. Because it is your family. It's my family, it's Malcolm's Family. All of your families in the Safe Zone, that is why you are here today. Because you are not going to let a tyrant like Octavius Atavus tell you what you can and can't believe. You are here today because you aren't going to let a fleet of anyone, Muslims, Christians, doesn't matter, it could be ships full of Christians, and had they come to take over our city, in hopes to slaughter everyone, I would be here all the same.

'We hold these truths to be self-evident, that ALL men are created equal.'" I said a line from the Declaration of Independence.

"As Americans, no, as people, we are all entitled to life, liberty and the pursuit of happiness. And it was our government's responsibility to protect those rights, but they gave that up when they handed it to Octavius, when it's ignoring this fleet that is sailing here. So it's our jobs to protect the people we love, we may be weak in numbers, but we are strong in purpose. So when you sleep tonight, I want you to think about everyone you are fighting for, your mother, your father, your sister, your brother, your wife, your children, or just another person. Remember them; because I tell you now, they are going to remember you forever. Who would we be if we sat back and just watched our world fall to chaos without picking up a sword, without shooting a bow, without helping a friend? Who would we be? I'll tell you, we wouldn't be here!"

I looked around. Faces were lifting, spirits were being raised, the tension had left and now anxiety had come. They were ready for this battle.

"So throughout the rest of the day, as you eat, laugh, dance and sing, make sure you tell someone thank you, and remind them to remember you for you're giving your life up for them. Malcolm!" I said. "Remember me my friend, for I will give my life up for you."

Malcolm looked at me and smiled.

"Remember me!" Malcolm said to me. "My brother! For I will give up my life for you."

Everyone started looking around and repeating to one another. I walked through everyone into my tent, I was exhausted from the fight with Octavius and the flight with Leon. I rested my head on the floor in my tent and dozed off.

"General," I heard someone say. "General!"

They said it louder. I opened my eyes to see it was Azeem talking to me.

"Sir, it's time."

"What do you mean, it's still dark out," I responded.

"They are here. They are beginning to load their man on long boats to drive them to shore. They do not know we are here," Azeem said as he turned and left the tent. I got up immediately and got dressed. I armed myself with all of my weapons.

"Soldier," I said to a soldier walking by my tent.

"Sir?" Said the soldier.

"Have Colonel Malcolm and Major Zaviera meet me here please."

"Yes Sir!" The soldier said as he left.

This was the day. I still wasn't sure what we were going to accomplish, but if we could show the rest of the world that we were standing up against those who wished to persecute in the name of their religion then it would not be for nothing.

"Sir, you wanted me?" Zaviera said.

"Sir," Malcolm came into the tent.

"Yes. What is the status of the escape ship?" I asked to Zaviera.

"The ship arrived last night shortly after you went to sleep." Zaviera said. "It's gassed up and ready when we are. It has thirty crew members who all took an oath and received honorary soldier badges, we have twenty jet skis and ten speed boats. The Jet skis can take one person per trip fast, speed boats can take from five to ten, sir."

"Where's the wind?" I asked.

"It's blowing north sir," Zaviera responded.

"Good. Archers have range. I want your Archers focused on the long boats, we still have the element of surprise. I'm not sure if they have guns or not, if they have guns, we're retreating immediately," I said.

"They are armed like us," Malcolm said. "Canada is stricter on gun laws than we are. They couldn't even bring them over."

"Good," I said. "Malcolm, I want your men facing North waiting for Octavius' army. They'll be coming north from Route forty-four. When I give the notice to retreat, I need you to leave, no heroism. Both of you."

"Yes, sir," they both said as they walked out.

I took a deep breath as I put my swords in their sheaths, one on my belt, the other on my shield on my back. I walked out to see everyone getting into formation. The sky had an orange glow to it, morning was coming. I could see the ships in the shadows if you looked hard enough north. And I could feel Octavius' men coming.

"Remember me!" I said loudly, the soldiers all stopped and looked at me. "For I will give my life for every one of you."

I looked at as many of them in the eyes as possible.

"You remember me, sir!" said a woman soldier.

"You remember me too!" said another one.

And then everyone was saying remember me.

"Fight with courage and strike without fear," I said to them as we all continued to our paths.

The beach had a curve stretching from the northeast to southwest. The sandiest part was in the middle, about two thousand feet wide, the parking lot was big, and the only way to this was route forty four, which was probably covered by Octavius' men. I had archers lined up on the smaller portion of sand on the south west, the escape ship was near there in the deeper waters, they were to cover the jet skis and speed boats. I stood at the front facing North, I had a line of soldiers at my back that stood at the beginning of the parking lot, in four lines facing north with me. Malcolm's men were behind us facing south, waiting for Octavius. This is where it would begin.

"Never thought I'd see the day," Malcolm said to me.

"What do mean?" I responded as we stood back to back.

He was getting ready to go lead his men closer to the entrances of route forty four.

"The day that a Christian and a Muslim get together…"

"To fight Christians and Muslims. Yeah, I get your point," I said as I stuck my hand out to shake his.

Malcolm didn't reach back.

"Shake my hand tonight when we're celebrating our victory," he said as he turned and walked towards the front of his formation.

It began to snow lightly. I saw the Muslim fleet. They had about six long boats coming toward us.

"I've done a lot of things in my life," Eric said to me.

Eric was an older man, in his fifties. He didn't look completely fifty, but you could tell he was up there. He's a Caucasian man with a tremendous tan. He had blue eyes and short cut brunette hair. He kept himself in shape pretty well. He was a few inches taller than I, broad shoulders but he had a stomach on him. He's a really good guy with a raspy voice.

"We've all done lots of things," I said to him. "Be calm."

"I am calm," he said to me. "I just wanted to tell you this, when Octavius came on the television with that crap he spewed I was angry. I mean my wife and kids, they went to church all the time, I was at the dealerships. I didn't really care about going to church, figured I'd have time when I retired. I just wanted to make money. And now, well, I won't retire. I'm going to die on this beach. I don't mind dying fighting for something I believe in. But what is it all for? What is to happen of my soul? I mean, what will God say on Judgment day?"

"I can't tell you what God would say," I said to him. "But I can tell you, Ephesians two eight and nine say 'For it is by grace you have been saved, through faith, and this is not from yourselves, it is the gift of God, not by works, so that no one can boast.' So just have faith Eric. You'll survive today, and you'll hold your wife tonight."

He looked at me and smiled.

"You know what I've always wanted, but there's no time for it now?" he said to me after a moment of silence.

"What's that?"

"I've always wanted to be baptized."

"You've never been baptized?" I said to him.

"Nope. My wife and my kids always asked me, hey, come get baptized today, come to church with us, do this and do that. But no. Always too scared."

"Why scared?"

"Because baptism for me, when I got baptized, I wanted to be saved, not play saved. And I still loved the cigarettes, the naked girls at the strip clubs, and the taste of beer. Man," he said as he shook his head. "What I wouldn't do to die in the flesh right?"

"Get on your knee," I said to him.

I didn't know what to do or what to say when baptizing someone. It had been so long since I was baptized. There wasn't any holy water around so the lake would have to do. If Senior was in my shoes, he'd baptize Eric. So I should do the same. He may very well die, might as well die with a clean conscience.

"What am I getting on my knee for?"

"Get on your knee!" I screamed to him.

He got on his knee as the rest of the soldiers looked at me.

"Pray to God, in your head, apologize for your sins, and promise God that you are going to repent your worldly ways. Offer yourself to

Him, pray with all of your heart!"

He began praying, he was mumbling at first.

"Pray with all of your heart!" I said to him. "Do you accept Jesus Christ as your Lord and Holy Savior?"

"Yes!" He said beginning to cry.

I believe I was scaring him, but it wasn't the time for coddling.

"Do you believe the Jesus Christ, son of God, died on the cross for you to have forgiveness?"

"Yes!"

"Are you ready to give your life to Christ?"

"Yes!"

"Are you ready to die in the flesh!?"

"Yes!" I grabbed his arm and helped him to his feet.

"Then come with me," I said to him as I grabbed his forearm and ran towards the lake.

"Victor!" I heard Zaviera screaming to me.

The longboats were near; the Muslim fleet knew we were here. They began shooting arrows at Eric and I.

"Victor what are we doing?" Eric said sounding scared.

"You said you wanted to be baptized!"

"In Holy water!"

"God made this water, it's as Holy as it's ever going to be! Now hurry up!" I yelled to him as we hit the water deep enough so that he could be completely submerged under the water. "Confess with your mouth, do not be ashamed of Christ!"

"I believe in Jesus Christ as my Lord and my savior. I wish to be forgiven of my wrong doings." He said as the water splashed and arrows went by our heads.

I was too focused to concern myself with them. I didn't know if this is the right way to do this.

"Are you ready to die in the flesh for the remissions of your sins, and be reborn in the newness of Christ?"

"Yes!" he said.

"Then I'll kill your flesh in the name of Jesus." I said as I took his head and took him backwards into the water. When he was in there, there was a bright red light. I brought him up. He was breathing hard.

"Thank you," he said to me.

"Do you see that light?" I said to him.

"What light?" He said looking into the water as I was.

I dove into the water and the light was even brighter as I went in. I felt hot all of a sudden, and it felt like my body was being pulled. The last time I felt this way was when I fell into the water when I promised Jesus my life. The red light grew closer and I felt myself losing consciousness.

33

I found myself in a void, absent light, absent form, absent everything. I felt my body, I turned my head, I looked around, and I couldn't see anything. I took one step and it was as if I stepped through a portal. I found myself on a rocky island, what surrounded me was pure darkness. But there was a fiery light in front of me. I walked closer to the light to see there were four men, two holding one down and one standing in front of him. As I walked closer I noticed it was Leon they were holding down, two angels, dark with wings. And another person, mark of the serpent on his left back shoulder.

Satan? I thought to myself.

"You were a fool to come here alone," said Lucifer in Angelic tongue to Leon as he raised his sword.

His sword was red and curved like a Sabre sword. I was shirtless and wearing black pants with black shoes. In my hand I held a black long sword, it was a smooth handle with a wrapping so I could keep my grip, I couldn't put my hand on what material the sword was, I smelled the blade, it smelled of ebony wood smoothed out and polished with a mixing of onyx stone to keep it dense. I'd have to keep this blade. I had to get Lucifer to attack me quickly so that I could get Leon free.

"I saw Satan fall like lightening from Heaven." I said in Angelic tongue. Lucifer stopped and looked at me. *"How art thou fallen from heaven, O Lucifer, son of the morning! How art thou cut down to the ground, which didst weaken the nations! For thou hast said in thine heart,*

I will ascend into heaven, I will exalt my throne above the stars of God: I will sit also upon the mount of the congregation in the sides of the north: I will ascend above the heights of the clouds; I will be like most High. Yet thou shalt be brought down to hell, to the sides of the pit."

"*Silence!*" Lucifer said to me.

He was about as tall as Leon, with a dark golden glow about him. His hair was long, thick and black, he turned his head, and he had a normal face, no horns, no trident. He turned and attacked me as I needed him to. I hit his right shoulder with my left and spun and with my sword I cut down both the angels holding Leon to free him.

"Thank you brother," Leon said. "Never been so glad to see you."

"Well, I'm glad I was able to come. But you can call us even, you did catch me from what I'm assured would've been a bad death," I responded as two more angels walked from the walls of this place. "What is this place?"

"You're in the spirit, this is Hell. How did you get down here? No, never mind that, how do you expect for us to defeat him?" Leon said to me.

"Can you handle your own against them?" I said motioning to the angels that walked through the walls.

They were dark, absent of color; their wings were that of a bat, not an eagle or a wing like Lucifer's and Leon's. They looked more like what I would imagine a demon would be.

"*Of course, I was doing fine until he interfered,*" he said pointing at an irritated Lucifer. The only way I was going to defeat him is with the words of God, patience, and the absolute perfect defense and counter strike. I'm only going to get one chance, this is Lucifer. This was commander of God's army. This was Michael's predecessor. He was the original Archangel.

"'*You were the seal of perfection, full of wisdom and perfect in beauty.*'" I said to him quoting Ezekiel chapter twenty eight eleven through nineteen. I stepped towards him. He was aggravated that I was quoting the bible, especially his fall. He'll attack soon enough. "*You were in Eden,*'" I continued. "*the garden of God; every precious stone adorned* you: carnelian, chrysolite and emerald, topaz, onyx and jasper, lapis lazuli, turquoise and beryl. Your settings and mountings were made of gold; on the day you were created they were prepared.'"

"Hold your tongue," Lucifer said to me as Leon began to fight the demon winged angels behind me.

"'You were anointed as a guardian cherub,'" I said. "'for so I ordained you.'"

After I said that Lucifer raised his sword and began attacking me. He was quick, he was fast, and ferocious with every strike. I felt overwhelmed but I had to stay focused.

"'You were on the holy mount of God; you walked among the fiery stones. You were blameless in your ways from the day you were created till wickedness was found in you.'"

He began to strike harder; he was faster than anyone I had fought before. Leon must've felt that I was failing for he intercepted Lucifer's next strike with his own sword. Leon was probably as strong as Lucifer, or at least a lot stronger than I. I took the chance to take a breather as I cut down the two demons Leon was fighting with ease. More came out of the walls, I attacked Lucifer again only to get his attention away from Leon, I was not sure if Leon had the skill to defeat him. I would do my best.

"' Through your widespread trade,'" I said continuing the verse. "'you were filled with violence, and you sinned. So I drove you in disgrace from the mount of God, and I expelled you, guardian cherub, from among the fiery stones. Your heart became proud on account of your beauty and you corrupted your wisdom because of your splendor. So I threw you to the earth; I made a spectacle of you before kings. By your many sins and dishonest trade you have desecrated your sanctuaries.'"

Lucifer stopped and regained his calm. He looked at me with pure anger.

"What you do not understand Son of Adam," Lucifer said. "I am still the most powerful Angel in the world." He said as his eyes and sword caught fire and he attacked me with zeal.

I blocked the attack, but the clashing of metals and the ember from the fire was hot as we looked one another in the eyes for a moment until my eyes burned so I had to shut them.

"So I made a fire come out from you, and it consumed you," I said as I looked away, blocking site from my mind so that I could focus on noise around me.

I blocked out Leon's struggle with the demons and only listened for Lucifer's attacks. He attacked and I dodged a few, blocked the others. I had to finish this verse, I have a feeling he'll leave himself open to try to take me out.

"and I reduced you to ashes on the ground in the sight of all who were watching. All the nations who knew you are appalled at you; you have come to a horrible end" I said as he did exactly what I thought.

I was able to open my eyes for a second, he swung his sword with his right hand from left to right horizontally, I ducked the attack, he came back across from right to left but I parried the attack and his chest was open.

"and will be no more," I said as I started to thrust my sword into his chest.

"*Stop!*" Lucifer said as he easily pushed my sword away from stabbing into him with his hands.

I was rendered motionless. I tried to move but couldn't. Lucifer looked at me with his piercing eyes, then his flames went out of his eyes and his sword flames subsided.

"Give this to Michael's grandson," he said as he handed me a golden skeleton key. *"It is what he came down here for. Marcel trained you well Victor, but if I ever see you here again, you won't be leaving."*

And then he disappeared right in front of me. The demons that Leon was fighting flew off into the distance.

"I take that back brother," Leon said to me in English.

"Take what back?" I responded.

"You are a much better swordsman than me."

"You'll get better."

"Maybe I won't have to."

"Here," I said as I handed him the golden skeleton key. "What are you down here for?"

"'Then war broke out in heaven,'" Leon said to me quoting Revelation chapter twelve as he looked at the key. "'Michael and his angels fought against the dragon, and the dragon and his angels fought back. But he was not strong enough, and they lost their place in heaven. The great dragon was hurled down, that ancient serpent called the devil, or Satan, who leads the whole world astray. He was hurled to earth, and his angels with him.'"

"What does that have to do with anything?" I said to him following him as he stepped towards the darkness to the edge where the darkness immediately took over and I can see nothing but darkness everywhere.

"You ever wonder what happened to all the angels that fell with the devil brother?" Leon said to me as he held the key up towards his angel necklace.

"No. It never crossed my mind," I said as I looked at him.

"Jude chapter one verse six says 'And the angels who did not keep their position of authority but abandoned their proper dwelling, these He has kept in darkness, bound with everlasting chains for judgment of the great Day.'" He said as he put the key together with his angel wings pendent, as they fused together a bright light shined and I had to turn my head.

"And second Peter two four says 'For if God did not spare angels when they sinned, but sent them to hell, putting them in chains of darkness to be held for judgment!'" Leon screamed as I opened my eyes to see the darkness was fading away and you could see for as far as the eyes could, rows and rows of angels in chains.

They all looked alike, they favored Lucifer, they had a golden glow to them, all males, with different hair styles. They were all naked of clothing, just chains on their neck, wrist and ankles came out of the ground.

"*You did well,*" I heard a voice come from behind me in Angelic tongue. It was Leon's Uncle Xin, who was also shirtless with pants and shoes on.

"*Hello Uncle,*" Leon said to Xin without looking at him.

"*Finally, Lucifer's fallen Angels are mine,*" Xin said.

"*You mean mine?*" Leon said to him. "*I released them.*"

"*My apologies nephew,*" Xin said. "*Yours.*"

"*What do you plan on doing with them?*" I asked to Leon.

"Victor!" I heard Zaviera's voice scream in my head. I closed my eyes to see water and people fighting.

I opened my eyes only to see Leon and Xin staring at me.

"*I'm going to end this war Octavius started,*" Leon said.

"*Then the world,*" Xin said after Leon finished.

"*Awaken my brothers!*" Leon said out loud in Angelic tongue.

I looked at saw all the Angels beginning to wake. They appeared groggy. I guess that's a natural reaction after being sleep for centuries. Leon extended his wings and lifted himself up in the air.

"*Who are you?*" said one of the Angels, he was closest to us. "*To be down here with the Son of Michael and a Son of Adam. Who are you who to have the wings of an Angel? But looks like Man?*"

The Angel spoke of Leon not having their golden glow. Xin didn't have it either but obviously these Angels knew who he was. I didn't even know Angels could reproduce.

"*It's a rarity,*" Xin said pointing to his head as he listened to my thoughts. "*But it's possible.*"

"*I am the Son of Sin,*" Leon yelled loudly. "*Clothe yourself, arm yourself, and pledge your lives to me, for I have freed you from your prison. No longer will you have to wait for Judgment day, seek your vindication in the world of man, and one day see Heaven again!*"

"Victor! Get up!" I heard Zaviera's voice in my head again.

I closed my eyes to see three men from the Muslim Army charging where I was near, Eric was to the right fighting another one from their army, and Zaviera was fighting one as well.

"*You have our allegiance!*" The angel said as he broke free of his chains, the second he broke free of them, he grabbed one on his neck and crushed it, in an instant, he was clothed with a black robe, on his left was a black sword similar to mine that hung from his belt. The rest began to break free of their chains.

"*I'll see you soon brother,*" Leon said to me smiling in victory.

"*If I were you, I'd get my army out of there,*" Xin said to me as he pushed me towards where the Angels stood.

As I was falling I felt my body being pulled again just like it felt when I was in the water. I took a deep breath. I rose out of the water and drew my bow, I took an arrow from my quiver and shot it at the one of the three Muslims charging in the water, I repeated the same shot two more times. I unsheathed my sword, ducked and stabbed the Muslim fighting Zaviera in his stomach, and I turned and cut the back of the one fighting Eric.

"It's about time!" Eric screamed. "How did you just come up and take down five of them when I couldn't even get one of them down?"

"You were down there forever." Zaviera said to me. "How are you even alive?"

I took a moment to look around at what was happening. It was an all-out battle, in the water all of my soldiers were battling their army, I looked back and Octavius' men were fighting Malcolm's and driving them back towards us.

"Call the retreat," I said. "We have to go."

For what was coming, I was afraid no one is ready for.

34

For the next few minutes Zaviera and I did the best we could to sound the retreat. We helped many people onto the speed boats and jet skis. Minutes felt like hours, I didn't know when Leon would come up with his Angels; I didn't know how long we could withstand both the Muslim fleet and Octavius' army.

"Malcolm isn't going to hold up much longer!" Zaviera said to me as we were defending some retreaters from attacking Muslims.

I was reserving my energy for when I needed it, I didn't want to take any lives that I didn't have to right now, I just wanted to get everyone to safety, well, what's left of my army. I stopped for a second and looked around and all I saw was death, my people, Muslims and Octavius' Christians, just everywhere, dead, blood ran through the waters and sand. It was a sad day.

I saw Eric was helping one of the soldiers up after they had fell and a Muslim man was coming behind him to attack him. I ran as fast as I could and I was able to push the Muslim down. He was a Caucasian man, with blonde hair and eyes like Octavius and Elizabeth. He had to be Elizabeth's brother. He swung his sword wildly, I dodged it and kicked his left shin and he fell into the water. I put my foot on his back.

"What is your name?" I said to him.

He didn't answer, I pressed the back of my heel into his hamstring and he moaned out in agony.

"I said what is your name?"

VENSIN GRAY

"Alexander!" he yelled out. "Alexander Tatopoulos!"

I took my heel off of his hamstring and let him get up.

"You're going to pay for that you miscreant!" he said to me as he charged me with his eyes closed.

I did a round house kick to his face rendering him unconscious. I was surprised he survived this long.

"Eric!" I said to Eric.

"Sir!?" he said to me.

"Take him to the cruise ship and restrain him."

"But, sir. He's one of them."

"He's one of us now," I said to him. "Now go! Get out of here, I don't want to see you back here."

I just baptized him. I want him to go and tell his family that he is baptized; I want them to be proud of him. I looked up to see that Malcolm was one of the few remaining of his men still battling out with Octavius and his men. I ran up the sand to help him. We ended up back to back and being surrounded by Octavius' men, Malcolm ducked as I swung high and he went low, we cut them all down in a manner of a few swings. More were coming but I ordered them to retreat. Let Octavius men fight the Muslims, let them destroy one another.

"I won't leave my men!" Malcolm said to me as he continued to fight.

"They will come with us!" I said to Malcolm as we stopped to see Wajeeh fighting four of Octavius' men at once.

We both ran over there to help him but it was too late, one of them tripped him and I saw two swords enter his chest. He was gone.

"Nooooo!!!!" I heard Malcolm holler out as he became enraged and swung his sword ferociously at anyone he could land his sword on.

"Pull yourself together!" I said to him as I stopped one of his attacks with my shield.

Octavius' men started marching towards the water to meet the

Muslim fleet who was out in full force now. I ran with Malcolm to the escape route.

"That's mostly everybody I can see," Zaviera said to me as Malcolm went to his knees and started to cry.

"Now's not the time for this Malcolm!" Zaviera screamed to him. "We have to go!"

Her eyes got wide. I turned in defense to see who she was looking at. It was Senior wandering around in the battle field. I didn't hesitate, I ran to him as fast as I could. As I got closer to him, a Muslim and a Christian were both about to attack him; I quickly put both of them down.

"Victor!" Senior said to me. "My grandson!"

"What are you doing here!?" I yelled at him.

"I had to tell you something."

"It couldn't wait?" I said scanning around making sure no one was attacking us.

"No. No. It's important," he said breathing hard. "On my phone there's a voicemail from…" as he said that I heard three arrows shoot at us. I blocked out what he was saying as I drew my sword and was able to cut two of them down. I looked for the shooters but couldn't find them, I wanted to be prepared for another attempt. The third one must've missed I said as I turned to see Senior looking at me. "There's…"

He said choked up in his words. Tears in his eyes.

"There's a voicemail from Sa'Rah on my phone," he said handing me his phone. "I…" He said in between breaths. "I think you need to listen to it."

He went down on one knee.

As I looked at him, I noticed that the third arrow didn't miss. It hit Senior in his back. I quickly went to grab it but Senior's hand grabbed mine.

"No," he said as he looked at me. "Leave it." He said breathing hard. "I knew the risk coming here but I had to get that to you. I wanted to tell you goodbye. I didn't say it the last time we saw one another."

He was coughing.

"I'm sorry grandson," he said as tears ran down his eyes. "I never wanted any of this for you or Leon. I thought that what happened all those years ago was it. I looked around and all I saw was death. And I thought that one of the bodies I would look upon would be yours and my heart couldn't bare it knowing that the last time I saw you, was wordless."

His eyes began to fade.

"Save your strength," I said to Senior. "I'm going to get you to the boat, and we are going to remove that arrow and get you patched up."

He was growing shorter in breath.

"Come on, Senior, I need you to be ok. I can't do this without you," I said to him.

All my life, he had been there for me and everyone in the family. And the one time I could be there for him, I missed. Didn't matter what was going on in life, Senior knew how to find the answer through the word of God. He has helped millions with his words of passion for Christ. He taught us all how to love. He was the leader of this family, and he was in my arms struggling for life. But he wasn't struggling, he was letting go.

"Be..." he said as he caught his breath. "Be strong... be strong in your faith... be strong in your faith."

"No!" I said to him. "I need you to fight!"

"Not anymore grandson. Not anymore," he said shaking his head at me. "I go to be with my father." He said smiling at me and looking at me in my eyes. "I go to be with Christ."

His face had the look of satisfaction. He closed his eyes.

"I love you Victor. I love you Leon. Two of the greatest grandsons a man could ever ask for."

He muttered as his words stopped. His breath stopped, and he died in my arms.

I was paralyzed with shock. Everything around me stopped. I

didn't hear anything, I couldn't see anything. I could only see Senior lying there motionless. A man who taught my father everything, a man that saved my life, a man that I wanted to be like, I was named after him. I am him; there is no life without him.

"Victor!" I heard Zaviera's voice in the back but I didn't hear her.

I didn't hear anything. I faded away.

"Come here, grandsons," Senior said to Leon and me as we were wrestling on the beach.

"Get off of me!" I shouted to Leon who had me pinned in the sand.

"You have to get stronger little brother," Leon said to me smiling as he got off of me and helped me up before tripping me in the sand again and running to Senior laughing.

"Come here you," Senior said as he helped me up from the sand and brushed the sand off of me and in my hair.

I am nine years old; it was a cool night in the spring time. We are on the beach in Euclid. The stars were out, the brightest I've ever seen them in my young life, the breeze was mellow as it caressed my cheeks. Leon and I followed Senior on the smooth rocks that lined up on the beach. We walked to the edge and we stood and looked around.

"Ten years ago a great man brought me here," Senior said looking at Leon very hard and smiling. "Well, you wouldn't call him a man, you would say he's in the stars."

"Where is he now?" I asked Senior.

"In Heaven with his father," Senior said smiling. "What I wouldn't do to get to talk to him again. Hear his wisdom, accept his guidance. What I wouldn't do to see my own father."

"You'll see him again," Leon said to him. "In the afterlife."

"Right you are, grandson," Senior said to him rubbing his head. "Right you are."

Senior laughed a bit.

"You both are my grandsons. And that makes you cousins, or brothers, or just really close friends. I want you to always look after one another. No matter what."

"You have my word, Senior." Leon said to him. "I'll protect Three."

"I don't need your protection!" I said to him.

"Don't be like that Three," Senior said to me. "Although you two may not share the same parents, you two are brothers. 'A man of many companions may come to ruin, but there is a friend who sticks closer than a brother.'" Senior said quoting a bible verse. "Can anyone guess that verse?"

"Um…" Leon said. "Proverbs chapter eighteen, verse… verse… twenty four." Leon said smiling and looking at me.

"You are correct." Senior said to him.

He pulled us both closer to him.

"I know you won't believe me, but that man that I spoke of earlier, he saved my life on many occasions, he brought me closer to our family, and opened my eyes to things I never would have thought of before. There would be no Leon without him, there would be no Three without him. There was a moment, a time, a second, where I was going to give my life up for him. For John in the fifteenth chapter thirteenth verse says that 'Greater love hath no man than this, that a man lay down his life for his friends.' A friend can be anybody, your grandmother is my best friend, brothers can be allies, and brothers can be enemies, but friends that become brothers, they last forever," He said as he looked both of us in the eyes.

I looked at Leon, and Leon looked at me. He smiled and I smiled.

"This is my brother first, friend second," Leon said to me. "And just like you were willing to fight for your brother, I'll fight for mine."

"It's not always about fighting or protection," Senior said to us. "It's about being there for your brother, supporting him during a tough time, not betraying one another, being there when he needs you the most. Do not gossip about one another, defend one another, and always be one another's strength. Yin and Yang, an Indian and Chinese philosophy in which Yin and Yang means dark and light, and basically it's how two complementary opposites, unseen and seen, that interact within a great whole. Light cannot exist without darkness, and darkness cannot exist without light."

"Just like, there's no Leon, without Three," Leon said as he put his hands on my shoulders.

"I love you both," Senior said as he hugged us.

"I love you too, Grandpa," I said to him. "Promise us you'll be with us forever."

"I'll always be by your side," Senior said.

"Victor!!!!!!"

35

When I came too from my day dream I looked up to see Leon standing over Senior and I. His wings relaxed and he was looking down at Senior in disbelief.

"What is this!?" Leon said breathing hard barely controlling his emotions. "What is this!?"

He dropped to his knees and grabbed Senior from my arms and put his head on Senior's chest to hear a heartbeat that wasn't there. Xin walked up behind him, Xin was back into his all black attire compared to his winged self in Hell. Leon started groaning as he cried over Senior's body, his groans were of pure anger, and the temperature rose dramatically. Xin was standing with another Angel who looked like the one who addressed me as Son of Adam. He was robed in a black robe like garment that went across his chest. He was looking at Leon.

Everyone who was fighting the war had stopped. Octavius had revealed himself, and everyone was staring at the angels, Leon crying, and the one next to Xin. I was frozen on the ground. I couldn't believe what just happened. One second Senior and I were talking, and then, he's gone, and he smiled at death. He didn't fear it.

"How did this happen!?" Leon yelled out to me.

I didn't answer; I just sat there looking at Senior lying there motionless.

"Answer me, brother! How did this happen!? Who did this!?" Leon said to me. "Senior no! I love you!"

He was crying even harder.

"They've killed Victor the Victorious," Xin said in Angelic tongue to the Angel next to him. *"Kill them all."*

"AHHHHHHHHHHHHHHHH!!!!!" Leon let out a loud roar of pain and suffering.

As he did that, the waters behind me splashed loudly as you heard wings coming up from them. Leon's Angels had awoken and came from their prison to do Leon's bidding. They began attacking the Muslim Fleet and Octavius' men. They were killing them quickly and in massive numbers. I knew it was time for me to go, Zaviera and Malcolm were waiting on me.

"Victor!" I heard Malcolm scream as he ran up to stand by my side. "We have to go, brother."

Leon looked up at Malcolm and he frowned. He stood up and drew his sword and attacked Malcolm. The Angel standing next to Xin stepped towards Malcolm but Xin held his hand out for him not to attack. Malcolm did the best he could but Leon was angry. I tried to move but I couldn't, it was as if when Senior died so did my desire to live. Leon punched Malcolm in the face and then he thrust his sword through Malcolm's stomach. I heard Malcolm groan in pain. Xin and the Angel were smiling. Leon took his sword out of Malcolm and was going in for the finishing blow. I saw Vita running towards us. I picked up my sword and stopped Leon from finishing off Malcolm.

Obviously angered at me stepping in between them, he shoved me but I parried his shove and kicked him in his stomach as hard as I could. Leon fell backwards and tripped over Senior and fell down. Vita stopped by me as I helped Malcolm up on to her. The other Angel had stepped out now but I was in no mood to fight an Angel. In the past few days I'd jumped out of a window, got sucked into Hell, fought Octavius, Lucifer and Leon. I was tired of fighting for one day.

Leon stood up. I slapped Vita on her hind for her to take off, she ran as I jumped to get on top of her the Angel lunged towards us with his wings spread. I took out my bow. I pulled an arrow from my quiver as quickly as I could and shot it right before landing on Vita. The arrow hit the Angel in the chest and the angel fell back to Leon's feet. Xin and Leon didn't pursue me, they just looked at me ride off. I rode Vita to the waters where there was a speed boat waiting with Zaviera in it.

"Is Malcolm going to be ok?" Zaviera said to me as she helped me get him into the speed boat.

l examined his wound, it wasn't a fatal stabbing, he would be fine if we could get him on to the ship, stop any internal bleeding and close his wound.

"He'll be fine," I said to her.

"What happened up there?" Zaviera said to me. "Who are all those winged creatures?"

"They are Angels," I responded to her. "They are my brother's Angels. Let's go."

I didn't mention Senior's death. I didn't cry, I didn't shriek, I just sat there on the boat. As we got to the ship, it was a large cruise ship, similar in appearance to a Carnival ship.

"What are your orders General?" said the captain of the ship.

"I want anyone who can shoot a bow and arrow out on the highest deck. Take us to the port in Downtown Cleveland. Tell the Pilots to get out of the plains, we are taking the ground, stay out of the air. Take Colonel Malcolm to the medical center. It's imperative that his life is saved."

Malcolm was taken away on a stretcher, Zaviera followed them. I followed a ship crew member to my room.

The room was off of the third row of the ship with small window. It was nicely decorated, about eight feet high, twelve by twelve foot box room with a full size mattress. I went to the bathroom and took a quick shower. It wouldn't take us that long to get to Downtown Cleveland from there in the water.

My shower was quick. I only wanted to get the blood and sand off of me. When I got out of the shower, I dried off, wrapped the towel around me and walked into my room to find Elizabeth on my bed. She quickly got up and came to hug me.

"I was so worried," she said as she pressed her head into my chest.

She smelled really good. Her hair was down and she was wearing a soft red robe. She had on perfectly applied red eye shadow and red lipstick that accentuated her beautiful lips.

"Why are you here?" I said to her as I walked to the dresser in the room to see that I had some clothes placed in here already.

Elizabeth grabbed my arm to turn me around and she kissed me. Her lips were so soft, and her touch was so warm, it reminded me of kissing Fawzia. I stopped her.

"You saved my brother," Elizabeth said smiling at me. "You promised you would."

She went and laid down in my bed.

"I gave you my word," I said to her as I walked near her.

I looked at her directly in her eyes, she looked very seductive. She licked her lips and looked at me from the corner of her eyes. My heart was weak right now, I couldn't resist her. I knelt down and kissed her, this time our tongues collided passionately. I put my hands around her back and held her tightly, our skin touching sent my mind into more aggressive behavior. I kissed her longer, and deeper, I grabbed her and groped her tighter and firmer. My hands went to her legs as I kissed her neck. She moaned in my ear as I felt myself beginning to want to thrust into her. I rubbed my hand up until I felt how moist she was and I stopped.

"What's wrong?" she said to me breathing hard.

"Nothing is wrong," I said to her.

"Then… why did you stop?"

"I want my first time to not be on a day like this," I said to her. "I want my first time to be with my wife."

I stood up and sat right back down.

"What do you mean a day like this?" Elizabeth said to me rubbing my back.

I took a deep breath.

"I have to go to my family," I said slowly. "And I have to tell them that Senior is dead."

Elizabeth gasped.

"I thought that Victor was in Michigan," Elizabeth said.

"I don't know how he got to the beach. But he was there. Three arrows were shot at me. I cut two of them down but the third one hit Senior. His last words were 'I love you Victor. I love you Leon. Two of the greatest Grandsons a man could ever ask for.' That's what he said to me. Then I fought Leon to save Malcolm, as I watched his Angels slaughter thousands of men," I said as I began to put on clothing.

I didn't care that Elizabeth was in the room. We would make port soon and we had to go.

"I'm so sorry, Victor," Elizabeth said to me.

She sounded sad, but she didn't cry. I'm glad, I haven't cried, and I know that my family is going to be difficult to handle. But someone had to do it.

When we got to the port, everyone got into the buses without issue. There wasn't any sign of any angels, or any threats from anyone. The ride to the Michigan Safe Zone in Midland was quiet. Malcolm survived surgery and was resting. Zaviera didn't leave his side. A lot of the soldiers were injured, the ones that wasn't went to their families the second we got to Michigan.

I took the long walk to my family's new house area. They were staying in my old dorm. When I walked into the front room, they were all watching Leon's Angels on the news as they ransacked the rest of Cleveland and officially made the city theirs. Grandmother Patrice was sitting on the sofa with Christina. My father was standing up near the kitchen area; my mother and Grandfather Persy were sitting at the card table near the kitchen. Aunt Victoria was lying down on the couch, and aunt Victory was walking back from the restroom.

They looked at me, and Grandmother Patrice asked me where Senior was, I didn't say a word, I just looked at her and she knew. She grabbed her chest and instantly started to cry. Aunt Victoria burst out into tears, Aunt Victory went to hug my father who dropped to his knees with his face buried into his hands. My mother went to hug her father, and I stood there as they all poured their eyes out. I eventually left out of the dorm.

"Is your heart that hardened, Victor?" Elizabeth said to me as I walked out of the apartment. "It sounds terrible in there. Do you have any words of comfort, a touch, a hug, anything?"

"No," I said as I walked away from her.

I didn't have time to mourn, I had people who are depending on me for survival, I had angels to defeat, and I had a brother to calm down. I didn't have the luxury like everyone else to just cry at the drop of a dime the second sad news came.

"Octavius called me," she said as I stopped walking and turned around and looked at her. "Your brother spared his life. He's appointing Octavius to be the Ambassador to the human race. Apparently Leon wants to kill every human besides you and your family."

"He wants vengeance for Senior," I said as I looked up to the sky.

"Octavius told me to remind you to remember your promise," Elizabeth spoke of my promise to Octavius that if the worst happened I would get his son from Egypt.

I looked at her and shook my head in agreement.

"How is your brother?" I asked of her brother that I knocked unconscious during the battle.

"He's ok. Grateful to be alive," Elizabeth said. "He said he's never fighting you again."

She laughed a bit.

"There's no easy way to put this Victor so I'm just going to say this. Octavius offered me and my brother to stand by his side. And we said yes," she said to me as she walked up to me and softly kissed me on the lips. "We leave today."

She turned to walk away.

"Fawzia is coming with us."

I licked my lips and stared at Elizabeth for a few seconds then I turned and walked away.

"You're not even going to ask me to stay?"

"What for? You made your decision," I said to her. "You wanted status, you have your status."

"Don't do that to me!" she yelled as she ran to me. "I've stood by your side, I've been there for you all these months and you barely look at me!"

She was tearing up.

"All you think about is Fawzia, the woman who is pregnant with your brother's child! Your brother who just probably allowed his angels to kill everyone in Cleveland!"

I didn't have time to comfort her. She made a good point with her reasoning for leaving. But I have people depending on me.

"If you leave," I said to her. "I will visit you, where ever you are at. And you will always be welcomed here." I said as I walked off.

I walked to the fields where I trained all those months. It was cold here in Michigan and the air was crisper here. The trees were covered in ice. It's amazing to me how nature stays the same despite all the turmoil that is going on in the world of men. As long as there is rain and sunlight, plants will grow, water will flow, and animals will be animals. I took time to enjoy nature as I meditated in the middle of the field.

Over the next week, not much went down. There was heavy snow falls over the Midwestern part of America. At our Safe Zones, we trained many archers, for if Leon found out our locations and sent his Angels here, they would attack through the air. I spent time with everyone in my family, as much as I could. I didn't know how much of them I was going to see over the next few months as I had to plan to see what Leon was up to. He didn't raise all those angels just to defeat Octavius. Or rather, Xin didn't help Leon raise all of them to defeat Octavius.

Elizabeth, her brother and Fawzia all left. Octavius came onto the television and basically told the world that Leon was the new King of what he calls New Heaven, Fawzia is his queen and Xin is second in

SON OF SIN

command of his Angel army. Xin asked for my Aunt Victoria's hand as his woman to spare our family. Aunt Victoria reluctantly accepted despite my father's pleas for her not to. My grandmother Patrice was a wreck, she was crying every day, it took Aunt Victory to force her to eat and to come outside for her to get out of bed. My mother and Grandfather Persy were enjoying the quiet life of the Safe Zone. My father was slowly losing control of sanity, he had lost his daughter and his father in less than two months, not to mention finding his wife cheating on him. I talked to him daily, getting him to read the bible, and try to prepare for how life was going to be.

Octavius made an ultimatum to the world, bow to Leon, who calls himself King Leon, Son of Sin, or die. He said that you will bow to King Leon, proclaim him as your king, or your cities will be burned down, children will be killed, and existence erased from history, and he said that no one will remember them.

I'd just finished meditating, trying to somehow get guidance from Senior through thought. I saw Malcolm walking around with Zaviera.

"It's good to see you out and about," I said to Malcolm.

"Thank you for saving my life Victor," Malcolm said to me smiling.

"What was I going to do? Let him kill you?" I said.

"Well, yes," Malcolm said as he was walking, it still hurt him to walk after being in bed for almost a week.

"What do we do now?" Zaviera said to me.

"I have some unfinished business to attend to in Africa," I said to her as I took off my Generals patch and handed it to her.

"What is this for?" She said to me.

"I am no longer your general," I said to them. "You are the General now Zaviera, you recruited majority of the soldiers here. Now your task is to get enough to protect all of your Safe Zones, and save as many people as you can from Leon and his angels."

"Thank you," she said, taking the patch. "I accept this, humbly." She said looking at Malcolm.

"You are to promote Eric Anderson to Colonel," I instructed her.

"He and Malcolm will make a good team. Train as many archers as you can. Keep your religion, but do not force it on anyone. Don't want to turn any internal conflicts, right now, our enemy is the same."

"Are you really willing to fight Leon?" Malcolm said to me.

"I'll do what I have to do. You have my final orders." I said to them, they looked at me in agreement.

I shook Malcolm's hand; Zaviera gave me a hug with her eyes watered up.

"Take care of yourself, General," I said to her.

"What about the original thousand you had?" Zaviera asked me in regards to the original thousand men I received to help during the war that I used to establish the Safe Zones.

"One hundred of them will stay here and watch over my family. I'm going to take another one hundred with me; the other eight are all yours to do what you will with them." None of the thousand fought in the war, they were all stationed around the city as look outs and went to the Michigan Safe Zone when it was time for the war to start.

"What are you going to do with your hundred?" Malcolm said to me.

"Make them angel killers," I said to him as I walked off.

I went to my family's apartment. They were all getting ready for Senior's funeral later on today. They are given safe passage to and from the funeral at Leon's request.

"Hello, son," My father said to me as he was tying his tie. "Will you be traveling with us?"

"I won't be traveling with you," I said to him.

"Ok son."

He gave me a hug tightly.

"I love you son."

"I love you too, Father," I said to him.

My mother came out of the room and gave my father a kiss and hugged me as well. I gave my Grandmother Patrice a hug and a kiss as she was resting before everyone was to leave. Christina was caught in between everything, on one hand, her son was the King of the world and on the other, and she knew it was wrong.

"You're going to have to eventually kill him aren't you Victor?" Christina said to me as she looked out of the window, eyes glossed over.

"I don't know," I said to her. "I hope it never comes to that. I'm not even sure I am able to kill him."

"You have the ability. You have the strength; you could've already if you wanted to. What are you waiting for?"

"He's my brother."

"But he's not your brother."

"He's my brother in every way that counts. And that's all that matters to me. He and I will talk. "

"I hope you don't have to kill my son."

"I hope not either," I said to her as I placed my hand on her shoulder in comfort. "He's asked you to stay there right?"

"My place is here," she responded.

"What time will you be coming to the funeral?" my father asked.

"I won't be attending the funeral," I responded.

"Why not?" My Aunt Victory asked as she was finish doing her hair.

There was no reason for me to make a public appearance. I was public enemy number one to every angel out there. I was Leon's most dangerous adversary, he knows it, Octavius knew it, and I was sure that Xin knew it. The only thing I was certain of was to go and get Octavius' son. From there, I'd decide what to do.

"I said my goodbye," I said as I left out of the house.

36

I rode my motorcycle to the funeral, it had been a very long time since I rode my cycle. I'd been mostly taking Vita everywhere, but I didn't want anyone to know that I was there. I didn't want my family to know that I would be coming. I wouldn't miss this for the world. I had to adjust to Senior not being there anymore. Senior was the man I went to with questions, now who am I going to go to? I love my father, but he still went to Senior for answers. It was a gray day outside in Cleveland. No snow, no rain, no sunlight, just a cloudy sky.

I arrived a little late to the funeral on purpose. I wore a hooded cowl robe that had a cloth to cover my face. The funeral was being held in the back of the Two Hundred Twenty Second Senior Community Center, right by the shore of the East Two Hundred Twenty Second beach. I heard that this was where they buried Sa'Rah at Senior's request.

I hadn't been to her grave since she's passed. I'd been too busy with everything else going on. I couldn't find the phone that Senior had given me with her voicemail on it. I must've dropped it saving Malcolm from Leon. I walked up the long driveway to the community center. There were cars parked everywhere and angels flying through the sky. Leon may have become dark, but he still had respect for Senior, and he allowed everyone who wanted to pay their respects to him to come.

I made my way through everyone who was standing. There was nowhere to sit up front as far as I could see. Leon's Angels were everywhere standing guard in attention, they didn't notice who I was with my covering on. I found my way to sneak on top of the community center. I went to the edge to see my family sitting in the front row. White chairs were provided for the funeral. I saw many member's from the church, Senior's sister, my grand aunt. I saw distant cousins and other relatives.

Senior's body was in a clear glass casket. From what I could see he was dressed in an all-white suit laying on top of white cushions. Senior's casket set at the center, everyone was facing the lake. Sa'Rah's tombstone was next to Senior's. Senior's was sitting on top of the platform to lower the casket into the grave. The chairs that were provided had a walkway from Senior's casket that was covered with a red carpet. At the end of the red carpet was some type of blue and gold jewelry box. Behind Senior's casket were two royal looking chairs, one for a King with red cushion and one for a queen.

There were several songs sung, Senior's obituary, and plenty of people who got up to talk about Senior. It was still early afternoon. The sun came out when my father got up to speak at the podium.

"Hello everyone." my father said somberly. "Thank you to Leon for allowing us to be here to see my father one last time before we say goodbye. I am half of the last remaining Victor Thomas' left. My father, ever since I was a kid, always tried to do the right thing by the Bible. Sometimes to a fault. I won't keep you here long, I won't sit here and tell you the thousands of times he's helped me in some sort of way, I won't tell you how good of a man he was, how he became my best friend, how I couldn't have asked for a better father. I'll tell you about the last time that I thought he was taken from us. I was sixteen at the time, and my father had just gotten into the most peculiar accident. He was in a coma for a few months, I visited him as often as I could before I went to Florida. When I came back, he hugged me, and he said 'Don't worry; I'm back.' I remember them like he said it yesterday. And all of my problems faded away there. But now that he's gone, I kind of keep expecting him to get up." He said as he looked at Senior.

"But I have to realize that he isn't getting up. And I'm not so sure that Thomas' are ready for life without Victor Thomas Senior. Is the world ready for life without him? I look around and I see one of his Grandsons." He pointed to Leon who was sitting in the Family section next to his mother with his wings not hidden.

"The other one is, well, somewhere. And I look at all these men, and women, and angels, and I can tell you that this world is definitely not ready for life without Victor Thomas Senior. I know I'm not. I love you dad and I'll miss you forever," my father said as he cried leaving the podium.

My mother went to meet him as he walked back to his seat.

Xin walked to the Podium with my Aunt Victoria at his side. Although my Aunt Victoria was almost forty, she didn't look a day over thirty. Her hair cut short, she wore a black dress with a black royal like robe over her that matched Xins. Behind them were Octavius wearing a black suit, Elizabeth in a black dress, and her brother dressed like Octavius. They stood to the left of Xin and my Aunt Victoria. Leon stood up as trumpets began to sound as Senior's body was lowered into the grass. You could hear the cries of many in attendance.

Leon had tears coming down his face. He wore a purple robe that allowed his wings to spread out as needed, with a black shirt on underneath and black pants. He stood to the right of Xin and watched Senior's casket be lowered into the grave. I breathed deeply as my heart dropped watching Senior's body be taken away forever.

When his casket fully descended into the grave. The trumpets sounded again. I saw a woman dressed in a purple Hijab walk to the blue and gold big jewelry box. It was Fawzia.

"You are all here today," Xin said loudly. "Not to only to bereave over the loss of the great man named Victor Thomas, whose life was told by all of those who loved him. Today you are also here to witness the crowning of Old Earth's, or rather New Heaven's new king."

Fawzia opened the blue and gold box. She removed a crown from it. From up here the crown appeared to be a single round band made of glass, or diamond that could fit around one's head. The orchestra that was sitting to the far right of the courtyard started playing a soothing but triumphant melody as Fawzia slowly walked up the red carpet towards Leon.

Leon knelt down on one knee in front of Fawzia who put the crown over his head. He stood up and looked her in the eyes; she grabbed his face and kissed him. The same way she used to kiss me, with passion and aggression. I felt my heart break a little bit, to say that I completely got over the feelings I had for her would be lying, it made it tougher that she was kissing my brother. I stood up a bit as I found myself not being able to breathe, Elizabeth looked at me, and tears ran down her face as she looked down and wept.

"You got your status Elizabeth." I said to myself.

"I give you all. King Leon!" Xin exclaimed loudly. "The Son of Sin!"

As he said Sin, thunder roared and lightning struck the lake in a distance, it was loud and bright and it got really dark outside. I looked down and Xin looked worried. Christina had gotten up, she went to hug Leon, he held her hand as she walked away crying. My father, my mother, Grandfather Persy, Grandmother Patrice, and Aunt Victory all went to say their goodbyes to my Aunt Victoria, who is now the Princess of New Heaven. Aunt Victory placed a flower on Sa'Rah's grave as they all began to walk out.

As they tried to leave an Angel came out of nowhere and landed in front of my father who led the way. I gripped my sword, I was impossibly outnumbered, with all of my soldiers waiting for me to set sail for Africa to get Octavius' son, where ever he was. Leon and Fawzia both saw me, Fawzia broke eye contact immediately, and Leon gazed at me. He was far away, but I could feel it, he is scared, he is angry, and he is sad.

"Let them go," Leon said as the angel moved out of their way.

"Everyone. Kneel before your King!" Xin said as the angels all kneeled immediately, the rest of everyone remaining kneeled as well.

Even Fawzia, Octavius, Xin, Elizabeth, and her brother, they all kneeled. Everyone but me. I stood straight up and Leon and I exchanged a stare down that you couldn't break with a two ton hammer. I turned my back to Leon and I walked off, I jumped off of the building as everyone was kneeling and walked into the backyard of someone's house. They had a bench back there, I laid my head on it to rest.

When I awoke, I looked at the position of the sun, it was beginning its descent to the west. The sky was clear and it was an orange glow outside.

"You're Victor Thomas' son aren't you?" said a male's voice behind me.

I stood up immediately and drew my sword only to see a man holding a plate of food and a tea cup. He was a short Caucasian man, with gray hair and dark brown eyes.

"No need for the sword," he said, startled a bit. "I knew your grandfather."

He set the plate and teacup down. It had some grilled steak, spinach and rice on it. The cup appeared to be tea.

"I figured you slept long enough you'd be pretty hungry when you got up," he said as he turned around.

"No sir, wait," I said as I sheathed my sword. "How did you know my grandfather?"

I sat down and ate the food that he had brought out to me. The steak was great, cooked just right, the spinach was good and the rice was good. The tea was fulfilling.

"You can say that he saved my marriage," the man said as he turned around to talk to me. "We took one of his first marriage counseling sessions, he was so nervous but he was really good. He taught us with the bible without ever using it or a scripture. He brought out God's values, without ever mentioning Him. He was a good man, a damn good man, and you're a good man too. " He said as he touched my shoulder. "I would say that I'm sorry for your loss, but it's everyone's loss, just like your father said." The man said as he walked back into the house. "I wish I could stay and talk to you, but it's cold out here. I don't know how you and the fella at your grandfather's grave do it."

He went back into the house.

"Thank you for the food," I said as he shut the door behind him.

I stood up to see a man at Senior's grave. No wings so he wasn't an angel. He looked a lot like Xin, but it wasn't Xin. I looked around; none of Leon's Angels were around. The park was completely empty besides the man and me. I walked closer as I drew my sword. I didn't know who to trust anymore.

"If I were you, young Victor," the man spoke in Angelic tongue to me. *"I would put that sword up. I assure you, I pose no threat to you."*

The man's voice was commanding but yet relaxing. I eased up my tension and put my sword in its sheath.

"Who are you?" I asked in the same tongue as he used on me.

He stood around the same height as me, maybe taller, he dressed in all black, derby hat, trench coat, black pants and black shoes. He stood over Senior's grave and didn't even look my way.

"Do you really need to ask that question?" he said as he looked at me.

He looked exactly like Xin except there was some white in his eyes. I couldn't make out the image.

"Sin?" I asked as he smiled and looked back at Senior's grave.

"Your grandfather was a better man than most people know." He said as he touched the top of Senior's grave and turned towards me. *"He had a love for this world that no normal man could understand. He was forgiving, passionate, empathic and courageous. Even in the face of death, he smiled."* Sin said as he walked away from the grave site.

"What are we going to do about Leon?" I asked him of his son.

"I'll let you handle my son." he said. "Young Victor…"

"Yes?"

"A man named Williams Penn said that 'They that love beyond the world cannot be separated by it. Death cannot kill what never dies," he said as he motioned his head towards Senior's grave. *"I'll be seeing you."*

I looked and there was the phone that Senior gave me before he died. I looked back to only see that Sin was gone. It was as if he vanished into thin air.

I walked towards the gravestones. Sa'Rah's read 'Sa'Rah Thomas Romans 14:8' It didn't have the scripture on it, but Romans fourteen verse eight says 'For if we live, we live to the Lord, and if we die, we die to the Lord. So then, whether we live or whether we die, we are the Lord's' It was a fitting verse. Senior's read 'Victor Thomas Senior, A man of God, A father, a husband, a grandfather, and a son.' Underneath 'a son' there was a carving, if I'm not mistaken, the markings were Angelic, it read 'A ProChrist.' I smiled to myself.

I grabbed the cell phone from on top of Senior's tombstone and knelt down at Sa'Rah's grave. The photo on the front of his screen was Sa'Rah, Leon and I after one of our basketball games. We were holding up Sa'Rah, Leon has his arm around me, we were all smiling as Sa'Rah had the number one finger sticking up towards the camera. I reached into my pocket and there was a paper in there. It was a poem from Sa'Rah. Must be the one she told me she wrote for me on my graduation day. It read:

I'm up waiting for you
Waiting for you to come home.
But you can't... And I'm all alone.
Waiting for this weightless numbness to fill me.
The feeling... this feeling.
I'm scared... then an Angel told me to say a prayer.
Is it something worth dying for?
It's inevitable, and I can't fight anymore.
It's so simple and pure... but yet so painful.
Tears rolling down my eyes, to question God is shameful.
What could be worse? It's just my divine curse.
It's the reason I was born, the reason why I was meant.
So that you can overcome... so that you may find your strength.
What have you given to get this? Where would you have gone to find it?

How many exceptions to your principles have you made?
How many lives will you touch? And how many lives will you hurt?
And think my brother, how many unexpected moments have you expected?
How many expected moments didn't happen?
And how many unexpected moments happened?
I'm just a girl waiting for the expected and the unexpected...
I hope my sacrifice is something you can understand
Because how do I present to you perfection in a flawed world with stained hands?
That is not a question your sword can match...
How do I tell you to believe me, when there's a liar presenting Christ as fact?
And if I don't do this, the world will only worsen
How do you show transformation to a blind person?
I want you to keep fighting, rise up till you can't stand
How else can you speak life to a deaf man?
Your ripples in the ocean of life will leave Demons shook
How do I cry without you believing its wolf?
So I'll give up my life, but it doesn't mean I'm done trying...
How can I save someone who doesn't believe they're dying?

"How can I save someone who doesn't believe they're dying?" I thought to myself as I pressed play on the voicemail. It was dated the night that Sa'Rah died.

"Will it hurt?" Sa'Rah said in a weeping voice.

"Never." Said a voice I have never heard before.

"Will I see him again in the afterlife?" Sa'Rah asked.

"I promise."

"What did Spurgeon say about fear of death?"

"He said that 'When the time comes for you to die, you need not be afraid because death cannot separate you from God's love,'" the man said as Sa'Rah began to cry. "Don't cry my child. We all have a duty to

God. Just sleep."

Then there was silence on the voice mail for a few seconds.

"I love you, Victor," Sa'Rah said finally, and the voicemail cut off.

I pressed the button that allows you to go back a few seconds.

"I love you, Victor."

I pressed it again.

"I love you, Victor."

And again.

"I love you, Victor."

And suddenly an array of pain, sorrow, regret, fear, and anger exploded in my heart as my eyes watered, the emotion was too great and I couldn't hold back tears anymore.

"I'm sorry Senior!" I said as tears began to flow from my eyes like the raging waters of a river no longer damned. "I'm sorry Sa'Rah!"

"I love you, Victor."

*Make sure you've read book one to the The ProChrist Series
"The ProChrist"*

*Visit www.vensinGray.net
Watch out for Angel King and other books coming from Vensin Gray!*